The Prepper Road Compendium

By Ron Foster

**ISBN-13:
978-1466490123**

**ISBN-10:
1466490128**

Printed in the United States of America.

Acknowledgements

Subscribe, like and favorite them, a great bunch of guys who have taken the time to make a difference for us all.

Acknowledgements

Aprovecho Research Center
StoveTec

Goat Hollow

LowBuckPrepper

StayingAwake20

Cheryl Chamlies

The Prepper Road Saga

Contains the four novelettes.

Stewart's Bug Out

Ron Foster

1

The Thirsty Traveler

Stewart lay panting behind the garage in the backyard of an older house in the Cheshire Bridge section of Atlanta. He tried to listen to the street sounds over the wheezing of his over labored breathing for sounds of pursuit. *Crimy! He thought to himself. I have done more running and ducking and dodging in the last month than I ever did as a schoolboy in London.* His breathing slowed and he carefully peeked around the end of the old wooden garage towards the street. No sign of those blighters that had started to chase him. *How quick can walking down the street and minding his own business turn into a race for your life over some stupidity by the lawless ones? He thought to himself reflecting on how often it had happened over the last few weeks.*

The "Lawless Ones" was a word Stewart had personally chosen or coined for the groups or gangs of juvenile thugs that plagued his existence since he had came up off the interstate when he like thousands of others was stranded. It was bad enough that technology had failed from the solar storm that had taken the grids and technology away from the world and his normal existence, but these vicious teenagers were worse to deal with than the adults who challenged him.

Stewart thought back to himself about the incident that had created the rivulets of sweat running off his body and brow and despite his totally winded state, he grinned with some satisfaction to himself that he had once again eluded the dark side of humanity that seem sworn to do him in. Poor Stewart had been trying for days to work his way back towards the interstate and out of the city, after he had so foolishly had tried to seek refuge at the World Trade Center and not knowing the city, had run afoul of the lowlifes and criminally misguided kids that seem to inhabit the neighborhoods on the outskirts and downtown areas of the city.

He thought to himself that London had many neighborhoods that were just as deadly for the unwary to traverse, but he knew to stay out of such realms. Here, in America it was different. Crimie!, he didn't even understand what some folks were jabbering about before they tried to take his meager possessions or do him bodily harm.

After all, all he was doing was walking down the street , when those three young blokes come out of an ally and asked what he had in his little wicker picnic basket. He had answered them nice enough before one started to circle in back of him and another tried to reach for his tea satchel. *My Lord,*

I am glad I had that Tommy knocker hidden and handy in my sling pack or things could have gone very bloody wrong in a hurry. Stewart reflected.

The large 16 year old or so boy that had made a grab for his basket and tried to pull it away from him like he was snatching a purse, got the full crack of his stick on his wrist and had let go immediately while howling. The one younger one trying to sneak in behind him to trip him up possibly got a whack to the knee before Stewart started sprinting away.

"I hope I broke their bloody joints" Stewart muttered to himself while calming down at the lack of sounds or visual evidence anyone decided to carry on their robbery attempt or seek revenge.

Damn lucky, damn lucky indeed those boys were not armed or more of them of they would have beat me like a drum. Stewart considered.

Stewart was pretty much looking the worse for wear and exhaustion by now as the events of the last few weeks had drained what little energy and fortitude the 57 year old man had. What with the constant danger and the lack of food and water his ability to even forage for the necessities of life was dwindling as his physical health was failing from the ordeal as well as his age.

"They not plant me in the church yard just yet." Stewart said to himself with some resolve and studied his surroundings. He was happy he had run into a couple friendly strangers on the interstate after his car had broken down from that horrible solar storm that had stranded hundreds of millions of people when it fried all the electrical circuitry in the vehicles. He had been using the innate street smarts he had learned growing up in London to get

by, but he was forever grateful a man called Dave had taken the time to teach him a few survival tricks to get by in a land without water or food. Dave had said the term for what he had learned or was trying to do was to be a "Rural Ranger" but damned if a lot of it didn't apply and he wished Dave had taught him to be a City Survivor instead. *I bet that portable man mountain bodyguard he had with him knew a trick or two for the city dwellers but he had sense enough to get out of the wasteland this place is now with Dave.* Stewart mused to himself while dusting himself off and looking over to the next neighbor's backyard in order to cross it and hopefully trick or evade his possible pursuers further.

I should have gone with them boys; they were kind enough to offer me refuge. I must of just been plain daft to think the British consul would take care of me here in the colonies when really countries themselves no longer exist except what you historically call the area you are stuck in currently. Well no going home or speculating now, I am going to find them boys and become a colonist myself if I can ever get out of this forsaken place.

Stewart walked towards the formerly landscaped fence line to the neighboring backyard and found himself a hiding place to observe what the situation was in the next yard he had to cross over. He remembered to check for dogs or other troubles and to be patient in his observations just as David had taught him.

David he had decided was an enigma, the sort of person that would be just as happy associating with louts as aristocrats. He and that man "Dump

Truck" certainly made an odd pair. David was tall and lanky with grey hair and a persona about him that was both country wisdom and years of academia and military, while "Dumpie" looked more like a tattooed, shaved headed subculture type that spoke as if he was out of his element of just being a farmer that decided to run a bar over a cattle operation. Who knows, that guy might have liked the biker or skinhead look without realizing what it was. Stewart considered thinking about all the different fads he had joined or had an opportunity to join as he grew up. Needless to say he had decided a few weeks ago, those boys were both good hearted people and his best chance of survival now.

Dump Truck and David had found Stewart as they were bugging out to the country on the side of the interstate as he was heading in from his vacation holiday to Florida. They had shared food and experience with him and Stewart had used his little portable picnic basket case to make some good English tea and assist the best he could in foraging the car and truck strewn highway for the necessities they all needed to make their road marches.

It was David who had suggested that maybe Stewart could stay with Dump if things were too bad in Atlanta for him to get help with no family or friends. It was Dump who had welcomed him to his new "tribe" without a second thought or complaint and exhibited the best in humanity and what the people of this land called "Southern Hospitality". All Stewart could do was hope that they sure meant it because he was at his wits end how to make it more than a few more days before fate or death caught up to him.

Stewart sat in his vantage point in the bushes beside the fence for a half hour or more observing the house on the other side of the enclosure and generally resting up from his exertions. Last night he had slept in an abandoned car and that had been fitful sleep at best. Food had been a problem and the few broken in already stores he had managed to find had been stripped bare as the tragedy that had befell the world continued to cascade its misery on all. Stewart had been reduced to scavenging whatever he could find, be it a stepped on broken pack of cheese crackers or attempting to wheedle and beg those people who did not appear hostile to take some of the worthless US currency he had for some food or water.

Water was the big thing now, without it he would die. Yesterday he had looked over the lay of the land as David had mentioned to him to look for ditches and low spots and had dug a about 8ft from a nasty looking trash filled creek and waited hours for the hole to fill with water. He had strained it through his socks and a bit of gravel and sand before drinking it, but it still tasted odd and he hoped that David was correct and he had not poisoned himself. Hell, David said the earth strained it to the hole he had dug, but he wanted to be a bit more careful and took time to wash out his socks as a filter. David would probably tell him he screwed up in washing the socks in dirty water and that no amount of filtering would undue it but he couldn't figure out how to get water out of the hole he had dug without dipping the fabric in it and wringing it out.

"What else did that old crazy emergency manager and soldier tell you about water? Think Stewart, Think! Stewart tried to recall.

Dave had told him that particularly in the south humidity is high and to tie rags on his shoes and walk across a grassy field collecting water in the morning, he should also try to find a sponge; He told me some warnings about being careful of disease and worms doing that. The best advice David had given was lost in the dementia that lack of water or regular food would do to some people as Stewart forgot that a simple baggie or garbage bag could sustain him if he made an evaporative still or a solar still. David claimed there was much open creative commons info on this subject as well as he could teach me a few personal tricks. Dave reminded him he had been to many military survival schools as well as been consulted on books or evaluations.

Survival **Science: How** ***Evaporation*** **and Condensation Can Save Your Life! Above-ground Still**

To make the above-ground still, you need a sunny slope on which to place the still, a clear plastic bag, green leafy vegetation, and a small rock.

To make the still -

Fill the bag with air by turning the opening into the breeze or by "scooping" air into the bag.

Fill the plastic bag half to three-fourths full of green leafy vegetation. Be sure to remove all hard sticks or sharp spines that might puncture the bag.

CAUTION - Do not use poisonous vegetation. It will provide poisonous liquid.

Place a small rock or similar item in the bag.

Close the bag and tie the mouth securely as close to the end of the bag as possible to keep the maximum amount of air space. If you have a piece of tubing, a small straw, or a hollow reed, insert one end in the mouth of the bag before you tie it securely. Then tie off or plug the tubing so that air will not escape. This tubing will allow you to drain out condensed water without untying the bag.

Place the bag, mouth downhill, on a slope in full sunlight. Position the mouth of the bag slightly higher than the low point in the bag.

Settle the bag in place so that the rock works itself into the low point in the bag.

To get the condensed water from the still, loosen the tie around the bag's mouth and tip the bag so that the water collected around the rock will drain out. Then retie the mouth securely and reposition the still to allow further condensation.

Change the vegetation in the bag after extracting most of the water from it. This will ensure maximum output of water.

Below-ground Still

To make a below-ground still, you need a digging tool, a container, a clear plastic sheet, a drinking tube, and a rock (Figure 6-7).

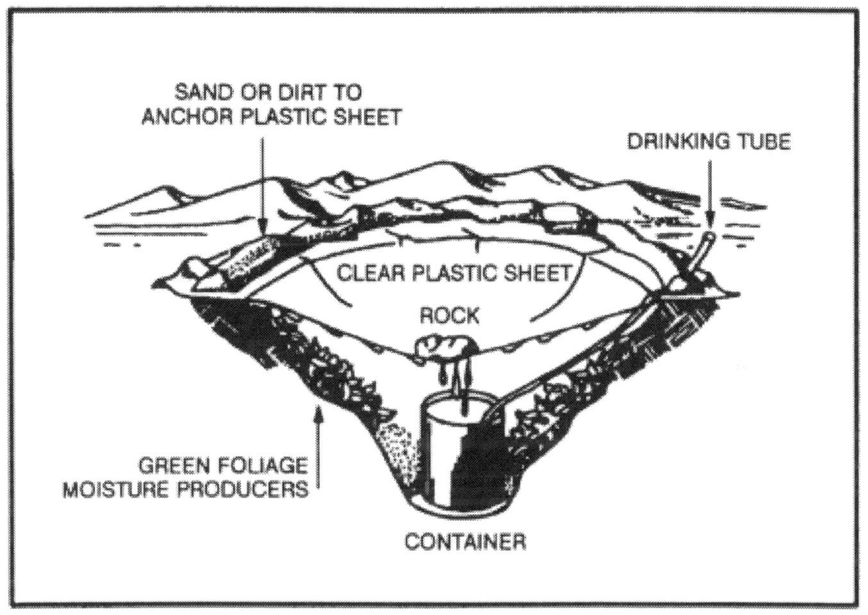

Figure 6-7. Belowground still.

Select a site where you believe the soil will contain moisture (such as a dry stream bed or a low spot where rainwater has collected). The soil at this site should be easy to dig, and sunlight must hit the site most of the day.

To construct the still -

Dig a bowl-shaped hole about 1 meter across and 60 centimeters deep.

Dig a sump in the center of the hole. The sump's depth and perimeter will depend on the size of the container that you have to place in it. The bottom of the sump should allow the container to stand upright.

Anchor the tubing to the container's bottom by forming a loose overhand knot in the tubing.

Place the container upright in the sump.

Extend the unanchored end of the tubing up, over, and beyond the lip of the hole.

Place the plastic sheet over the hole, covering its edges with soil to hold it in place.

Place a rock in the center of the plastic sheet.

Lower the plastic sheet into the hole until it is about 40 centimeters below ground level. It now forms an inverted cone with the rock at its apex. Make sure that the cone's apex is directly over your container. Also make sure the plastic cone does not touch the sides of the hole because the earth will absorb the condensed water.

Put more soil on the edges of the plastic to hold it securely in place and to prevent the loss of moisture.

Plug the tube when not in use so that the moisture will not evaporate.

You can drink water without disturbing the still by using the tube as a straw.

You may want to use plants in the hole as a moisture source. If so, dig out additional soil from the sides of the hole to form a slope on which to place the plants. Then proceed as above.

If polluted water is your only moisture source, dig a small trough outside the hole about 25 centimeters from the still's lip. Dig the trough about 25 centimeters deep and 8 centimeters wide. Pour the polluted water in the trough. Be sure you do not spill any polluted water around the rim of the hole where the plastic sheet touches the soil. The trough holds the polluted water and the soil filters it as the still draws it. The water then condenses on the plastic and drains into the container. This process works extremely well when your only water source is salt water.

You will need at least three stills to meet your individual daily water intake needs.

WATER PURIFICATION

Rainwater collected in clean containers or in plants is usually safe for drinking. However, purify water from lakes, ponds, swamps, springs, or streams, especially the water near human settlements or in the tropics.

When possible, purify all water you got from vegetation or from the ground by using iodine or chlorine, or by boiling.

Purify water by -

Using water purification tablets. (Follow the directions provided.)

Placing 5 drops of 2 percent tincture of iodine in a canteen full of clear water. If the canteen is full of cloudy or cold water, use 10 drops. (Let the canteen of water stand for 30 minutes before drinking.)

Boiling water for 1 minute at sea level, adding 1 minute for each additional 300 meters above sea level, or boil for 10 minutes no matter where you are.

By drinking non-potable water you may contract diseases or swallow organisms that can harm you. Examples of such diseases or organisms are -

Dysentery. Severe, prolonged diarrhea with bloody stools, fever, and weakness.

Cholera and typhoid. You may be susceptible to these diseases regardless of inoculations.

Flukes. Stagnant, polluted water-especially in tropical areas-often contains blood flukes. If you swallow flukes, they will bore into the bloodstream, live as parasites, and cause disease.

Leeches. If you swallow a leech, it can hook onto the throat passage or inside the nose. It will suck blood, create a wound, and move to another area. Each bleeding wound may become infected.

WATER FILTRATION DEVICES

If the water you find is also muddy, stagnant, and foul smelling, you can clear the water -

By placing it in a container and letting it stand for 12 hours.

By pouring it through a filtering system.

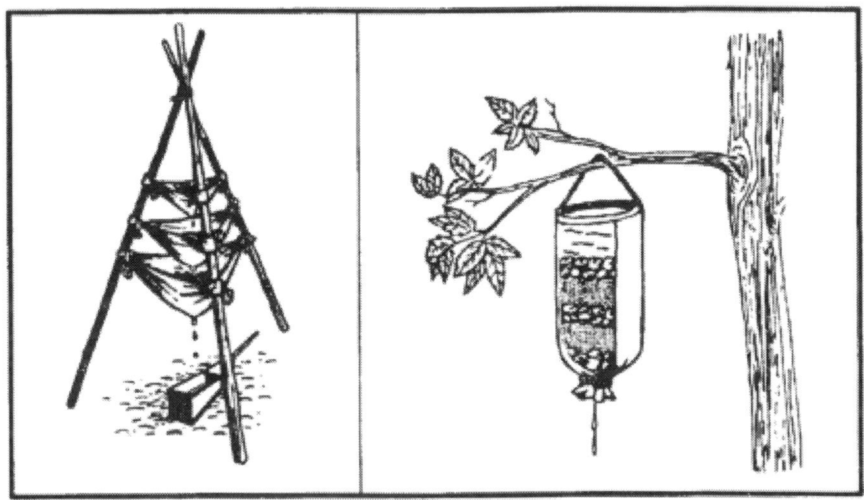

Figure 6-9. Water filtering systems.

Note: These procedures only clear the water and make it more palatable. You will have to purify it.

To make a filtering system, place several centimeters or layers of filtering material such as sand, crushed rock, charcoal, or cloth in bamboo, a hollow log, or an article of clothing (Figure 6-9).

Remove the odor from water by adding charcoal from your fire (brush the ashes off). Let the water stand for 45 minutes before drinking it.

A lot of this information Stewart had already known but that was why he liked David. David would reiterate things, customize them, let you gloss over what you already knew, or teach you to apply things to new conditions by challenging you with a new scenario to apply skills to. Who cared if he used a military manual to cover basics, he explained why to apply it and left you with a reference in case you forgot. The current challenge Stewart faced was how to apply country and military skills to this city environment. 'He had thoughtfully collected some of the clear trash bags found in most office buildings to make tree transpiration still. He also had remembered why David said he bitched about no one having these or other common available items in their so called bug out bags. "A plastic sack that gives water when none is there should be a trip to the kitchen to get one before you spend money on a water purification device or pills" the words still rang in Stewarts head. Another thing Stewart remembered was they can take your preps, they can take your options but for those that are prepared mentality, they can not take your mind. So out wit them, out source them, out think them and out survive them. Stewart had already decided to do exactly that and abide by his mentors belief in the first rule of survival was be prepared to lose everything. Stewart then began to look on his weariness in a new way, he was not tired of non availability, he was tired of people complicating the simple if they would just join together to share common survival items or knowledge. He knew if he had a pair of pliers for example he could tap no longer useful water heaters for water, yet people were getting killed over a bottle of pre disaster bottled water.

David had given him a beer inspired lecture that night on the highway weeks ago that basically said; let's say you need water in the worst of ways. You are lost in the wild or in this case the city or side of the road, you are at home but there is no running water, you are camping and can't find any potable water--what do you do? Here is a very easy thing you can do to get water. Build yourself a tree transpiration still. What the heck is that? Stewart had said. David had replied soulfully and scientifically, "A tree transpiration still takes advantage of the moisture that trees or plants expel from their leaves as they "sweat" or transpire. "Tying a clear plastic ***bag*** around a green leafy branch will cause water in the leaves to evaporate and condense in the ***bag***

There are two rules to remember about plants you put in this though for both the ground and tree still:

1. "Leaves of Three, Let Them Be"
2. Don't do this trick for plants with glossy leaves

There are a myriad of other ways to obtain drinking water, but you need more tools. If you're lucky enough to find grape vine, the liquid from the cut vine is drinkable. Once you've collected what you need, you can replant the severed vine and it will sprout roots

In North America there are no toxic grasses. If you cannot collect dew, you can chew the blades, extract the moisture and then spit out the pulp. Stewart had tried this once and was not apt to perform the experiment again unless he was totally desperate.

2

Melanie Says Maybe.

Stewart had spied what he thought was a grape arbor over in the corner of the yard he had been watching and he jumped the fence and headed in that direction. It was hard to tell now a day if houses were inhabited or not he considered as he made his way over to a rather large trellised structure that he could walk underneath of and get out of the sun for a bit.

Saints be praised he said to himself and ran to the arbor as he spotted several bunches of grapes growing on it.

Stewart started plucking grapes and popping them into his mouth as fast as he could and relished the sweetness and juicy texture of them as only a half starved and thirsty man could. Stewart had eaten about two dozen or more when he heard the backdoor of the house slam and saw a woman rushing towards him with a revolver in one hand and an aerosol can in the other.

"GET! Get out of here right now!" The women hollered at Stewart who looked at her astonished and put his hands up while backing away. Stewart tried to answer her but he was having difficulty with a mouth full of grapes and choking on a seed all at the same time.

"You leave my muscadines alone" the woman

shrieked at him and sprayed a stream of liquid at Stewart that caught him on his hands and neck and began to burn him.

Stewart had regained some of his composure and was still backpedaling trying to get away from this mad woman when he tripped over a tree root and smacked hid head against a large pine tree.

"I am going! I am sorry!" Stewart called from the ground trying to regain his feet and his eyes tearing up from what ever foul liquid the women had doused him with.

The women heard his British accent and looked down at the disheveled man more intently.

"Are you Ok? I didn't mean for you to fall and hurt yourself" she said anxiously looking at the blood starting to come from Stewarts scalp.

"I be alright momentarily miss and be on my way, Please don't spray me with that stuff again." Stewart said rubbing the knot on his head and noticing the blood.

"I am sorry, I just wanted you to quit stealing my grapes" the women said to Stewart.

Stewart regained his feet and holding his head turned to go get his picnic basket and sling pack that was made out of an old piece of canvas.

"Wait a moment, let me get a towel and some water to clean that cut on your head" the woman said looking after him.

"Id be obliged mum, could you spare a bit of water to wash off this burning oily stuff too? " Stewart said trying to wipe his neck with his shirt.

"Oh that's wasp spray, I am glad you didn't get it in your eyes. Be careful with your hands." I will be right back

Wasp spray? Do I look like a big bleedin bug? Stewart thought to himself.

The woman returned shortly with a big stainless steel bowl of water and a couple towels.

"I am sorry but that is all the water I can spare right now. My names Melanie, lets get you fixed up" she said and dabbed the edge of one the towels in the water.

"Stewart's my name. Can I get a sip of that water before we dirty it up? He asked.

"Oh what was I thinking, sure. You want a glass?" she replied.

"No the bowl is fine" Stewart said and took several big swigs from the bowl and returned it to her.

"I don't know what I was thinking chasing you around like that. Those grapes are about the only food I will have soon and I guess I just got over protective." Melanie said while patting at Stewarts wound with the towel.

"I wasn't thinking either miss, I just got overwhelmed when I seen them. Been rather meager with the rations myself these days" Stewart said wincing as she cleaned the scratch.

"You must be in an awful state, were you living or visiting here when that sun flare went off?" Melanie asked while applying some antiseptic ointment to the wound while Stewart wiped off the bug spray as best he could.

"I was traveling back from a bit of holiday in Florida when old sol decided to shut everything down" Stewart replied.

"Oh you poor man, I am really sorry to have put you through all this on top of what happened to you already" she said wringing out the cloth.

A loud voice suddenly yelled out from the street in back of her house drawing both of their immediate attentions.

"Have you seen him yet?" they heard while listening and heard a reply from a bit of a distance further away. "No, but if he ain't run off too far we will find him",

"I suggest you go back in your house Melanie. That be some young hooligans I had a run in with earlier" Stewart whispered while starting to rise.

"Are they armed?" Melanie asked while looking intently at her back fence and drawing her pistol from its holster.

"They weren't a half hour or so ago, but not telling what or who they got with them now. I best be on my way." Stewart said and started to gather up his possessions.

"You can come hide in the house until they quit looking. Hurry now" Melanie said and guided Stewart towards her back door.

Once they were safely locked in, Melanie told Stewart to have a seat and she peered out the kitchen window watching her back fence and grape arbor.

"I have seen them dang kids snooping around this street before. Old man Harvey up the street threatened them with a shotgun, when they tried to break into his neighbor's house. Those folks are not at home, but he has been keeping an eye on the place." Melanie said reluctantly leaving her look out post to sit down with Stewart at the kitchen table.

"If you got the means to heat it and a bit more water, I can make us a spot of tea. I got the fixings right here "Stewart said motioning towards his picnic basket.

"I would love some tea, I am afraid we will have to use charcoal to heat it though. I been saving it best I can by putting the lid back over the fire after

I am done and only cooking once a day. I guess this little run in deserves a cup of tea. We can split a can of soup if you like, too." Melanie replied

"You think we should be cooking on the barby with them blokes about?" Stewart asked

"I thought about that. Some of these neighbors are armed and our street has not seen very many problems yet and one has to eat so I guess we just go on living huh?" Melanie said and rose to get a can of soup and pointed Stewart towards a 5 gallon water cooler that was half full.

"You lucky you had one of these in your house" Stewart said unpacking his tea pot from his basket and moving towards the cooler

"Hey that is a neat little setup you got" Melanie said eyeing the contents of Stewart's basket and admiring the way everything was securely tied in.

"That has been my traveling companion for many years and has served me well. I had not contemplated all its uses until now and it seems to be becoming more useful all the time." Stewart replied and followed Melanie to her front porch after they both surveyed the backyard one last time.

"You said you had a run in with those street punks. What was that about?" Melanie said as she busied herself with lighting the grill.

"Oh they thought they needed my tea service and I gave them a few raps with my knocker to set them straight, before I went to running like a banshee was after me" Stewart said chuckling but still watching both ends of the street for the little scumgullens.

"What's a 'knocker'?" Melanie asked and scrutinizing Stewart's knuckles for signs of clouting someone.

"Oh I call me billy club a Tommy Knocker; I think you Yanks call it a 'Tire Thumper'." Stewart said sitting back in a lawn chair and waiting for it to burn down enough for him to put his kettle on.

"I know what a billy club, is but I never heard it called a tire thumper before." Melanie said settling into a chair next to Stewart.

"I never heard it before either, until two nice mates on the highway introduced me to one. It seems the 18 wheel truck drivers use one to check the air pressure in their tires. There were lots of broke down trucks on the road and they helped me get one, so I could have some protection from the two legged and 4 legged predators out here" Stewart said while considering going back in the house to get it , but instead keeping his chair and relying on Melanie and her pistol instead.

"Ha! That is how I learned about using Wasp spray as mace from two guys wandering down the road. One of them didn't happen to be a big bald guy with a bunch of tattoos did it?" Melanie asked looking at him intently.

"Yes it was. The other was a tall lanky grey haired bloke named Dave" Stewart said excitedly.

"Was the big one called Dump Truck?" Melanie asked laughingly.

"That he was. Friends of yours?" Stewart said with his eyes sparkling in anticipation of finding them sooner and closer, rather than farther away.

"Well no, not really. They helped me out of a bind when some punks tried to take my bottle of water from me not long after the solar storm hit" Melanie responded.

"I heard about that! We spent a very pleasing evening and morning talking about everything that had happened or might happen, because as David put "The Shit Has Hit The Fan". Stewart recollected.

"I wish I had more time with them, what did David say to expect? He is a pretty character." Melanie inquired.

"Well the biggest thing he warned me about besides the obvious ones of shortages of food and water and people rioting and looting, was to watch out for the number of stray dogs that will occur and start packing up and becoming a huge threat to us humans" Stewart answered, while going to check on the fire to see if he could put his tea pot on yet.

"He gave me some warnings and survival tricks, too. We ought to compare notes, don't you think." Melanie replied enjoying this Englishman and having fun sharing common acquaintances with him.

"David is smart about that sort of thing. He told me to think improvisation, the ability to use things for other than what they were originally designed for, is an important survival skill. It's not what things were that's important, it's what they can become, what they can be used for like garbage bags. They also gave me directions to Dump Trucks cousins' house, if I got in a bind here in the city and that is where I am headed, as soon as I make my way back to the interstate." Stewart said with some determination in his voice

"Dumpie said he was going to Newnan when I met him, is that where you are headed?" Melanie said studying Stewart

"That I am. I was hoping to somehow acquire a bicycle for the trip. I got some money; you have any thoughts where I might be able to make an offer on one?" Stewart said hopefully.

"Its possible, I got an extra one in the garage if the tires are not flat from sitting up too long. But I want to talk about why they said for you to go there first; before we talk about possibly making a deal." Melanie said while accepting her cup of tea from Stewart and motioning for him to have a seat quicker, because she wanted his full attention.

"Well, I am not exactly clear on all that, we broke into a beer truck that day and things got a bit hazy after Dump Truck asked me to join his "tribe" and gave me an invite to go along with them. Oh, I was properly daft not to have accepted then and there. It seems Truck has lots of farmers in his family and that they were going to be somehow alright; no matter what, even if the grid never got back up." Stewart advised while enjoying his first cup of tea for the day and relishing every drop in the company of this interesting and friendly woman, "How remarkable that we know the same helpful gents."

"I thought about trying to go north to my Grannie's house. They used to farm, but have not set a crop in years and … she had a pacemaker" Melanie said letting the last word dangle and tearing up.

Stewart realized that the electromagnetic pulse produced from the Coronal Mass Ejection or CME by the sun was probably a death warrant for all those people who rely on such medical devices, and so he hesitantly offered his sympathies. He also told her that no one could be sure just how the EMP would effect a pacemaker, and reminded her that some are 'demand only,' which meant that maybe her grannie is alright.

Melanie regained her composure and sipped her tea thoughtfully after thanking Stewart for his kind words.

"Stewart, things are getting out of hand around here and I need to think outside the box here for a minute. Grannie's house is 60 miles north and I don't know what I will find when I get there, but I got some blood relative rights to be there and I can raise a garden. You want to consider maybe entertaining the thought of trying to make the trip with me?" Melanie asked speculatively.

"Well you have taken me off my feet and beside myself, that you would offer a total stranger, let alone not one of your countrymen, such a grand opportunity" Stewart said confused by this turn of events.

"I am not offering this proposition to you out of pity or passion. It's strictly for selfish reasons, that circumstance requires me to consider. I do not have anyone else to help with the farm work or help with dangers of the road. And, I think maybe you might be the one I can trust; and in your present circumstances, that you might agree to such an offer." Melanie said while watching the changing nervous expressions thought processes that Stewart's face was betraying.

"I am honored you would suggest such a thing but, I think my lot is best thrown in with David and Dump Truck. Them Gents got a good spirit, I don't see why they would not welcome you too, if say you arrived with me self to take them up on the generous offer afforded me." Stewart said contemplatively.

"I don't know, Stewart you do not know what they might feel like after a month of food stores going down and no hope in sight. Besides, David said he was going to try to make the trip all the way to Montgomery and might not be there. How he is going to walk 180 miles home I don't know, but he seemed dead set to try" Melanie advised Stewart who was pouring them both another cup of tea.

"I wouldn't sell Dave short, if anyone can make it, he probably could. He might have looked at his options and stayed with Dump. Either way it's a shorter trip and from the little bit I know about the way Dump Truck described his relatives, those are all working farms and that would be the best bet for survival" Stewart replied resolutely.

"What you are saying makes sense, but lets talk inside about this further; I see a group of folks just rounded that corner up the street and we don't need any confrontations" Melanie said hurriedly grabbing the pot off the grill and putting the lid back on the barbecue.

Stewart helped gather up the sauce pan that contained a can of soup that had been warming on the edge of the grill and their cups and followed Melanie back into the house.

"Bloody hell, it is just not right that two people can not have a peaceable moment over a cup of tea without some yahoos spoiling the moment" Stewart growled while peering out one of the windows to see if the group would soon pass.

"That is my main reason for wanting to leave soon. Things are only going to get worse and I am also faced with not knowing what to do when I eat the last can of beans on my shelf" Melanie said standing vigil at another window.

"I will just check the backyard and be back in a moment" Stewart said as he went back in the kitchen and collected his Tommy knocker and gave the backyard a quick look over before returning to his peering from behind the curtains in the front of the house.

"You recognize anybody" Melanie called in a stage whisper to him from the window to his far right.

"I seen that young boy with the pants falling off of him with the ones who tried to waylay my kit, but I don't see the others" Stewart said eying a group of six assorted aged people walking the street and eying the homes surrounding it.

"That one that looks like the leader with the bandanna hanging out his back pocket looks like he might be a gang banger, but I don't know, That color is supposed to signify some kind of gang affiliation, but I don't remember which one" Melanie said as Stewart noted she had her pistol out and ready.

"I see you found your Tommy Knocker; sorry I can't offer you a pistol or something." Melanie commented looking over at Stewart.

"I am sorry I can't be more useful, my friend; but I will give you me best if the waterloo comes about" Stewart replied grinning.

"I never get tired of your accent Stewart, but I am glad I had a history minor to figure out your allusions at times" Melanie said re-holstering her revolver, but only after it seemed the possible danger was passed.

"I only got this six shooter, a speed loader and about 10 extra rounds of 38 special, so we definitely lack firepower, if someone was serious about getting in here. Let's talk about your counter proposal over that soup before it gets cold. You showed some of your mettle, Stewart, by going to get your stick to fight off them punks and I'm pretty sure you checked out back before coming back in here. I like that; we're going to get along just fine." Melanie said smiling charmingly at him.

'Probably would have died trying, but I was all in for ya Missus" Stewart said in his best cockney accent with a tip of an imaginary hat.

"That's all it takes" Melanie jibed back at him and gave his shoulder a squeeze, as they wandered back into the kitchen.

"If both those bicycles work, how long would it take to reach Newnan you suppose?" Melanie asked as she filled the two bowls with soup.

"I am not sure, mum. Look at this map and tell me if you recognize the landmarks. I really know very little, but to pass the exit marker by on the main interstate. This goes a back way I am unfamiliar with." Stewart said producing a brown paper bag with directions and a crude map drawn on it.

"What's this map drawn on the back?" Melanie asked turning the bag over.

"David said that was where his "Bug Out Mobile" was parked at. He said it was 50/50 if it worked or not, because it was a 1985 GMC Jimmy 4x4 that used a carburetor instead of electronic fuel system. He gave me the key, in case I needed bug out supplies or camping stuff, if I got over that way, whether it started or not." Stewart explained his voice full of awe and gratitude at the kindness of the almost stranger named David.

"What is Bug Out Supplies?" Melanie asked looking confused.

"Bugging out, he said, just means leaving an area for whatever reason. Bug out supplies are basically camping goods that help you, if you're thinking you might have to rough it in the woods. I think that was how he explained it." Stewart said trying to reflect on the conversation.

"Why didn't he go get his stuff?" Melanie said studying the drawing.

"He said it was 20 miles in the wrong direction and could not justify the 40 mile round trip going back for it" Stewart said remembering how testy David was about the loss of his preparedness gear and dependable old Jimmy 4x4.

"That is about 12 miles from here; I don't have any camping stuff or know much about it. What do you think he has in that truck?" Melanie asked trying to think if it would be worth bicycling in that direction for an unknown value.

"I am not sure, I asked a similar question and he just told me it was enough for whatever was going on, short of getting nuked, as he put it. He said there is a pistol in his hotel room, but its one of those electronic key card things and unless I busted the door down it would not do me any good. I never seen a semi automatic pistol anyway and he said did not matter and explained what he called basics to me, if I could gain entrance." Stewart explained and wondered where the conversation was going.

"You can go to Newnan or Lithia Springs from over there down an alternate Georgia state interstate. Maybe Dave not being from here didn't know that. Thing is though we got to consider will that truck work," Melanie said to a thoroughly confused and possibly misguided Stewart.

"So you are saying, if we go to Dump's it might be worth an extra day or two to try Dave's "Jimmy" is that it?" Stewart said searching for the word for a different version of a Blazer truck that was popular before SUV's.

"Why did Dave give you a 50/50 on it? I seen some military trucks running, but I thought that was because they might of thought about shielding them from Nuke EMP. I find it hard to grasp why anything works or doesn't work at the moment." Melanie said looking perplexed.

"David was bitching about having to park in a parking deck and the little I know about shielding from things says that those layers of concrete and asphalt might just have given that type of vehicle another chance." Stewart said following his new found friend's drift.

"If that vehicle works, we could check out Dump's place in an afternoon or be well on our way by evening to Grannie's. If it does not work at all, we would maybe have some tools we need to get by in this or other environments." Melanie said getting enthusiastic towards going on a mission.

"What about that bicycle in your garage that we discussed? We can not even talk much further regarding details without finding out if the tires hold air. Do you have a pump by the way?" Stewart said warming to the idea, but still speculating and cautious.

"There is one attached to my 10 speed that will work, that is if the tires are not rotted on the other one. Let me ask you a question. Did you go in that garage in back of my house before you jumped my fence? I saw you do it by the way, but you appeared to be eating more than I was willing to give up was the reason I sprayed you with that wasp juice." Melanie said being reproachful but still apologetic for spraying him with the wasp spray.

"No. I just hid my lily whites from possible mayhem. I did not even try the door. Why? What might be in there?" Stewart said with an 'I am not beyond a necessary acquisition or requisition attitude'.

"I don't know where the couple is that owns that house, but they had a bicycle built for two they used to ride around here with a detachable trailer for carrying the two kids they got." Melanie said beaming a beautiful smile towards Stewart

"Cranky, I say we go investigate further! If you got an axe or hammer or something that we might use as a key to this possibly useful mystery to get the lock off, we maybe strike gold" Stewart said rubbing his hands together and looking pleased.

"I got a regular hammer, if you think it will serve the purpose at hand." Melanie said while going to a kitchen drawer to retrieve the tool.

"That looks like it will do nicely. If that bicycle is in there, I say we just pass it over the fence and not be riding it on that back street." Stewart said looking at Melanie for confirmation.

"Sounds like a plan, lets do it"." Melanie said while moving towards the back door.

Melanie and Stewart climbed over the fence and after a quick look up and down the street in front of the house that the garage belonged to and set about prying the lock hasp off the door. After some initial difficulties Stewart managed to pull the screws out of the wood and take off the mechanism lock and all.

There inside just as Melanie had advised was a red bicycle built for two and a little two seater kiddie trailer.

"Bingo" Stewart said as he rolled the bike out and Melanie pulled the trailer out.

After a bit of a struggle Stewart and Melanie managed to get the tandem bike and its trailer over the fence to her backyard.

"That was a bit of a workout" Stewart said sweating and gingerly touching the scratch on his head that was stinging from getting salt in it.

"Well part one of our escape plans is here, we can load up that trailer with what food I got left and some clothes and stuff. Can you think of anything we might need to take Stewart?" Melanie said as they moved the bike into her garage.

"I say you pedal your bike along with this one, if we don't overload that trailer I think I can manage to pedal it by myself if we keep the pace down" Stewart said regarding it.

"I will keep the weight down best I can" Melanie said

"Bring your winter clothes too, no telling when you can get a winter coat again" Stewart said sagely.

"I hadn't thought of that, what else can you think of?" Melanie asked.

"A good butcher knife would be right smart. I wish we had time to make some sort of sheath for one, but we got other matters to deal with" Stewart said running down a mental list of what might be needed.

"I built me a bug out bag of household stuff like David suggested when we met, for the eventuality of this day so I am already pretty well packed" Melanie said and went to show it to Stewart.

Basically what she showed Stewart was a large shoulder beach bag with some essentials and a blanket tied to it. The whole setup didn't weigh more than about 18lbs.

"I just got a sauce pan in there for cooking stuff and boiling water. We could lighten the load but how can we be sure David's truck is unmolested? I would hate to not have what we need because we depended too much on an unknown probability" Melanie said to Stewart who was looking through her preparations.

"I agree wholeheartedly, hey you got an apron around? We could use it to hold that wasp spray and some other incidentals like a bottle of water etc. as sort of a field gear setup while riding the bikes." Stewart advised.

"I got a couple, but you going to look dang funny in either one of them" Melanie said while going to a Kitchen drawer and producing a Blue one with embroidered flowers and a pink one that had "Kiss the Cook" emblazoned across the front.

Stewart grabbed the Kiss the Cook one and tried it on for size while Melanie stood giggling at the spectacle.

"If me mates saw me in this, I would never live it down" Stewart said and did a comical pirouette.

"I got a floppy beach hat you can have to finish the effect" Melanie said now outright laughing at Stewart's appearance and antics.

"Well how else am I going to carry some water and other essentials while riding a bike? I can't be stopping to get in the trailer for water or trying to get to my Tommy knocker." Stewart said removing the unflattering apron.

"Hey I know, you can use one of my purses' Melanie said and went to get him a Hippie Chic looking carpet bag one.

"This is much more fitting for a gent. Thank you" Stewart said and draped the purse over his shoulder.

"Well, I must say that is an improvement, But I will miss all the fun of hearing what Dump Truck would've said to see you in the other get up." Melanie said chuckling and giving Stewart an evil looking smirk.

"Now you'll not be telling him I was thinking of

wearing a pink apron to greet him." Stewart said playing along with the joke.

"Oh I just might, you better be good to me on the road trip." Melanie retorted back.

"That I will, mum! Hey, maybe we can trade that big bag of charcoal you got left for some more stores. Didn't you say some of these neighbors were friends of yours?" Stewart said contemplating a barter situation.

"That's a good idea; we will go see that old man called Harvey up the street that ran off those young punks with his shotgun. He fancies himself a ladies man, but he has got to be at least 80. He is a World War II vet and I believe he spent some time in London, if I remember right" Melanie said while contemplating what else she might have to trade him.

"We can only carry so much water. I got another full 5 gallon water jug and I guess since we're leaving, he may as well know the bathtub is full as well as a few more pots and pans of water." Melanie said finally committing fully to the notion she was going to be gone most likely forever from her home.

"May as well trade him the dispenser too if he has a mind to take it. We could get it down to him some way" Stewart said warming to the notion that he was going to get to participate in some haggling.

"Well lets lock up and go, when should we say he can have this stuff, if we arrange a deal?" Melanie said with a smile that soon faded as she had not considered when they would depart.

"I say he could have them today or at latest tomorrow morning. We should be off from here and about our business as soon as we can." Stewart said a bit anxiously at how leaving so soon would be received by Melanie.

After a bit of a tenuous pause Melanie responded.

"You're right; the time to go is as soon as possible. I'd just soon do it at dawn in the morning and hopefully be out of here before anyone notices we are gone" Melanie said committing to the bug out concept.

"Well alrighty then, I know it's your stuff, but would you mind me doing a bit of the negotiating? I got a lifetime of haggling with fish mongers and such." Stewart said with a wink in her direction.

"Have at it, but he is a crusty old geezer and I don't think it will be easy to get the better of him." Melanie said writing down on a note pad the goods she wanted to trade.

"You just leave it to me, I only want a fair shake for a farthing and I will do us proud, you will see" Stewart said and picked up the 20lb bag of charcoal and headed towards the door.

"That's his house over there on the corner, it looks like he has company" Melanie said as she watched several old women seemingly carrying goods into the house.

"It looks like he may be doing some business already" Stewart said looking at the old folks bustling around Harvey's porch.

Melanie spotted Harvey carrying a box from one of the neighbor's houses along the way and called out to him.

"Hey, Harvey! You're starting a block party without inviting me?" Melanie said to him cheerfully.

"Hi there! No I am collecting me a harem of all the sweet old ladies on this block that think I need taking care of. Actually they want my protection but we let them think what they want." The barrel chested old fellow in khakis said.

"You been flirting with every old bird on this street for years. They look like they moving in with you, or are they just centrally locating supplies?" Melanie said amazed this old goat was still so spry

"Welcome to Fort Grogan, the last bastion of southern hospitality and manliness' Harvey said grinning.

"We old folks got to stick together so me and old Luke over there talked to these six fine ladies and invited them to stay in my princely abode" Harvey said full of himself and his gaggle of new tenets started to wander over to meet Melanie and Stewart.

"This old gigolo made some sense with his offer to band together, but he don't know we're all going to lock our doors to his advances" A feisty silver haired woman with a large bun hairdo said.

"I am Dotty Rawls and this is my roommate and friend Lorelei Pierce" she said indicating a smiling woman of about 70 years of age.

Stewart set down the bag of charcoal and was soon overwhelmed by the chattering sounds of the group of old people introducing themselves and asking him how he got stuck here away from his homeland.

Harvey finally put an end to the good natured banter and asked what he could do for Melanie.

"We are leaving tomorrow Harvey and wanted to know if you had anything to trade for some charcoal and water. I know times are tough but heat and water got values so we thought maybe you had some cans of food you would be willing to let go if you thought the offer was right" Melanie said as Stewart tried to get closer to the conversation.

"I just might, Stewart you look like you want to get in on this deal, what are you offering?" Harvey said as the tenants to his fort got back to the process of moving in.

"Oh nothing much, being a former member of the diplomatic corps and the traveling companion to Miss Melanie here, we thought it best to let me tell you our needs and see if we can meet your terms." Stewart said getting poised to try to evaluate what might be offered for scarce goods amongst the survivors.

"Well I haven't taken inventory of what all we got but you are offering two things we need a lot, let's do a little dickering and see if your expectations are up to snuff." Harvey said indicating some porch chairs to his quests.'

"Not wanting to speculate too much mind you, but I say 1lb of cooking briquettes for 1 can of food" Stewart offered.

"Well on a good day, that offer sounds fair but in these bad days, why would I do that when wood is aplenty and just as useful to boil a pot?" Harvey said taking the wind out of Stewarts sails and recalculating the worthiness of Stewart's goods to his disadvantage.

"Indeed sir you have me not considering that one cannot eat coal, but we got purified water and a dispenser to add to the lot" Stewart said while mentally setting the fire starter fluid aside to try to equal up the barter terms.

"This is going to be fun, I haven't bartered with a Brit since the big one, I was in London and India you know, as well as Sicily and North Africa" Harvey said to put Stewart on his guard and warn him he was an experienced trader.

" I be thanking you for your kind service and the worlds freedom, knowing that you are a well traveled man you must see the value in having a household water dispenser one can monitor visually and accurately in times like these" Stewart countered.

" I don't see shit except that it needs to be filled about right now and we got short sheets to do it, if you understand my meaning" Harvey groused but willing to listen to any proposals.

"I might be able to tell you where to obtain sufficient supplies of water to keep your "harem" was it? Surviving in times of need like this. You can gather it and refill the dispenser so that it might be rationed until better resources avail themselves." Stewart said confidently.

"You're not from here. How are you going to tell me where to get water from to help my group? Don't get cocky with me Limey, spit it out and take my offer or be done" Harvey said in his flashback to harder war times.

"Watch the Limey Yank, I got a fair offer for you on an intellectual scale you might not have considered" Stewart said rising to the occasion.

Melanie was not used to this type of male banter and tried to intercede but got hushed by both of them and decided to wander off and check out the other inhabitants of the house.

"So I am listening, where is this water at that you know better than me about" Harvey said regarding Stewarts smug look.

"It's everywhere and no where mate, just like the lack of goods you offering me on the table. What exactly are we trading for? I showed part of my cards and you for all I know want to trade cans of French cut green beans or something. Give me something of more substance so we can get this pig out of a poke." Stewart said sensing he might be getting the upper hand.

"The value of that dispenser is unreliable, if you leave I get it, if you destroy it you're just being an asshole and I might not try to trade for that reason. Give me a taste of info or a clue you can actually produce this mythical water you claim to have." Harvey said still trying to get his upper hand back from Stewart.

"Ok, a small sample only and only for the short term. There is a dialysis clinic about two miles from here that has about 500 gallons of water in a tank that is already filtered." Stewart said rubbing his brow.

"Can you see this old folks convention I got going here walking every other day to get water 4 miles? Half of us would be dead in a week." Harvey replied disgusted he didn't get anything very usable, *Hell he thought, that's good but now that he knew this he could just get his Yellow Pages out to locate it.*

"Show some cans man, I said a small sample and what I might tell you will not require walking so far "Stewart said getting aggravated with the obstinacy of this man.

" Fine, a can a pound for the charcoal, 5 cans for the 5 gallon jug of water plus the dispenser and if you quit being so damned mysterious about the water sources I might sweeten the deal on can selection" Harvey countered knowing he wasn't going to win in this trade.

"I have yet to see the food in question but let us put that aside for the moment. I know where a grape arbor is that you could harvest both fruit and water from, does that make the pie tastier to you?" Stewart said regarding his new barter buddy.

"Now we talking, is that your hole card you been hiding?" Harvey told him thinking he could get an advantage back.

"Only some icing on the cake my friend, 50% meat in those cans and I show my hand for the day. I would dare say the deal can be satisfactorily resolved to our mutual benefit" Stewart told him sitting back and looking serious. He looked at Harvey a moment before extending his hand to seal the deal and after a moment's hesitation Harvey grabbed it and gave it a hardy shake.

"Ok you old lobster back, what's up with the water tricks?"" Harvey said glad to be done with negotiations.

Stewart explained for the next 30 minutes or so what appeared earlier in this book that David had explained to him about using solar stills and tree transpiration in the city to get water and left Harvey breathless with the possibilities of something so simple but ingenious to survive long-term in the desert conditions it seemed the city faced now.

"Most folks are dead or already dead just from no way to produce water right Stewart? Harvey said becoming aware it was just a matter of time his old ass could outlast the punks that were demonizing the community.

"As simple as that mate, in three days after someone does not get water you can fight them like you were twenty again if you are hydrated at your age." Stewart said mentally thanking his mentor David.

"I got an old bayonet I took as a memento off one of the Huns that I would be pleased if you would put to good use protecting Melanie. These old biddies be a joke trying to use it but I think you could put it to good use. Take it with my compliments and I am glad to have the chance to team up with a Brit again to wage. a war." Harvey said taking Stewart off guard with a hug and leaving him sitting speechless as Harvey went to retrieve it.

Harvey returned shortly and gave him an old German sword bladed bayonet that looked about two foot long to Stewart's eyes.

"I wish it was an Enfield rifle but this is the best I can do" Harvey said presenting his piece of war memorabilia.

"This is a mighty fine honor you have given me and greatly appreciated" Stewart said admiring the long piece of steel with its cut out blood groove. Battle weapons picked up by you on the field makes this a greater prize than I can imagine." Stewart said forming a newer and stronger bond to the old bleary eyed soldier.

"May it serve you well? Let's see if we still got a drink around here and quit this namby pamby recollection. "Harvey said rising from his chair and going back to his persona of joking with his "girls" and old marching buddy Luke.

"You seem to have done some good" Melanie said saddling up to a touched Stewart.

"Aye, I did, but no one might ever know what this short sword had seen." He said reflectively looking at the deadly and heavy knife in his lap.

Stewart considered that Harvey gave him a knowing smile and a leg pat when he presented the bit of history and defense that was personally his now, and wondered at how many times this tradition had passed down thru the ages.

"Melanie, our deal is done but for the collecting and delivering of the goods. We need to hook that trailer up to the bike and either in one trip or two give the water and delivery unit to Harvey." Stewart concluded.

"Did you get what you asked for?" Melanie said questionably.

"Yes me bucko, that and more. Are we ready to start the transference or do you need more time?" Stewart said pushing the bag of charcoal back to the edge of the house with his foot.

"I am done but for the good byes to those sweet old ladies. We leave on the morning tide, is that right Stewart?" Melanie said with a half smile.

"Would be if an ocean was here about, but I guess if we count the tides of humanity it's an appropriate saying" Stewart said indicating he wanted a "high five" by raising his hand.

"Stewart, are we doing the right thing?" Melanie said looking pleadingly at him.

"Best we can with the lot delivered, these folks be alright and maybe we see tomorrow a bit longer than they, but life's wheel will always keep turning" Stewart recognized.

"Sometimes Steward you make no sense or all the sense in the world. Let's go get your trade items and finish with a cup of tea. By the way, did Harvey tell you that he is a widower from the era and his wife he met during the war liked tea?" Melanie said with a sparkle in her eyes.

"No, he didn't, that explains a lot. What did you talk about in passing?" Stewart said befuddled.

"He gave me a big tin of tea and a tea ball for as he said your "brewing pleasure" for taking care of me on a distant road as he termed our little trip. I was not supposed to tell you till later but that old man likes you and gave something from his heart" Melanie said regarding a speechless Stewart and evidently the old ladies present were in on the gift as they all smiled and waved their farewells as Melanie escorted him back home towards the collection of promised goods.

Stewart and Melanie managed to load both the water jug and dispenser into the bike trailer and delivered it to Harvey with a round of applause from those present that saw them bicycling for two down the tree lined street with it in tow.

Melanie's grape arbor and whole house possessions passed to the "stay on" group of elderly residents in a tearful and meaningful series of good byes, and Stewart and her readied themselves for tomorrow.

Dancing With Dump Trucks

Stewart awoke the next morning as the sun was just coming up and thought "this is it! The great adventure begins as they were all in to achieve a goal. What a lucky man he was to have happened upon this neighborhood irregardless of those that would hate him for being different.

Melanie heard him stirring and mentally readied her self for the day of new challenges and opportunities. Old Dumpie was not the nicest person she had ever considered a kindred bond with, yet there was something in his eyes that intrigued her. I am being silly like a school girl she chided herself; I got probably 20 years on him and a world of social class difference. Yet she still thought of the exciting possibilities of this younger mans evident interest in her. Stewart was nice enough and a possibility for a mate but some kind of weird chemistry was going on if her "Dumpie" still had a shine in his eyes for her.

Melanie heard Stewart go out the front door and trying to resurrect the few remaining coals in the grill ostensibly to get his morning tea she mused. What is up with the English and their tea, I guess it's the same as our morning coffee ritual she suspected but still was amused on the number of times she had heard they did it a day.

They had inventoried and collected their bags the night before and Stewart busied himself securing the load on the trailer he had attached to the tandem bike. Melanie walked out to see Stewart casually leaning over her back fence and surveying the street for signs of miscreants,

"Top of the morning to you missus" Stewart said quite loudly when he heard the door open.

"Your up bright and early, I heard you making tea earlier, lets have that and be off." Melanie said welcoming the new day and adventure.

"It's me own blend we be having until she runs out, but I am mightily grateful your man Harvey seen to my affection for a cup of leaves" Stewart responded happily back.

"I hate long goodbyes, can we just put it in mug and start peddling or I might cry." Said Melanie wistfully looking around her place one last time.

"As short as you want mum, let me clear up my pot and we be gone if that is your wish. Stewart responded and returned to clear off the grill and repack his basket.

"That has done it then, you want to give the house one more looks over while I ready the transport?" Stewart declared" I am ready now and not looking back" said Melanie following his lead and they pulled up the kick stands and the new venture began.

Stewart thought this was going to be an easy ride despite the lack of another peddler on this tandem rig but soon realized that Georgia sun would take its toll on his best and worst expectations.

"You going to have to slow a might darling, these old bones ain't up to the task at hand" Stewart said after the first mile or so.

"You want me to give it a shot?" Melanie asked after seeing that a single rider had a handful driving that bike made for two plus a trailer.

"I will push on but the pace and this ducking and dodging cars and obstacles is getting me down" said Stewart huffing and puffing in his reduced state.

"Lets pull over and take a breather; I know I could use one." Melanie said just trying to placate his obstinacy of not showing how much the labor of driving that bike was taxing his energy.

"I guess not having a good sup is showing in me limbs, a break would do me right Stewart said letting the bike slow to a very slow coast on the next hill he had to surmount.

"We got nothing but time" Melanie said trying to reduce Stewarts exertions. She knew that men get their pride and ego confused but from this point on she was determined to make this half starved man measure his distance not in miles but in getting to a destination safely.

"How far we got to keep bumping this track missus?" Said Stewart, fading fast from the heat and pedaling towards an unknown distance.

"We've covered about 7 miles, I am guessing we go another at least 5 more before we find some refuge at David's truck. Its only 7:30 in the morning so let's take time to nibble something" said a concerned Melanie for Stewart's health.

"No I jut need a small break, I am not used to this heat. Be a good place for a water stand." Stewart said rasping out a chuckle as he dismounted and stood on wobbly legs.

They were lucky to leave at so early an hour and had no distractions as to their right of way to make a path down this broken-down-car stretch of highway. They had had the occasional fool holler at them from an overpass or chain link fence as they peddled along, but no threats so far.

Part of the reason Stewart thought he was so winded was the smoky haze that seemed more intense in the area they were in. Ever since the solar storm had hit there had been countless uncontrolled fires continually burning. Whether it was a product of the geomagnetic disturbance or the grace of God, the weather seemed to also have included numerous rainstorms that had most likely kept the whole city from burning down.

Melanie noticed the increase in smoke also but it was impossible to tell where it was coming from.

"You know Stewart we hadn't considered the possibility that we might not be able to access that area where David parked his truck" she said ominously.

"I was just thinking about that, you got any alternate routes in mind if it's too bad down that way?" Stewart said hoping that he would not have to retrace their steps.

"Yes there are many routes we can take but I would have to study on which is best if we somehow get diverted from our location." Melanie said pondering a worst case scenario.

"Well no sense putting off the inevitable, I am rested enough now. Let's see what cards fortune will deal us." Stewart said and they set off back on their journey.

They were going through the water they had with them much quicker than anticipated and Stewart hoped David had a decent provision of it in his truck if they made it that far. The only other thing he could think of was hole up somewhere until it got cooler and maybe they could travel early mornings and dusk.

They had been traveling for a couple miles when Melanie pointed ahead and said exuberantly "That's our exit! We were closer than I thought "which gave Stewart renewed vigor and speed towards the destination.

"That map David drew said it was about a half mile off this exit. Oh there is the Hotel sign up ahead" Melanie said gesturing.

The road off the exit was a jumble of crashed and stalled cars and it appeared a tanker truck had burned blocking the entire right lane. Melanie and

Stewart stopped and surveyed the carnage and tried to see a way round the huge mess.

"We are forestalled," murmured Stewart not seeing anyway around the mess unless they walked.

"If we go back up on the interstate and come in reverse from that On Ramp we can get through it looks like" Melanie said while Stewart scrutinized the odd cloverleaf.

"Looks like it to me two, oh well" Stewart said as he made a wide sweeping turn to go back and try a reentry.

Stewart and Melanie managed to weave their way towards the hotel and begin to approach its parking deck.

"What level did he say he was on" Melanie asked Stewart who was scanning the safety of the area.

"Third level, it's a red and white truck with Alabama plates and something called a deer rack attached to the back, supposed to look like a small welded tray to haul stuff in." Stewart said and then started pointing.

"That might be it" Stewart said catching a glimpse of the top drivers' side of a truck.

"These bikes will be too hard to drive up those ramps. You think they be okay down here? Melanie said looking around but not seeing another people about.

"Too bad we don't have any means to secure them. I guess we ok if we get up there and back quick" Stewart said and moved his rig into the first floor of the parking deck so at least a casual passerby wouldn't see it.

Stewart and Melanie made their way up the

parking decks ramps and gave each other a high five when the truck came into view.

"He certainly has a bunch of stuff in this thing "Stewart said as he approached the back hatch of the GMC.

"I like having the gear, but the big magic question is does it work?" Melanie said approaching the vehicle as Stewart fumbled for the key

"You want to do the honors?" Stewart said handing Melanie the keys.

"I feel like I should say a little prayer or something but here goes nothing" Melanie said inserting the key.

"He said to kick the gas several times before you try it" Stewart offered and watched Melanie do just that before glancing up and giving the key a turn.

Vroom, sputter sputter , and died the trucks engine sounded.

Melanie and Stewart looked at each other very hopeful and sure as she tried it again and the engine turned over and picked up an easy idle that was almost interminable over the whoops of joy and laughter coming from Melanie and Stewart.

"We Got Wheels!" Melanie cried reaching out the door to give Stewart a hug.

"That old Prepper Dave has come through again" Stewart said happily hugging her back.

"How much gas we got?" Stewart asked

"Only a quarter of a tank, but how much you want to bet there is a siphon hose in here"? Melanie said smiling.

"Knowing Dave he probably has at least two" Stewart said going over towards the passenger side door.

A quick search of a large plastic box on the back seat revealed a siphon hose as well as blankets, flashlights, a full 2 quart canteen and some other preparedness goods.

"Ha! Told Ya there would be one in here! He told me about this, you see that little brass bell on the end of this hose. He said you just stick it into whatever you want to siphon and just shake it. No sucking or blowing to get it to work" Stewart said showing Melanie the contraption.

Stewart quickly siphoned gas from the cars parked on the deck and thought what a shame it was he didn't have keys to try some more of them.

"Hey, he has a bunch of bungee cords and rope in here. We can tie the bikes on top of the truck so we can use them later or if something happens to the truck" Melanie said searching through Dave's goodies in the truck.

"Capitol Idea! I am almost done here and we can drive down and get them." Stewart said and started humming to himself as he finished his tasks.

Stewart and Melanie didn't even bother to take inventory of all the various items in the truck as they were sure by now if they needed it, it was probably in there. They secured the bikes on the roof top luggage rack and after some difficulty even managed to get the bike trailer tied down on top of the lot.

Stewart decided Melanie would be the best driver and happily relaxed on the passenger side as she maneuvered around the road trying to get back up on the interstate.

"Hey see if the air conditioner works: Stewart said grinning.

Melanie immediately gave it a try and they both thought the weight of the world was lifted off them as a stream of cold air began to blow and they didn't lose their smiles for many miles from the sheer joy of having it available.

Stewart and Melanie proceeded down the road at a snails pace as avoiding stalled cars made it impossible to go over a few miles an hour in some places and possibly 10 when they hit gaps in the broken down traffic.'

"I don't care how long it takes, I am enjoying this AC" Stewart said as Melanie groused at not being able to make any time at all.

"I guess I should be more than thankful too" Melanie reflected and brightened up as traffic greatly opened up upon leaving the city.

Melanie started telling Stewart to check the map and the landmarks as they got closer to Newnan and their final destination.

They were surprised to see an old tractor plowing a field as they progressed and chatted happily about the implications that might mean.

Up ahead of them they saw someone riding a horse or a mule and carrying a rifle or a shotgun and they slowed to almost a stop to talk about the possibilities of an encounter with the rider.

These days one couldn't be too careful about getting into armed confrontations. Then again it was now common for everyone to take up arms.

"We are supposed to be awful close to Dump's cousin's house. It might be possible that who ever that is might be related to him." Stewart said considering the dilemma.

"We could sit here and just let them move on" Melanie said advising caution.

"Just keep your pistol handy and try not to surprise whoever that is. Maybe we can get directions from him too" Stewart advised wanting to proceed.

"I will give it a try" Melanie said restarting the vehicle and driving slowly down the road catching up to the rider.

"Stewart could see from his seat that it wasn't a horse but a mule in front of them. The big man riding him looked as wide as the mule from Stewart's vantage point.

The rider heard them coming and turned in the saddle to regard them and Melanie and Stewart instantly noted the Tattoos on his forearm.

Could it be they both thought glancing at each other? Stewart was sure and climbed halfway out the window and hollered "Dump Truck! It's your old mate Stewart!"

A broad grin became visible from under the riders hat and he swung down from his mount.

"Stewart! Hey buddy good to see you, who is that driving" he said as they slowly rolled up.

"Melanie!" Dump yelled loud enough to startle his mule.

Melanie put the truck in park and both she and Stewart ran forward to greet Dump who just dropped his reins and looked like a smaller version of his mount running to great them and embraced both simultaneously once they got into his grabbing range. Dump managed to pick both of them up and was doing a happy snoopy dance that took both of their breaths away as everyone hooted with laughter.

Martha's Home For Wayward Preppers

Ron Foster

1

The Great Arrival

Stewart and Melanie finally caught their breath, after having had Dump Truck grab them both up off their feet in a bear hug and swinging them around in little circles, as he did a bit of a happy dance.

"How did you find each other? Is that David's truck? Are you ok?" Dump let out a stream of astonished questions to the pair's sudden appearance from the apocalyptic city of Atlanta.

"Well yes, that's David's truck; Stewart and I met by chance or fate and are both fine." Melanie said laughing.

"Good to see you, my old traveler buddy!" Stewart said beaming at Dump.

"I have been thinking about you guys off and on for so long now. I been worried to death that I could have done something to make it easier on you; but you know times being what they are, it's a miracle we even got a chance to meet again." Dump said, putting his arm around Stewart and grinning like no tomorrow at Melanie.

"It's been a rough go of it, that's for sure. Does the offer still stand to join the Truck clan?" Stewart said tapping Dump on the shoulder and smiling at him.

"Sure it does! My cousin Martha will be happy to

see you both. I told her all about the two of you several times. Boy is she going to be surprised you have made it here, and with David's Truck to boot!" Truck said looking over the old 1985 GMC Jimmy 4x4 that had somehow miraculously started, when 90% of the cars in the world didn't.

"We just picked up that vehicle a few hours ago. Otherwise, you would have seen us on those bicycles a day or so from now." Melanie said reaching out to pat Dump's Mule who was taking an interest in the meeting.

"That's old Saul; he's pretty friendly for an old beast, just as long as you are not asking him to do some work." Dump said, as Stewart also gave the animal a pat.

"He knows he is going to have to work, when Martha puts that stupid straw hat on him; he doesn't much like the sound of horns either, so I am glad you didn't blow yours." Dump said still wearing a smile as big as the Kool Aid pitcher promotional guy.

"I've been around Horses and such, so I didn't want to spook him. Not sure it even works, the radio is fried, but check this out, Dumpie... it has AIR CONDITIONING!" Melanie said, like it was the biggest treasure in the world. Dump guessed it was indeed quite a wonderful and rare item to possess these days.

"You are going to have to let me and Martha sit a spell in it this evening; this heat is trying to parboil us and I'm sure she would find it the biggest blessing in the world to just have a few moments of cool air." Dump said looking over the load it had on and in it.

"You bring any food?" He said looking at them inquisitively and hopefully.

"We brought a pillow case full of can goods, plus David probably has several day's worth stashed in the back of the truck there. Is food tight?" Melanie said worriedly.

"Oh, we short on a few things and long on others, but we're doing ok. Martha and the folks been helping out some travelers here and there; so arriving with any kind of food to help lengthen the pantry will insure you'll be well received. Right now, we don't have any house guests; the Hop Sing's are in the shed. And there is one Prepper couple staying down at the old Halstead place, though they're leaving out in a day or so, after getting some rest. Martha is kind of particular about who she lets stay a day or so, and who has to move on." Dump said still enjoying the wonder of it all in seeing his two new friends return to the fold and feeling relieved as to their well-being.

"What are Hop Sings?" Stewart asked trying to understand southern colloquial English.

"I was wondering that, too." Melanie said waiting for Dump to explain.

"Oh, that's just what we call them. They are a nice Asian couple I found on the roadside one day; they just sort of stayed on and moved in. It was about to start raining and I was riding old Saul here back from Philburn's, when I saw them on the side of the road. Old Papa san had the biggest meat cleaver I ever seen and his wife had a wok she was threatening to bean me with; and they both sort of dared me to mess with them. I think that boy of theirs would have jabbed me with a chop stick, too; if I hadn't convinced them I was friendly." Dump said laughing at the memory.

"Anyway, we kind of did sign-language at each other about how it was going to rain, and how I would give them a roof over their head and something to go in that fancy Chinese frying pan they had. Then, I took them home to Martha's. They don't know very many American words, but the man started jabbering at Martha, when he saw that big wood stove in the house. 'Me cook, me cook' says he, and she said 'he looks like Hop Sing off the TV show Bonanza; the cook that used to work for the Cartwright's on the Ponderosa'. Get this, every time Martha tries to do some work around the kitchen, that wife of his starts saying 'Me do! Me do!' so we call her MeDo. Her son we call HeDo, because once old Hop Sing saw me going to feed the chickens or gather eggs, he started saying "He do! He do!" I about got stuck with a new name, too; since when they want something, they come to me and say 'You Do! You Do!'" Dump said laughing hard enough to make his belly shake at how the family had got adopted and named.

"Their real names we can't pronounce, so we sort of shortened them so it won't sound so much like we're picking on them; but they answer to most everything with nice smiles and understanding. They can't say Truck, so I am 'Dimpie' and Martha sounds like 'Moutha' and Ray is 'Way'." Truck said, obviously fond of his rescued highway charges.

"Sounds like you got a house full already, we don't want to impose." Melanie said thinking once again about going to her Grannie's house in the opposite direction.

"Don't give it another thought. We got plenty of room and options, you both are most definitely welcome." Dump said putting his friends at ease.

"Sounds like the Hop Sings' are right handy to

have around. Hope we will be, too." Melanie said giggling and enjoying how warm a reception Dump had given them.

"Oh, I know it's going to be nice having *YOU* around." Dump reassured her and his face colored a bit, as he thought how maybe he had said something wrong.

Stewart picked up on Dump's discomfort and remembering a conversation with David that maybe this big old boy had a schoolboy crush on Melanie, he decided to poke a bit of fun at him.

"Hey! I am here, too!" Stewart said smirking and feigning hurt feelings.

"Well, I... I mean... I meant... Damn you Stewart, you know what I meant." Dump finally said huffily.

"We know." Melanie said charmingly and patted the big behemoth's shoulder, totally disarming Dump and deepening his blush.

"Well, we're only about a half mile to the house; let's go get you moved in. Martha hates Hop Sing in her kitchen, so get ready for a battle of who cooks for you. Either way is good eats.

"Ray and I got a small still going on her stove that might interfere with her cooking up supper, but I doubt it slows her down much." Dump said explaining the 'summer kitchen' set up they were using for most meals.

"I'd just as soon not be making 'shine' in the house, but Hop Sing won't let us near his stove and Martha won't let us brew down her blackberry wine without her near-constant supervision."

"Oh, you're making brandy!" Stewart said smiling.

'Exactly, liquor is getting hard to find and we thought we would start making up some trade goods or something for personal consumption.' Dump said giving Stewart a high five.

"When the Hop Sings came to stay, Martha put them in the Shed next to the barn, and because they fought over the kitchen so much; Old Papa San moved the wood heater out of the house and everything else in the shed to the fence, while they cleaned it out. He left the stove out by the fence and cooks out there all the time now, I guess not to heat up the house. Even has as his own setup to use the well water for washing up, dishes and laundry.

"He really can cook I give you that, I often wander by and get me some double dinners." Dump guffawed and explained that Hop Sing would cook for him and his families at times then bring food up to the house for the rest of the clan to eat. Even though Martha made faces, when he did this, she had to admit he was a whiz with spices that rivaled her own award winning country fare.

Dump told them that having the Hop Sings around wasn't always good food and friendly kitchen rivalries though. They insisted on fertilizing their small plot of ground that, through many confusing hand gestures and pleadings, they would help work the main fields that supplied the farmstead; but that they insisted they have a kitchen garden next to their house of their own. They use animal and human manure for their fertilizing in their little garden, and as bad as they thought it wasteful for the other residents of the farm not to do the same, the food harvested from their garden was equally distasteful to the western minds of those it was offered to. Particularly bad were the constant offers by HeDo to collect any manure in sight from the animals and his not understanding that the house had indoor plumbing that didn't require his attention. Martha had freaked one day, when the plumbing was being worked on and she had to use the old outhouse and came out the door to see HeDo standing there holding a blue plastic kid's sand shovel and bucket and thinking he was going to do his duty to harvest any night soil available.

Dump warned Stewart and Melanie, "That little bastard will watch you if you go off to the bushes to relieve yourself and will collect anything that hits the dirt to go into Papa San's growing collection of compost piles around the place."

"You figure out what part of Asia they are from yet?" Stewart said contemplating his travels and people he had met.

"I tried and every one else has tried that, but we are lacking good communications. They say no Chinese, laugh if you say Japanese, get mad about Vietnamese, makes faces about Korean and looks at you like you are stupid, if you say Philippine. Ask if from Thailand, they put their hands together and bow a bit, but shake their heads 'no', so we are at a loss. Hop Sing just looks at you and puts his thumb up and says something like 'Mong' and goes back to silly grinning at you and agreeing to anything, if you try to ask more.

"Ah, they sound like Hmong, maybe; mountain people from China, Vietnam, Laos and Thailand borders." Stewart said astutely.

"The tragedy of the Hmong people was that they fought with the US against the North Viet Cong and then basically got abandoned after the war; except for the lucky ones in camps along the borders, who managed to escape and immigrate to the U.S." Stewart continued, relying on the histories he had heard of through the U.N. interventions of mistreatment or from people he had personally met and been exposed to.

"Well, that's interesting to know. I was wondering how they might have gotten here and what nationality they might have been." Dump said, as he held the reins on his fidgeting mule that was eager to go home.

"Martha's house is just up around the corner up there. Just follow me and I will introduce you, before getting you settled in." Dump said mounting his mule and then taking off at a quick trot.

2

Martha's Home For the Wayward

Stewart and Melanie pulled up into the driveway and parked next to the front Porch of the house. Martha came bustling out the front porch screen door and looked over the visitors.

"Who did you bring home this time, Bill?" Martha said while smiling down at the pair. Martha never used Dump's nickname and neither Stewart nor Melanie had ever heard his real name, so they were taken aback for a moment.

"This is the Stewart and Melanie I been telling you about." Dump said happily to his cousin.

'"Well, land sakes. I finally get to put faces to the names. Why, there ain't a day goes by, that Bill doesn't retell the story about you all and David's adventure." She said hugging Melanie and then grabbing onto Stewart for good measure.

"Come on up and have a seat on the porch and tell us what you been up to and how you managed to find us." Martha said escorting everyone to the line of rocking chairs and benches arranged along the front porch.

"That's David's Truck, Martha." Dump said beaming a smile.

"Well, where's David then? Is he back, too?" Martha said confused, but happy at the thought.

"We don't know where David is, Martha. He and Dumpie, I mean, Bill drew me maps to find the truck and to find this house, if I needed to leave the city." Stewart said wishing for more news on David for himself.

"When did David leave?" Melanie asked.

"Oh, he has been gone better than a month or so now. He got on an old tractor that still ran and lit out for Montgomery." Dump said hoping David was all right.

"Well, I be gob-smacked. I bet that was a journey I sure would like for him to tell me about someday. David riding the highways on a tractor. Ha! That would have been a sight to see, too." Stewart said chuckling at the notion.

"Well, if anybody was going to make it, it would be David." Martha said for some reason defensively.

"Aye, that he would indeed. I just meant that would be an amusing sight, to imagine David rolling up to some stranger on that god forsaken interstate and trying to give them a lift. I bet he had the bonnet of that old tractor covered with riders sitting every which way hitching a ride home." Stewart said smiling at the mental image he had created for himself.

"It was a pretty danged old tractor; he might've busted down somewhere and had to walk himself home." Dump said worriedly.

"Don't listen to Mr. Sunshine here, David made it home just fine. I got me a premonition." Martha said speaking of her feminine wiles and eerie knack for knowing about the health or welfare of someone she liked.

"Where are Ray and the Hop Sings at?" Dump asked Martha.

"Ray borrowed that old 1940 dozier off Philburn; they are gathering up all the manure from the cattle to probably put in one of those poo pits them Hop sings seem to like so much." Martha said talking about the compost heaps.

"Never have seen a bunch of folks like doody, as much as them Hop Sings. They should be along directly, its getting close to meal time. At least I didn't have them under foot, while I was getting lunch close to ready; which reminds me, I better go see to a few things. 'Me Do' butchered me a couple chickens; I had a feeling we were going to have us some company today, just didn't know who. Bill did you warn them about them veggies the Hop Sings grow? You be careful, if that old scallywag Mr. Hop Sing offers you anything raw. Cripes, be careful if it's cooked, too. I know Me Do saved them chicken feet and gizzards for something, and it's liable to end up on your dinner plate, if you don't watch out." Martha said rising and going back into the house.

"Martha fusses about them a lot, but she actually treats them more like naughty pets at times than she means to, 'cause it's so hard to understand them and their ways. She couldn't get by near as good as she has it now, without all their help. She said Me Do is going to have a baby and now she has new arguments to grouse about her trying to help out with every little thing. Hey, here comes Ray now. The Hop Sings be along shortly I guess. Did I tell you to expect them to dress up for dinner, when we got guests? Now, that's a sight to see!" Dump said chuckling and everyone started to walk down towards the barn to greet Ray.

Melanie looked at what had to be the oddest tractor she had ever seen pulling up. She hadn't seen many tractors in her time, but she was sure that it must be one the odder makes of its vintage.

"Hey, Ray!" Dump bellowed. "You ain't going to believe who we got for house guests today!" Dump said moving quickly towards him and reminding him that he had friends named Stewart and Melanie.

"I am pleased to meet you. Dump has told me lots about you." Ray said extending his hand to Stewart and then doing the same with Melanie.

The group chatted about how interesting it was to reunite like this and waited until the Hop Sings wandered up to join the group.

He Do immediately shyly grabbed Dump Truck's little finger and held onto his big buddy's hand as introductions were made. A lot of hand gestures, funny mispronouncing of names, and laughter occurred, as Stewart and Melanie met the charming family. Melanie became Minnie and Stewart finally settled on Stewie, so they could be called something somewhat resembling their names by the Hop Sings.

"You Do" Papa Hop Sing said to Dump, as he

gestured for him to follow and Truck made a 'who knows' face and followed the little man off in the direction of the Sings home.

Dump tried to figure out what Hop Sing wanted, as he gestured towards some cracked corn chicken feed in the barn. Evidently, he was asking Dump if he could have some for himself, but Dump for the life of him couldn't figure out what for.

"Sure, you can have some." He said gesturing and the little man looked pleased.

They left the barn and went back up to the house, where Martha and Me Do were busy setting plates on the outdoor picnic table. He Do followed Dump around like a puppy and was often seen holding on to Dump's shirt or hand or pants leg in some fashion, as he curiously surveyed the new strangers in his world.

Martha had really made a good spread of food for everyone from the produce off her small farm; and Melanie and Stewart ate fried chicken and biscuits, until they thought they would burst.

Hop Sing managed to sneak into Martha's kitchen, under the guise of bringing in the dishes, and made off with a small bag of pickling lime.

"That was the best meal I ever had." Melanie said to Martha, who beamed from the praise she got from her and everyone else.

"Well, we can't have Sunday dinner all the time, but we make do pretty good around here. I am going to make a sweet potato pie for dinner later on today and Hop sing can make the dinner on his stove." Martha said and Hop Sing brightened and said "Me cook!" and pointed to himself.

"But no Chicken Feet!" Martha said adamantly, while making her hand into a claw and waving it at him, which he definitely didn't understand and mimicked making soup out of them.

"NO! NO chicken feet whatsoever!" Martha scolded, waggling her finger and shaking her head to a less than happy, but understanding Hop sing.

"Motha come." Hop Sing said heading towards the house, ostensibly to get permission for something or other out of the kitchen.

"Did he just call her Mother?" Melanie said to Ray.

"No, that's the way he says her name." Ray replied chuckling, but obviously as fond of the family as his Martha.

Hop Sing indicated to Martha he wanted about a dozen or so eggs, some flour, and garlic and then started looking over her canned goods. He settled on a can of chicken broth and indicated he wanted more, after much gesturing Martha indicated she didn't have any more, and offered him some chicken bullion instead. He evidently didn't know what it was, so Martha showed him the tablespoon and told him how many spoons equaled a can of broth, when added to water. He looked at her skeptically, but took a few spoonfuls back with him in a little baggy. He gathered up several eggplants that were sitting in a basket from today's garden harvest and gave Martha a 'thumbs up' gesture.

Martha and Hop Sing returned and sat at the picnic table with the group, who were discussing what was going on in the surrounding towns. Hop Sing chattered at his wife and son for a minute, and then HeDo picked up the supplies and headed back to their home to get the materials out of the sun and go on some other errand his father had been seen to be explaining to him carefully.

"I got no idea what he is cooking for dinner, but it has lots of eggs in it." she said regarding the cook for the evening.

"Not Hot, Not hot," she said in his direction indicating her tongue.

Hop Sing evidently understood her and held his hands up and nodded his head, while smiling like he was assuring her whatever culinary thing he had in mind wasn't going to be too spicy for her.

"Bill you keep an eye on him when he is cooking and watch what he does. I don't have time to supervise him, because I got my own baking to do. Try to make him get vegetables out of our garden and not his, too." Martha advised him thinking in advance.

"You know he don't like me hanging around when he cooks, Martha, just like someone else I know." Dump said complaining.

"Well, you try and watch him anyway. What's he got HeDo doing, I wonder? He should be back by now" Martha said looking off in the direction the boy had gone.

"It will be fine Martha, quit your niggling." Ray said patting her on the leg.

"I just don't want to end up with the squirts or worse from some strange dish he can come up with." Martha said eying Hop Sing again, who noticed he was being talked about.

"Number 1 Cook, Me.' Hop Sing said pointing at himself and having his wife repeat the same phrase pointing at him and holding up her finger in a 'number one' gesture.

Stewart decided it was time to change the subject and asked Ray what was going on with the Preppers that Dump had mentioned staying up the road. Stewart had not realized before talking to David, that some folks had been preparing for this sort of event for years; and he just now had started wondering what he would have put in his own bug out bag, if he had had the opportunity. He wasn't too worried about that now, as he had David's preps that he had yet to investigate thoroughly. He had better reconsider that thinking, he thought. Melanie somewhat had the rights to some of those too, even though David had given him the keys and blessings to take his stuff, if he could make it to that location, which he might not have been able to do without Melanie's help.

I will think on this more later, pretty much everything is now shared and I shouldn't be thinking in terms of mine or yours. Stewart considered.

"Those folks should be leaving in the morning. I told them I was going to come by there later and arrange to transport them a few miles down the road in the wagon to save them some boot leather. The big decision is whether they want to go to Philburn's trading post or stay on their current direction of travel. I hope they just want to keep on going, because I don't like setting folks off in that direction, but their supplies are short." Ray said.

"Why don't you like that direction?" Melanie asked trying to understand Ray's reluctance.

"I tell you why. That damned Sheriff over there now hangs out around the trading post and has taken it upon himself to require you to register, when you go on the grounds. You have to check your guns and he searches your stuff. He's got some prisoners that he rents out to do farm work; some of them are folks that we dropped off in that direction. He decided to give them sentences for stealing food from a vendor or whatever else he accused them of. Thing is, he decides how long is fair that they have got to serve, and he is becoming somewhat of a bully." Dump said with an angry scowl.

'Well, he ain't that bad, but those deputies of his are a bit high handed. They just showed up one day and started to sort of take over. Philburn says he can't do anything about them, but I think they are in cahoots together. They say the outlying towns around there have hung a few people, mostly strangers for one thing or another, too." Ray said, acting like he didn't want to get into those stories.

"Blimey, things haven't been out of control that long that the constabulary should be creating fiefdoms." Stewart said shocked.

"It's a lot worse than you might think Stewart. Folks had been streaming through here, even though we are off the beaten path, in groups of two to twenty. The resources are not here to either feed or control them. We helped everyone best we could at first, but there are just too many mouths to feed and too many folks think being able to walk down the street carrying a rifle makes it the Wild West again. Ordinary folks that lived here their whole lives, now got to contend with folks that think they got a right to survive better than somebody else, because they are hungrier. We had to hold up in the house for weeks, because some cowardly fool would take a shot at you and think about robbing your body or house. The signs in front of the road David had us put out deterred a lot of folks; but the way the signs were treated by those that they didn't send on gave us an indication of their intentions. I don't know if it was good or bad to have the signs up for those that just didn't care and looked for targets." Ray said thinking about a particularly bad day.

"I know it's been rough in the City, but I had not thought about being on the outskirts. People that make it at least this far must be desperate enough or not thinking enough for anything." Stewart replied.

"You need to learn to shoot Stewart. I got a 12 gauge double barrel coach gun you can use for now that doesn't require too much finesse, but armed around here everyday is a necessity. That prepper couple is armed with a shotgun and 22 rifle and not knowing them as well as we should, we got them staying in an abandoned house for our safety. I don't like folks I don't really know on the property to be armed." Ray replied considering his offer of arming a yet unknown guest.

"These are friends Ray. Martha said we got to have more folks, if we going to hang on and protect this place. She also gets whoever stays in that old house, to do some work on it to make it better for the next. Those Preppers down there, I would think would side with us in a heart beat, if we needed them; but they heading towards their own bug out location, so we just playing way station, like with the old stage coaches." Dump said.

"I didn't mean anything against your friends, Dumpie. I am just saying I got a problem with Martha's adopt a puppy attitude towards those that are of the Prepper ilk. She is damn sure mean enough to those that have nothing and look like they won't contribute. No offense, Martha." Ray quickly said and then clarified the position.

"I know we got to draw the line in the sand somewhere, just to look out for our own survival. Where that line is drawn, I just don't know. We got to manage our own, but I think telling everyone with just the shirt on their back to just keep moving is wrong in some ways." Ray said.

"There is a mineral spring about a quarter mile from here that just needs a bit of a cleanup and a sign to give folks water. Used to be folks from miles around in the old days would come by to get some 'healing water'; we could fix up the area and make a sign for that says courtesy of the "Truck clan" and explain it's safe to drink and to avoid our house as a favor." Dump said.

"That work about as well, as what got your and your half cousin's place burned. I told you not to be too forceful in your messaging on signs and somebody went and firebombed it at night." Martha said thinking about how the skull and crossbones etc. on signs had probably just made someone scared enough to get particularly nasty about how they were going to rob it.

"Don't go there." Dump said and remembering how lucky he was to be alive, because he was out that night fishing and arrived to find the cousin dead and houses burned to the ground.

"I am a plenty sorry Bill, but these people we see nowadays ain't no stray dogs that follow you home with manners and gratitude. They humans and sons of Satan, when it comes to being unappreciative; robbing you or murdering you in your bed is more in their character." Martha said resolutely and ending the conversation with a no answers back look.

"I don't see the difference between giving them a cup of water, so they don't fall out in front of the place, or driving them off at the point of a gun when they desperate for one. But I give you my promises and it's as you want." Dump said and then looked at Melanie for support.

"What kind of mineral water are you calling healing waters, Bill?" Melanie said directing attention to his mention of the spring.

"Well, we are right up the road from Lithia Springs and this water that comes out an old pipe on the side of the road is supposed to have some similar properties of minerals and such that are good for the body. It tastes kind of like if you poured water into a glass after you got done drinking the milk in it. It's supposed to be good for you." Dump said happy that Melanie had an interest in taking his side.

"I would like to see this place, Dump. How long has it been there?" Stewart asked while Martha squirmed at possibly being corrected.

"About 1890 they say, used to be folks would do the 'take the waters' thing, to insure health or recover from diseases we didn't have cures for back then, at spas all over the place." Dump said happy he was the center of attention in a positive light at the moment.

'YOU SAY IT'S A FREE FLOWING SPRING?" Stewart said anticipating a possible new project to make some needed money.

Dump laughed heartily and reminded everyone of the 'waters free, rent a cup a dollar' stand, where he and David first met Stewart. "By that twinkle in his eye, I imagine he has an equally enterprising idea to benefit the Truck Tribe and still help the vagabonds."

Before Stewart could form a reply, HeDo came running up to Hop Sing pulling a battered, but freshly scrubbed old Radio Flyer wagon.

"What do you suppose that is for?" Dump said pretending to admire how good the kid had cleaned it up, to the adolescents' evident joy.

"He is too big to want a ride in it; maybe he wants you to put something in it." Melanie suggested.

"Yeah, but what?" Martha commented.

Hop Sing looked it over and evidently approved as MeDo patted her son affectionately.

"I have no idea what they are up to." Stewart said as he watched Hop Sing start towards the white and red GMC they arrived in and peered into the back and came back momentarily to pull on Dumps arm saying "You Do."

"I guess he is going to help you unpack." Dump said following him towards the Truck.

"See if you can get him to understand, take out only the small packs holding our clothes. I see an advantage leaving David's Prepper bug out bags in there for now." Stewart said.

Dump opened the hatch on the back and quick as a shot; Hop Sing grabbed the big orange water cooler like you see on the back of utility trucks and looked confused when the ice chest he wanted too didn't move, because evidently it had something heavy in it.

"What's in this Ice chest?" Dump called as everyone started towards the truck to see what was going on.

"I don't know; we didn't get into it" Stewart said as he was walking up. David had put a Flectar camouflaged rain jacket over most of it and had a rucksack parked in front of it, and they hadn't checked all the prepper goodies in the vehicle yet.

"Damn thing weighs a bit; watch out Hedo let me snatch this thing out." Dump said moving the boy who was trying to be helpful, but was just in the way, bodily aside. Dump pulled it over an assortment of loose, as well as arranged gear, and opened it up and looked inside.

"Looks like a bunch of MRE bags and some kind of candy bar looking things." He said to his gathered audience. He pulled a couple bags of it out and read labels aloud such as, Pound Cake, Chocolate Chip Cookie and the candy bars things were something called Millennium bars.

"Looks like he's been collecting desserts and snacks out of military ration packages. Those silver looking packages, I recognize as emergency water I used to see in overboard bags, when I was in the Navy." Ray said joining in the investigation of the contents of the chest.

HeDo already had placed the water cooler on the back of the wagon and was waiting impatiently for something to do, while listening to the babble of foreign voices and looking at his father for direction. Hop sing reached out and looked at a few packages of MRE and mocked putting them in a big sack towards Dump.

"I think he just wants the cooler. There is a box of garbage bags in here we can transfer to, but I say we just bring the whole thing up to the house and add it's contents to Martha's pantry and get them out this hot truck." Dump said looking towards Martha for approval.

"I guess that be best, but throw it in the root cellar for now; I am not eating that stuff unless we need to." Martha said wringing her hands at whether or not it was still fit to eat in her opinion.

Dump picked up the over hundred pound container like it was a sack of potato chips and started towards the house, which upset the Hop Sings no end. Dump set the ice cooler down and said irritated, "What? You want something?"

"Hop Sing and the rest of his brood touched the cooler and said "Me, Me" and waited for him to respond.

"They want the cooler." Stewart said.

"If it's all right with you, they can have it; but I think the food in it will store better at the house." Truck said trying to figure out what was transpiring.

"That ok with you, Melanie?" Stewart asked his intrigued, but confused travel partner.

"It's David's, but yours now I guess. Stewart, do what you want." She said making Stewart's job of who had rights to what easier; but how do you tell someone they can borrow, but not keep it, if they don't speak English.

Stewart pointed at himself and all the Hop Sings and then the cooler and then back to himself and made a small bit measurement with his thumb and forefinger indicating a short amount of time. The Hop Sings gabbled a bit to each other and Hop Sing senior extended his hand to Stewart to shake evidently to agree to some unknown or understood terms.

Dump picked up the entire thing and a quite irate Hop Sing clan chattered at him all the way to the porch, before he put it down and said "NO!" like he was telling a misbehaving cat not to do something, which started HeDo to start crying and Dump was beside himself what to do next, as he started patting and trying to console the boy.

"He thinks you are taking the box away from him, after Stewart said they could have it." Martha said gathering the boy up in a loving and smiling hug. Just start taking everything out of it; they will put up the contents themselves once they understand." She said as MeDo walked up and hugged Martha and the boy looking at her imploringly.

The contents of the ice chest were soon emptied on the porch and the boy laughingly ran to get his wagon to retrieve his hard won prize, as Papa San Hop Sing came up and grabbed Dump's hand with both of his and then put his hands together in a praying position and touched his forehead and smiled and once again gestured with praying hands at Dump and said something like 'Siddi'.

"He is giving you a Buddha blessing." Stewart said doing the same motions back to an amazed Hop Sing, as he wife also repeated the motion in gratitude to Dump and Stewart.

Hop Sing looked perplexed and thinking for a moment, he then imitated someone firing an automatic rifle, puffed out his chest and pretended to give a salute and then touched Stewart on the chest.

"No soldier me. You?" Stewart said patting Hop Sings shoulder, speaking in Pidgin English.

"Good GI." Hop Sing said proudly, making sure he carefully touched his shoulder where two stars indicating rank would have appeared had he been in uniform.

"I think he might have been a general or something, hard to say what a foreign rank is." Stewart said, while doing his best stiff Brit snap and polished salute interpretation complete with a raising of both feet and stomping, which made everyone laugh and got a completed correct response from Hop Sing with a grin at the end of the performance.

Dump placed the cooler in the wagon and HeDo gave him a hug, while the rest of the Hop Sing clan chattered happily.

"I don't know what they got in mind, but evidently they needed those items for something." Martha said watching the Hop Sings heading back towards home.

"You say somebody named Philburn was the last to see David?" Stewart asked Dump.

"Yeah. Why? I pretty much told you all we know." Dump said.

"Oh, I don't know. I kind of feel a bit obliged to him and that truck runs, so maybe someday maybe we could take a road trip and go see him. Not that I am any hurry to give him back his stuff." Stewart said laughing.

"Ha! That would be a big day if you, me and Melanie showed up in his truck at his doorstep around happy hour." Dump said chuckling at the notion.

"From the notes we compared, I think David declares happy hour at first opportunity, because as he used to put it, 'It's got to be 5 o'clock somewhere.'" Stewart said laughing

"I bet he would flip, if he saw that alcohol still me and Ray got going." Dump said waving to Ray to come over and join the conversation.

"What's up?" Ray said wandering over with Martha in tow.

"Stewart wants to go see Philburn and see if he knows where David went to." Dump said seeking approval from Ray and Martha.

"Last we heard he went to Montgomery, I never asked Philburn if he left any kind of address." Ray said.

"You steer clear of the Sheriff, Bill; I need a couple things from the trading post, if they got them and don't cost an arm and a leg, if you do go up there." Martha said.

"Let me find out what those Preppers want to do up at the house and we can either take them with us or drop them off going the back way and leave tomorrow. Come to think of it. I can deal with them and meet you there; I got to take Philburn1s tractor back to him anyway." Ray said watching Hop Sing walking back up to the group.

"I love this guy, but I sure wish we could learn him some English." Dump said as Hop Sing motioned Dump towards him.

Hop Sing pointed at the tractor and then at himself and said "We go" and waited patiently while Dump tried to digest what he wanted.

"Come here Stewart; see what this guy is talking about. Ray I think he wants to either borrow the tractor or leave." Dump said anxiously.

"We go Philboo." Hop Sing said as Stewart walked up.

"He wants to go back with you to Philburn's," Ray said as recognition set in.

"He must understand that we trade at Philburn`s and wants something." Ray said.

"What's he got to trade with I wonder. I guess he going to use some of the wife's jewelry, but what does he need he hasn't got here?" Dump said pondering the inscrutable face of Hop Sing.

"We are going tomorrow." Stewart said pointing at the sun and making a gesture like it was going down and coming back up and then pointing at himself and Hop Sing.

Hop Sing pointed back at his family and held up three fingers saying he wanted him and his family to go also.

"Melanie, you want to go to right?" Stewart said

"You bet sounds interesting. That truck is going to be packed with you, me, Dump truck and the

Hop Sings though. Melanie said thinking about the seating arrangements.

"Well, we definitely going to have to do some unloading, but we can fit everyone." Stewart said looking forward to a new adventure.

"Philburn's going to have a fit, when he sees you got a running vehicle, let alone one with Air conditioning that belonged to David." Dump said

Martha called out from the Porch and told Dump to come to her. Dump shrugged and headed in her direction.

"MeDo wants a bunch of those jars we got and I can't seem to tell her they are no good for canning, but she can have some regular mason jars." Martha said perplexed looking at the table which had a case of Ball brand mason jars and a box full of left over mayonnaise, Skippy Peanut butter etc. jars on it. Dump signed that mason jars were good for heating up in a canner and the other kind break, but MeDo was adamant she wanted the other ones.

"Well she can have them, but I got no idea what for. She also wants some of those old baby food jars." Martha said while MeDo was happily gathering up her goods.

"Well like I said before, half the fun of having them around is seeing what they get up to next. By the way I think we having Rabbit for supper, I saw HeDo coming out of the barn with one and yes he knows which ones we eat and which ones are for breeding." Dump said

"Normally I would say one rabbit for all of us wasn't much of a meal, but that Hop Sing can stretch a piece of meat a country mile and make you think you're full." Martha said in a rare compliment to his cooking. Martha had lived in the country her entire life and had not been exposed to any kind of Chinese cooking, so it was an adventure any time she got nerve enough to partake of Hop Sings cooking his ethnic dishes.

"They got something going on over there, usually they are getting cleaned up and getting ready to put on their fancy duds to have dinner with the guests. Today though it looks like they got every pot and pan we lent them filled and bustling around like a bunch of bees." Dump said and then wished he hadn't.

"I told you to watch them, quit standing here jawing with me and see what it is they making." Martha said pushing Dump towards the door.

"Geez, they ain't going to poison us. I am going." Dump said huffily and started walking back towards the Hop Sings outdoor cook house.

"Where you going, Dump?" Melanie called out from the picnic table under the big old oak tree.

"Martha said I got to keep an eye on the Hop Sings cooking, you want to come?" Dump said hopefully.

"That sounds like fun" Melanie said cheerfully and rose to follow him.

"It ain't that much fun, we got to pretend like we not really watching Hop Sing or he gets mad and shakes that cleaver of his at me.

"'Chop! Chop! Dimpie'" Dump said mimicking Hop Sing and making Melanie burst out laughing.

"We will just pretend to be passing by and I will play with HeDo for a minute, if he isn't busy doing something." Dump said walking towards the Hop Sings and getting an instant scowl from the patriarch of the family.

MeDo rushed over and took Melanie by the hand and guided her towards a big stoneware crock sitting on the bench in front of their place.

"Minnie" MeDo said while ladling up some syrupy looking liquid into a baby food jar and smiling the whole time.

Melanie took the small jar and figured out that MeDo wanted her to take a sip and did.

"UMMM...Peach nectar. This is good Dump." Melanie said gesturing him over.

MeDo made it evident that Dump could only have a little bit knowing his appetite for all things sweet and food in general and reproachfully stood guard over her crock of Peach Nectar.

"That is good, they haven't made that before. I bet that's why Martha is getting low on sugar Dump said going to get another Jar full, but being playfully chased off by MeDo using her ladle like a fly swatter to wave him away.

"Oh hell Dump, I just saw Hop Sing putting Chicken feet in that pot of boiling water." Melanie said.

Hop Sing evidently saw her observing him and made a comical face and waved both his hands around like arthritic claws. "Moutha, No" Hop Sing said grinning.

"I ain't so sure what he meant by that, but at least he knows not to serve them to Martha." Dump said as Hop Sing pointed to his chopper and wagged a finger at him.

"See I told you he would threaten me! Yeah, I know Hop Sing. 'CHOP CHOP Dimpie'" he said laughing and gesturing for Melanie to follow him away from Hop Sings outdoor kitchen.

As the approached the barn to get out of the heat, they saw HeDo stirring a large pot that evidently had come out of a military chow hall at sometime and went to have a look.

"What is that?" Dump said looking at slurry of corn and some kind of whitish liquid.

"Ha! Dump, thought you were a country boy. He is processing hominy. Basically its corn and lime or other alkaline solution, see how the kernels are starting to swell?" Melanie said giving HeDo a pat.

"Well, Ill be darned, I have eaten a bunch of it, but never seen it being made. I don't know that Martha going to appreciate them using chicken feed to do it though." Dump said still regarding the process, but uncaring himself what it was made out of as long as it tasted good.

"Let's go see what Ray and Stewart are up to." Melanie said and she and Dump headed back to the porch.

Stewart and Ray had been debating about how long they thought it would take before any measurable recovery took place and basically couldn't come to any measurable agreement. There were just too many variables to consider. They had decided that Ray should stay with Martha and help guard the homestead while Stewart and Dump went to Philburn`s. The preppers would just have to wait an extra day, if they wanted a ride somewhere. That evening when they sat down to supper they were delighted to find Hop Sing had made egg drop wonton soup and had filled the wontons with rabbit meat. Not traditional, but they sure were good. He had a big side dish of garlic flavored eggplant to go with it for everyone and the meal ended with a piece of Martha's sweet potato pie. Everyone was quite thoroughly satisfied.

"Well, I didn't see any chicken feet in the soup, and it did taste great." Martha said unknowing of Hop Sing having used the feet to make part of the chicken broth stock for his soup.

3

Philburn`s Trading Grounds

Stewart and Dump wandered out to the GMC truck and noticed that Hop Sing had already loaded a little red wagon into the deer rack on the back of the truck and had secured a water cooler and ice chest into it.

"What do you supposed he has in there?" Stewart said.

"No telling, he has it tied down tight. so I guess we get to see later. Maybe he packed us a lunch." Dump said hopefully.

Martha had made a huge stack of pancakes and allotted each of the farm's resident's two pieces of beef jerky for breakfast.

"See if you can get any flour, Bill. Buy as much as you can get; I doubt we're going to be able to find any for sometime to come. I got no idea what prices are these days, but I am sending you with three hundred dollars and just buy whatever groceries you can with it." Martha said.

"I got a few hundred to donate towards the cause." Melanie offered.

"I can donate the same." said Stewart

"Well, every bit is going to help. I don't think you will be able to spend all that, but get what you can. See if Philburn has got any wheat for planting. We could solve the flour shortage, if we could put a few acres in." Ray said.

"What is that Hop Sing got loaded in back?" Martha asked.

"I bet its Hominy and Peach nectar, we saw them making it yesterday. I guess he has a mind to trade it for something." Melanie volunteered.

"Hominy? Where did he get the corn for that?" Martha said looking at Dump.

"He used about a half of sack of chicken feed corn I told him he could have. We still got plenty and with the chickens free ranging these days, we won't miss it." Dump said looking at Martha and making sure she didn't get in a huff with Hop Sing.

"Chicken feed? Well, I guess corn is pretty much corn, but I hadn't thought of that. I bet you that devil been in my pantry and got some pickling lime, when I wasn't looking." She said looking at the Hop Sings.

"Try to find more of that too, Bill. I am going to be making green tomato pickles later this week and we might get pretty low on that, too." Martha said adding to Dumps shopping list.

"Well, we better get going, I am going to stash the truck at Philburn`s and ride a horse or a wagon to the trade grounds. No sense in having that vehicle seen there or that danged Sheriff trying to appropriate it." Dump said and they loaded everyone up and took off on their trip.

"Man! That Air Conditioner feels good!" Dump said relishing coolness he had accepted he might not get to feel again.

Stewart, who was driving this time, agreed with Dump and enjoyed having almost no stalled cars on this stretch of road.

"Philburn`s place is just a few miles ahead. You know I got an old eight track player in Martha's garage; I want to see if it still works and, if it does, we can install it in here." Dump said while advising Stewart to turn off in front of a big colonial mansion looking house.

Philburn came out the back door with another man following him wearing a Stetson cowboy hat.

"Hi Philburn! Roland, when did you get here?" Dump said rushing to shake hands with him.

"Rode in last night. Dang ain't you the lucky one, where did you get the truck?" Roland replied.

"That's a story in itself, let me introduce you to everyone first." Dump said and proceeded to do so.

"Hop Sings? Well, I guess you got to call them something but only your country ass would come up with those names" Philburn said laughing.

"You come on a social call or business?" Philburn said quizzically, like Dump had something in mind for bringing the Hop Sings with him.

"Oh, we are going to the trade grounds and wanted to leave the truck here and borrow a team and wagon or something." Dump responded.

"Yeah, I wouldn't bring that truck onto the grounds. Trading is kind of light over there just now, but maybe I can save you folks a trip. Roland brought in a wagon load of trade goods he has managed to collect. "What do you need?" Philburn said.

"Uh, is it Roland's stuff or yours Philburn?" Dump asked, because he knew he would get a much better deal with Roland.

"Well, you might say some of both. I will make

sure he don't skin you too bad, Dump." Roland said grinning at Philburn.

"Now you know I always make better deals for family members." Philburn said starting to protest.

"So make him a GOOD deal then!" Roland said escorting the group to the back porch which had a large buckboard wagon covered with a tarp out front.

"You got any flour?" Dump asked

"About 75 pounds worth. I also got some sugar, dried beef, some corn meal and assorted canned goods." Roland recited, much like a seasoned peddler.

"How much is flour?" Dump said and Philburn immediately said "$3 a pound, I get $4 for it at the trade grounds."

Hop Sing and his family had been looking over the wagon and its wealth of goods and had been jabbering back and forth amongst each other arriving at some kind of conclusion. Hop Sing wandered back over by Dump and motioned for him to follow him away from the group for a moment.

Dump and he walked to the far side of the wagon and Hop Sing gestured to include all its contents, then produced two heavy gold 22 karat chains and said, "You Do Philboo?"

"You want me to trade him for the whole wagon load"? Dump said mimicking Hop Sings offer to which he shook his head in agreement.

Dump placed the chains in his overalls front pocket and went back to the group.

"What does he want?" Roland said upon his return.

"He wants me to trade for a few things for him." Dump said watching Stewart and Melanie talking to

Philburn and hearing David's name come up.

"Well, I will be damned. Roland here said he saw David about a week and a half ago. He has moved up to the lake with his family and some prepper buddies." Philburn said excitedly.

"That's David's Truck?" Roland said brightening.

"Sure is. I will get it back to him one day, meantime we are settling in at Martha's. She has access to an old house that she has been fixing up and that will probably be home for us for awhile." Stewart said.

'Well, he certainly is going to be glad to hear you all made it out of Atlanta. Small world isn't it for him to have touched so many lives." Roland said smiling.

"How much is gold going for these days, Philburn?" Dump asked nonchalantly.

"You got a ring or something to trade? I will give you the same or better than the trade grounds would." Philburn said with his eyes sparkling at the thought of acquiring another piece of gold.

"I mean how much is it an ounce these days?" Dump responded.

"Well, it was almost $2,000 an ounce, before the collapse, and of course I need a profit. Why you got a few pieces to trade?" Philburn said getting interested.

"I might." Dump said looking over at Roland, Melanie and Stewart happily chatting about what David had been doing, while the Hop Sings went back to the back of the truck and apparently were unloading the water cooler.

"Roland how much in dollars you reckon you got on that wagon?" Dump asked, like it was an innocent inquiry; but Philburn smelled a deal of some sort being made.

"Oh, I guess once it gets traded out, a few thousand dollars. Hard to say with prices the way they are and accepting barter or cash." Roland said like he was just answering a curious relative.

"Ok. I was just wondering." Dump said and watched the Hop Sings, who were indicating they were offering everyone a drink.

"What is this?" Philburn said accepting a baby food jar of it.

"Its fresh homemade peach nectar." I think they are going to try to sell some at the trade ground.

"Hey, this is good!" Roland said sipping the refreshing beverage.

"You got any wheat for planting, Philburn?" Dump asked.

"I got some feed wheat you could probably use, never tried planting, it but I bet it would work. It is $25 a 50 lb bag." Philburn said.

"Dang, price was six bucks before the collapse; but okay, I will try a few bags." Dump said.

"Hey, I bet that nectar would go especially good with rum." Roland said winking at Philburn.

"He wants to show off some ice he brought with him; he made it back at his farm. Its getting pretty melted, we might as well use it up." Philburn said and motioned everyone inside.

"Dump tell your Hop Sings, I will give them $25 for the rest of that nectar." Roland said.

The Hop Sings agreed and the deal was struck after Dump made it clear the price didn't include the cooler.

"Do they drink?" Philburn said holding up a bottle of Rum and indicating the elder Hop Sings, who understood and nodded their heads assuredly 'Yes' they wanted a drink.

When everyone had a drink and they were

relaxing on the back porch, Dump told Roland and Philburn he had a proposition for them.

"I will give you about an ounce of gold for that wagon load." Dump said and produced one chain out of his pocket.

"Let me see that." Philburn said reaching for the chain and examining it closely.

"You get this off the Hop Sings? We don't have jewelry like this in this country." Philburn said.

"Well, actually yes I did." Dump said uncomfortably, not knowing if that made any difference.

"Let me see that, Philburn." Roland said feeling the heft of the piece.

"That's about an ounce; yeah, Philburn I know you got a scale or something around here." Roland said as Philburn started to go into the house after something.

"Yeah, I will do it. You can't fit all that stuff in your truck, so I guess I got to deliver it, too." Roland said joking, like he was going to get the short end of the deal.

Philburn came back with a set of postal scales and weighed the chain, while Hop Sing watched him intently.

"This is just a hair shy of an ounce, but close enough to call it a deal." Philburn said.

Dump shook his hand and indicated to an amazed Hop Sing to do the same.

"That's one happy Chinaman you got there, Dump." Philburn said laughing, as he finally retrieved his hand from an exuberant Hop Sing, who continued to happily babble at his family.

"How far is it to David's place?" Stewart asked Roland.

"It's about 70 miles or so, I guess." Roland said

watching Hop Sing checking out his haul. "I will be seeing him a week or so probably I will give him your regards." Roland said looking back at Stewart.

"You draw me a map and I might go see him in a week or two; depending on what it's going to take to fix up that old house Martha offered up." Stewart said.

"Well, come armed and be careful. No telling who you might meet up with on these roads nowadays. It's gotten a little safer, now that there are not so many folks moving around; but people are also getting more desperate." Roland advised him.

"I can imagine. Hey, is that Martha's old bike I heard so much about?" Looking over at HeDo and his mother eying it, where it had been left under the house eaves after David left.

"Yeah, that's that ugly old thing. You reckon that boy wants it? I would love to get rid of it. Tell him he can ride it, Dump." Philburn called over.

"Trade it to Hop Sing for some Hominy, I think that's what he also was bringing to trade this trip." Stewart advised and He Do perked up sensing something was up involving him.

"I like hominy and I would love to get rid of that bike back to where it belongs. Dump, see if they got any hominy they want to trade for that bike?" Philburn added.

Dump took Hop Sing back to the truck and asked him to see into the ice chest and he showed him about two dozen jars of hominy. Dump tried to get him to indicate how many jars he was willing to trade for the bike and Hop Sing indicated he would give a dozen each to Roland and Philburn. Probably he was guessing they had a joint interest in the deal.

"He says you can have 2 dozen for the bike, but wants Roland to have half." Dump said.

"Well, tell him done deal!" Philburn said. I would of taken one jar for it; but considering he wants to be generous, why not." Philburn said thrilled to get such a deal.

Hop Sing unloaded the jars and replaced them with about 8 bags of sugar from the wagon and said "For Moutha."

"Was he saying that he is going to give those to his mother? You got more of his relatives at your house?" Philburn asked.

"No, that's the way he says 'Martha.' Wow, that kid really likes that bike!" Dump said and smiling at the boy riding it around the backyard.

Melanie asked Dump if they were still going to the trade grounds and was told it could wait a day or two, because Roland wanted to get the wagonload delivered and get back to Philburn`s before sundown.

"I guess we can chip in for supplies next time then." Stewart said and watched Roland start to hitch up his team of horses.

"Seems sort of weird to have a car in a horse drawn society, doesn't it?" Melanie said.

"Strange times indeed." Philburn said somberly.

"We will see you again in a couple days." Dump said and went to try to tell the Hop Sings what he had in mind and to give them back their other chain.

Stewart got everybody loaded up and drove slowly back, with Roland following with his team and wagon, towards Martha's and as he'd started thinking of it, 'home'.

About a half mile down the road Roland waved for them to stop and Dump walked back to see what was wrong.

"Damn, Dump! You can drive a team; you take this wagon and let an old man ride in the air conditioning." Roland said laughing and handing the reins to Dump.

"Sure thing, Roland; sorry for not thinking of it myself." Dump said and took control of the wagon.

"I could get used to this. Bring Dump, when you go to see David, and he can drive my team to the trading post down that way, while I ride in style." Roland said chuckling.

End Book 2 of the Prepper Novelettes

1

Our End of The Lake Revisited

David shrugged off his pack and waited for Sherry to catch up. They had both been out on one of their almost daily "borrowing trips" and the distance they had to go to find a vacant house that might have some supplies in it that someone else had not snatched was getting further and further away. It seemed everyone's primary job these days was to gather up whatever usable stuff they could before somebody else snatched up what little their was left.

Security was at an all time high now to, which just made matters more difficult. If you left your stuff at home unguarded, it was a pretty much a reasonable assumption that you would get cleaned out before you got back. David's clan had enough people to allow some of them to guard and some to foray out on scavenging missions, but that practice in itself was dangerous. You never knew if a dedicated group would attack your homestead while you were undermanned, let alone someone might be lurking about somewhere to waylay a passer by for the meager possessions they had.

Today's haul wasn't too bad, just heavier than hell. Try throwing 20 cans of food and some other essentials in a pack and having to walk a few miles under the Alabama late summer sun.

Hell David muttered to himself. I was getting old and out of shape before this solar storm hit.

David was much leaner and harder now that a considerable amount of exercise went into just going about living life everyday and doing small tasks, but the current sun up to well past sundown routine of being ever vigilant was stressing him out.

"How are you doing Sherry?" David said as he watched her catch up carrying her share of the days searching and pilfering through abandoned houses.

"I am fine, just hot. That and trying to keep up with those long legs of yours is wearing me down a bit." Sherry said dropping her own pack and reaching for the canteen David offered.

"We don't have too much farther to go. We are lucky that on this end of the lake to have so few people still around on our side. Boudreaux and his bunch are starting to go out past 10 miles scavenging the countryside"

"I suppose it will get worse before it gets better. When do you figure that people will stop bugging out of the towns around here? It was pretty quiet for several weeks and then it seemed everyone started coming towards the lake in mass, as I guess all their food ran out" Sherry said scanning their back trail.

"I wish the danged fools would quit shooting at

anything that moves. They got the game around here so spooked I got wonder if the animals haven't migrated back into the swamps or something" David said mopping his brow with a big green bandana.

"We been lucky to have so few come up on us at home, but that don't mean we are in the clear. I over heard that damned Elroy down at the trading post talking about trying to figure out where our end of the lake was, because we brought in so many barter items" David said.

"I wish someone would just shoot him and be done with it. Everyone knows he probably is robbing folks for the stuff he carries in. Nobody leaves jewelry around like he supposedly just "finds." Sherry said like she wouldn't mind an excuse to throw some lead his way.

"Well Bernie said that we are going to try and start a constable force of some type in order to deal with Elroy's sort. I know he won't go on Boudreaux's turf though, they already had some words over that and Boudreaux told him flat out if he smelled him anywhere near his house or the Point he was going to peel him like a potato. I wouldn't want that crazy old swamp fox after me, I will tell you that." David said eyeing the woods around them for any signs of trouble or game.

"We would make a lot better time getting into these houses if we didn't have to stay off the main roads so much. I heard Beverly say that some exit watchers were set up outside of Alex City playing highwayman with whoever came out of town until they got in a big shoot out with some Guard troops. They killed two of them but 4 others are among the missing and most likely headed in this direction.

"Well at least they got some local National Guard over there, no telling how long they going to stay on duty though and then we got to worry about them too going rogue. FEMA has started up a bunch of those displacement camps around the bigger cities but who knows how long they can sustain them with food. They also got that so called civilian labor force thing going but that's basically prisoners growing food for other prisoners if you ask me. That stupid Patriot act allows them to conscript labor if they decide they need it." David said angrily.

"I doubt that you will ever see any of us get desperate enough to get around one of those camps. You can't trust the radio news anymore; it just drones propaganda all day. That bit about that radio announcer saying the other day, we got another solar storm coming and to shield all working radios got me skeptical too, but what do you do?" Sherry said contemplating basically a news blackout until you got nerve enough to try a radio in the coming weeks.

"We are probably better off not knowing what's happening or not happening. You about rested up?" David said starting to sling his pack.

"Yeah, onwards and upwards" Sherry said grunting as David reached down and took her hand and pulled her to her feet.

"I got to find me some good hiking boots one day in my size. I didn't think I could wear out a pair of tennis shoes so quick, but when you are on your feet all day tromping around the lake doing something it doesn't take long until they get the worst for wear." Sherry said regarding her shoes that had begun to fall apart.

"I placed you a standing order for some and some winter clothes at the trading post. I got to pickup Boudreaux tomorrow and go over there, do you want to tag along" David said while making his way down the side of the road leading back to their camp.

"You taking the sailboat? " Sherry said instantly wanting to play captain for part of the trip.

"Yeah we can, most of what we been finding is staying in the pantry, but we got to still trade some stuff too." David said considering what they needed to bring. David had just soon keep pretty much all of their ill gotten gains, but others needed stuff too and he was still accumulating a bit of cash also incase America finally ever got rebooted sometime far off in the future...

"We staying the night or coming back?" Sherry inquired.

"That will depend on what's going on over there. Sometimes it's a party atmosphere, but most times its just misery trying to trade for a dollar. With no banks to get money from anymore it's amazing what folks think has value or that's all they got to offer. There usually is a big pot of fish soup or something we keep going on the fire for those less fortunate, but it can really wear on you to be around so many desperate people begging and pleading." David said shuddering at how miserable some of the lost souls that showed up there were.

"I keep forgetting about that, it's hard to think about it when you're so removed from it." Sherry said getting ready to start skipping rocks down the road in the direction of Jack's listening post before they came into camp.

"You keep Jack away from those peaches we found. I want to save them and get Beverly to make us up a pie when I get another can or two. He ate the last ones before I could even get over to see what she would take for doing it. That woman can cook! I have no idea what her secret is but I have been craving a slice of pie from her ever since I had that sliver of one from our last little lake party." David said mentally drooling over possibly having a big piece for himself.

A rope with a series of metal cans rattled in their direction and Sherry called out Sonoma which was the password chosen for today and got the proper response back from Jack who was behind a small fortification off the main road.

"Well all quiet on the western front" Jack said joking and coming down to great them.

"We did pretty good today Jack, I got you some crackers, you got any beer left to trade?" David said hoping his little mutual exchange system he had worked out with Jack would benefit them both.

"No but I got a bottle of peppermint Schnapps I can trade you" Jack said unslinging his SKS and leaning himself against a tree.

"Dang, I don't have that many crackers" David said considering the options.

"Gimme what you got and you can owe me," Jack said wanting some of them right then.

"Here you old chow hound" David said good naturedly and opened his pack and presented Jack with 5 probably stale as hell mini packs of orange peanut butter crackers which Jack instantly pounced on ripping a pack open with his teeth.

"Just tell Lois to give it to you when you get back in camp." Jack said to David regarding his end of the trade.

"We haven't seen movement all day, I guess you can come back to the night watch position and I will relieve you in a bit." David said motioning for Jack to follow them, if he could stop munching his crackers long enough.

"MMPfff... sure" Jack said trying to talk around a mouthful of dry crumbs.

"You got my permission to take out one of those geese Jack. I keep looking at them like somebody in one of those cartoons where you see them already plucked and roasting as they walk by." Sherry said craving some juicy meat in her diet, already tiring of their mainly fish fare.

"Oh this now? From someone that been protecting them and keeping me from spitting one from the first day we got here?" David said laughing and waving to his friends that were gathered at the dock at their base camp.

"Its weird, I always hated greasy food and now I crave it." Sherry said having a hard time getting used to their greatly reduced fat intake of food.

"How about some "Fry bread" for supper. I got a recipe from an Indian friend of mine off the reservation that might help your taste buds out. We still got plenty of flour." David said volunteering a side dish for whatever the rest of the girls had cooked up for dinner.

"I don't know what it is but just the sound of it is wonderful." Sherry said getting interested.

"I can make it a couple ways; I will tell you the basic recipe:"

1cup flour
1/2 tsp. salt
2 tsp. baking powder
3/4 cup milk

Mix ingredients adding more flour if necessary to make a stiff dough. Roll out the dough on a floured board till very thin. Cut into strips 2 X 3 inches and drop in hot cooking oil. Brown on both sides. Serve hot with honey.

Pumpkin Fry Bread

Add the following to the ingredients shown above to make Pumpkin Fry Bread

2 cups fresh pumpkin or 1-16oz. can pumpkin
1 tbsp. milk or water
3/4 cups brown sugar
1/4 tsp. cinnamon
1/4 tsp. nutmeg
1/4 tsp. vanilla

Drop into hot cooking oil and brown on both sides. Serve hot with butter or powdered sugar.

"That sounds yummy, we got some canned pumpkin but I bet it be good with Seminole squash, that's sort of pumpkin flavored and texture." Sherry offered.

"Those danged Seminole squash are threatening

to take over everything. I bet some of those vines stretch 60 ft or more. I warned you all about them sturdy plants. They will climb a tree, too; but I haven't got the hang of making them do that yet. Did I tell you I had one fruit sitting on my counter for a year and a half and it didn't go bad? It might have lasted even longer if the stem hadn't gotten knocked off. They are great storage and prepper food." David said looking at the vines stretching out to and down the road reminding him of Kudzu or as he like to call it, mile a minute vines.

"Looks like we are having tortillas again." Sherry said watching Lois and David's Mom using a couple galvanized cast iron tortilla presses that Sherry and Dave had previously stored in their preps.

"Question is what are they putting in them things today?" David said testing the air with his nose and hoping it wasn't fish...yet again.

"Hi! TVP Taco Night, David." his Mom said already knowing what he was going to ask.

"That stuff ain't bad if you add enough onions to it." David said wishing he had bought more freeze-dried and dehydrated onion dices from one of the long term storage food companies before the storm hit. Onions could make anything taste better he had decided awhile back; and although he thought he had decent supply, they were being used up amazingly fast. Hopefully, we can get something out of those onion seeds I bought instead of the sets I am used to planting.

"Add some hot sauce and I can't tell it from ground beef." Jack said looking around to see if there was going to be a side dish or not.

"I got some refried beans cooking on the fire

Jack." his wife Lois said.

"Sounds good to me, got our own little Taco Bell going on around here. I think it's neat the way David and Sherry made up them boxes to have everything you need to make a couple dishes up and putting the cans all in one case. I guess we will be having the same thing for lunch then tomorrow or you going to open a different box and space it out a bit" Jack said not really caring but David got tired of some of the monotony of the same kind of food when you were trying to use up number 10 cans.

"Sherry and I won't be here tomorrow so have at it, I got some MRE in my bug out bag but I am hoping to get a meal out of Beverly and Boudreaux tomorrow. If not, I will get something at the trade station." David advised everyone.

"I need me some sewing needles and thread. I don't believe you all can't find some when you're out scavenging. I guess it's not something folks think to bring to a lake house" Lois said regarding the piece of sheet metal they had on the fire heating up to cook the tortillas on.

"I got one of those mini travel sewing kits if that might possibly help" Sherry offered.

"Well thanks, but I need a bunch of thread. I got in mind to make something for the trading post. My granny taught me how to make sanitary pads for women out of old sheets and I figure in these days and times the demand for such will come back." Lois replied

"That's a great Idea! Betsy and I could help you sew if that's not interfering with your personal trades." Sandra said walking up on the conversation with Betsy tagging along.

"Well it's got to be tight stitches for obvious reasons, but we could make a lot more of them if we pieced out the work." Lois said looking appraisingly at the girls to try to gauge if they could come close to her seamstress work.

"Well I am not the best at stitching I guess but I can cut the patterns and do the stuffing or something." Betsy offered and then the girls went off to themselves to happily babble about the birth of their new cottage industry as dinner was getting ready.

"You see any sign today David" Jack said as the two wandered to his house to drop off the days haul. Jack knew that after 2 months of playing point man on borrowing trips and hunting the old scout was getting back into the zone of noticing everything in his environment.

"Two people passed a couple miles from here a day or two ago heading towards that holiday place the Air Force had on the lake. They had hiking boots on but I can't tell if they were issue military or not. I been out of service too long and haven't seen a confirmed sign what the lug pattern on them is anymore." David said back tracking in his mind over the days foraging trip.

"I saw some deer sign that looks like they are starting to use a trail regularly again. Next time we short on meat I will put a couple snares on it." David said opening the door to his house and making a beeline to his bar to get a drink.

"The weatherman said he wants you to find someone to move into that house next to him. He said he would share supplies with them. He said it's just too hard doing things over there on his own and not safe either being so far from our camp." Jack said talking about the couple that lived across the slue from us and then starting to prowl David's kitchen to see if something tasty was left laying around.

"Bottom drawer left Jack; you can have 1 bag of MnMs. That's my personal stash and I am going to put a lock on that drawer so don't get any ideas." David said chuckling at the saucer eyed look Jack got when he saw the drawer full of snacks David had in there.

"Where did you get all this?" Jack said in awe of the bounty he saw before him.

"I actually forgot I had them in my preps. Sherry and I bought two of those 72 piece survival snack packs off sportsman's guide awhile back that have pretzels, peanuts, MMs, pound cake and the like just to have something around for a sweet tooth or give to kids and I just unpacked them the other day.' David said watching Jack choose the peanut candy and trying to palm something else at the same time.

"I see that Jack, grab some pretzels to, buts that's it." David said taking a big swig out of his drink.

"Damn boy, you got eyes in back of your head" Jack said sheepishly.

"All the better to watch the munchies thieves with Jack." David said picking up the binoculars and giving the lake inlet a quick survey.

"Shit, I am going scavenging tomorrow while your gone and come up with some beer or something before you get back. " Jack said contemplating trading for some of David's stash.

"I would rather you didn't Jack, we will be two guns down and Betsy's attention span when on guard duty leaves much to be desired. Cut a deal with Donnie across the slue. His wife gets along fine now with the girls and he is a bit more agile than you and can leave her here while he makes a foray." David suggested

"Who goes out with him?" Jack said thinking on the possibilities of which one of the ladies to send on a trip to help the weatherman do security and collecting.

"I don't care, see who wants to go." David said fixing himself another drink and glancing to be sure his snack drawer was closed from Jacks wandering fingers.

"Tell Donnie not to draw attention to us by taking pot shots at any game he sees. I don't know what it is but I got the feeling there are lurkers about over on the main road. Its hard to tell where the wood smoke smell is coming from these days with everybody using them to cook and probably half the cities around burning down." David said paying attention to the uneasy feeling he had been experiencing lately.

What's the old saying David? Live by your first instinct and die by your last. David said to himself to rely on his intuitions that had served him well so far. The first instinct a man has when the doctor spanks you on the butt when you are born is to breath, The last one you will ever get is to stop breathing so if you follow your instincts your whole life you wont be second guessing yourself till you die.

How many young soldiers have I tried to teach that too in the past, David thought?

"Yeah, that boy is still trigger happy and not to accurate but you wont let anybody get much range time in lately because of security" Jack said taking up the more powerful pair of binoculars and looking over to see what the inlet neighbors were up too.

"There is more than one reason for that Jack. Keep this to yourself though; my right eye was diagnosed with cataracts before the solar storm hit and its getting worse. I am carrying this Ruger single action pistol because I can still see the sights and also instinctively shoot it. I don't however, need to be missing on the firing range and trying to teach. I think folks would pick up on that quick and lose confidence in me." David said tossing a mostly full drink down and going to mix another while waiting for Jacks response.

"I sort of guessed you couldn't see as well as you used too, but I didn't know what was going on. I thought just maybe you needed more vitamins or since you decided to go back to wearing your hair long it took some getting used too." Jack said considering a new predicament with what used to be the designated sniper.

"Short distances I am still ok with somewhat, I have also been practicing dry fire with my left eye but I am definitely at a disadvantage until I find out if I can actually hit well being a lefty." David said regarding his old partner seriously.

"Well its not like you can get it fixed anytime soon. You always been an iron sight guy, I noticed you put a scope on that AR of yours. Does it help any?" Jack said looking seriously at David.

"It helps immensely but I only have taken one shot with it. That scope is still factory sighted in and I am not sure what kind of accuracy I can achieve. I am going to switch to the AK with that big side mounted scope, I can shoot that thing left or right eye the way it's mounted." David said letting Jack figure out on his own, if the noticeable difference in weapon and gear might make folks question the choice.

"I don't think anyone will say much except to ask you about the technicalities of why you switched, and you can bullshit your way through that." Jack said ending the conversation with a mutual understanding.

"Ok we swap out gear tonight and let Sherry carry that SKS unless we are going to go deer hunting." David said relieved he could confide in someone about his new shortcomings that had worried him.

"Hey, Boudreaux is over at Frank's" Jack said glassing our inlets neighbors dock and handing me the binoculars.

"What the hell is that he is trying to get out of the boat Jack?" David said watching Boudreaux dancing about the boat while his dog Bear stood on the dock barking encouragement.

Jack took the binoculars and stared across the inlet at the neighbors for a moment.

"He has got something in a trash can that's turned over in his boat that he is not wanting to get too close too. Grab them other binocs, Frank is handing him a boat paddle and his wife is looking like she is going to lasso something" Jack said handing a pair of binoculars to David without taking his eyes off his own while watching the interesting spectacle occurring about a half mile away.

David finally got the binoculars in focus on what was happening and saw Boudreaux extending a boat paddle towards the insides of a big galvanized 55 gallon garbage can and noticed Boudreaux's "Pirogue" as he liked to call it was full of water. All the sudden Boudreaux grabbed the paddle with both hands and started to wrestle with something on the end that looked like it required some great strength.

"Snapping Turtle, it looks like. Biggest dang one I ever seen." Jack said giving the more powerful binoculars to his friend David in a gesture that meant you need them more than me.

"Holy shit, that thing got to weigh in at more than a hundred pounds. Why its shell got to be 3 foot long" David said excitedly.

"I don't know how he got him in that garbage can but evidently it turned over in his boat and that's one pissed off turtle" Jack said watching Boudreaux pull the snapper out of the can and towards the middle of the boat and almost falling overboard as the turtle let go of the mangled paddle.

Even across the lake David and Jack could hear Boudreaux hollering some garbled French at the turtle and an occasional Cajun yell as he did battle with the monster who looked like he wanted Boudreaux's feet for his dinner.

Franks wife made a few bad casts with her rope before Boudreaux finally said hand it to him as he danced about the boat and poked at it with the splintered stick that once was a fine birch wood paddle.

Boudreaux finally lassoed the snapping turtle's long neck and jumped up on the deck and proceeded to haul it out with Frank and Boudreaux's dog bear all pulling on the rope.

Out came that big old Arkansas tooth pick knife that Boudreaux was never seen without and he buried it in the turtles head while dancing away quick.

David and Jack heard a happy "YAHEEE" come from Boudreaux as he grabbed the still moving turtle by the tail and commenced to drag it off the dock back toward Frank's with his dog grabbing one long nailed scaly foot and tugging with him.

The battle of Boudreaux and the mega turtle evidently had an effect on the neighbors witnessing it as the couple hugged each other and Boudreaux did an impromptu dance as the dog barked at the beast of the waters to tell his master they had bested it.

"Damn, that was better than a movie" David said setting down his binoculars and grinning at Jack.

"Sure was! Well I know what you're having for dinner tomorrow but, it's questionable how he is going to cook it" Jack responded.

"Hey, you remember the video I bought off Buckshot's Camp that showed him trying to clean one a day after it was dead with its head cut off and it still moved?"

"Yeah, that was a kinda morbid video but it was interesting to learn how to clean a turtle" Jack said.

"Boudreaux must have gone up one of those back creeks to find that thing. Anyway let's go eat and we will decide later what I need to bring to the trading post' David said wandering back to their outdoor community cook house.

"Veggie beef, lunch room hamburgers. I still can't get over the concept but it was one of my best purchases on the limited budget I had" David said biting into a savory taco flavored tortilla.

2

The Exchange Club

Sherry and David set sail to go over to the far side of the inlet to pick up Boudreaux and go to the trading post. A series of signals had been worked out to communicate across the lake as well as reverting to just writing signs and having the neighbor view them through binoculars. David had laughed with Sherry that they didn't need to see Boudreaux's simple TURTLE SOUP sign to already know that was what was in the pot over there that day.

Sherry sailed the boat up to the pier and Frank and his wife came down to meet them.

"That was fine show you all put on yesterday" David said laughing and shaking Frank's hand

"You saw that? I keep forgetting you spy on this place. I best keep my shades drawn" Nancy said giggling and welcoming Sherry

"Where's Boudreaux? Is he down at the boat landing?" David asked as their friends escorted them towards the patio deck.

"Yeah, he is down there doing the community

meal thing with that turtle he managed to catch. If times were not so tough I am not sure he would have many takers to eat it though." Frank said laughing about how some of the residents on his side of they lake made a face at the prospect of having turtle for lunch.

"Ah they will get over it when they taste it. If you don't keep an eye on that crazy Cajun cook, you won't taste anything but spices and red pepper anyway." David said remembering he always had to tell Boudreaux to tone it down with the pepper whenever he watched him cooking for the group.

"Boudreaux said he wasn't even looking for a turtle when that one got hung up in a raccoon trap he had baited on a creek bank" Frank said

"I would have liked to seen him put it in that garbage can the first time. I bet that would have been a sight to see and remember." David said smiling at the prospect of that unlikely battle between man and amphibian versus a stew pot.

"I hadn't thought of that part of the scenario. That would have been a sight to see alright." Frank said offering David some hot sassafras tea his wife had brewed up.

"Nancy, you get just a little bit better with that lasso and we can have us a turtle rodeo." David said poking fun at her.

"That thing was scary David. Did you see the mouth on that thing? I am not sure I even wanted to lasso it." Nancy said laughing with amusement

"I missed the fun of actually watching it, but Jack and David couldn't stop talking about it last night" Sherry said sharing in the humor of the moment.

"I told that Boudreaux not to bring another one of those things around here. I don't think that dog of his Bear likes them much neither. When that garbage can turned over and that gargantuan thing got loose, Bear jumped right out of the boat and acted like he expected his dumb master to do the same." Nancy said smiling.

"Ha! Ha! I missed that part of the battle. I did see him helping pull on the rope and drag that thing to shore though." David said with his eyes sparkling with mirth.

"That is one smart dog Boudreaux has. If it can be carried or pulled on and helps his Master, that dog lives to do it." Frank said admiring the clever old hound dog.

"I have been using that trait of his against Boudreaux as a practical joke when ever he puts his fiddle down. You just have to say "fiddle fetch" and the dog will bring it to you leaving Boudreaux in a quandary as to where he laid it down at. Boudreaux said for me to quit doing it though, because the dog slobbers on the strings." David said chuckling.

"See if you can find me some Alka Seltzer or Tums when you go to the trading post David. This new kind of food and cooking has been getting to my stomach." Frank said patting his tummy and looking sickly.

"I got some across the lake you can have, Maalox, the Pepto Bismol pink stuff, you name it we got it. Seems to me about every house over there had a bottle or two of something in it." David said

"That figures, you are on kind of the retiree end

of the lake. That is probably the reason you got so many vacant houses over there to go through." Frank advised

"I sort of figured that, furnishings, equipment etc. is old or hasn't been used in years in them places. The few houses that have clothes in them look like something from the fifties." David replied.

"Have you seen anybody trading a rifle at the Post David? I need something for deer, preferably with a scope." Frank asked hopefully.

"I have seen a few. A lot of folks thought they could just move into the woods or one of the houses around here and live off the land. They end up trying to trade their weapons for either something in a better caliber or just for food, if they are desperate enough. I got no problem with giving them a bunch of food for a gun, it usually means they are pretty much disarmed and one less desperado to deal with. They also just trade them if they are heading to a FEMA camp, because you're disarmed there with no profit to be had. They are going to regret it when those camps run out of food one day." David said thinking about all the reasons people would give up a gun in these days and times but guns were plentiful, if you could find the ammo.

"That cruiser model shotgun of mine ain't worth nothing to hunt with. Not having a stock on it sucks, unless you just using it for defense." Frank said about his impractical 12 gauge.

"What are you looking for caliber wise?" David asked looking forward to the answer and some prepper banter about what might be appropriate.

"What kind of ammo is most plentiful these

days? David, you got any recommendations?" Frank asked seeking advice.

"Well shotgun shells are plentiful and a shotgun can do multiple duties. We got Deer, Turkey, Ducks etc. around here for now until they get over hunted. Your idea of a rifle is a good one, because it's going to take a longer shot to get them as they become more wary. What kind of budget we on?" David asked because prices were whatever somebody was willing to accept or give these days.

"Well the wife has some diamond rings..." Frank began until David cut him off.

"These days I haven't seen anybody put a value on diamonds, just the value of the metal in the setting and you're probably better off holding on to them. What else we got?" David asked

"You didn't let me finish, I wanted you to maybe talk to Donnie to see if he would lend me some silver against them." Frank said watching the wheels turn in David's head.

"Humm, that's a possibility. He can play pawn shop I guess as well as be the bank. But let's look at alternatives here, how attached are you to that shotgun you got now?" David said contemplating a solution.

"Well I love the hell out of it for sneaking around the house when I hear something go bump in the night, but other than that, I am not too attached to it. What do you have in mind?" Frank said regarding David.

"Well you know Bernie and I got a business arrangement with each other, so I am pretty sure I can get him to swap you even for it, or maybe with a bit of something thrown in he will see as a profit.

No, tell you what, even trade. That shotgun is very practical for the Trading Post guards. You can borrow my .380 pistol until I get back and I will pick you up a decent hunting shotgun at the Post. You got anything to trade for some more shells or slugs?" David offered.

"Well let me think for a minute. Kind of hard to think of something I am not using that would still hold value these days." Frank said scratching his head to think of something.

"You are one of the few lake residents that live here year round, so I know you got some stuff around here somewhere we can use. You got any extra coats stored? It's going to be a long cold winter and those will be valuable. "David said contemplating how unprepared most of the people that got stranded at the lake in midsummer were going to be.

"You a smart fellow Dave! I got a few to spare I am sure, let me go get them and you can give me a guess as to their value." Frank said rising.

"That's going to be hard to do when its 90 now and not 35 later." David said mulling over how to set a price this time of year.

"Let me see them, they aren't some kind of weird yuppie colors or women's pink jackets are they?" David said half joking.

"No, they are civilized and practical" Frank said smiling back

Humm David thought to himself. If I started now I could own a coat concession of sorts at lower prices and make some decent profit this winter maybe.

David's musings were cut short as Frank

returned a lot quicker than he had thought.

"I had these in the hall closet, probably got a few more scattered through the house. You know what? While I was getting these I started thinking about how my kids are going to be out growing theirs pretty soon and they are going to have to either wear something too small or way too big this winter. Maybe we ought to try to trade in kind like you doing with my shotgun now for anticipated needs. "Frank said trying to guesstimate what his family might need, because living at the lake in the winter time was definitely colder than being in the city.

"You and your wife must ski" David said looking at a couple heavy parkas you wouldn't normally see in Alabama.

"Oh yeah we used to go to the slopes every year. You got any market for ski boots?" Frank said chuckling.

"That one I can't help you with." David said grinning back

"I tell you what, go grab any coats you want to barter on and I will make you a deal for entire lot right here and now.' David said committed to his winter coat project.

"What are you all doing?" Nancy said coming back from the garden she had been showing to Sherry.

"Bartering" David said smiling towards them.

"For winter clothes? Dang David, you getting ready for Christmas all ready" Sherry said knowing the old Prepper fool probably was.

"Hey, I got to have me a Thanksgiving Sale first off." David retorted, while grinning at Sherry and her knowledge of his love of all things to make a buck by thinking ahead.

"We are going to need warm clothes of our own this winter Frank. What do you have in mind?" Nancy said doing the hands on hips routine all men dread seeing.

"Oh, I already know that Nancy. These are some of the outgrown or extras and we are thinking about how to get the kids a bigger size before they are needed" Frank said disarming Nancy before she could possibly scold him.

"Well that sounds like some clear thinking to me" Sherry said backing up the two gents that smiled at her knowingly and appreciatively.

"I must say, it sure does. I am sorry Frank, you been doing a fine job so far of anticipating our needs and trying to provide." His wife said lovingly and giving him a hug.

"I tried to sell David here on some used or almost new snow skis and some boots but he didn't bite." Frank said smiling at his wife.

"You should have tried water skis first; they might have sounded more useful." Nancy said grinning back at him and then smirking at David.

"You know what; I could take some ski poles off your hands." David said contemplating a project they might be suitable for he had in mind.

"What would you do with them David?" Nancy said curious about what invention he was going to come up with next.

"Now if I told you that. I would be showing my hand a bit early in the game, wouldn't I" David said sitting back and getting ready to do a bit of "see how cheap I can get it for" bartering.

"Well if you want some, we got some; I will give you a cheap deal on them, but let's get back to these coats at hand. You got five pieces there and I will consign a few of the kids coats to you also for a fair even exchange for a bigger size, Christ on a crutch, we gotta be thinking about shoes too Nancy." Frank said the days of going to shoe city or the mall were over until Lord knows when.

"Watch your blaspheming Frank, but your right. I have a hard enough time thinking about what we are going to eat from one day to the next, let alone what growing children are going to need." Nancy said wistfully

"There are lots of flip flops around, but I can't recall ever seeing a pair of shoes left in any of these cabins." Sherry said commiserating with her friend Nancy

"We might have to make that trip to one of these outlying towns before winter sets in, David. I know you have been dreading to do it, but there are just some things we can't get for ourselves up at this lake" Frank said causing Dave to flinch at the prospects of getting near a mass of starving and desperate people.

"The longer we wait, the safer it might be for us. I hate to say it, but I am counting on a heavy die off of folks before trying to enter one." David said not relishing the thought of what they might encounter in a town these days.

"I didn't mean we would have to leave tomorrow or the next day. You said some of those traders make regular forays into the so called civilized world searching for items. Do you reckon they could take some kind of appointment to fetch back certain things we in need of?" Frank asked, while looking speculatively at David and then to his wife for approval.

"We take orders all the time, but the roads are desperate now and not safe to travel. Roland doesn't take that trade wagon out in most directions without 8 armed guards loaded for bear and you got to feed and pay them to boot. Simple items like what you want are going to be costly if they have to wait around a town to find them." David said thinking about his supply chain and how one bad encounter with armed locals who had set their sights on robbing a supply wagon could leave this whole side of the lake without any resources.

"Well once again back to the diamonds and colored stones, rarity has had value for thousands of years, why can't I purchase what we need?" Frank said.

"I think you answered your own question Frank, a diamond might be rarer than kid's shoes but which is more practical and valuable now? What's rare at the moment on the lake is to get a new good fitting shoe for a diamond." David said trying to let the concept sink in.

"Hell, your right David "Frank said as a realization struck him. " I think if you wrap that entrepreneurial brain of yours around my problem, you or Donnie can come up with a solution." Frank said not willing to give up the notion diamonds were no longer expensive or desirable.

"I will have a talk with Donnie on that subject, but right now I am just stating facts. The reality is that we are running flat out on the highway to hell, and that societal collapse has already happened and that ain't negotiable. "David said getting huffy

"Calm down David, it was a legitimate question." Sherry said trying to play peace keeper.

"Your right, but most folks in America only have a vague understanding of what it takes to survive in this world we find ourselves in now and it ain't something that you can buy yourself out of based on old commodity values." David responded

"There is a food crisis going on, he means Frank. Those with the food like they old saying for gold, make the rules. The irony of it is you cant eat gold or silver but if you got enough food you can survive to spend everyone else's wealth if the economy ever recovers and precious metals or diamonds for that matter again have intrinsic value." Sherry explained.

"Its like this Frank, You see these two hands? You can't see my knowledge of farming but combined with these two hands I got value. A gem cutter or a miner only has wealth if I produce more than everyone else and have a surplus for trade with them so they are worth less than me at the moment. There are no surpluses of anything on this lake other than tears and misery right now. A new day will dawn and like art, we will have time to value and appreciate other things. Just not right now buddy." David said hoping he had explained the current position well enough.

Frank looked angry and his wife looked concerned until Frank said "Teach me a skill David, all my degrees, experience and money in the bank mean nothing now. It's not like I can apply for a job or hope for unemployment to feed my family." Frank said tearing up because he doubted he could provide for his family with anything he was familiar with.

David put his arm around the mans shoulder and motioned with his head the women should go find something better to do while they talked and Sherry lead his distraught wife away reluctantly.

"Frank it's just like regular life but you now need, more so than ever to specialize. Find one thing and be the best at it you can be and know the subject well enough to be the come to guy to help those that know less" David said trying to placate him while he dreamed something up.

"That's all well and good for you David, you managed to bring your own supplies and family and friends here but I only got me to try to support the family" Frank said trying to control his sobbing that he had held in through the worst of the fix we were all in.

"Look my friend, Donnie and the rest of us have been trying to restart an economy, it ain't even close to easy or predictable. We knew this and talked to everyone here how best to adjust to our new circumstances and offered you a make shift bank to assist with any reasonable attempts to help commerce start." David said as Frank dried his eyes and went back to being the stalwart man he was.

"I been thinking on that, but I don't have any back to the land skills to apply to it. Cripes, I don't even fathom how the old pioneers got by." Frank said desperate for alternatives.

"Ok I got two suggestions; the first is addressing your own needs and get what you need for free by selling it to someone else. That's shoes if you following my line of thought and Donnie and me will back you with silver to do that." David said attempting to come up with a rational conclusion that would help the community and Frank.

"You are telling me to open a shoe store? Where would I get stock?" said an incredulous Frank

"Hell, where do we get barter goods for the trading post? We get someone to specialize and supply things. If you get known for one thing the customers come to you." David said as he considered all the different folks that brought goods to the enterprise Bernie, Roland and he had set up in the aftermath of the solar storm.

"I guess I follow you here, your saying pick a niche and gain a following and you and your group will support it. Sort of like you did with the mail service you started at the trading post." Frank said remembering what David had created after he remembered about a bygone era when public notice boards were a major tool of government in the days before electricity.

David decided he was going to be the post office one day when confronted with the request to get a message through to another town to swap some goods and it had worked out well with him so far.

He had taken a sheet of ply board that he prized off a shed up the road from the Trading Post and gotten permission to nail it at the front of the Post for a 3% allowance on the traffic he generated.

He got a woman he had somewhat adopted to Post public policies on his company's behalf that Bernie and Roland had agreed upon they wanted for behavior in the establishment and its grounds, or trade directives in one section and "good advice" such as water purification procedures in another.

Another section of the board contained news items picked up on a shortwave or from other communities that David had decided was his news service he might make a nickel from later.

David stuck another board up on the other end of the trading post, sort of as a public option he considered necessary. It was made open to the public simply because he deemed it necessary and a goodwill gesture to the community. He remembered that folks have no reliable communications means and may need to link up with missing relatives or communicate with other community members if their paths didn't cross regularly.

This board was a good way to do this and substituted for a public mail service to get a message out locally.

David had then proceeded to set up a drop box situation with a padlocked lard can for personal messages (which was controlled by someone that he gave a small stipend to that worked at the trading post sort of like old Sam Drucker at the general store on Green Acres TV show) This individual maintained a list of people with "refugee mail" on the public notice board. That way, if someone wanted to send a letter or something to anyone else, they would drop an envelope in the drop box and pay with whatever they had and write the addressee's name (and a date) on the public board. When the addressee came to pick up his mail, he would cross his name off the list and give an egg or ten minutes of labor sweeping the front of the post or something. David was good about seeing to it if a person or trader traveling to a nearby town could carry the mail to that town.

"Hey I am game, you said there was other alternatives too I think." Frank said seeing some light at the end of the tunnel.

"Well that is working for someone else or contracting your labor. I got an idea but I got to talk to Boudreaux first" David said before he offered another option.

"Ok. Well holler back at me and I will think over what you have said so far" Frank said saying farewell to David.

3

Planning for the Future

Sherry and David said good bye to Frank and Nancy and sailed over to the boat landing around the bend.

This area had become sort of the public park and gathering place for the families surrounding it.

David moored the boat and they walked up to see what was going on in the picnic area and look for Boudreaux.

Sherry and David saw Boudreaux sitting over at a concrete picnic table talking to the local residents who had arrived early to get something from the community cook pot. David thought about how lucky this community was to have banded together and appeared so far to have a good chance of surviving. Most communities are doomed these days because they were never set up to be self sustaining. The majority of any American cities or towns are basically artificial constructs entirely dependent on modern society to keep them running.

It is pretty easy to tell if ones town can survive

or not by looking at the population density, arable land, water supplies and other resources available in its general proximity. A smallish town with a good water supply and a lot of working farms not dependant on too much fertilizer or electric powered irrigation would be an ideal place to be these days, but that resource of America had been getting scarcer for years

Some people have nothing of value in this new economy all except their labor and at least here in this little enclave, the community at large tried to take care of them and find odd jobs for them like garbage disposal, tree cutting and such in exchange for food. Any finance system has to be able to allow people to exchange what they need for what they have or it will fail and the economics of this system was still struggling to find ways to make it sustainable.

Boudreaux greeted David and Sherry warmly as they came over to supervise his cooking efforts.

"Smells pretty good" Sherry said looking at several pots and pans arranged around the fire presumably containing mostly turtle meat and whatever else could be scrounged up.

"Everyone throws what they can in these here" Boudreaux said indicating the collection of cookware. "Maybe a handful of rice, a measure of beans, some dried minced onion, possibly a can of corn and the world lives another day." Boudreaux explained hoping for some donations to the community larder.

"I can throw in about 10 cans of food." David said noticing how bad things were getting over on this side of the lake.

"It be a blessing for sure, things are most lean

here about" Boudreaux said with his thick Cajun accent.

"I will see what Bernie has to spare for the common good when we get to the Trading Post but I expect its going to be the same story of too many mouths to feed and an excess of nothing" David remarked.

"She is going to be a long cold winter coming to snuff out many." Boudreaux said thinking about those less fortunate than us today.

" Its hard facts that's for certain and unfortunately I don't have any answers except to protect our own as best we can as long as we can" David said hurt, but hard about not being able to assist more than what little they could for so many.

"We going to go here in a few, I want to finish giving instructions to Paulie over there on how to make Jerky out of some of this turtle meat." Boudreaux said looking at a makeshift smoker they had rigged up.

"Turtle Jerky?" Sherry said making a face.

"You can make Jerky out of any meat. Don't turn your nose up so quick, He be pretty good" Boudreaux said smiling at Sherry

Boudreaux went over to the group gathered around the smoker and gave some last minute instructions and told David he was ready to set sail as soon as he retrieved his trade goods from a friend's house.

David liked how the community on this end of the lake was trying to work things out. They pretty much avoided giving "handouts" to anyone. It was pretty much of a consensus they needed everyone to work as hard as they can. The community needed everyone to use their incentive and creativity to try to do for themselves. Handouts that compete with the local economy are counterproductive and destroy human dignity David had advised awhile back and tried to offer other solutions so people could help themselves. Finding those solutions or food to pay for someone's labor was hard enough these days. The incentive to immediately start farming, hunting, and otherwise adding to the public larder was readily apparent. The trading Post community worked similarly. The Post would pay for labor and services with "ration cards". That ration card entitled its workers to eat a single meal at a community soup kitchen, or it entitles them to a set amount of grain or other commodity on demand from the Trading Posts warehouse. In essence anyone needing community resources "works for the community" and gets to eat at the mess hall of sorts that had become a centralized relief point on the boat landing and main road into this section of the lake. It would be great to keep everything capitalist but they had to do some things socialist until they could come up with a better way of doing things.

Without machinery, manpower was our biggest resource we needed to take advantage of. The plan and understanding at the Trading post was to cherish each unemployed citizen. The Post made them work for their pay and used them to build capital for the future of the community we were striving to build. They were directed to labor in food production, foraging, military duties, messenger services, trash collection or anything else that needed doing. Everyone was free to come and go as they liked, but the idea of a free lunch everyday was quickly discouraged.

"Boudreaux came back to the boat with a wheelbarrow full of goods that David helped him stow and lash down in the sailboat. Boudreaux had to tell his dog several times to go lay down as the dog attempted to "help" with any line David or Boudreaux took up to secure the cargo.

Deciding everything was ship shape, the group set out on their journey up the lake towards the ferry point and trading post about 6 miles away on the opposite side of the lake.

"Bernie is supposed to be up to the Trading Post today. Roland brought him down a week or two ago to set things up while he organized the trade wagons to go over and see Philburn to see if we could get some back and forth trade" Boudreaux informed David and Sherry.

"That is going to be an interesting arrangement. I knew Philburn and Roland were related, but I never thought of trading that far north. Makes sense though. Philburn has farmland and equipment that still works and Roland runs cattle and trade down this way, so why not. I am going to have to go see old Philburn again one of these days just for fun. That old tractor of his that got me home and up here is still serving us well. Not that I would risk driving it back to Philburn though" David said smiling at the notion.

"Having resources definitely makes a difference and ties groups together. What was it you wanted to ask me about? You said you had some kind of proposition maybe." Boudreaux said relaxing on the gear stored in the well of the sail boat.

"How good are you at catching fresh water

mussels?" David said

"You mean "footing it "or otherwise." Boudreaux said talking about looking on the floor of the lake for the swirl patterns in the mud or sand they made when they moved and walking around feeling for them with bare feet.

"I mean the way they used to harvest them commercially. I never seen it done but I heard about it before" David said as he helped Sherry adjust the trim of the sails.

"When I was a boy, them old Clammers used to set up makeshift encampments each summer to collect a harvest. They spent the mornings dragging the riverbed for shells.

Musselers, or 'clammers' as they sometimes called themselves, made 'crowfoot' hooks using simple kits they constructed. The crowfoot bar was an invention of the inland waterways. Crowfoot hooks were attached with chains to a 10-to-14-foot crowfoot bar that was lowered into the water. It took up to 150 crowfoot hooks to outfit a single crowfoot bar. Most of them old boats were equipped with two bars. After lowering the bars, the clammer then lowered a thing they used to call a 'mule.' The river current filled this underwater sail and moved the johnboat sideways downstream, over the mussel beds. The crowfoot hooks dragged the bottom of the river, snagging mussels, which faced upstream with their shells slightly open to catch food. The dull barbs would prompt the mussels to clamp down and be dragged along on the hooks. The bar was periodically lifted and the mussels removed. I seen a lot of different types of rigs used. Some of them looked like wires with little balls welded on the ends for the mussels to grab hold too. For collecting mussels where there was no current, those gatherers used dip nets. They also Dived with goggles or masks and sometimes they tried wading with a glass-bottomed bucket were two other common methods of finding and picking mussels up from the bottom" Boudreaux said remembering his childhood days and ways people made a living off available resources.

"I think I can make a rig out of ski poles possibly. You think it would work?" David asked considering the possibility.

"Ha! I bet you could. Where the hell did you find enough ski poles around here to even dream that one up" Boudreaux said grinning at another one of David's crazy but workable notions.

"I got me resources" David said mocking Boudreaux's accent and then explaining what he had in mind for a possible joint venture with Frank.

"Sure, I can teach him how to do it and find the beds. I got an acetylene torch that maybe we can weld something up with. I can't do any aluminum welding but I can make up some drag hooks and work out something with them" Boudreaux thought

"Well no one has harvested mussels around here for who knows how long, there should be plenty of them" David said thinking of an untapped resource to exploit.

"You might just have something there Davie me boy. I bet you can get a boat full of them tasty mussels if you just had the right rig." Boudreaux said up for the challenge and excited about the prospects of an easy way to feed the residents.

"I want to give it a shot if you up for it. I like eating mussels better than fish anyway." David said giving Boudreaux a high five.

"Sounds like we do a good business. Sherry let off on that sail line an inch or two, you got that water getting a bit close to the edge for my liking." Boudreaux said as the heeled over sailboat zipped along towards the Post.

"Spoil Sport! I will slow down some" Sherry said grinning and having fun with being able to captain the boat today mostly however she wanted.

"That girl, she got jumping beans in her feet. She ain't ever still and likes things to go too fast "Boudreaux said liking a more relaxed way of dealing with things at leisurely bayou pace.

"She got a need for speed, that's for sure" David said already having been on a few harrowing sailboat rides with her.

"You don't miss so called civilizations much do you Boudreaux" David said watching him relaxing with his dog on the canvas covered trade goods.

"Me? No I miss a car and a juke box, but I been an outdoorsman most of my life. Beverly misses the hot water out of the tap the most but ever sense you started making them hydraulic ram pumps and indoor plumbing got easier she don't complain much. Boudreaux said patting his old hound and enjoying the boat ride.

Hydraulic Ram Water ***Pumps*** have been used for many years to move water without electricity and can be made from PVC pipe or regular plumbing fixtures.

"How about a little mouth organ music, Boudreaux. You got that harmonica of yours with you?" David said digging into a bag that held a couple six packs of beer that were semi cold from soaking in the lake previously.

"That I do, as soon as you let me wet my whistle with one of them beers. I am sure going to miss a good beer when we drink up what's available for now" Boudreaux said reaching for one that David was passing to him.

"I been dreading that day myself, but I might manage to find some for some time to come if I can keep trade flowing." David said offering Sherry one and watching her wanting it but not willing to give up the tiller or the mainsail line to drink one.

"Just let me have the main sail line and you can have one. I am not into racing over to the trading post if we can have a more leisurely sail and some fun on the way" David said wiggling a can at her.

"Ok, you got me. Here take the line and let me have one. Boudreaux play something soft first if you would when you get around to it and not that one Bear likes to sing to." Sherry said wanting to relax and have a leisurely trip instead of Boudreaux and David gearing up for a party this early in the day.

"David, how do you see this all panning out? I mean after they someday mange to get the power back up" Boudreaux said adjusting himself to look at Sherry and David at the rear of the sail boat.

"The way I see it we might be better off as a nation for living through this if we got enough folks left to just hang on. It's my thought that since everyone has had to get their hands dirty to eek out a living; they are not going to allow the government to take 30% in taxes for so called services we got by without until 1930. No the money grabbers are not going to get back in for awhile. No money to snatch anyway if barely anyone has a regular job or income to speak of as we rebuild.

Folks are reeducated now in the values of life and we will probably revert to the original intent of the Constitution." David said expressing a good sentiment.

"If enough of us are still alive you mean. Didn't you say the government predicted a 90% die off rate within a year after an event like this?" Boudreaux said solemnly

"Yeah, but that was not considering our end of the lake now was it? They didn't figure in any Boudreaux's and David's into those statistics, or any preppers like Sherry here. We stack the odds in our favor by our hard work everyday and beyond by just planning and preparing for ourselves and others. Who would have thought we would have a fellow named Bernie as our Mayor? When he gives up the reins we might have a Boudreaux next as president." David said chuckling at the notion.

"Hey! I like the sound of that. President Boudreaux! I could declare you all learn French when the schools got opened again." Boudreaux said laughing.

David started to say something nasty to him in Cajun French but behaved himself and told Boudreaux it would be better to learn Cajun cooking in Home Economics to which Boudreaux laughed uproariously.

"We got to think about starting a school David to educate the young ones." Sherry said seriously

"You want to teach school darling?" David said curious about Sherry having an interest in such.

"No, not me necessarily but the old saying it takes a village to raise a child comes to mind. How about until we find a regular teacher if everyone devotes a day a month to teach at a school we set up. The basics of math etc. a lot of us are fine with and the skills you and Boudreaux and others are just as important to teach now as learning the crap they used to try to force feed the kids in the past life. "Sherry said correcting for the wind and heading towards the trading posts landing.

"See you already got the head of your department of education on board." David said to Boudreaux who had sat up to view their arrival at the dock and smiled at the joke.

"Well I am sure sorry we didn't have time for a bit of a concert on the lake with my harmonica but. I think we covered some good stuff to discuss with Bernie that might need doing." Boudreaux said getting ready to heave the lines to the Dock attendant.

"Who is that on the dock?" David asked eying the man.

"Used to be the owner of the gas station, but he is out of food and money these days." Boudreaux said waving at him and casting him a line.

"Hello Pete, how are things?" Boudreaux said stepping up on the dock.

"The usual, I am sort of harbor master and soda jerk now." Pete said indicating a little stand that offered various juice drinks produced locally that Bernie had set him up with.

"Well I am sure we can all use a drink. Any suggestions?" Boudreaux said looking at the menu.

"Blackberry juice been a best seller" Pete said pouring Boudreaux a sample.

"Hey that's pretty good, give us three cups please" Boudreaux said and waved for Sherry and David to join him.

"You want to pay cash, barter or trade dollars" Pete said looking over at Boudreaux.

"I will give you some cash. $1.50 does it?" Boudreaux said digging in his pocket.

"Sure will! Thank you I appreciate it" Pete said relishing the thought of getting a small bit of hard cash to put away.

"No problem, Is Bernie up in his office?" Boudreaux asked.

"He was earlier. Do you need help unloading your boat? "Pete said looking to maybe make a tip for helping, even though there were plenty of hands around to do the task.

"You could fetch us a wheelbarrow if you would.'

David said starting to go back the boat and unlash the cargo.

"I will get you one right away" Pete said and hurried off to go get one from the loading dock at the general store.

One of the Trading Post guards wandered down to the dock and reminded them to keep their weapons on safe and holsters snapped while they were at the Post. You pretty much got shadowed by the security as you shopped at the trading post. With everyone going around armed it required this high level of vigilance to avoid any accidents or confrontations.

"We set up a Tavern since you were last up here Boudreaux. Weapons get checked at the door and if a customer gets too much to drink, we decide when you get them back, other than that it ain't much different than any other bar. We got a few pool tables and occasionally got some live music." The guard said and then went back to lurking around the post.

"Who has the bait store concession, these days?" David asked Pete.

"Charlie does, he was running a bait store before the storm hit and pretty much does the same thing now except he also got a group of guys fishing for him you might say commercially." Pete replied

"I need to get something like that going on our end of the lake. I want to look him up later" David said starting to unload the boat.

"Just ask around, he usually comes in once a day" Pete replied and started to pitch in and help bring the items up to the main building where the two shopkeepers began to inventory them and record the goods on a ledger.

David had been through this routine several times before and knew that the shopkeepers were quite honest and they didn't have to hang around for the count.

"Is Bernie upstairs?" David asked one of them

"Yes, he is up there. You want to stick this on your balances or do you need some personal goods?" The shopkeeper asked

"Let Sherry give you our list and I will be back later to settle up" David said following Boudreaux to the stairs that lead to Bernie's office.

"Hi guys! Long time no see" Bernie said standing up from his desk and coming around to shake hands with his visitors.

"Yes it has been awhile. Glad you were in today.' David said sitting down in a big easy chair.

"Looks like you got the place working pretty well. Any problems? Boudreaux asked.

"The usual petty stuff but nothing major. There are just too many danged people to find something to do for." Bernie said tired from trying to figure out a new plan for how to handle the number of indigent people that showed up at the post.

"I guess we should look into setting up some kind of employment agency so you don't get stuck with that burden" David said thinking he might know someone for the job.

"That's a great idea. David a messenger came in last night with a note for you." Bernie said producing an envelope.

"It was addressed to the post so I already read it" Bernie said with a deadpan face that didn't reveal what the contents were.

"No who would be sending me a message" David said and rose to get the message from Bernie.

David opened the message and began to read the contents.

Dear David,

I am at Martha's with Melanie and Dump Truck. Your truck started mate! What a blessing it was and outside of the radio not working she runs fine. I met Roland and he drew me a map to get to his place and I will be down in a couple weeks. Looking forward to seeing you again. Everyone is very happy to hear that you made it and are doing fine. We got lots of stories to share my friend and I will be returning your stuff to you and including myself as a package. Ha! Ha!

Your comrade of the road.

Stewart

"Well this is just wonderful news!" David said jubilantly and handed the message to Boudreaux.

"You hear anything else? How the hell did Stewart end up with Melanie I wonder?" David said excited to hear about his friends,

"I just know what the note said; I got a rider going back that way in a couple hours so you can send a reply. I guess we need to combine your mail service with my trade messaging formally and that little post office thing you got going can have more regular service." Bernie said

"Yeah sure, I will knock out a note in a few. Well I never thought I would ever hear from any of them ever again. I can't believe Stewart is bringing me my Truck back either! This calls for a celibration; I hear you got a tavern built now, Bernie?" David said joyously

"Yeah I got one but seeing how you sitting with the owner I can get a barmaid to bring you something up here if you want. I know you're a good tipper and she needs the money." Bernie said thinking about how service had gotten taken to an all new level with so many folks willing to just work for their daily meal.

"Well sure, drinks are on me. Get one of those bean counters downstairs to run me a tab against my account and we will have us a little party." David said.

"You all can stay the night with me and eat over at my place. I got me a fulltime cook when I am around and he cooks almost as good as you Boudreaux " Bernie said laughing and not telling Boudreaux he had some how acquired a souse chief who had got broken down here while vacationing at the lake.

"He can cook the Cajun food? I no believe it; I taste his cooking and tell you what he do wrong."

Boudreaux said miffed that his authentic cuisine could be compared to someone else's not from his home state.

"Boudreaux, tell your dog to take this note to Sherry" David said and put the message back in the envelope and handed it to him. Boudreaux stuck the message folded over the dogs collar and opened the door and sent him on his way.

About 5 minutes later Sherry arrived with his dog and both of them looked like they wore the same grin.

"That's great news for you David! I know how fond you were of that bunch and I feel like I almost personally know them after all the stories you told about them" Sherry said beaming.

"We going to stay the night and have us a little party in the meantime mixed with a bit of business" David advised her.

"That's fine. Boudreaux you need to teach that dog some manners. I was leaning over looking in a box of can goods when he poked me in the butt with that big wet nose of his to get my attention. "Sherry said to a greatly amused group.

"Ahee! He don't mean nothing by it, just doing a favor for his Paw Paw" Boudreaux said laughing and rubbing the hound's ears.

"I am not so sure you didn't teach that to him. That's the third time that dog has poked his nose in my butt." Sherry said at first put out but then seeing the humor in it evident by the looks on everyone's faces.

"Does that old truck of yours have air conditioning David" Bernie said rubbing a couple days worth of beard stubble on his chin.

"It did have, Stewart didn't say if it still worked

or not in his note. Wouldn't that be great if it still worked?" David said thinking what a luxury that would be.

"If it does you going to be giving me a bunch of rides." Bernie said chuckling but serious he was going to make David repay some past favors.

This is turning out to be a fine day David declared to himself. I best start writing a note to Stewart he decided and reached for pen and paper.

The End
Book three of the Prepper Novelette

Roland`s Post Apocalyptic Railroad

by

Ron Foster

1

Hop Sing`s Hoe Down

Stewart, Roland and the Hop Sings drove along slowly as Dump Truck drove the trade wagon along at a brisk trot. Roland had commented many times how it was a miracle David's truck still ran and had of all things a working air conditioner.

HeDo had got permission from his family to ride on the wagon with his big buddy Dump and everyone was somewhat patient about Dump occasionally letting the boy take the reins, as Dump attempted to teach him how to work the team of horses pulling the wagon. This was no small feat as the boy didn't understand English and seemed to want the horses to go faster by slapping them with the reins, which Dump quickly took from him when he did so.

The child was beaming and laughing though, and Dump was grinning himself and turning and waving at everyone that he had things under control, as the horses sped up and then he slowed them back to the pace he wanted to maintain, so as not to overtire the team.

"What do you reckon he is going to do with all that food?" Roland asked Stewart.

"I don't know them that well, but I guess they will share some and keep some for their personal use." Stewart said glancing at the Hop Sings quietly chatting in the rear of the truck in that odd to western ears sing song voice of their native land and language.

"I reckon they fancy themselves going to be traders, if they can get Dump to help with the lingo." Roland said contemplating how they were prepared to start up some kind of business when he first met them.

"I wouldn't put it past them; they are quite clever and industrious. I just hope that those trade ground folks don't try to take advantage of them or be mean to them." Melanie said considering how some of the country folk in the south had preconceived notions or prejudices towards anyone they deemed foreign. *Hell, she thought. Some of these small towns just didn't accept anyone moving into them unless your great grandfather was buried in one of the town's cemeteries.*

"I doubt anyone would bother them, if that big heathen of a man Dump was around." Roland said laughing while looking at He Do trying to sit with his arm around Dump. He might as well have been trying to hug a Volkswagen for all the reach the boy had on Dumps girth.

"Roland, you said the roads were bad around where you came from. How did you manage to make it safely here?" Stewart said contemplating traveling the same roads towards the lake and David's group.

"We brought in two wagons and had 4 guards on horseback too. We travel a bit off the main roads when we can and run messengers up and down the roads in advance mostly." Roland said thinking about how even that level of security was not much if someone had actually decided to ambush them. You can't get a horse rig turned around on a road very easily, and skirmishing off a horse was not like how the old westerns on TV showed it.

"I suspect someone could just sit off in a field and take us all out sniping, if they had a mind to. We brought along a couple dogs and they can kind of sense danger or smell folks, but it's a precarious situation anyway to move about. A lot of folks now are just plain sick in mind and body these days and although there are less of them to worry about, you still get groups of crazies to worry about." Roland said watching Dump speeding up the team to give the boy a thrilling ride.

"He better not get them horses lathered." Roland said starting to roll the window down and stick his head out to holler at Dump but he realized he wasn't going to get them up to a full gallop.

"When are you coming back again?" Stewart asked.

"I have been thinking on that. I might hang around Philburn's and Martha's a week or so and then, if you had a mind to, you could take me home in this truck and I could show you the way myself to get to my place." Roland said playing with the air conditioner vent so it blew right on his face.

"I think we could arrange that. You don't live too far and I could make a day or overnight trip out of it and be back to Martha's in a flash." Stewart said contemplating an interesting road trip.

"We turn off up here, that is if you don't know already, but wave at Dump to stop the team now so I can talk to him." Stewart said.

Roland hung out the window and hollered at Dump to pull over and Stewart stopped the truck.

"Dump, I have a notion to go see that Lithia spring you said wasn't far away, before I go to Martha's if you don't mind." Stewart told him.

"Sure you can do that. Roland can show you the way, I am not sure if I can tell the Hop Sings what it is that's going on though." Dump said looking at the smiling faces anticipating how Martha and Ray would be surprised to see them back so soon with so much bounty in the horse wagon Dump was driving.

"I hadn't considered that, I can go over there later on today, after we get unloaded and rest a bit." Stewart said and then told Dump to just carry on down the road with his heavey wagon load.

"I want to see Martha's face when Hop Sing gives those six pounds of table sugar to her." Melanie said smiling in anticipation.

"Me Too! That old country gal's probably going to squish that little fellow to bits while hugging him in thanks for it." Roland said chuckling at his mental image of the event.

"That solar storm and EMP certainly made for some odd arrangements and relationships to be shared." Stewart said turning into Martha's driveway as he followed along in back of the wooden wagon.

Ray and Martha were sitting on the porch when the horse team and truck turned in. Stewart and Melanie noticed they picked up their rifles and brought them with them in a cradeled postion to greet the travelers.

"Do my eyes deceive me, or isn't that Roland Stiles vsitting in that vehicle?" Martha said opening her arms in a wide embrace with a lever action rifle in one, and what appeared to be a mason jar full of something dark and possibly alcoholic to drink in the other.

"Hey you old goat roper!" Ray called and chased after his Martha to greet Roland carrying his own mason jar of spirits with him.

Roland attempted to fend off Martha's exuberant embrace and Ray's bone crushing grip as he shook hands, but was soon taken in about how happy they were to see him and returned the greetings almost as wildly going from one to the other to reciprocate the enthiuasm of this eventful meeting.

"Land sakes Roland, never in a month of Sundays did I ever think I would set eyes on you again! I take it you were over at Philburn`s?" Martha said bubbling up with questions.

"Yeah, got there yesterday. Damn, Ray you been eating your Wheaties cereal or something; you dang near broke my hand squeezing it so hard. Good to see you all!" Stewart said standing back and looking at the pair with a huge grin.

"We didn't expect nobody back until dark and been tippling a little. You want a drink Roland?" Ray asked not minding another himself.

"I thought I smelled a bit of whiskey in that kiss Martha gave me. You been corrupting her again Ray?" Stewart said laughing at this happy reunion and playfully chiding Martha.

"Hey! That's right, you ain't heard yet! Me and Martha got ourselves married by David over two months ago." Ray said escorting him back to the porch.

Dump unhitched the horses with the Hop Sings supervising the whole ordeal after he did hand gestures to ask them where they wanted to leave their wagon full of goods they had gotten in trade for a gold chain.

"I did hear about you all getting hitched. Philburn told me and get this now, David did to!, I mean he told me about the ceremony." Roland said with his eyes sparkling as he watched Ray and Martha looking shocked he had spoken to David.

"Where's David? When did you speak to him last? How did you come to meet him and where?" Martha gushed and her and Ray almost backed Roland over the Porch rail trying to get as close as possible to him in anticipation of some news of their friend they had waved goodbye to what seemed like so long ago now.

"You all just back off a mite now; you got me losing my balance and I have not even got me my drink yet." Roland said smiling and touching the couple's shoulders to move them back some from him and give him some breathing room.

"Ray, get him a drink now please. Sit down quick now Roland and start telling me the story." Martha said pushing Roland towards a chair.

"I want to hear about it to, I aint going no where. Melanie, the jug is on the kitchen counter. Bring it out here if you would and get Stewart to bring cups for everyone and that crock of spring water." Ray said sitting down in a chair next to Martha and giving Ray his rapt attention.

"Glory be, I forgot about my Hop Sings neighbors. You reckon they are going to want me to store something they got in that ice chest they're toting this way?" Martha commented as she watched MeDo and HeDo carrying it towards the porch, while an animated hand gesture conversation was going on at the wagon between Dump and Papa Hop Sing.

"They just might, it appears they got something on their minds. " Roland said knowingly with a small smile that told Martha he knew something he wasn't going to say or talk about just yet.

Hop Sing had climbed on top of the canvas covered wagon and was shaking his head no emphatically at Dump and making a gesture that measured the whole wagon and then began pointing at his head as if to tell Dump to think about what he was trying to say before he got confused about his meaning before gesturing some more.

Hop Sing jumped off the wagon and walked towards the middle of it and said "Chop Dimpie" Chop, and drew a line down the middle with his finger." The he made a motion with his arm and hand indicating half the wagon load of goods.

"He wants something off that wagon of yours Roland" Martha said always having a hard time understanding her adopted special guests and began again to be looking puzzled as to what it was under the canvas Hop Sing evidently wanted to cut a portion off of.

Dump regarded his friend and somewhat sort of understood the intent, but wanted confirmation from a third party and told Hop Sing "Stewie Do' using the name the Hop Sings had chosen for Stewart and pointing at him on the porch.

"AH!" Hop Sing said and gabbled something to

HeDo across the yard and HeDo ran up and took Stewarts hand and led him towards the wagon happily repeating "you do", along the way.

"What's up Dumpie?" The Englishman said as he was lead by the boy towards the two people who watched him intently and himself still figuring out ways to get a mutual understanding amongst everyone.

"I think maybe, he is telling me he wants to save half of these supplies in the house for him, but Martha doesn't like him in the Kitchen Pantry or root cellar and I would say the barn would be better for him to store them in." Dump said pointing at the barn and then in the direction of Hop Sings little house.

Hop Sing shook his head vehemently no it was not his intent and did the "Chop Dimpie" thing again with his hands and pointed towards Martha on the porch. He definitely had her attention by now and by observing the Tower of Babble conversation as she liked to refer to these misunderstandings in the biblical sense, she was at odds to try to explain why it was so difficult to accomplish things with non English speakers herself.

Stewart regarded the sun darkened Asian man who was busy now, scampering about undoing the ropes securing the canvas and who was also looking up at him patiently once in awhile, possibly apparently thinking that he, Stewart, would somehow figure out what he wanted eventually and for the life of him Stewart still couldn't figure it out.

Hop Sing had a realization apparently and pointed at his head like a light bulb had just gone on and smiled. while doing another hand gesture for understanding

"You do!" and then Hop Sing pointed at Stewart and motioned for him and Dump to walk to the porch.

He looked a bit comical to Ray as he was kind of marching towards them with his chest poked out and Dump and Stewart were conversing confusedly in back of him following in his wake not looking nearly as convinced to the mission he was on or possibly intended.

Hop Sing mounted the stairs and moved his wife MeDo and son HeDo who were sitting on the cooler to the side of the stairs away and then had them standing in almost military formation beside it , time he was done looking like he was posing for a picture with them when everyone was arranged.

Hop Sing Said with a flourish of jis hand touching forehead and heart "For Moutha and Way" opening the lid of the ice chest and handing Ray a pouch of chewing tobacco and Martha a bag of sugar and indicating that the contents of the whole chest were theirs as a gift from him and his family he cherished.

"Well isn't that the nicest thing. He traded with you for that Roland, did he?" Martha said doing her best impression of a thankful Buddha blessing by putting her hands together in a prayerful fashion and nodding at each one of the Hop Sings before she gave them all hugs and a wet sloppy kiss on Hop Sings face that he could have lived without.

"" Dang he give me 5 pouches of Redman Chewing tobacco" Ray said reaching for Hop Sings hand before the little man made sure he didn't return the shake without Ray remembering to be gentle in his grasp, which Roland found hilarious watching Hop Sing make a painful face mimicking what a Ray not knowing his own strength if he had a few, could do to your hand.

Hop Sing motioned for the group to follow and once again lined his family up and stood next to them.

"Stewie, you do. Chop half." Hop Sing said in a gesture that meant honor and benevolence towards the wagon and the division of goods.

"He wants you to have half what he bought!" Stewart said as the realization came over him and he waved at everyone indicating whether or not just for Martha and Ray or was it a gift for all in order to get the message right.

Hop Sing considered for a moment and chattered with his wife and motioned at everyone but clarified it with "Moutha Do" meaning she decided distribution of the supplies he had gifted for them all.

Martha teared up as she understood and scooped them all up in her ample arms and hugged the Hop Sing family tightly much to their discomfort.

"Ha! Told you she would squish them! "Ray said sipping on his drink and smirking towards Stewart and Melanie.

"Well that's the nicest thing anybody ever wished me. Bill you tell them Hop Sings I love them and Thank them with all my heart" Martha said dabbing at her eyes while MeDo happily patted her once she got her spine readjusted from the embrace she had just received.

HeDo made everyone laugh as he directed Dump with a "You Do!" to pickup two 50lb sacks of flour and haul them towards Martha's porch like a little general to which his father shook a finger at him but still smiled at the kids audacity to order his big friend around.

Dump playfully picked the kid up and put him under one arm while still carrying a sack of flour with that hand and grabbed the other sack of flour and headed towards the house while the boy laughed and everyone looked on approvingly of the way the giant handled his "little buddy".

Melanie thought how rare it was that a man of Dumpies stature and background would take the time to teach and befriend a boy he had nothing in common with. That's what she liked about old Dump, if you got through the bar bouncer appearance and the scary brawn, he had a heart of gold that lay in that body, if you could recognize it, she mused.

"Me cook?" Papa Hop Sing said tentatively in Martha's direction indicating he wanted the honors tonight.

"Me help?" Martha said grinning at him and attempting to do his accent.

"Get him to come with me Dump. He has a bonus he doesn't know about. Up under that front seat on the wagon,I got two big slabs of salted pork ribs from a hog we butchered a month ago. He needs to soak them in water first to get some of the brine off, but that's the closest thing to fresh meat I got." Stewart said while Hop Sing studied what he thought he might be included in, regarding this conversation.

Dump made a pig noise, pointed at his ribs and at Hop Sings cookhouse or the barbecue pit and led an elated Hop sing off to investigate what was under the front seat of the wagon.

"Damn Roland, remember to tell me a slab of ribs is a whole hogs worth" Melanie said watching Dump and Hop Sing examining a burlap sack that looked like someone had taken a circular saw down the middle of a pig.

"That was one of those old land racer long sows I had at my place. They got more length than a regular pig and she was getting a bit old to give me any shoats. She going to be good eating though, if he gets that salt off of her. It would be best to soak it 24 hour like a Virginia ham but I used about as much sugar as salt so it should be tolerable in about 4 hours if you swish the water around and turn it a lot. You think I should do the cooking?" Stewart asked as Dump evidently was having trouble making Hop Sing understand the need to leach some of the salt and nitre out of the meat.

"That man understands things his own way, but when it comes to food, he pretty much can do miracles. He will be ok, as long as he keeps that stinking garden of his out of it." Martha said giving an approving look at MeDo and still scrupulously watching Hop Sings next efforts to make Dump understand what he had in mind to do in cooking the lagniappe he had missed knowing about in his trade with Roland.

"Tell him that fire won't get that taste out Dump." Roland said evidently understanding that Hop Sing meant that a hot enough fire might sear it out in the cooking process by Hop Sings hand gestures.

"Gotcha, I think he is saying he wants to cook it long and slow if it's ok. Hang on, I think he saying he going to make 5 dishes out of these ribs." Dump said watching the elaborate motioning of the hands and pointing out of different cooking stations Hop Sing was doing.

"Just let him cook and help him, but watch that danged garden of his "Martha said thinking of the penchant of the Hop Sings to use human manure in their kitchen garden distastefully.

MeDo evidently picked up on the aversion Martha had for her home garden and directed Martha to follow her to the kitchen where she indicated she wanted a large quantity of the few onions she had left. Martha hesitated and then motioned Medo could have what she wanted and that the kitchen could be hers for the evening ,to which HeDo asked where was a bigger "Chopper" indicating a small meat cleaver Martha had thrown in a kitchen drawer years ago.

"No chop, I do" Martha tried to make him understand that she didn't have a big cleaver like his daddy, but she was willing to cut up the onions herself with a butcher knife.

Dump and the rest of the men came carrying various trade goods in and Ray was directing their placement as MeDo gently escorted a reluctant Martha out of the kitchen.

"Feels like mothers day, although I never been a mother" Martha said to whoever was paying attention to her in the ant line carrying stuff into her home, as she somewhat relaxed and drank her drink on the porch watching the procession.

Hop Sing sat down next to her and motioned that he wanted a drink of whiskey too and Martha mixed him a light one from the half gallon sitting on the table. He regarded her with solemn eyes for a moment after nodding his thanks to her for the beverage and a mutually shared grin at his grimace as he had not acquired a taste for such liquor yet.

"You do Moutha" Hop Sing said as he handed Martha his last gold chain and gestured it was all he had left in this apocalyptic world, but he trusted himself and his family to her good graces.

Martha had never understood this enigma of a man before, but understood he was placing his life and his fortune in her hands. She regarded the chain and began stroking the links lovingly and touched his cheek as if to say , it will be alright you can stay forever as she pointed at the home she had lent him and his family.

Hop Sing looked deep into her eyes then grasped and kissed her chafed and reddened hands in gratitude and understanding that can only be shared with those of mutual intents.

A toss down of a drink by Hop Sing, a hearty laugh from Martha and a hug, and a deal was sealed without a contract or a word spoken.

"What are you all looking so seriously about?" Dump said walking by with a case of canned potatoes on his arm and Ray riding HeDo on his shoulders and the boy carrying a sack of precious peaches on his shoulder.

"They are kin now, that's their home. We traded I think to love and honor each other foreverm so we call them family npw in front of folks so they know we are all in this together." Martha said in her style of adopted protection.

"I do that anyway, why the change Martha?" Dump said setting his load down and looking at the two, who wore secretive smiles in their eyes.

"I don't know, Bill we sort of promised each

other and gave each other trust like when animals adopt masters but that ain't what I mean. Hop Sing placed his wealth in my hands to do what is right and share our home. Nobody will ever, ever, bother this man or his family while I am alive and you heed that Bill. He has more honor and nicety in him than anyone I ever met and we bonded and promised to give support, the same as any other family does. I don't know what tomorrow will bring, but from now on, we live together and die together, just like we and our blood kin do now. Ok Billy?" Martha said distraught but adamant in her convictions.

"You give him PawPaw`s old forty five to seal the deal, better yet you let me seal the deal and show my worth." Dump said

"Done and DONE." You go get that gun and some ammo for him. You get him a rifle or something too. He's probably seen combat in his country Stewart had said; and I would be pleased to see him armed and on our side." Martha said watching Hop Sing trying to absorb any bits of foreign words that assured him and his family were now fully accepted into this tribe.

Dump went into the house and returned with a Colt Commander 45 and presented it to the Hmong man sitting next to Martha, as well as gifted him an old Lee Enfield .303 rifle he had chosen for the occasion.

Words could not express what occurred behind the older mans dead set eyes, as he looked from one face to the other and weighed the gravity of the honor and relevance on the gifts bestowed upon him.

Hop Sing touched his forehead, his heart and

waved across his body signifying he was there for them forever and then embarrassed Dump by kissing his hand, then also did the same to Ray's and Martha's as a gesture of blind protection and held up the weapons to his family for their approval.

Stewart had been standing on the inside of the door listening to the exchange and looked so touched by it, Melanie asked him if he was alright.

"David told me a story of allies one time when we were out on the road and I have never forgot it" Stewart began.

"He told me back in the days of Vietnam, that the US Special Forces would put the mountain tribesmen called the Montngyards or YARDS, as the G.I.s called them in the front foxholes on the line knowing they would never retreat. You see what they did was put the whole displaced family in one foxhole and knew the man would fight for his family to the death, before anyone could get to them. That sounds horrible until I remember David say how happy they were to be together as a family, and had a better chance of surviving with American firepower backing them up. US soldiers would use those few extra seconds of defense to call air or artillery support, so that everyone could live another day and the husband wouldn't be offline checking on his family when death by Viet Cong walked over his trench." Stewart said somewhat realizing the way he had arranged his and Dump Truck's bunks while they were sleeping that first night of the disaster that befell the world.

"He probably been around more crap than we can even comprehend," Ray said regarding that Hop Sing had already strapped on, checked the pistol and was regarding the rifle as something nasty that needed cleaning after inspecting the bore.

"This is a good day, don't spoil it!" Melanie said drawing attention her way. "We are now a worrying group that needs food and friendship over a bullet or was that called a round David said? Anyways, if he was here, he would have unloaded that bike of HeDo`s and been encouraging him to go and play I think." Melanie stated to bring folks back to a different and more pleasant reality.

"Show him where we keep the gun cleaning kits Dump. He appears to be the type that is meticulous about his weapons." Ray said watching Hop Sing checking over the rifle.

"Ok." Dump said motioning for Hop Sing to follow him inside.

"Stewart you want to go and make a long trip out of it and go see David up at the lake for a day or two"? Roland asked.

"I have been thinking on that. You say there are lots of vacant houses up there also?" Stewart said carefully.

"Sure there is. David's side of the lake is pretty much deserted. Are you possibly thinking about getting you a lake house up there, Stewart?" Roland said smiling.

"Well to be honest with you the notion does appeal to me. Maybe I could trade David back his truck for one of those empty houses. "Stewart said laughing

"You are considering leaving us already?" Melanie said looking a bit shocked

"Well just looking at all options, I need to find me something useful to do and thought maybe I would have a little talk with Dave about it." Stewart said nervously.

"You and David could come back and forth to see us couldn't you"? Dump asked not really knowing what to think about Stewarts change of plans.

"I didn't mean to upset anyone, I was just sort of thinking out loud. I am at a loss with myself being so far from home and hearth and I think a little working lake vacation might be just the thing to set my mind at ease, so I can try and plan for the future." Stewart said wringing his hands.

"Now when you look at it that way, it sounds pretty good" Melanie said somewhat relived.'

"Sure Stewart, go have yourself a holiday as you say. Maybe Melanie might need a break too." Dump said flinching at the idea of losing his friends companionship so soon.

" Well I certainly would like to one day, but if Stewart swears he will be back one day, I just soon have my rest here on the farm. I been on enough adventures to last a life time and don't really want to start another one just now." Melanie said to Dumps champion smile of relief.

"Might be, you will be able to take a train down there someday" Roland said to the astonished group.

"See I had me this little toy truck conversion to a train on my mantle and John got to looking at it one day and said he could build us one similar to it" Roland said and then began to describe the setup

"I got him and some others working on building one now. We figure there should be lots of trains stalled on the tracks here and there, nobody has got around to looting them yet and we could get lots of trade items and food stuffs. Of course, that will also mean a lot of tracks are impossible to pass, so we are building little go cart looking affairs to go explore the rail lines." Roland said sitting back and letting the ingenuity of it all sink into his very interested group.

"That's cool as hell! I should build me something like that. There are bunches of rail lines going into Atlanta running here and there not far from here." Dump said pondering the notion.

" I tell you what, next time a trade wagon comes this way, I will send you one of the go cart train wagon things and you could do some exploring for me and my trade company" Roland offered.

"That is neat, is it big enough to take Hop Sing as another rider with me to help?" Dump asked thinking about an enterprise.

"Yes sure is. I will talk to John when I get back and see what modifications are available he has come up with, since I have been gone and send you one with the latest improvements. "Roland said looking forward to what might be a very lucrative enterprise.

"Is David in on that?" Stewart asked.

"Well no not specifically. The rail lines run through the little towns around him, but not down by the lake. We got a regular little trade wagon route to him though, so he will benefit from it" Roland advised him.

"I am going to see if Martha needs me to do anything in the kitchen and be back in a bit." Melanie said excusing herself.

"Why a man that runs up on a freight train full of goods would be set for life." Stewart said with his eyes sparkling.

"Thinking of staying now?" Dump said laughing.

"You just leave some for me buddy. I might be back sooner than planned though. I was considering doing something with that mineral water spring, but I just got my sights set a wee bit higher." Roland said smiling.

"Our original idea is to send spotters out on them go-carts or as John likes to call them "skimmers" and when somebody finds a good haul we send the truck locomotive after the haul and carry it out to the trading posts by wagon. I guess some small time freelancing is ok, as long as you don't get too greedy about it. "Roland said trying to figure out an equable way to share what started out as a monopoly.

"I wonder how long Hop Sing is going to cook those ribs. I am starving" Dump grumbled.

"I am ready for them myself; I think I will go wander over to his kitchen for a look see." Ray said.

"He doesn't run you off near as quickly as he does me. Give me a report when you get back." Dump said.

"So does Roland's Railroad have a name, or is that it?" Dump said chuckling.

"That's pretty much it, we are going to call that truck locomotive the apocalypse express though." Roland said sipping on his drink.

"I like that!" Stewart said thinking about the apocalyptic times they were living in.

"Looks like we are getting ready to eat." Melanie said wandering out on the porch.

"I am certainly ready. I have been smelling things cooking for hours." Dump said heading over towards the picnic table with the others.

Martha and the Hop Sings had sure put on a great spread. Hop Sing had out did himself with several different tasty dishes and a huge feast was had by all.

2

Johns Junkyard

Stewart had been looking forward to his trip to Roland's all week. He had visited Roland at Philburn`s a couple times and Roland had sent his wagon back with the other trade wagons heading out. Today he and Stewart had gotten together early and were heading towards his farm.

"I like that scatter gun Dump gave you, reminds me of the kind they used on stage coaches." Roland said looking at the short 12 gauge double barrel coach gun leaning on the floor between them.

"I am liking it too; it's not much for distance, but it is devastating up close. I had Dump give me some lessons with it this week and am pretty comfortable with it." Stewart replied.

"I think we left early enough that we won't encounter anyone on the road, but you can never tell." Roland said watchful of the road as well as it sides as they traveled onwards.

"I hope it stays quiet, I was really getting pretty

relaxed at Martha's. I see why Melanie wanted to stay there for now. I used to like to take a nice drive in the country, but there is nothing nice about traveling these days." Stewart said wary of his surroundings and uneasy about going into a new territory.

"Well at least we are out in the country. I doubt I will get close to a city ever again." Roland said considering what state those places must be in these days.

"Believe me; I kick myself every time I think I was fool enough to go back into Atlanta, instead of going off with Dump and David. I almost got killed or badly hurt, I don't know how many times. I can not comprehend how anyone could still live in one these days." Stewart said thinking of the fires, the murders and thieves, not to mention the lack of water and food in those death traps.

"John has been tinkering on something or inventing something pretty much everyday since he moved into the cabin, that I got out by the pond. He pretty much has my barn starting to look like a junkyard; so I got some carpenter neighbors of mine to start building him a shop, so I can get my barn back. I swear he can pretty much make anything mechanical that we can dream up, or have a need for." Roland said directing Stewart to turn in the next driveway about a half mile up.

"This is a big spread you got Roland. You ain't had anybody try to rustle any of your cows?" Stewart said looking over at a small herd.

"No, I know most folks around here and I am sharing meat with them some. They also know we got an armed contingent around here, so they steer clear of my place. Every bit of a cow is getting used nowadays except the Moo. Marrow bone soup is back on the menu for sure. The offal gets ground up by a guy that used to be a butcher and he has been making up a sort of dog food for them that have hunting dogs." Roland said getting out and unlocking his gate.

The pair pulled up to the house and John and Sarah came out to meet them.

"Hi there Roland! The traders said to look for you today. You must be Stewart." John said reaching to shake his hand.

"I have heard about you, too. Roland said you're the Einstein of this little enterprise." Stewart replied.

"Oh he is just being kind. I just like to play with old machinery to make it do something new. This is my wife Sarah." John said introducing his wife who also shook hands with Stewart.

"I hear you been building a train of some sort." Stewart said looking around at the barn that john had come from.

"I basically got that one done: but it wasn't until today, that I figured out how we might build something we can take on and off the tracks easier. I got to thinking about some of those freight trains which are extremely long and could block us from miles of track we could use. I got the idea thinking about Sherry's Bobcat loader. I designed us something we can get on and off the tracks, using its own power and being able to travel the roads as well. Check this out." John said as his wife handed him a pad she had been drawing on for him.

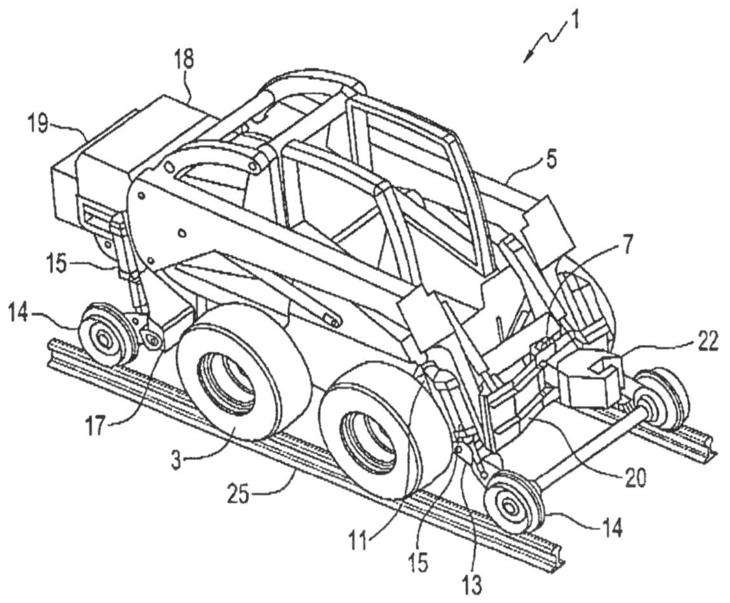

"Sherry is going to want to drive that thing you know. That is a pretty slick idea you came up with. Now, we just got to convince her to let us borrow her Bobcat some." Roland said admiring the plans.

"Well they don't use it much at the lake and I can build them something to maybe replace it for transportation purposes." John replied

"I think they will go for it easily and if they need a front end loader, you can add the blade back on cant you?" Roland asked.

"Oh sure, I will make it an easy on and off affair." John said eying his drawing.

"What have you been up to Sarah?" Roland asked.

"Oh I have been making herbal tinctures and looking for medicinal plants." Sarah told him.

"You find anything new?" Roland asked her. Roland took a great deal of interest in what local plants could be used for what and had learned a lot from Sarah.

"Yeah, I found a plant called Motherwort. I left the page of my herbal open for you at the house." She said walking towards the back patio with the group.

"Great, I would like to see that." Roland said going to retrieve the Herbal and began reading.

Motherwort has been used for centuries to treat conditions related to childbirth. Motherwort has the ability to act as a galactagogue, meaning it promotes a mother's milk flow. It also has been used as a uterine tonic before and after childbirth. The herb contains a chemical called leonurine, which encourages uterine contractions. Motherwort is also claimed to be an emmenagogue, or an agent that promotes menstrual flow. It has been used for centuries to regulate the menstrual cycle and to treat menopausal and menstrual complaints.

Motherwort is also a mild relaxing agent and is often used by herbalists to treat such menopausal complaints as nervousness, insomnia, heart palpitations, and rapid heart rate. The herb may help heart conditions aggravated by nervousness. Because of its ability to improve mental outlook and reduce the effects of stress, some herbalists feel motherwort tea can help minimize the risk of postpartum depression. In such cases, motherwort combines well with linden flower and ginger tinctures.

Motherwort sometimes has been referred to as a cardiotonic. Motherwort injections recently were shown to prevent the formation of blood clots; which, of course, improves blood flow and reduces the risk of heart attack, stroke, and other diseases. It is good for hypertension, because it relaxes blood vessels and calms nerves. Motherwort also may correct heart palpitations that sometimes accompany thyroid disease and hypoglycemia (low blood sugar). Motherwort is useful for headache, insomnia, and vertigo. It is sometimes used to relieve asthma, bronchitis, and other lung problems, usually mixed with mullein and other lung herbs.

It is also seen as a remedy for heart palpitations, it has a strengthening effect, especially on a weak heart. The antispasmodic and sedative effects promote relaxation rather than drowsiness. The leaves are antispasmodic, astringent, cardiac, diaphoretic, emmenagogue, nervine, sedative, stomachic, tonic and uterine stimulant. They are taken internally in the treatment of heart complaints (notably palpitations) and problems associated with menstruation, childbirth and menopause, especially of nervous origin.

"Wow that is a very useful plant to find. Maybe we can cultivate it, too." Roland said passing the book to Stewart.

"I need to find more bottles somewhere, so I can bottle it up for the trading posts." Sarah said pouring everyone some tea.

"I will put the word out and see what we can find." Roland replied.

"Well, I guessed that was something useful for mothers, so I guess I was right! MeDo could use some of that I bet." Stewart said handing the book back to Sarah.

"Who is Me Do?" Sarah asked.

"An Asian woman staying at Martha's, I will explain to you later." Roland said settling down into a patio chair.

"John, you need anything for your projects?" Roland asked.

"No I got traders out hunting a couple things, but I am pretty well stocked for now." John replied patting his wife's hand as she sat down next to him.

"We are going to go see David at the lake. You want to tag along and talk to Sherry about letting you use that Bobcat loader?" Roland asked him.

"Yes that would be great, we could use a day off and I wouldn't mind getting a little fishing in to. Sarah will probably want to visit Mary and share herb lore with her." John said thinking about what he wanted to bring with them to the lake.

"Jack said he could use some input from you in his shop on the projects he has going. I think he is having a bit of trouble with the hydraulic rams they are trying to use to deliver water to their houses." Roland told him.

"Sounds like fun. Remind me honey, though, we are supposed to be having a day off for us, so Jack don't lock me up in that shed he calls his "Skunk Works" all day fixing what they been trying to make." He said smiling at Sarah.

For a couple who had broken down on the side of the road in an RV when storm hit, they had been extremely lucky to have bumped into David and had Roland take them in. John and Sarah had been at wits end to even get their next meal, until David had helped them to learn a few skills and shared some food with them. That reminded him; he needed to give David back the book that he had lent them.

"Roland, remind me to bring David's Rural Ranger book back to him. I certainly found some useful things in it and know why he valued it so highly. If it were not for that book, I wouldn't know anything hardly about trapping and snaring, and the simplicity of that window heater in there I doubt I could have ever come up with." John said watching Roland showing Stewart his "Schrade Old Timer Buzz Saw Trapper Knife", that Stewart had taken an interest in, when he had pulled the tweezers out of it to remove a burr or a tick from his dog.

"I got it by my bedside, that thing might not be edited all that great, but knowledge and good skills don't need editing for using, or good advice that is practical and handy to have." Roland said getting up to go get it.

"I am going to trade you out of that knife one day" John said grinning at Roland on their on going battle to keep it out of John's pocket, any chance John got to forget to "return it", when he borrowed it for running his snare and trap line.

"No way, No how! Hell I value it twice as much now that I read that book and can manufacture snare triggers so easy. I used that pin awl on it the other day, in order to clean the paint out of the eye of a fish lure. You might try to put a trader's bounty on one, if they could find you something like it, but I doubt you will ever see another." Roland said exaggerating putting it back into his own pocket.

"If that thing was made like the old time fishing knives with a hook disgorger/scaler blade it would be the all time perfect fishing and hunting tool.' John said wishing for such an item.

"I got this knife out of David's Bug out bag". Stewart said producing one of the old style fishing knives John had mentioned.

"That's a beautiful thing," John said examing it and admiring the plastic abalone look scales on the sides of it. That's what I like about Dave; he seemed to be more practical than tactical. That hook removing blade is a must for fishing these little perch and such around here. It might not be considered a fighting blade, but that fillet blade on it would be plenty for most things." John said handing it back.

"Can I see that book, please?" Stewart said as Roland returned and handed it to Sarah to keep up with it for John.

"Sure, I have read it too, it tells you how to take a piece of string, a baking bag and a box and catch your dinner and cook it to!" Sarah said approvingly as Stewart started to flip through it.

"Well I know what I will be doing while folks are snoozing tonight!" Stewart said forcing himself to put the book down and be socialable.

"I couldn't find any aircraft style cable anywhere out here, or something similar, for those commercial snare replacements David wanted. I guess he is going to have to just make do, after he uses up what he has in his preps. I thought he just wanted some more for deer until I saw what a raccoon could do to a brand new one he had given me. That thing was totally unusable except for the swivels and such, after I only used it once and caught that big boar of a coon who twisted and kinked it up beyond recognition." John said remembering how he had been warned by Dave that often time's snares were not reusable no matter how strong of materials they were made out of.

"He has been having a blast trying to out do Boudreaux in the game catching department. He used a trick one day that Boudreaux clamed he knew about, but that it was an Indian trick only to be used for emergencies and David had cheated by doing it. I don't think he knew about it at all until he had back tracked David's trail and figured it out from the signs and tore up ground everywhere, where the animals had fought the snares." Roland said settling back in his chair to begin telling the story.

"Hey, before you get started, I bet Stewart here would like to have a drink of something better than sweet tea". John said using Stewart as an excuse to partake, before the official happy hour was announced for the day.

"Go do the honors John, you heard this story before. I could use me one to. "Roland said squashing any objections from Sarah and watching Stewart brighten up at the prospect.

"The way David tells it, when game got to be too scarce around a tribe's camp and people began to starve, one of the better hunters of a clan decided it was time to move, but he needed to get enough meat for the march to a different location. Now this Brave had been observing animals his whole life and knew their ways and habits of communicating in the wild. He got him a sack and went collecting the scat of all kinds of different animals he could find and went to a clearing in the woods and commenced to throw shit every which away and then broke trails and set snares on them, channeling towards the clearing by arranging brush on them like funnels." Roland said as Stewart leaned in closer with interest to envision how all this worked.

"Thanks for the drink John" Stewart said as he forced back a grimace of how strong it was, so as not to let on to his wife,, John had leaned on the bottle considerably when pouring it, but she caught it anyway.

"It ain't even sundown yet, don't be getting all smashed this early in the day, I should of done the bartending." Sarah said looking at the men reproachfully.

"I am maintenance drinking only; I wasn't sure how Stewart liked his drink. You can taste mine if you want to." John said chagrined at being publicly scolded, but knowing his only occasional drinker wife would forgo checking his glass for the same potent mix.

"Well you boys play nice and no wrestling later when you get a buzz, you ain't any spring chickens no more. I guess I will have me one also, so I can tolerate you later, but I will mix it myself." Sarah said rising to go to Roland's bar and trying to camouflage her attempt at seeing how full the bottle was now and would be later to monitor the level of imbibing that was going to go on. Roland had already figured out this ploy by now and he and John came to the conclusion that they would leave one bottle out for her to watch and one bottle hidden for them to monitor and pour from freely.

"Go right ahead Sarah; let me get back to my story." Roland said cheerfully and resumed the tale.

"So this Indian fella commenced to sling shit to the four winds and then went back down the trail and climbed a tree to use as a deer stand to settle in and wait. Well this old boy knew that every animal in the woods monitors every other animals poop for what's going on in the forest. Mr. Animal as he was going down the trails starts smelling crap, lots of crap, all kinds and every kind of crap, and thinks to himself, there is a party going on over here with all these different kinds of animals and it must relate to some kind of plentiful food source and he goes to investigate.

Why would so many different kinds of animals be going back and forth to the same place and then crapping everywhere, unless they were getting something good to eat that was plentiful? Mr. Animal thinks and though caution says don't go there, his curiosity gets the better of him, so off he goes down the trails or off the trails, being directed and drawn towards this great animal feed station he has never seen before. Why there are rabbits and deer, turkey and possum, foxes and Bobcats, rats and mice and every other critter he can think of going in this direction.

Must be cautious Mr. Animal says to himself, predators follow prey, but that is the nature of things and natures way. How old are these signs? All different, some animals have come and gone before, but they all came for something. Did the herbivores find a bounty? Did the predators just follow the congregation of plant eaters? Maybe there are fruits aplenty; something is happening that's for sure to be so many animals coming to one location and Mr. Animal wants to know what it is regardless.

Man has been here lately also, must be extra careful, but his scent is light and he has not urinated or pooped here abouts. Hurry go see what it is, Mr. Animal thinks, but the predators, the meat eaters might have a claim, or the big fruit and plant eaters could be a danger or a rival. Caution, Caution! But hurry before what it is that attracted everyone is gone. Stop, listen look, smell, move a step. Why did Deer poop where rabbit went? Why is Fox telling Bobcat this is his territory? It is just all to confusing to Mr. Animal's mind and need over caution hurries his brain. He smells death though and watches and waits against his instincts to run to the clearing.

I can't smell food! What is it? What is it? He asks. There must have been a storm or something to take out so many trees, the paths are clogged with brush but so far he has found clear paths.

"Dang vine, I got to get to this place he thinks, as a noose settles over his neck, Mr. Animal thinks it will just break it" was the last thing of this world he thought on, before he got strangled and dangled from a sapling." Roland said finishing the story, but waiting to tell them that the animals only fall for this once and it can't be repeated in the same hunting grounds for quite sometime.

"You had me on the edge of my chair." Stewart said contemplating the lore, as well as Roland or David's story telling ability, he did not know which.

"I respect the taboos and will not try it unless needed; but supposedly, David picked a forlorn place to win a contest with Boudreaux on and created a critter convention of animals for a lake party eat fest, that they still talk about today. David always says "I will teach you everything you know, but not everything I know." Roland said laughing.

"He is quite a character, but I never heard that one." Stewart said admiring David's wood lore.

"He always says he is a wealth of useless information; but I tell you now, that guy has skills I never thought of, or heard about, until you get to talking to him over a drink." Roland claimed.

"I have seen him get more fish at the end of the dam one day, where he had us put those rocks under that overflow pipe that goes into that pool, than I got fishing all day. I don't know why fish go out, or get flushed out of that pipe like that, when the pond rises, but they hide themselves between those rocks and David has the balls to just reach in and feel them between the stacked stones and fill up a bucket with the biggest pan fish I ever seen in 20 minutes." John said remembering how David had learned the trick growing up on Air Force bases and an old Sergeant had taught him this at the Base lakes.

"He has a knack for making things easy for you to catch game with a trick or two, I give you that. Boudreaux thinks he is the king of the lake trappers and fishermen, but David can sure give him a run for his money." Roland said thinking about what they were going to do for lunch.

"Sarah what were you thinking about making for lunch?" Roland asked her knowing it was going to contain most likely some kind of foraged greens or something.

"I found a bunch of cattails and have been

experimenting with them. There is so much to know about cattails that a book could be written just about them, my new motto is "You name it and I'll make it from cattails!" Cattails are the supermarket of the wilds. The young cob-like tips of the plant are edible as is the white bottom of the stalk, spurs off the main roots and spaghetti like rootlets off the main roots. They have vitamins A, B, and C, potassium and phosphorus. The pollen can be used like flour." Sarah said proud of her find and now being able to substantially stretch their food stores.

"David told me about them in case I found myself walking to Dumps place. He said that if a lost person has found cattails, they have four of the five things they need to survive: Water, food, shelter and a source of fuel for heat—the dry old stalks. The one item missing is companionship. The other thing he pointed out is that no matter where the water flows, down stream is civilization in North, Central and South America. He told me to remember that when you are lost in the Americas. "Stewart said showing he had listened and remembered a thing or two, he had picked up about surviving in the woods even though he had rarely ever gotten out of the city growing up." Well I have been making starch out of them to add to things. In Euell Gibbons' Stalking the Wild Asparagus, his chapter on cattails is titled "Supermarket of the Swamp." The way you get the starch is to clean the exterior of the roots and then crush them in clean water and let them sit. The starch settles to the bottom then one pours off the water. It may take several drains and settle sessions to get rid of the fiber. The flour will begin to separate from the fibers. Continue this process until the fibers are all separated and the sweet flour is removed. Remove the fiber and pour off the excess water. Allow the remaining flour slurry to dry by placing near a fire or using the sun once you have just the starch. It is excellent for cooking as you would any flour. Getting starch that way is quite labor intensive. Here is another way I read about to get to the root starch: Dry the peeled roots (peel roots while they are wet--they are difficult to peel when dry). Chop roots into small pieces, and then pound them. When the long fibers are removed, the resultant powder can be used as flour. The roots also can be boiled like potatoes then the starch chewed out of it, or you can also roast the root in a fire until the outer spongy core is completely black. Then chew the starch off of the fiber. The book said not to eat the fiber. I haven't gotten around to trying that that way doing it yet." Sarah said and then explained what she was going to make as a side dish today.

Scalloped Cattails

Scrape off two cups of brown cattail tops and put them into a bowl with two beaten eggs, one-half cup melted butter, one-half teaspoon each sugar and nutmeg and black pepper. Blend well and add slowly one cup of scalded milk to the cattail mixture and blended. Pour the mixture into a greased casserole and top with grated cheese —optional — and add a dab of butter. Bake 275 degrees for 30 minutes.

"Of course we don't have a regular oven but I can use that Coleman box oven pretty good now, so I will try it with that." Sarah explained to the group.

"Well you can use that goat cheese I got in there and I think I will butcher us a Duck for the occasion if they are not off in the pond at the moment" Roland said thinking about having a welcome to his home Stewart party.

" I will go get you a duck, they gotten used to seeing me around and I have fed them a few times like you told me to some grain so the slowest one going to get cooked today." John said laughing.

"I think I will get the smoker going to cook it, unless you all are starving to death and want to eat something quicker? " Roland said thinking that a late afternoon supper sounded better to his liking.

"We got some biscuits left from breakfast and some jelly to tied us over until it gets done" Sarah offered.

"That would be fine with me" Stewart said enjoying just sitting around and soaking up bits of information and news of the lake.

"Well that's settled then. Stewart, Dump said you were pretty short on clothes. I got some things that will fit you and when you feel like it you can get a hot bath. John and I rigged up a solar hot water heater as well as a fire assisted one so you can soak as long as you want" Roland offered.

"You don't know how good that sounds." Stewart said smiling.

"I got some bubble bath you can use, that Roland got me at the trading post" Sarah offered.

"I have died and gone to heaven, smoked duck, clean clothes and a bubble bath all in one day? I must have lost track of the time, is it Christmas already?" Stewart said jovially.

"I will give you access to a bottle of Scotch to take with you while your soaking your body, so you can soak your spirit also. I know you been through a lot and to me, nothing beats a good hot bath and a little bit of the hard stuff, to make a mans worries as well as his aches and pains disappear for a time." Roland said graciously.

"Well if I started right now, you might see me get out of that tub by dinner time." Roland said accepting the offer and thanking Roland for his hospitality.

"I bid you adieu" Stewart said mimicking tipping an imaginary hat to John and Martha and followed Roland inside, to be shown to his big treat for the day.

"That's a nice fella, shame to be stuck so far from home and no way of knowing how his family is making out." Martha said to John who was thinking the same thing.

"I haven't got the heart to tell him that David said he heard on the radio that half of London was burning. He said that it seems that the food riots got totally out of control and that the fools basically burned themselves out, because the fire departments could no longer respond and the military just got overwhelmed trying to contain the rioters. He didn't get much news, he was listening to a shortwave operator that had been monitoring the space weather channel on the internet and had secured his radios before the solar storm hit." John said regarding his beloved.

"Oh don't tell him, he got enough worries. You tell Roland to keep David quite for a bit to, we don't know what part of the UK he is from, or where his friends and family might live." Sarah said upset that she felt a need to hide something from someone.

"I won't say a word. I better go get that duck for Roland. He has the hang of butchering them things. They got more feathers than a chicken, but that thing he has hooked to a drill and an inverter makes short work out of plucking one." John said rising from his chair.

"I am staying here of course, that's not a task I care to be around" Sarah said and John gave her a little knowing pat and was on his way.

"Stewart is in the bathroom humming some kind of British ditty." Roland said as he came out the backdoor smiling

"That's nice; I know when I got my first soak in that tub, I could have sung with joy too." Sarah said remembering the experience.

"John go after that duck, or is he in the barn?" Roland asked.

"He went for the duck. Roland, John's birthday is coming up and I wanted to give him something but for the life of me I don't know what." Sarah said seeking advice.

"I already got you covered, he mentioned something about his birthday a week ago and Bernie came up with the perfect gift for him that he had stored back at his lake house. A slide rule!" Roland said enthusiastically.

"That is perfect! No calculators to be had these days and he knows how to use one. Oh that's perfect Roland. Can it be from all of us?" Sarah asked hopefully.

"No, you give it to him yourself. Bernie and I are giving him his very own tool set that we drug out of a garage. We were going to give it to him anyway but since it's his birthday, we saved it and will throw him a party and butcher a steer for the occasion. A man needs his own tools and we figured he would like that." Roland said to a beaming Sarah.

"You folks sure are big hearted. I don't have much to trade you for that slide rule, unless you take some of my tinctures." Sarah said contemplating what she might have to offer.

"Think nothing of it, our gift to you and your gift to him. " Roland said affectionately to the old woman who had become an integral part of his home and farm.

"Well that's awful sweet of you all. John is going to love it and I will bake up some nice things for you and Bernie's sweet tooth for being so nice." Sarah said appreciatively to Roland who had begun to reach for his 30-30 as he noticed someone riding a horse come up to his gate in the distance.

" I cant make out who that is from here, beat on that pipe hanging over there a couple times to tell John and the field crew we got company." Roland said getting ready to go to the barn and bareback a horse in that direction.

"Only looks like one man." Sarah said but proceeded to beat on the pipe with the rope attached piece of angle iron anyway.

Roland got one of the horses and rode towards the gate as Sarah moved into the cover of a brick archway leading to the patio. Stewart came out dripping wet and clad in only a pair of jeans shortly there after and carrying his shotgun.

"What's going on?" a bewildered Stewart asked watching Roland riding towards his gate and John driving towards them, on one of his weed eater powered go carts.

"Probably nothing Stewart, a rider is at the gate but Roland said to sound general alarm, sorry to get you out of your bath." Sarah said scanning the gate and surrounding area.

"No worries here, I heard that alarm and saw you leveling that rifle and knew it wasn't a dinner gong you had in mind." Stewart said watching the goings on, as the field crew started heading in their direction carrying an assortment of long arms.

Roland turned in the distance and gave the everything is well, all clear sign and resumed talking to who ever it was at the gate about 600 yards off. John mean time had seen the all clear signal from Roland and had passed them and was proceeding in the direction of the gate to find out for himself what was up.

Sarah motioned to the hired hands that it was alright and they went back to whatever it was they were working on. Stewart told her he was going back inside for a shirt and a towel while Sarah settled down to watch Roland and John talking to the mounted rider at the gate.

The pair eventually waved the rider off and returned to the patio wearing somber looks.

"What happened?" said a concerned Sarah

"Trade wagon got ambushed heading towards the lake. They took the team and wagon. The drivers said the people that took it didn't appear to be familiar with driving a team. Had to have been someone local did the deed, so we are probably going to find them. We don't even use guards around here because it's been so calm. Thing is, that who ever did it, is pretty damn stupid to even try it and that worries me." Roland said pondering who it could have been.

"Wagons are scarce as hen's teeth right now and so is the harness. Supplies we might be able to replace, but not the other equipment. Lew said he was going to gather up some men and go looking for who ever did it, but I assume its all going to end with shots going to get fired and there will be somebody getting killed or wounded, most likely." Roland said disgustedly.

"Why in the world would somebody rob a horse drawn wagon they can't even drive?' John said

"Who can gauge the stupidity of people? I don't know what that posse plans on doing with them if they can manage to talk them into surrendering when they find them." Roland replied thinking lynch mob.

"Well I got to go re-catch a duck; I turned him loose when I heard the alarm sounded." John said not looking forward to now having to deal with wary domestic ducks dodging the dinner pot.

"Stewart, change of plans, if you don't mind. We will leave out early while the patrols are out in the area and maybe see if we spot that wagon further out than they are searching." Roland said wishing that things had turned out different for this day.

"I understand, just give me a wakeup call in the morning." Stewart said and went back inside to straighten up the bathroom he had left in disarray.

"I think I will fix us some corn fritters to go with dinner, that is, if you think we got enough cooking oil." Sarah said speculatively.

"We got enough, but you know how rare that stuff will be getting. I need to get with John and figure out how we can produce some, when the store bought stuff runs out." Roland said thinking about how that consumable was probably best just used in baking instead of deep frying like most of his favorite recipes required.

"He will figure out something for us I am sure. Well let's get everything together and make an early night of it so you and Stewart are fresh for your trip tomorrow.

3

CHAPTER TITLE

This is pure hell. We really need to find a more perfect way to water the garden. These raised beds will need a couple of seasons to get easier to work in, as well as improving the soil. Carrying buckets of water is a piss poor way to kill every morning. Even the morning is hot, but this is the south and summer time. The squash looks good this morning and the cucumbers are getting big. Need to find some supplies.... *Jack thought to himself.*

"Hey David let's get together after breakfast" Jack said. "It is somewhat muggy feeling today already."

David looked at Jack, "Sounds like a plan, why don't we talk some while we check the trot lines. We promised the trading post some fish as soon as we can to help those less fortunate."

Breakfast this morning consisted of grits, powdered eggs and some biscuits. While breakfast was being consumed, the clan gathered and people began talking about the day's chores and projects. Sherry talked quickly about finding some more mulch material for the raised beds in the makeshift gardens. Louise was prepared to do some sewing and clothes repair. Dave's mom was interested in finding some more herbs for tonight's dinner. The rest of the motley crew seemed bent on doing something or the other just long enough to cover their desire to go swimming later.

The group was lucky enough to have salvaged a good aluminum canoe. The canoe was stable enough to pull fish up from the lines and jugs they had taken some additional time to put out, inorder to help the less fortunate survivors.

Fish was an easy enough protein source to harvest and had helped Dave's group feed a great deal of people passing through or remaining on the lake. Hunger is always the beast at the door and one that makes normally sane people crazy.

The first bank line rig was not too far from the dock and the discussion about the housekeeping had wound down, when Jack proffered, "David we are going to have do a bit of salvage beyond just the houses on the lake. We have needs beyond just getting food and supplies."

"OK, so tell me what you got on your mind? I know the time you spend on guard duty allows you plenty of reflections on inventing, to convert it into planning to make it." David said who had been waiting for Jack to start pushing for things beyond just the start up phase of survival. They had many discussions before the EMP strike about what would be needed to not only survive but to help bring about some type of long term recovery.

"Dave I know we have a really good group here. We have more food than most and we have better transportation than most of the folks at our end of the lake. We even have a good community, where we have the beginnings of a strong common defense. This area is beginning to run out of easy foraging houses close by. We need to start looking at possible long term defense ideas also, because we really have no way of knowing when the threats become unlikely. We should begin to look at making life more livable and an easier pace. It would be nice to have a better flowing water system. Running water for gardening and hot water for bathing would greatly raise moral." Jack began.

"Whoa, slow down and let's explore just one of those ideas before jumping into everything at once. Just tell me how you plan on providing running water so you don't have to bucket water to the beds every other morning. I know you, all work and no play makes for a dull Jack." David laughed.

"Well you know we have discussed the idea of a ram water pump with a bit of specific foraging and some luck we should be able to supply for all the folks at this end of the lake enough water for gardening. The real trouble will be finding storage tanks. The internet had lots of plans for using PVC pipes to make a pump but there are some large manufacturing facilities that should have galvanized pipes which should be much stronger. The further the drop the better the pump works. The more pressure we can produce the greater area we can water. It is just simple hydraulics

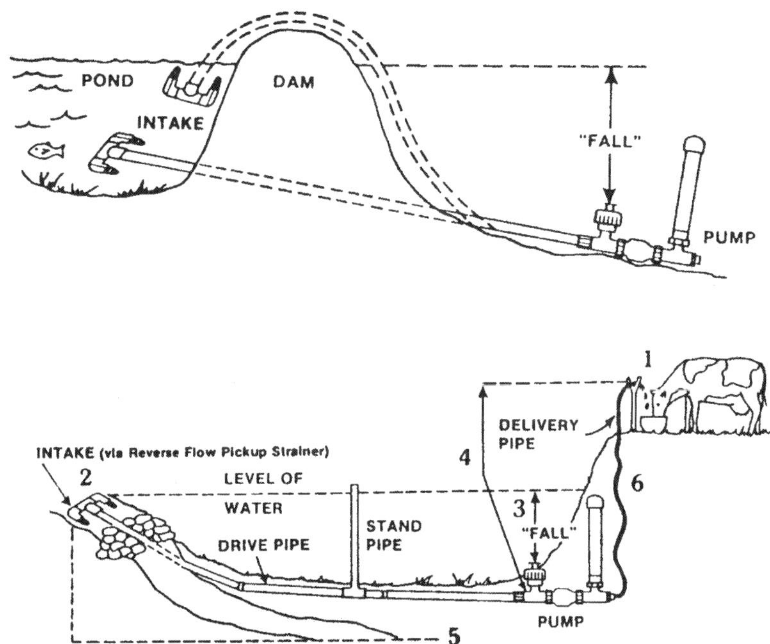

We need to create plans to start producing food for ourselves year round. Our raised beds will help, but with a regular and easy supply of water, we can take the uncertainty of rainfall out of the equation. Here in the south we can make four crops and perhaps five. "Jack looked like he had more to say but, about then the friends were confronted with a big channel cat and had to focus on fishing. The hooks were eventually all reset and put back in the lake and them it was time for the slow paddle back to the base camp. "We got what five fish this morning one of them looks about 12-15 lbs. What do you think we should do with this haul?

"Sherry and I will be going up to the trading post and will donate them to the communal fish stew. How long will it take for you to get the type of ram pump you want up and going? Do you think we can make a couple of them and perhaps do some trading for them at the post?" David asked.

"After we find the parts, it should not take but a few hours to get it them somewhat put together. We will have to get a bunch of people in the digging mode, inorder to make the infrastructure needed for them, lay some pipe etc. , but once we get it in place, we should be able to support a goodly number of the refuges with garden surplus or just can it for ourselves." Jack said and then thought of the 60 or 70 acres of hay field that was about 5 miles up the road that could be used for some legume production maybe.

This was already cleared land, but not without a great deal of work and time could it even be remotely considered for production. He would have a talk with Bernie and Roland about that, they had the extra manpower, seed and tools to possibly get it done.

Meat and fats made up a large portion the southern diet normally, but it takes lots of protein from the plant kingdom to grow animals for food. The rest of the world understands this and many cultures use the protein and carbohydrates from wheat, rice, soybeans, and corn for their main staple food. Sustaining life is easier for a person who gets most of their food from the plant kingdom. Variety and many vitamins and minerals are provided by the rich abundance supplied by vegetables and greens that are well known amongst the people of this southeast region.

Being a leftover at the lake was fraught with advantages and disadvantages but so far everyone on this end of the lake had great prospects for making it long term.

CHAPTER TITLE

Stewart and Roland headed out, just as dawn was starting to peek over the horizon. They had rehearsed their plans if they encountered any problems on the road to the lake and Roland had talked momentarily to the posse that was out looking for the lost wagon and advised them he would also have his eyes peeled for any signs of its whereabouts.

John and Sarah had decided to forgo their trip to the lake this time, because of possible trouble lurking on the roads and had remained behind.

Roland had Stewart stop at a few likely places along the route that might have been where he thought the thieves might have taken the wagon to, but was unable to discover anything of consequence.

"Well they didn't come this way, that's for sure. We would have seen some fresh manure or something on the road, maybe even some wagon tracks going into a driveway. I will send a messenger back from the trading post and tell the vigilantes not to worry about this direction." Roland said relaxing.

"I am glad for that, I am ready for my vacation now Mr. Stiles" Stewart said flashing a grin at Roland and relived the tension was off for now.

"Too bad John and Sarah decided not to make the trip, but I can't blame them. Never trouble trouble unless trouble, troubles you are one of John's mottos and a good one if you ask me." Roland said now enjoying a leisurely drive but still monitoring the surroundings.

"That is a good saying and although I never heard it before, I guess that would be my own philosophy too." Stewart said enjoying the coolness of the morning with the windows rolled down.

"Damn! You see that deer just run across the road? I wasn't even thinking about collecting one on the way. Oh well, they getting a bit scarce anyway. Maybe that young buck can live through the winter and help repopulate the herd around here." Roland said still looking back to see if the does were following the buck, versus the normal routine these days of the buck following the does so he could escape if trouble in the form of a hunter was encountered.

"You got any news about what is going on over the pond? London and the UK I mean." Stewart said thinking about his homeland far away.

"No, it's hard to get news about even stateside stuff. The radio used to report on the riots in the big cities, but there must be a news blackout on that sort of thing these days. Pretty much the only thing you hear about is. that constant droning of where the FEMA camps are trying to be set up and the occasional Homeland security threats of retaliation on looters, or a doubtful President address that things will be ok someday coming off those hardened AM emergency transmitters." Roland replied and in agreement that none of their group wanted to be the bearer of bad news at this stage of the game, with Stewart recovering from his ordeal.

"It's the not knowing, that bugs me. Although it doesn't take any stretch of the imagination on my part to envision how things are in the big cities of Europe or here. I suppose I might never know, I guess." Stewart said resolved that the worst possible thing he could imagine, can and was happening right this minute.

"We should be getting close to an outrider station soon. We try to keep a guard or trail watcher 5 to 10 miles away from the trading post on all the roads that lead to it, in order to look for trouble approaching or to guide refugees in. There are not enough horses or riders to have one at every point, but we do pretty good relaying messages the old fashioned way with signal fire or beating on something like a drum." Roland said looking for anyone that might be in the area.

"That's funny, or not so funny to think the mighty US is reduced to the old Jungle telegraph to talk to each other at a distance." Stewart said envisioning an African tribe or Native Americans communication systems of old.

"Hey. We going to have us a real telegraph once we figure out how to wire it together and Bernie already located a Boy Scout manual that has Morse code in it." Stewart said proudly of the herculean tasks that everyone was doing to try to get a semblance of civilization back together.

"Somebody needs to start an artifact retrieval service from all the old museums. That and try to locate any historians or curators that know what that old stuff was used for. or how it worked." Stewart suggested.

"That's the thing, we thought of that somewhat, but cities are still too dangerous and that kind of knowledge is too scarce. I wish I had done more than think how archaic something was when I went to a museum as a kid, instead of how it worked or how it was made." Roland said noticing a spotter up ahead and telling Stewart to slow to a stop.

"This be Roland! Who be you?" Roland called out using the old style speech, chosen by the trading post to identify people who were regulars around the trading post versus newcomers.

"I be Travis Dupree if you please." The man called back and started down the ridge he had been posted on.

Roland and Stewart waited on the man to make it down the ridge and noticed another man coming up the gully beside them.

"Tommy O'Dell coming up." The man called out as he went up the embankment.

"Is that an Irish brogue I detect?" Stewart said smiling to Roland.

"That it is!" Roland said trying to mimic it. We are somewhat of a very worldly group in some ways, but we southerners got you all greatly out numbered. The lake gets hundreds of thousands of visitors from all over, every year as tourists and residents. Add the travelers on the highway that broke down and there is no telling who all is represented here. We got Swedes, Canadians, Japanese, and Mexicans to name but a few nationalities represented. Most likely almost every state in the union to include as far as Alaska. That Solar storm made a bigger melting pot of new so called Americans now in this area, than you can imagine." Roland said getting out greeting the employees of the trading post community.

"Roland you never cease to amaze me! You got you a running lorry with an English chauffer now!" Tommy said walking up with what was evidently someone's fine skeet shooting shotgun.

"I don't know about the chauffer bit, seems I am missing the cap for that." Stewart said good naturedly enjoying the old banter between Englishman and Irish and shaking the hand of the closest compatriot he had seen or heard of in awhile.

'It is indeed a pleasure to hear a familiar accent, you be an unexpected blessing to our little community that's for sure." The smiling Irishman said watching his fellow guard skirting the thorn bushes that lined the road in front of his deployment.

"The same here, we got to share stories one day. I am guessing that an Irish Pub is out of the question to do it in over a pint." Stewart said grinning.

"If you count me front porch and don't have none of them lordly ways that them tourist Englishmen sometimes have, it could be arranged." Tommy said enjoying the moment.

"Ha! Lordly ways is it? I didn't know I was privileged with royalty" Roland said and greeted Travis as he come down smiling at the banter, between his backup and Stewart.

"Roland, I have one of those old trucks. How

come yours runs and mine don't?" The old country boy said shaking hands with Stewart and him.

"Something about being under a parking deck and the age of the thing. I don't really understand it myself. If you got one, let's see if the mechanics can fix it. From what John tells me, since you have an old carburetor on it instead of electronic ignition, if we find the parts it might be able to make it run again." Roland said to which the man took immediate interest to.

"Is that possible? I mean I gave up hope of ever seeing a running vehicle again except something older than dirt like a Model T." Travis said speculating on how his luck in life might have changed at that moment.

"You wouldn't be needing an Irish chauffeur now would you? That is to say, if John gets your lorry running." Tommy said smiling and pretending to dust off an imaginary uniform.

"Well I never thought of having one, but if that truck works, you and I are not going to be sitting here swatting mosquitoes working one week on and off no more." Travis said in his deep southern accent to his trusty foreign friend who had helped him defend the small community that was in its infancy.

"What is the word on the trade post, these days?" Roland said searching for news.

"Look out for that stolen trade wagon and divert travelers if we can to the new trade post Bernie is starting away fro the lake." Tommy answered still studying Stewart and wanting more conversation.

"Do what? We can hardly supply what we got! When did he start creating another one?" Roland said a bit miffed he had not been consulated about it.

"A trader came in that found one of those little railroads yellow utility transports and rode it down as far as the junction and got interviewed by the roving guard over there when they saw him siphoning gas out of a car. They put two and two together and brought him to Bernie who cut some sort of a deal." Travis said telling Roland everything he knew.

"I guess it sounds reasonable then, did he say how clear the tracks were, ordid the guy have a bunch of any one item?" Roland asked contemplating what this information might lead him to.

"That is all I know, we watch, we guard and get stuck out here with shit for food, unless a hunting gathering party comes by and then have a few drinks and decent chow back at the post and do it all over again." Tommy said complaining and shrugging his shoulders and comparing notes with Travis.

"No sign of the wagon but be watchful. You want a snack of pickled pig's feet?" Roland offered.

"Normally I would tell you that would make my asshole suck a lemon, but in these days and times, I am willing to try anything." Travis said enjoying the look on the Irish Mans face that had never hear of what some folks in the south considered a delicacy and had huge jars of them around some country stores or bars.

"A what? What does it taste like? Oh hell, I will try one. A Porkers foot pickled in Lord knows what, is it like vinegar on fish and chips?" Stewart asked not knowing he had the jar included in the cargo Roland had loaded.

"Me too I guess, is their salt in it? I am craving salt for some reason." Tommy said still looking like he wanted to be sick.

"Just try one" Roland said getting the keys from Stewart and opening the hatch on the back of the truck to retrieve a giant jar.

"Well when you get over the looks and smell I would say can I have another." Tommy said pretending to attack his shared responsibility buddy with the remains of one bone chewed piece of cloven hoof and actually enjoying eating the weird things.

"Were off, you can have 6 more if you want and put them in a baggie, there is a box of then in the back. I got to get down to David's and the Post today" Roland said watching the two fishing around in the jar for the bigger ones with a hobo knife's fork and a disreputable looking pocket knife of no brand name that looked rustier than hell and the reason he gave up that whole jar eventually to them.

"Well thanks!" The pair chimed and went back to their private squabble about who got what foot as Roland and Stewart pulled off.

"Damn, I didn't see that piece of crap Travis put in the jar until it was too late. I hope they don't get lockjaw off of it. I would never in a million years expect a country boy to have such a nasty knife." Roland said making a face and spitting out the window.

"Just because you're from the farmlands don't mean you're a farmer." Stewart said agreeing with him and understanding the implications of tetanus if you stepped on a rusty nail these days for example. There would be *not be anyone around at a hospital to save you from a dumbass lazy stun,t like not keeping a knife sharp and clean in case you cut yourself, he remembered his father saying to him as a boy, when he was first gifted with the responsibility of a blade.*

"Stewart, we got a pecking order around the trading post and I am not trying to put on airs by telling you to observe it. David I guess said it best, in that you can't get too familiar with your troops or they take advantage of you. Don't be overly friendly to the help, or to the refugees. We got to have order and command principles respected and them not think of us as just friends in power. Handling objections in the human resources sector you might say, is an art and the old adage of " A comparison other, Its who folks compare themselves too in the hierarchy of things, such as pay and work ethics, even though they have not yet, or will not ever attain that spot by acting like them anyway. You got to lead by example anyway you can to make the difference in your own success or failures and not compare the lower standards of some workers, to yours regardless of pay status."

Stewart remembered David had said "Work, easy, work smart, and if you can, wprk for your own pocket" regarding things like knowing the tricks of a trade to produce quality and craftsmanship, as well as not wasting efforts in its production. Once people recognize you consistently out do others, then your opinion is valued over your hand skills and you get paid for just opinions. Otherwise your opinion is worthless to most, unless you are working under your own banner.

Weird guy David, but smart, Stewart considered,

remembering the man had once been a highly paid diamond and colored stone appraiser after his stints in the military. Damn I would take a hundred and ninety dollars an hour for telling someone they screwed up buying something, humnn, isn't that what lawyers do? David had said and had decided to charge them double for his credentials and specialized opinions they collected extra money for?

David hated lawyers and would give free opinions or assistance to people all day in the retail jewelry shops, but he said lawyers were the ticks on society and would drain them professionally, if they required assistance from him; just like those ambulance chasers thought they had some right to a person's pain or injuries to profit from.

"See that sign that says boat landing? Turn in there and we are at the trading post." Roland said glad to be arriving with no more mishap than the loss of a jar of pig's feet.

"Roland! David come in a half hour ago with Sherry at the ferry boat landing." The gate guard said swinging back a heavy oak log that was counterweighted to raise it easily from the entrance.

"Our lucky day! Saved some miles before we got to his house. Is Boudreaux with him?" Roland asked?

"No, Boudreaux is on the outs with Beverly for some reason and he has been holed up in the tavern last couple days. I told David to go help patch things up and get that crazy Cajun out of here, so the guards didn't have such a handful when he got on the whisky trip." The unofficial Sergeant of the guard said nursing what evidently was a shiner from Boudreaux or someone he fought with in his current state; Roland couldn't tell which, and the man was hesitant to say.

"Ill get go him, as soon as we get settled, should be a 'don't feed the Boudreaux' sign in there, instead of the bears." Roland said dreading that chore of tackling a swamp critter on whatever poison of choice the liquor stocks allowed in the drinking establishment.

"He ain't getting that pig sticker of his or his gun back for a day or two and an apology." The bar's bouncer said coming up out of nowhere.

"You will set them in this truck, with none of your sass or be answering to Me." said Roland not sure what he was defending other than the official administrative end of who made the rules around here.

'I just meant he ain't fit for normal company. I know he was just playing, but he lassoed me and hog tied me last night like I was some kind of gator in his Bayou and I ain't putting up with that shit." The big burly man said embarrassed that Boudreaux had caught him off guard.

Roland tried to stop himself from chuckling at such an unlikely spectacle, but offered some sage advice to the bouncer. "He couldn't have done it on his own and likely had plenty of help setting the trap or pulling on the line that strung you up. You better be thinking about who you pissed off lately or has got a grievance with you; before you blame Boudreaux for pranking you. Hell that man brought you in here for the job, and no disrespect, but it is his bar, even though Bernie and I and Boudreaux said to toss his silly ass out when he gets in his cups too much." Roland said remembering the old man played too rough and was too strong for anyone one to wish to have him around them at times.

"Well he is outdoing himself and I am going to take him out if you can't convince him to leave..." The bouncer started to say.

'You would rather sand paper three wildcats ass in a phone booth than take on Boudreaux and me at the same time. You're off duty for the day! Go home, rest up and come back tomorrow." Roland told him not giving him a break.

"I will go see about him now but, YOU gotta go on vacation for the day." Roland said reminding him he could still dance with the fisty cuffs and that Boudreaux was the proprietor of that establishment and Roland's word was law at the trading post.

"Merry Christmas!" Was all Stewart said leaning against the truck with that old twelve gauge coach gun and a malevolent look about him, as the bouncer looked around to the folks observing the confrontation for support.

"I guess it's appropriate to say happy New Year and go on vacation now." the deflated bouncer said.

"I would suggest that." Roland said not worried about him any more and thinking about doing a snatch job on Boudreaux, who was somewhere in the cabin in front of him.

"Who has his knife?" Roland said before the big man could exit.

"I do," he said reaching down and pulling up his pant leg to reveal its hilt.

"We talk about keeping you or not tomorrow. That is what probably pissed him off and he saw you stash it there. I would be mad too; if I thought your fat ass was sweating on my blade. Leave now, I will get him out and thanks for the restraint, but remember he owns the place." Roland said squaring himself up to go deal with what was described as a raging Cajun.

"Go get Bernie and Stewart, you sit this one out and hold my hat." Roland said to a mystified Stewart and a young girl in the crowd and started towards the tavern.

"AIHEE! Where that tush hog that got me knife?" Boudreaux said staggering from the bar.

"Roland! Roland me friend. Tell them Boudreaux must have his knife before he leaves." Boudreaux said weaving and wobbling and holding on to the newly placed hitching posts for support as a couple faces appeared in the doorway in back of him.

"I already got it Boudreaux, I want you to settle down now and meet David's Stewart." He said gesturing at the Brit, but watching the wily Cajun closely for signs he was in a blackout.

"Stewart? Stewart? Oh the Englishman with a cup for rent," Boudreaux said finding his legs and marching forward to greet a poor Stewart that got caught in an unexpected bear hug, This be my Dog Bear, Where is Bear?" Boudreaux said looking around for his hound, forgetting he was not allowed in the bar and looked confused his ever present side kick was not available.

"He is probably sitting in Bernie's office or pleasuring some other hound. David talk to you today?" Roland said trying o get the lay of the land.

"No, Sherry she did," Boudreaux said trying his best to sober up and see why things were not fun no more. They ain't been in but an hour and she got her two drinks and left. That who has my buddy dog? He is a sucker for women and she gave him a treat. You seen Beverly? She no love me anymore, I tried to make peace, but she no listen." Boudreaux said and to him the old Dude actually made a growling and whimpering sound.

"Settle down Boudreaux, Stewart and I am going to drive you home later on. You can take a nap in the guest house in the mean time." Boudreaux said seeing Bernie, Sherry, Bear and David making their way towards them.

"DAVID! " Stewart cried and rushed to meet him.

"Hi Stewart! Good to see you!" David said shaking his hand and then giving the man a hug.

"I will be back in a minute" Bernie said and walked over to wear Roland was talking to a greatly subdued now Boudreaux.

"What the hell you got into now Boudreaux." Bernie said looking perturbed.

"I am alright now, going for a nap. Come on monsieur Bear" Boudreaux said calling for his dog and weaving off in the direction of the guest house.

"I take it him and Beverly had them a falling out again?" Roland said watching Boudreaux and his dog making an unsteady line for some much needed rest.

"I wish they would get married or build them a wall between houses." Bernie said shaking his head at how inebriated Boudreaux had gotten himself, over whatever had gone on between the pair.

"He doesn't get that way very often, but when he does it's usually over her. Can't tell him to drink at home when she's next door, and their ain't another bar for him to go to. Ha! I am going to tell him to go to David's next time he wants to tie one on." Roland said chuckling.

"Oh yeah, he would appreciate that alright." Bernie said watching David and Stewart's happy reunion.

"I can't believe he made it all the way back here from Atlanta and with my TRUCK still in running condition! David said as happy as one man could be, to Roland and Bernie as they walked up.

"You got luck going for you both, I give you that." Roland said to a pair of Cheshire cat smiles.

"Most of my stuff still in there? You didn't have to trade too much off?" David said walking towards the vehicle with the group following along.

"Its all there, just as you left it, except Dump confiscated that big old pile of MRE you had in the cooler.

"He and Martha said to give this to you as full payment for them, but you owe Hop Sing and me some change." Roland said producing the heavy gold chain Hop Sing had given to Martha.

"Who is Hop Sing and why do I owe both of you?" David said confused but studying intently the heavy piece of jewelry.

"Well that is sort of a story in itself, but the gist of it is, Martha gave me the chain to grubstake me for this little adventure, to bring you the truck back to you. We all sort of formed a trade company with me as the head agent, or trader, representing our interests between them and the lake." Stewart said watching Bernie reaching for the chain David held to examine it closer.

"Well we can certainly work something out. You are going to stay Stewart?" David asked hoping that he was.

"I just got here! I haven't had a chance to look it over yet. But yes that was sort of the idea. See me and that truck come as a package deal, you get one. you get both of us." Stewart said smiling.

"I would be honored to have you stay Stewart. You know that. This calls for a celebration lets go have a drink." David said starting for the bar before Stewart asked him to hold up a minute.

"How many Boudreauxs do you have in that bar Davie?" Stewart said speculatively and everybody laughed and made fun of Stewart a bit.

"We only got one like him on the entire lake and when he sobers up, he will probably be one of the best friends you ever had. You wouldn't know it to look at him for the first time, but that old ornery cuss spends his days and nights out hunting and fishing, just because he feels the need to help feed all these folks around here, that sort of depend on him for a meal." David said still smiling that Stewart thought Boudreauxs came in bunches. Well come to think of it, in some parts of Louisiana they do, but thank the lucky stars they only had one good hearted one to deal with.

"I will protect you." Sherry said grinning and took his arm to escort him to the little honkytonks.

"Roland looks like you got replaced." Bernie said grinning.

"Hold up Sherry, you going to protect the guests you need the hat." Roland said offering his Stetson which she put on and tried to imitate Roland's cowboy swagger.

"This is going to be a fun party. If that darned Boudreaux wasn't cross-eyed I would get him to play his fiddle so Stewart could see that dog of his dance the two step" David said escorting them into the cooler confines of the drinking establishment.

"I get first shot at converting that chain into trade goods or dollars before you get that Banker of yours involved David. I don't know why you all wont merge banks with me, but I will beat any price within reason he offers." Bernie said still holding on to it.

"Put it around your neck and keep up with it for us." David said using an old jeweler's trick to increase Bernie's desire to not part with it later and increase his negotiating powers if need be.

"I can wear it? How does it look?" Bernie said modeling it for the group.

"Like a million dollars." David said looking away and smirking at Stewart slyly who picked up on the pun.

"Looks right smart and handsome, shows you're a man of means." Stewart said playing along.

"Philburn has got one he might part with" Roland said spoiling David and Stewart's fun at how rare a prize it was.

"Is there more? How many are available?" Bernie said pouncing on a possible advantage.

"Just the two chains that I know of." Stewart said off handily and looking at Roland to not spoil his and David's, negotiating.

"Dump owes us for a doodlebug or works for us now." Roland said acknowledging Stewart and changing the subject.

"You gave him an option? I am not sure I like that." Bernie began.

"What's a doodlebug?" Sherry inquired.

"It's an old name for a railroad service car that rides a few folks to help maintain the tracks or the engines. By the way John said for us to talk about borrowing your Bobcat loader later." Roland said accepting his drink from the waitress.

"I am going to challenge you to a game of darts later Stewart, but we got some reminiscing and planning to do for now. You folks mind if we go off to a private table for a few, we won't be long?" David said to the table.

"Why are you rushing off, David, plenty of time later to have a talk?" Sherry began before the look she got from David said hush and she figured he had something on his mind of importance.

"Go ahead Dave, Sherry was telling me about maybe trading me a couple live geese for some pork chops before Boudreaux decided to show his butt and interrupted our conversation." Bernie said figuring David had something to discuss that couldn't wait.

"Just be a few minutes." David said collecting his drink and moving with Stewart to the far corner of the bar.

"What is troubling you Dave?" Stewart said looking concerned,

"Did you get a chance to go through that bug out bag?" David said sipping on his drink looking at Stewart in a regarding manner.

"To be honest, I barely glanced into it. I have been too busy and didn't have any need to." Stewart said flatly at the accusing tone he thought David had.

"I was just curious, we need to be sure that trucks locked up anyway but it can wait. The guards will see nobody molests it. I got me a little stash of a couple 2 ½ dollar gold pieces, a roll or two of mercury dimes and some generic round silver pieces in it. The thing I was concerned about was a mans diamond ring I picked up awhile back for scrap value that has Bernie's name written all over it if I can get him wanting it also. It won't fit him as it sits and I haven't quite decided how to get it sized, but I can tell John the process as I have seen it done many times before maybe." David said smiling.

"So you think maybe it would be a good time to put it on the table?" Stewart said speculating on David's intentions.

"He is getting happy now and into jewelry mode for his personal use and he is enjoying the new company, meaning you. Go out to my truck and lock it up after arranging the stuff in the back. You will find my little stash in the false back pocket of the bag where a pistol normally goes. Welcome to our end of the lake, that will pay you back for your loyalty, honesty and honor in returning my truck." David said extending his hand to an incredulous Stewart.

"Dave! It's too much, I..." Stewart said flustered.

"Lower your voice." David hissed

"Look my friend I want to do it. Those baubles only work in trade if you're a good trader and got somebody that wants them these days. You got talent and a future as a trader in these end times, for a new beginning or an end to a means. Take them with my blessing and I won't discuss it any more." David said doing the cheers motion with his glass towards Stewart who reciprocated and smiled his thanks.

"As a matter of fact the whole bug out bag is yours, I got a lot of spare equipment and don't you get separated from yours like I did. Keep tabs on it always and keep it close to you." David said rising from his chair and heading back to the party.

The End. Book Four of The Prepper Novelettes and the beginning of The Prepper Road Saga which will be occasionally updated to show the lives of the characters living in their post apocalyptic world of hope and possibilities for the future.

CHAPTER TITLE

A Prepper Prepares For Christmas

Ron Foster

USA

1

CHAPTER TITLE

"I hate duck weather" David grumbled to himself, miserable up on his tree stand in a misty rain over looking the trail. It had been one of the coldest and wettest winters he had seen for sometime. He wished he could have been back at home in front of a warm fire, but that was not to be. Necessity drove him out today to try and bag a deer. Food supplies were dangerously low as his group had consumed all the preps Sherry and he had stored for an occasion like this. They had put up a years worth for the two of them; but with five other mouths to feed in their group, the preps had dwindled quickly regardless of what they had scavenged or hunted.

I can't begrudge everyone eating up my chow though, they are my friends to the end on this little road trip down life's hard path, that had thrown everyone quite a few curveballs lately. I bet I could sit here all day and not see one deer in this over hunted and trapped area. Hell, the deer were probably bedded down and not moving about today, but hopefully they figured humans wouldn't be out in this mess and take the opportunity to browse some. I would do the candle under my poncho trick to warm up a bit, if it wasn't for the smell, no just got to tough it out for an hour or two then warm up checking the trap line on the way home. He thought gloomily.

He had talked to Roland and Bernie about the need to boost moral of the community and do something about everyone's cabin fever making things worse, but they hadn't come up with much in the way of ideas. The boat landing, where everyone normally gathered, was just to damn cold to stay out at for very long. No one wanted a ton of house guests either, because you didn't want to show what you had or risk someone coveting your possessions, if they were openly visible. Tools like axes and saws had a habit of wandering off if not watched carefully these days. An extra clean pair of socks was to be treasured and could be quickly pocketed by someone who was desperate for them.

Christmas wasn't far off and everyone was trying to keep a positive outlook on it, but the doomer thoughts still pervaded every waking moment, like this cold making its way to his marrow. Then there are the kids to consider. 'Sorry boys and girls; Santa is going to be awful stingy this year.' Though overall, kids have seemed to be handling the change of everything better than most of the adults were. This was the first Christmas after the solar storm hit that wiped out the grids and most modern technology and conveniences.

Times were much harder now on folks just trying to survive. The strong were still prevailing, but the weak spirited had left the theater and had passed away in droves. David was surprised at the number of suicides, and of course there was that one guy who murdered his whole family and then himself. No one talked much of those people that had gone to an early demise by their own hand or by that of some deranged and desperate man. David had been the one to come upon that gory scene from Hell and shuddered whenever he thought about what could possess someone to do such a heinous act. It certainly wasn't out of love as the man's note had said, because he didn't want his family to suffer, David remembered reading. David and Jack had gone back to the house and just torched the place and let the bodies' burn after saying a little prayer. David tried to avoid the scorched area whenever he could in his wanderings, because the haunted looks of the occupant's faces still troubled his sleep to this day and an air of forlorn dread still hung about the ruins.

Summer had ended on a pretty much positive note of hope and reconstruction. We even had a few community baseball games to entertain and to gather the tribes together. That's what most of us are now, little scattered tribes just trying to get by and defend one another. We need something to draw us all together and get the communities back to interacting with one another.

If it wasn't for Roland's Railroad project, we would have lost 75% of everyone in the last few months as everything that could be scavenged food wise had been consumed already for miles around.

People had started to just drift away from their homes in the pursuit of their next meal and that had caused more confrontations than David cared to think of as desperate and determined people moved into the area with no scruples about robbing others, if it meant they themselves would live for another day. No one could survive alone; you had to have a community for protection and to produce what was needed. David needed some younger blood in his camp to help with the hunting and chores, but was reluctant to bring any outsiders in, because at the moment he had problems enough providing for his group. Trade was doing almost nil these days as no one wanted to get out on the roads due to weather and rumors of increasing prevalence of mad highwaymen.

That's just what they are is mad; mad not as a March hare, but as a mad dog, David considered recalling hearing about a group of cannibals that were caught preying on unwary travelers between the lake and Alex City. *When someone decides they can eat another human being, they have lost all sense of reason and sanity and no one is safe from their perverse appetite,"* David mused as he climbed down out of his tree perch and gave up attempting to hunt deer for the day.

David began his trek back to home in a meandering way, checking his snares as he went.

Two rabbits were all he had to show for a full day of wandering and freezing in these wet woods. Well, at least the chances of catching rabbit fever from handling the carcasses was reduced after the first frost, if that old saying was true. So far no one had gotten anything like it; but you still had to be careful. David's group had a good supply of penicillin in the form of FishMox, which is a manufacturer's brand name for one of the products containing amoxicillin, he had bought at a pet store to cure this and most anything else needing a powerful antibiotic to cure it.

So, what is Tularaemia? Also known as "rabbit fever" and "deer fly fever," it's an extremely infectious bacterial disease that commonly infects hares, rabbits, muskrats, and voles. It has also been found in foxes, bears, beavers, and squirrels. Additionally it's a known biological warfare agent. How do you get it? The most common way humans get it is by being bitten by a tick or deer fly that has fed on in infected animal. You can also get it by handling an infected animal or by eating a poorly cooked animal that had it. Antibiotics are the most effective treatment. Streptomycin is the drug of choice. Gentamycin and Doxycycline are also effective against Tularaemia.
Field treatment consists of maintaining hydration (for intestinal symptoms). And prevention of further infection of skin ulcerations.
Tularaemia is NOT transmissible from human to human, but universal precautions (gloves, mask, gown, eye protection) should be used if there is a risk of contact with body fluids of an infected individual.

A rabbit carrying tularemia often has a spotted liver and so far no one has reported finding any such infected animal, hope our luck holds, David thought as he picked up his pace in anticipation of home and warm hearth.

2

Visitors

David returned to camp and saw Roland, Jack and Bubba sitting on his porch close to the fire in an outdoor fire pit he had made and laughing about something they had found funny in their conversation.

"Oh great, there goes my whiskey stock" David thought to himself seeing Bubba with a large glass of what appeared to be whiskey and water.

" I bet that damned Jack let him access my bar" David considered, seeing that Jack had the keys to his place and was supposed to be throwing an occasional log on the fire to keep the place somewhat warm until David returned. David liked Bubba, but Bubba liked the sauce as much as he did and that didn't bode well for his liquor cabinet. Bubba usually stayed over by the trading post so he must have some news or have brought something interesting over from the post for trade.

He was an interesting character and damned lucky he had managed to find David after the collapse. Bubba, his dog Harley and His wife Cat had ended up in Birmingham of all places when the solar storm had hit. They had come all the way from Arizona on a road trip to visit friends along the way and finalize their trip in Panama City Florida for a vacation. He had been out walking Harley at a rest stop when the poo hit the fan and immediately recognized it for what it was. David remembered the story Bubba had told him how he and his wife had weighed their options of what to do after the fact of being 1700 miles from home had deeply set in. Bubba decided he would set out for Montgomery and try and find David. He didn't have an address, he just knew David lived somewhere around there and would find a phone book and roll the dice as to finding him. He figured it was a dumb plan in some ways, because David was probably in the process of bugging out or had bugged out by the time he got there; but it was his only option. Birmingham is only an hour and a half away from Montgomery by car, but on foot it had taken the couple several weeks to make it to David's doorstep. Luckily David's neighbor recognized him as a Prepper and had allowed him to use David's house for some much needed rest and healing up after that extremely long and tiring hike. He shared some of the food David had left behind and took him with him for a food drop that the National Guard used to do. Bubba hung around for a week and then began the long arduous trip to the lake using a hand drawn map David had left as to his whereabouts for the neighbor.

It took Bubba about two weeks to make as far as John's old RV parked by the interstate and they had considered staying there, because of the large pond and the ability to have some undisputed shelter to rest up in, but had finally decided to keep pushing on. Bubba's supplies from his bug out bag were long gone and trying to hunt and fish after such an ordeal was pretty much a losing proposition as starvation was already taking its toll and sapping his strength. They could make it to David's they figured in another few weeks, the Lord willing, Bubba had thought and they had elected to trudge the rest of the way to the lake before it became impossible to do so, as their last reserves of energy dwindled.

One of Roland's trade wagons had found them and brought them to the trading post. Stewart had found Bubba a few weeks later crushing up mussel shells to make egg laying mash for chickens, in order to pay off his bar tab and had finally alerted David that one of his buddies had arrived as the trading post residents didn't know exactly where he lived and also knew that the "Our End of The Lake" clan was very secretive and suspicious of anyone inquiring about their whereabouts.

Bubba sort of worked for Stewart and Bernie. I say sort of, because it was hard to pin down exactly what Bubba did and why. You see Roland had found a freight car full of alum and Stewart had acquired it, because he knew how to make a solution out of it to fire proof fabrics. He had remembered that in Victorian times, women had used such a solution to fireproof dresses, curtains and table cloths and such to guard against the ever present danger of fire from open hearths and candles.

Bernie had passed an ordinance that everyone within a mile of the trading post was required to fire proof their house as best they could and clean their chimneys. That's when Bubba sort of became the official fire marshal of the volunteer fire department and also went around cleaning chimneys and fire proofing things. He had a wagon that Harley could pull containing a big washtub, his chemicals and chimney scrubbing brushes and could be found most days out roaming the countryside in pursuit of his trade. The deal was that, as a tax for the fire department to serve you, You had to feed Bubba and give him a drink or two of something alcoholic if you had it, in payment for his services helping you get your house fireproofed, but Bubba also traded for Stewart along his route, sort of as a traveling salesman and he also delivered messages for David's postal service. He also checked on the residents and had found more than one family that in their beds, too malnourished or sick with dysentery to take care of themselves. The great death taking place in the world did not even spare the residents surrounding the lake.

From the book, "INQUIRE WITHIN UPON EVERYTHING", first published in 1856 by Houlston and Stoneman in Great Britain.
Page 3, Tip # 28.
PREVENTION OF FIRES, add one ounce of alum (Alum is inexpensive and available at any good drug store.) to the last water used to rinse children's dresses and they will be rendered uninflammable, or so slightly combustible that they would take fire very slowly, if at all, and would not

flame. This is a simple precaution, which may be adopted in families of children. Bed curtains and linen in general, may also be treated in the same way.

He also had an easy way to keep soot from accumulating in the chimney pipes.

Mix 1 cup salt with 1 cup zinc oxide powder (available at ceramic shop or drugstore) and sprinkle on hot fire. This will help keep the chimney flue clean.

"Hey guys! What's up?" David asked setting down his rifle and catch, catching them unawares of him walking up on them.

"Damn David! You the sneakiest snake in the grass I ever seen." Bubba said sputtering in between chocking a bit on a piece of ice he had swallowed and raising up to greet his friend.

"Fine bunch of guards, you all are" David said smiling to the group and shaking Bubbas hand.

"Before you ask, Bubba brought his own booze" Jack said anticipating my unsaid question.

"Cool! Got any extra?" David asked slyly, just to see the look on Bubba's face as he contemplated sharing his stash with a fellow lounge lizard.

"Hey! Matter of fact, Bernie sent you some off my tab, but you can't have it until you quit picking at me." Bubba said pretending to be indignant.

"Bernie was probably anticipating if he added to my liquor supply I would keep you around with me a few days!" David said laughing and still poking fun at his drinking buddy.

"Let me go get me a drink and I will be back in a second" David said removing his poncho and hanging it on a nail to dry before entering the house.

"Hurry back, I got news for you" Bubba said trying to keep Harley from following David into the house in anticipation of begging a treat.

"He can come in" David said, as a very happy Harley zoomed in the door and headed towards the kitchen before David could get all the way into his house himself.

David got Harley a piece of deer jerky and himself a drink and wandered back out to sit with the rest of the folks enjoying the comfort of the fire.

"David, Bubba said they going to do a Christmas play over at Phil burn's trading post" Stewart said grinning about something and allowing Bubba to relay the news himself.

"They are going to do Scrooge! I bet you all ready know who is playing the part!" Bubba said smiling.

"Philburn!" David said laughing at the mental spectacle of Philburn dressed as Scrooge and how fitting the old skinflint had decided to play the part.

"You got it! " Jack said grinning.

"The also going to have a Santa Claus for the kids" Bubba started to say before David interjected.

"Ha! Don't tell me, let me guess. Dump Truck?" David said knowing he had to have been correct.

"Correct! And the HopSings are going to be his elves!" Stewart said laughing at what could only be another hilarious spectacle.

"That's what Bernie sent me over for, we going to have a little Christmas Pageant of our own. We going to get the Goat Man to be Santa and Bernie is going to put on that Leprechaun suit of his and be an elf!" Bubba said hardly able to contain himself with mirth.

"I can see that now, Santa Claus driving his Elf around in his side car" David said chuckling.

"Bernie said Dump raided a Dollar Store on the Outskirts of Atlanta and has been filling up Bernie's and Philburn`s warehouses with stuff for last month or so. He wants you to give classes to the children on how to make bug out bags using those types of items just before Xmas and he will let the parents have credit in Bernie bucks and sell them the stuff at cost for gifts if they want." Bubba said and then took a big swig from his drink.

David thought this was a great idea. Before the Storm hit the internet was full of Prepper contests to make the best Bug Out Bag out of Dollar Store materials.

"The parents will like that, they been pestering me about ideas about presents or bemoaning the fact of the lack of being able to celebrate in any meaningful way. Hey, we got enough rolling stock that I can bring just about everybody to the trading post, if Bernie will lend me some guards to watch our places for a few hours" David said getting into the spirit of the season.

"We could have a Parade" Stewart said thinking about the variety of vehicles and horse wagons that would be needed to transport our little community.

"Yeah, folks would have fun decorating them in Christmas motif if we wanted to" Jack said thinking of the possibilities of how his lawnmower would look decked out in garlands and a set of fake reindeer horns.

"What are you all laughing so much about?" Sherry said wandering over from the girls' cabin to join the little party.

David explained it all to her and Sherry rushed back to the other cabins to spread the news and bring the rest of the group over to share in the excitement and planning.

"You know them women are going to drive us crazy getting ready for this party and creating new little tasks or chores for us to do" Jack said watching a gaggle of happily babbling women heading in our direction.

"I see you brought May with you, you in for it also" David said seeing Bubbas wife talking to Louise and measuring something with her hands.

"Well this little party can't stay out here anymore, not enough room on the porch around the fire." I guess we go inside for a bit. David said dreading that many people in the small confines of his home, but not having any other choice.

"We will sneak back out here after a bit and leave the women inside talking" David said with a conspiring wink to Stewart and Bubba.

"Is Goat Man over at the trading post or up at Roland's?" David asked Bubba as he mixed them a new drink and watched Jack escorting the ladies in who were full of questions and plans already.

"He sent you some cheese, but he said he was going back to work on some project with John." Bubba said hugging his wife as she walked up.

"Sherry said she wanted to take the boat out while there was still light and tell the folks across the inlet about the news" Cat said to Bubba.

"Why don't you go with her, David and I got a few things more to talk over." Bubba said deftly avoiding what was sure to be a hen party ride over to the landing where he would be stuck being the only male in attendance coming and going.

"I already figured you wanted to stay" Cat said knowing her man and giving her order to Jack who had decided to play bartender.

Stewart had somehow managed to get himself corralled in the corner by Sherry and her gang and was cut off from the bar temporarily, as he tried to extract himself from a barrage of questions and suggestions as to what everyone should be doing to prepare for the event.

David managed to distract the girls for him a moment by announcing that someone needed to clean the rabbits for dinner and responded to their grumbling of a task no one like of his deal with everyone, that if he caught something they would clean it.

"I would like some of that Rabbit Fricassee and biscuits if you wouldn't mind Lois." David said making a suggestion to Lois to put a bit more effort into dinner because of the guests.

"Sure David, I know that is one of your favorites" Lois said and proceeded to explain to Cat how she made it.

A fricassee is a creamy dish often made at home with white meat (usually a whole chicken cut into eight pieces), vegetables, and a dense white sauce. Rabbit meat can be substituted for chicken for a similar flavor. There are lots of different recipes for it, here is one.

Ingredients

- *1 dressed rabbit (about 3 pounds), cut into pieces*
- 1/2 cup *vegetable oil*
- 2 tablespoons *all-purpose flour*
- 1 tablespoon *butter, melted*
- 1 teaspoon *lemon juice*
- 1/2 to 1 teaspoon *hot pepper sauce*
- 1/2 teaspoon *celery salt*
- 1/2 teaspoon *salt*
- 1/4 teaspoon *pepper*
- *1 egg*
- 1 cup *evaporated milk*

Directions

- In a skillet, brown rabbit in oil; drain. Cover rabbit with boiling water; cover and simmer for 30-40 minutes or until tender. Remove meat and keep warm. Bring cooking liquid to a boil; boil, uncovered, until reduced to 2 cups.

- In a bowl, combine flour and butter until smooth; gradually add a small amount of cooking liquid. Return to skillet. Whisk in remaining liquid. Add lemon juice, hot pepper sauce, celery salt, salt and pepper. Bring to a boil, stirring constantly; cook and stir for 2 minutes.
- Reduce heat. Combine the egg and milk; gradually whisk in sauce. Cook for 1 minute or until thickened and mixture reaches 160°. Pour over the rabbit. **Yield:** 4 servings

3

Snared

The girls were reminded about how quick it got dark around here this time of year and even though asked to put off the trip across the inlet until morning due to the weather, they insisted on carrying their gossip and news over anyway and out the door they went heading for the boat slip.

Not that the men folk minded, they could go back to their own gossip and news and were not being set upon with new chores of gathering decorations or ideas for the party that always seemed to be steadily be adding to the already over taxed load of things to do daily, just to survive around here.

"Where's my cheese?" David asked Bubba, hoping he had not entrusted it to the always ravenous and liberty taking Jack.

"'I gave it to your Mom" Bubba replied looking miffed that all the ice was gone from Jacks small battery powered icemaker after everyone had gotten a drink and Jack had used it up.

"Ok, I will get some later." David replied. I don't

know why I crave cheese so much lately. I remind myself of that rescued castaway in that book Treasure Island that was always asking if someone had a bit of cheese about them.

"The Goat Man said he has about got that project of yours done, David" Bubba said poking at the fire to gather the coals up and get it burning better in the fire pit before he added more wood.

"What do you have them building now, David?" Stewart said not knowing of any projects going on other than David and Jacks skunk works when they had the time.

"It's a secret for now." Is all David would say and changed the subject back to asking questions about the other full time residents by the trading post.

"What is Swede up to? I heard that little foraging party he took over to that little local airport dang near got their asses shot off trying to get out of town" David said moving closer to the fire and still feeling chilled to the bone from the days exertions out in the weather.

"Oh, that was one big misunderstanding. He went there to try to find some aircraft cable wire to make something with, and get a pair of what he called lock wire pliers, for some project he and John were creating, when his group come up on another group of free rangers that were roving the countryside and some trigger happy kid setoff a firefight between them, before the group leaders could even find out why they were in the area, or who the other one was, before all the lead started flying in both directions.

"Luckily Swede and someone named Billy Davis

started hollering cease fire, before it got out of hand, but it was a very close thing that no one did the dirt nap over it" Bubba said.

"Did He get any cable?' David said, instantly interested in replacing his hardly serviceable stock of commercial animal snares.

"He said he has about a thousand feet, but he is having difficulty with getting what he needs for snare lock parts." Bubba said advising Harley to lose his fixed interest in the dead rabbits hanging off the post that the girls had managed to get out of cleaning.

"Tell him to do it the old way with penny locks" David said and explained himself.

"Pennies work good for snare locks. Clamp em in a vise and bend them to a 90 degree angle, then drill 2 holes for the wire or cable. Cheaper and easier to find than a washer." David said motioning towards Jack to fix him a drink if he didn't mind, while he explained how to do it to Bubba.

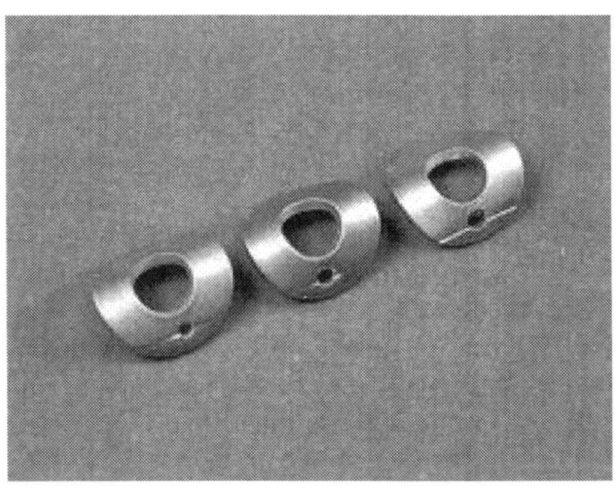

I got a sheet printed off from Backwoods home that Allen Easterly wrote that shows you the gist of it to make a ground hog snare, David said and went to retrieve from his library.

Material list

5 feet 7x7x3/32-inch cable
2 1/2-inch nuts
1 dime diameter flat washer
6 inches #9 gauge wire
1 penny diameter flat washer
2 to 3 inches #12 gauge wire
3 feet #11 gauge wire
1/2-inch #12 or #14 gauge wire
2 feet 1/2-inch rebar stake

Snare assembly

1. Create a cable end stop by slipping one of the nuts over one end of the cable and smash it flat with a heavy hammer. The threads of the nut grip the cable preventing other parts of the snare from sliding off the cable.

2. Slide the dime washer from the open end of the cable to the stop. This washer will allow the cable to rotate freely

and help prevent kinks and twists and allow more freedom of movement for the trapped animal.

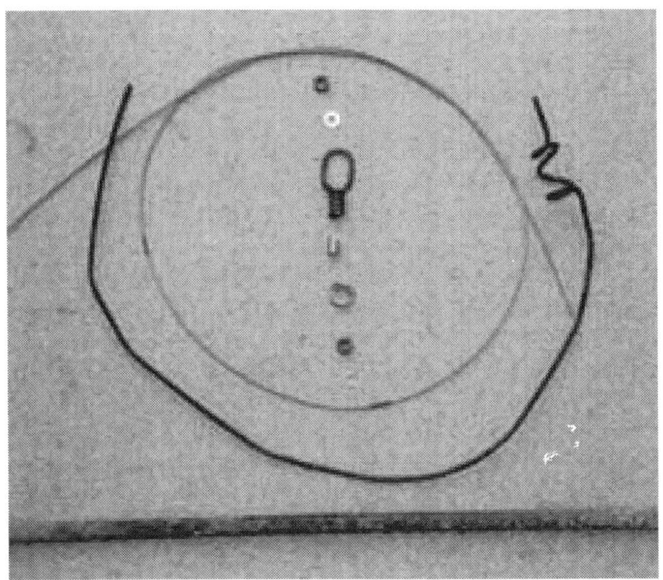

These are the only parts you need to build your own groundhog snare. From the top: cable, end nut, dime washer, completed swivel, completed snare lock, drilled penny washer, end nut, snare restrictor, snare support, rebar stake.

3. Place a screwdriver handle or similar item at least 3/4" diameter in the middle of a 6" piece of #9 wire. On the opposite side of the screwdriver handle, hold the base of a 1/4" drill bit or similar diameter metal rod perpendicular to the handle. Pull both wire ends around the handle until they meet the drill bit. Twist the ends of the wire around the bit to create a swivel as shown in the picture.

Thread the swivel, loop-end first, through the cable until it rests against the dime washer. The loop should extend beyond the cable end.

4. Make a snare support connector by temporarily placing the #11 wire against a portion of the cable. Wrap the long piece of #12 wire around both the #11 and cable five or six times, keeping each loop tight against the other. Remove the #11 wire, leaving the connector on the cable.

5. The next step is to make a snare lock that will allow the cable to close tight around an animal yet not loosen without your assistance. Lay the penny washer flat and drill a 1/8" hole in the side. Place the washer in a vise, leaving the half with the drilled hole facing up. Bend the washer over to a 90-degree angle. Remove the washer from the vise, and hold it in your right hand with the drilled hole up and the outside of the bend facing left. With the left hand, pass the end of the cable through the drilled hole about a foot. Bring the end of the cable back through the center hole of the washer about six inches. Apply the second nut to this end of the cable as in step 1 to create another stop. With a pair of pliers, bend the cable at the stop to a 90-degree angle.

6. If you have goats, deer, or other animals that might accidentally get a leg tangled in a snare, a snare restrictor should be applied. With the snare loop open, pinch the 1/2" of #12 or #14 wire around the cable at a point where it will stop the loop from tightening around the animal's hoof or

foot. Large-hoofed animals such as horses and cattle should be separated from the trapping area since a restrictor set for those animals would provide a closed loop too large to hold a groundhog.

7. The last item you will need to make is a support for your snare. With a pair of pliers, hold the #11 wire about an inch from the end and tight against an object 5/8" in diameter. Wrap the wire around the object a couple times, remove it, and you're done. The whole process to make a complete snare set-up takes only 5-10 minutes

"I will give him this if that's okay, but it's so simple I could probably explain it to him." Bubba said still studying the drawing.

"Sure take it with you. Hey, you think Goat Man can train those goats of his to pull one of Roland's Dog carts? I would love to see Bernie or Him making a Santa sleigh pulled by goats instead of reindeer" David said chuckling.

"Goat Man could probably do it, he been trying to sell off what he calls "pack goats" to the hunters, but Bernie ain't getting near one I bet, after that Billy Goat of his decided he didn't like Bernie making faces at him and took a run towards him with those big old horns" Bubba said laughing at the sight of the old man being put in his place by a goat.

Goat Man was an enigmatic character that had come to stay with Roland.

He would be the perfect Santa Claus stand in for Bernie's trading post. John and Roland one day had been working to attach an old hand operated pump to a gas stations tank when the Goat Man had driven up on his old military surplus motorcycle and said to the incredulous pair "Hidey Ho! You two open for business?" Like nothing in the world was wrong.

After John and Roland got their wits back about themselves from seeing this motorcycle vision from the past complete with a scabbard attached 30 cal carbine rifle, they noticed a goat kid sticking its head up out of his side car.

Roland, who was not to be put off by anybody or anything, asked if the rider had packed his own lunch as he tried to sneak towards his 30-30 next to the adjacent pump before being warned off politely by the Goat Man putting his hand on a belted .45 and inquiring again if he might buy some gas.

"You can have all you want, if this pump we installing works" John said in a more relaxing manner.

"Sure, I got lots of time. That's an interesting pump you made there, think its going to work?" He said moving his hand away from the pistol to an obviously relieved Roland who could have been easily outdrawn.

"It should; worked at home pretty good, but this tank has lots of moisture build up in it and using this garden hose to get it out, I am not so sure you want to put it in your ride till after I check it out better. Roland here assed up the threads on the bolt holding the cover cap on and we were pondering what to do to muscle it in place without blowing ourselves up when you surprised us by pulling in here so quick." John said taking a tentative step in the rider's direction.

"I got a nut breaker in my tool box, but I doubt that would do you much good now. Mind if I look?" Goat Man said dismounting his bike, himself relieved by John's demeanor, but still cautious of Roland who had managed to lower his head and hide his eyes now under a well worn cowboy hat.

'Wouldn't mind it a bit, where are you headed?" John asked as the rider approached and looked at the mangled threads on the bolt from a safe observation point, out of Roland's grasp.

"I heard tell outside of Newnan that a second trade post was down this way by a lake and was going to check it out. A big old boy on a mule named of all things Dump Truck said I should maybe seek out some civilized folk down this way?" Goat Man said looking speculatively at the pair for a reaction.

"You met Dump? How did that happen?" Roland said evenly and still being standoffish as he avoided eye contact from under his hat brim.

"Nice fellow, he was riding with an Asian boy down the road and come up on my road side camp. I heard them mule hooves clomping in my direction and he had either seen or smelled my fire and we come to a meeting of the minds for me to quit hiding in the woods and come out and parlay. I seen the kid and figured he wouldn't put the boy in danger, so I come out and we had us a talk and he explained to me that even though things were not as they should be, some folks were reorganizing and trying to rebuild." Goat Man said carefully latching his pistol so this meeting could get more relaxed, based on this gesture.

"Did you meet Martha?" Roland said still not quite convinced of the strangers' presence, but willing to raise his brim and look directly at him and get some eye contact.

"No but I know who you are speaking of, he invited me to come up to the house, but I had already passed it and was making my way south after that earthquake set Tennessee and the surrounding area in a permanent flood state." The rider said while reaching down to feel the ruined bolt threads that looked like they had been taken off with an axe or a cold chisel.

"What Earthquake?' Roland said totally relaxed now by the stranger's amicable and helpful nature.

"Well, some say that Solar Storm set the New Madrid Fault off, or they reckon it was just a matter of time until it went on its own, either way the Mississippi reversed itself like it did a long time ago and washed out a bunch of states. I only know this from trying to find my way down here and talking to a refugee once in a while. I have not heard any radio news in a long time, you all hear anything? GM said going over to his side car to release its passenger for a respite from its bleating protests of being confined when the machine was not moving.

"Not a lot, we got us a trench radio we try to listen to once in awhile, but don't get much from it" John began.

"What is a trench radio? Is that like one of those POW things they used to make back in WW II in the prison camps?" GM said inspecting the pump flanges and coming up with an idea to possibly give a solution to the problem of mounting the pump.

The author has provided the following excerpt from Bizarre labs for your education and use. Skip over it, or read it. I wanted to be able to have some written accounts on how to do this out here, just in case someone needs it.

Building a foxhole radio is rewarding and the basic setup is very simple. It is, however, difficult to adjust, and it may take several attempts to find a proper razor blade for the detector. This is a project that requires patience and much trial and error, but it will pay off once it begins to work. It will help to be versed in the construction and operation of crystal sets before building one. It will be especially helpful to read the introductory notes about the coil, detector, antenna, and other components. These sets are extremely simple in construction, but tuning and modification require some basic understanding of theory, as well as practice. All sets presented here are based on old articles, notes, and people's recollections. There are fairly major variations in design and materials among these plans. It must be remembered that these were improvised under often adverse conditions; there was no "standard" design. With this in mind, take this entire article as a whole, and use it a bit here, a bit there, to build towards a design that works best using modern materials.

Set 1

GI's, during World War Two, built these sets which took advantage of (comparatively) readily available materials. The instructions are purposely lacking in detail; these were a project designed with improvisation in mind. It will help if you have had some experience with crystal sets before undertaking this project. It is very tricky to tune and properly set the detector. But once you get it working, you will be amazed that you can actually receive signals through so crude a device. This design has survived mostly thanks to the article *Build a World War II Foxhole Radio* by Lance

Borden, as it appeared in the Electronics Handbook vol. XVII, p. 47.

The basic components are:

- Razor blade "PAL Super Single Edge" by American Safety Razor Co., or a regular rusty one
- Cardboard toilet paper tube

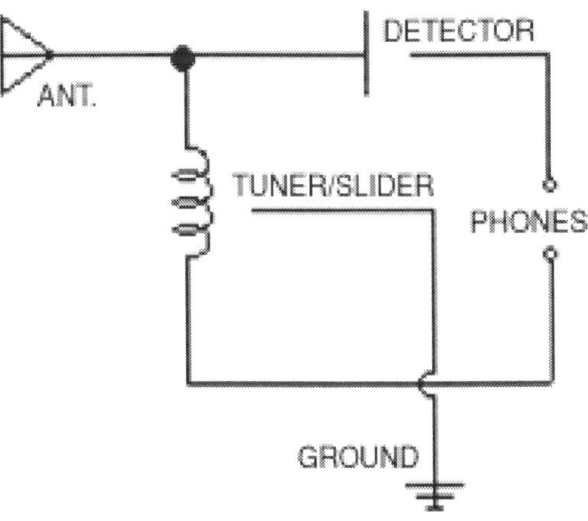

- Wire coat hanger or other handy strip of workable metal
- Headphones or earphone (2 - 4 K ohms)
- Large safety pin
- Lead from a wooden pencil
- #22 AWG (or so) wire
- Something for a base (small scrap of wood)

- Lacquer, glue
- Small tacks or screws for fastening components

Refer to the schematic for wiring and connections. Wind the coil 100 turns around the tube. #22 AWG wire is recommended, but it is likely that whoever was in the field used whatever gauge was in the scrap coil, motor, or transformer they were cannibalizing. Spray / paint the coil with lacquer (or whatever is handy) to set it firmly. Scrape off whatever paint or varnish may be on the wire used for the tuner/slider. Spread the safety pin apart and bend the head 90 degrees to use it as a base for attaching the pin to the base. The pin should stick up from its bent head, then down to its point where the pencil lead is attached with some of the wire left from winding the coil. The sharpened pencil lead is the detector, which touches the razor blade, which is in turn attached to the base at one of its ends (through the hole) with a screw or tack. The tuner should be mounted so that it is free to pivot and slide across the coil (see the crystal radio page for basic construction tips). Use a scrap of paper or cardboard as a template for getting the tuner/slider the correct size. Sand off the varnish on the coil where the slider will touch it. Connect the ground and antenna, hook up the headphones, and through much patient adjustment of the detector and slider, you should eventually be able to pick up broadcasts. A capacitor (.001 - .002 uF) between the earphone terminals improves performance. I have seen more than one example where a cap was improvised from cigarette foil, cut into strips and stacks (the paper backing served as the insulating layers). Simple variable capacitors (condensers) may have also been easily improvised.

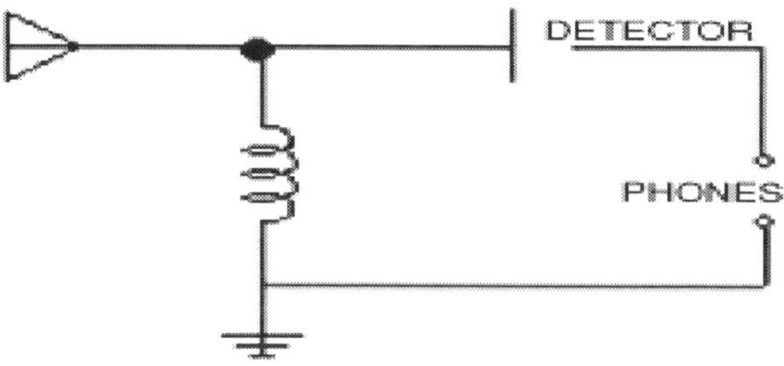

Another reader writes that he had success using a blued hacksaw blade (he didn't specify how big of a piece) and a hard drafting lead. These days, a blued hacksaw blade is much easier to find than a blued razor blade!

Set 2

The simplest of these wartime sets didn't include a slider/tuner arm, and were therefor capable of only tuning in one frequency. An article appeared in a 1944 issue of QST, and is faithfully reproduced in the D J Adamson Collection pages, so I won't go into a lot of detail here except to include the schematic. I highly recommend visiting Mr.

Adamson's pages if you are interested in old radio (or stereography).

Not much can be said about so simple a design. The coil was 120 turns around a 2" form (toilet paper tube). The whole thing was tacked down to a

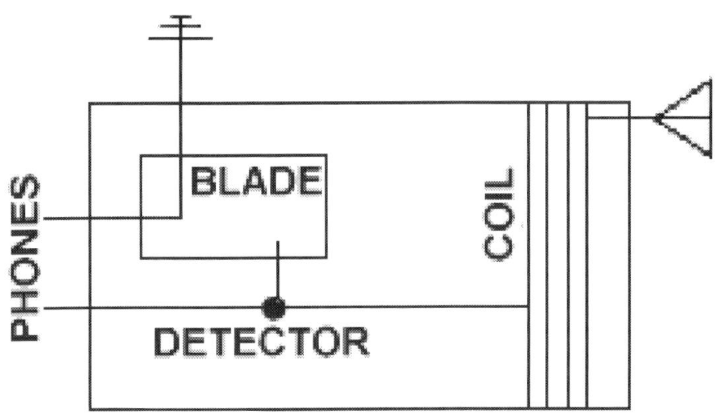

board. Pencil lead wasn't used at the time, instead the safety pin point directly contacted the blue (or rusty) razorblade. There is no tuner, of course, so only one signal will be received, and only if there is a station broadcasting near the correct frequency!

Set 3

I have been told that often these radios were constructed even more simply. The whole thing would have been built on a small, thin piece of wood or shingle, about 1/8 to 1/4 of an inch (3-6 mm) thick, 1or 2 inches (25-50 mm) wide, and 3 or 4 inches (75-100 mm) long. The coil was wound around one narrow end (I am not certain how many times... start with 100 and experiment). The blue razorblade would have been screwed or tacked down (at one of its ends) at the other end. The safety pin and pencil lead (if there was a pencil lead, which there probably wasn't) would have been rigged up in the same manner as in the above sets.

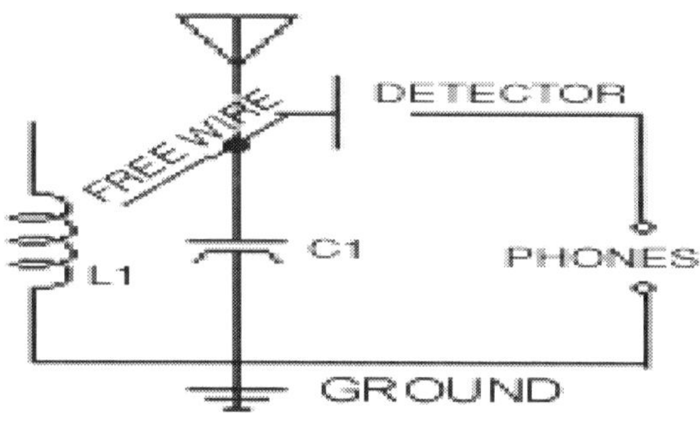

From what I can tell, there would have been only 3 terminals, one securing the antenna wire and one end of the coil; one with the detector (bent safety pin head) and one of the headphone wires; and one with the razorblade, ground wire and the other headphone lead. I have not built one of these. This is based on a sketch I made which in turn was based on the description of someone I briefly chatted with a long time ago, who himself constructed the thing much earlier. It is possible something was left out, so it may take a lot of tinkering to get it to work (if it works at all). Once I get around to building one of these myself, I will add to this page whatever tips I can (assuming I can get it to work!) I would also enjoy hearing if anyone else completes a working model.

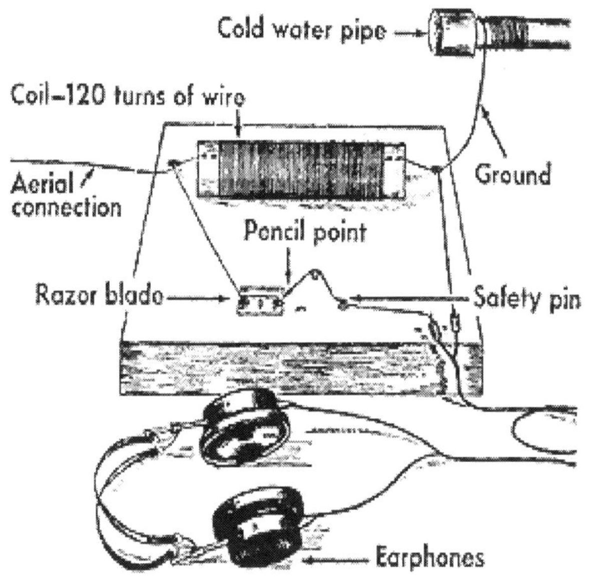

Set 4

I have recently come across a sketch of a set that looked exactly like set 2 on the Crystal radio page, except it had a razorblade/pencil detector where the diode would have gone.

There was no "standard" design. They all used razorblades, usually blue, but the other components and configurations varied greatly. I have even seen a reference to a set that uses two blades, stuck with one business end in the board, and inch or so apart. I don't have any details about the circuit, but wires ran from each blade, presumably either between one of the headphone terminals and the antenna, or between the ground and the antenna. A pencil lead spanned the blades, resting on the sharp edges.

Set 5

This is paraphrased from the article "How to Build a 'Foxhole Radio,' " from *All About Radio and Television* by Jack Gould, Random House, 1958.

The illustrations are by Bette Davis (a different Bette Davis, I imagine). The book is long since out of print, and too dated for most libraries to hold a copy. It is a simple set, much like Set 2, but curiously it does not include a slider for the coil, even late in the article after the razor blade is dropped for a crystal and a condenser is added.

Tools required are:

- A hammer

- A pair of pliers
- A pocket knife

Parts

- Board, at least 8 inches by 6 inches (200 by 150 mm)
- Cardboard tube, 2 inches in diameter by 6 inches long (50 mm by 150 mm)
- Insulated (enameled) copper wire, 28 gauge
- Pair of crystal earphones (which in 1959 cost 2-3 dollars U.S.)
- 3 new nails
- 4 metal thumbtacks (not plastic push pins)

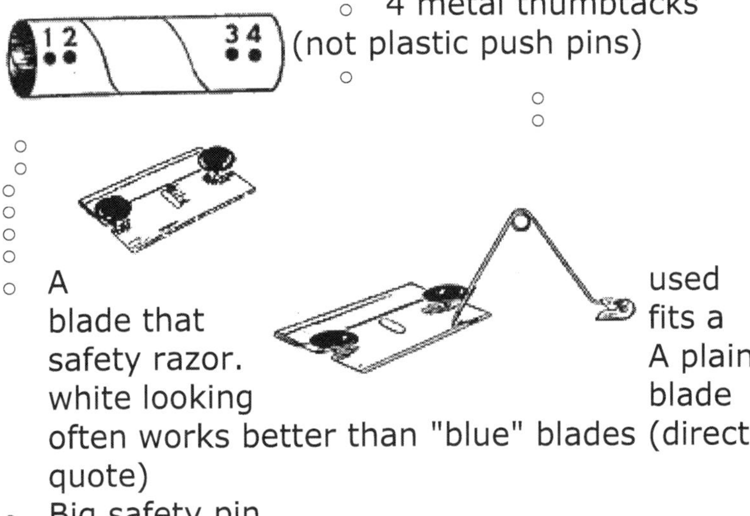

- A used blade that fits a safety razor. A plain white looking blade often works better than "blue" blades (direct quote)
- Big safety pin
- Pencil with a fat lead

Make 4 little holes in the cardboard, 2 at each end, with one of the nails. Push about 6 inches (150 mm) through hole 2, and then pull the wire up through hole 1. Wind the wire around the tube, making sure the turns lie side by side and not on top of one another. Wind for a total of 120 turns. Afterwards measure off 6 more inches of wire at the end and cut. Push the end of the wire down through hole 3 and up through hole 4. Lay the coil on its side at the back of the board. Fasten it to the board with 2 thumbtacks, making sure the thumbtacks do not touch any of the wire.

The razor blade is placed in front of the coil. Lay it on the board, and gently fix it in place with two metal thumbtacks. Do not push the thumbtacks all the way in.

Sharpen the pencil so there is a long piece of lead showing. Break off the lead, and wire it to the tip of the safety pin. Bend the head of the pin back so that it will lie flat on the board. Place the pin to the right of the razor blade. Hammer a nail through the head of the pin until it almost touches the pin.

Remove the insulation from the ends of the wires coming from the coil, as well as from the ends of all wires used to make connections. Hammer a nail just to the left of the coil. Leave it sticking up just a bit. Wrap the bare wire from the end of the coil around this nail. Take another wire and wrap a bare end around the thumbtack holding the left side of the razor. Push the tack all the way down to make contact. Take the other bare end of the same wire and wrap it around the nail.

Hammer a nail to the right of the coil and attach the coil wire as above. Use another wire to connect from this nail to one of the terminals of the earphones. Take another wire and wrap the bare end around the nail holding the safety pin. Hammer this nail in to hold the wire in place, but not so tightly that the pin cannot move a little. The other end of this wire attaches to the other free end of the headphones.

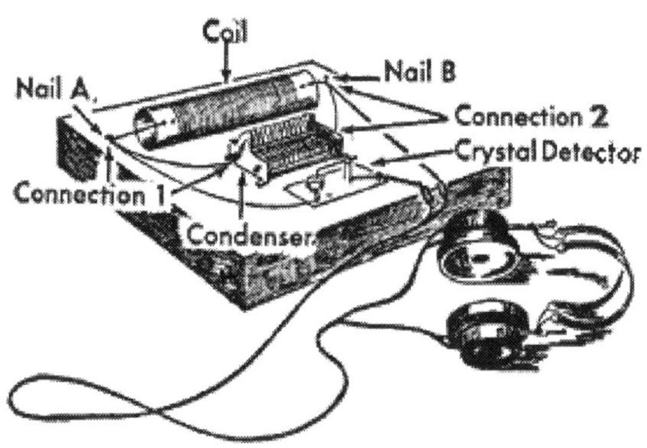

The antenna attaches to the nail that connects with the coil and razor blade (A). The ground wire attaches to the other nail, where the coil connects with the earphones (B). Hook up the headphones, and gently move the pin and pencil lead across the razor blade until you hear a broadcast. Once you hear it, don't move the pin, because you are more than likely going to lose it if you do. If there are more than one stations nearby broadcasting near the same frequency, you are likely to hear overlap.

To solve this, you can add a condenser. A variable type can be used, as in the illustration. It is recommended that it have 17, 19, or preferably 21 plates. Or you can use a fixed capacitor of around .002mF, or you can build your own (see the condenser article on the Crystal page). If a variable condenser is used, the post attached to the fixed plates should be connected to the nail that connects the coil to the blade (A). The condenser's

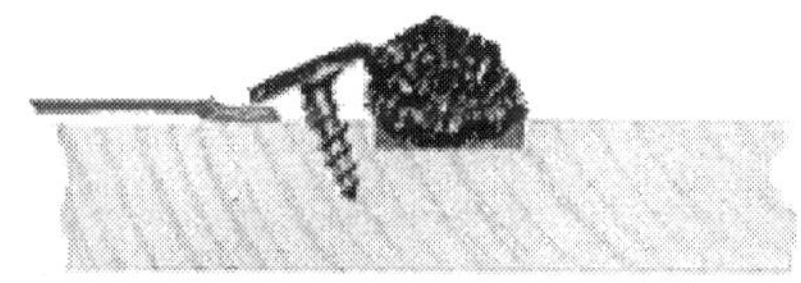

other post is attached to the other nail (B). Once a station is found using the pin and blade. The condenser is turned until the signal becomes clearest. Also note that in the illustration a crystal and detector have been substituted for the razorblade. The wire that was attached to the blade is attached to the crystal's post, and the wire that was attached to the pin is attached to the detector's post. A safety pin can still be used instead of the cat whisker (see the introduction of the Crystal page).

POW Radio

Prisoners of war during WWII had to improvise from whatever bits of junk they could scrounge in order to build a radio. One type of detector used a small piece of coke, which was a derivative of coal often used in heating stoves. The piece of coke used was small, about the size of a pea. A small board was used and a depression was cut into it near one end to hold the coke. A screw and, if available, a screw cup were used to hold the coke in place. A wire lead to the receiver was run from this to the coil/aerial (see Set 5).

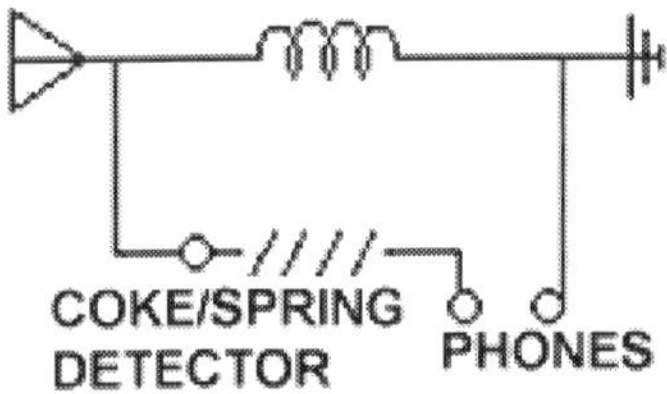

A foot or so (30cm) of steel wire (guitar wire, piano wire, etc.) was wound around a pencil, long nail, or similar, leaving about one inch (25 mm) unwound at each end. The wire should be somewhat springy. A second screw and screw cup is set about 3 inches (75 mm) from the first.

Attached by this screw are one end of the steel wire spring and a second lead, which is connected to one lead of the headphones or earphones (if anyone has any information on how earphones from these sets may have been improvised, I would like to hear about it). The steel spring wire was then stretched so that it just rested on the coke. After much adjusting of the point of contact on the coke and the tension of the wire, some strong stations would have been received.

If the POW was lucky enough to scrounge a variable capacitor, the set could possibly receive more frequencies.

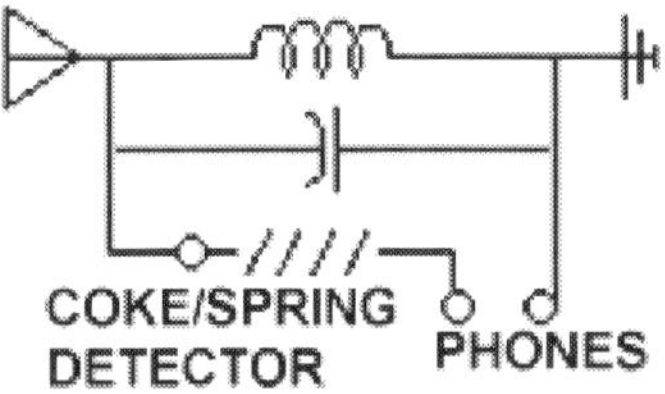

A POW camp radio's construction described

The Centre for the History of Defence Electronics Museum has posted an amazing interview with Lieutenant Colonel R. G. Wells, who built a rather elaborate set out of scrounged and improvised items while in a POW camp during WWII.

Improvised diode

The following appears word for word on my crystal radio page, but bears repeating here:

If you want to try your hand at making your own diode, Allan Charlton, of Sydney, Australia, adds:

"When I was a kid in a small town in Tasmania, Australia, our school was at the base of a hill, and the local radio transmitter was on top of the hill. We had lots of fun with crystal radios.

This is how we made our diodes:
Take a small length of glass or plastic tubing--an inch of the case of a plastic pen works well. Close

one end with wax, sealing a wire through the wax. Pour a little copper oxide into the tube: enough to cover the end of the wire. Fill the rest of the tube with copper filings or turnings. Poke a wire into the copper filings or turnings (but don't let it go down to the oxide) and seal the end of the tube with wax.

Can't find copper oxide?
Throw some copper wire into a fire. When it's cool, scrape the oxide off the wire. Yes, there are two oxides of copper, a red oxide and a black oxide, and they both work well. We preferred the red, but I have no idea why."

But what about the earphone?

Richard Lucas, who was a POW in Vietnam, built a radio in camp and was also able to improvise an earphone. He writes:

Four nails were bound together with cloth from our clothes.

Wire was obtained from wire used around the camp which I might add wasn't coated with varnish. It was bare wire, so we wound a layer and, using a candle, we dripped wax over the turns, which were spaced as closed as possible without shorting out (not touching). We repeated this process over and over again until we had about 10 layers of wire, which were insulated from each other layer by a strip of cloth and wax. Then we put this in a piece of bamboo and adjusted it so it was about a 1/32 of an inch from the end.

A tin can lid was positioned over the coil of wire and nails. Then connecting it to our "foxhole radio" (basic design as yours) we could here about three radio stations. Our antenna was the barbwire around the camp and the ground was wire laid along the ground to make up the ground. Best listening was at night and it had to be pretty quiet, because the earphone was pretty weak. If we had a magnet to set up a bias on the coil, the volume would have been a lot louder."

And Mike Barnard points out that "the headphones were almost always acquired from a tank crew's radio operator, and often one side of the headphone was cannibalized for wire to wind the tuning coil while the other was used for listening."

After this long dissertation, the Goat Man was intrigued, because he had found a new intellectual soul to share ideas and inventions with. He had surmised and rightly so, that this chance opportunity would set his future for life.

"Why do you have a goat riding shotgun?" Roland asked as it wobbled toward him and he gave it a smiling pat to calm it.

"Well his mama died giving birth, after she rode with me off the farm, so its only fitting that "Side Car" continued on with me. I am good with goats, and that's my thing, maybe this little girl can be the start of something one day, if I can find me some milk or substitutes for her." GM said wishing he had seen a milk cow instead of two other Tech redeemers on this road.

"I got goats" Roland said meaningfully and rubbed his chin.

"Would you mind if one of your nannies might be convinced to give suck to this poor baby?" Gm asked imploringly.

"Might be possible, you say you know goats and their natures do you? Roland said settling into his disarming country boy twang that John had learned meant a deal of some sort was afoot.

"I had a few on my farm at one time, what do you have in mind?" GM said carefully, wondering what options were on the table.

"That kid is looking poorly, I got me a nice Nubian that lost her baby that might adopt him if you could see your way clear to work off some grub and basics for me to take you on as a hired hand" Roland said taking his hat off and giving GM a full look at his thinning grey hair and expanding bald spot showing his age.

"I am not so sure I like the sounds of a hired hand, you got goats, I can more than pull my weight taking care of them. I got tricks of making cheese and utilizing whey, most never seen, I can produce drinking alcohol and help you create compost, but I BELIEVE GOATS ARE A FREE RANGE ANIMAL, which means I am not keen on having to clean a small yard of them." GM said eying a bolt on one of the pumps he thought might could be hammered down into place enough to bite the underlying bolt enough, so that a grip on another bolt threaded into the nut exposed could be used to do the task.

"Shit, that's clever" John said picking up on Goats backyard fix and thinking he could tap it with a cold chisel so it would never loosen by pushing a bit of metal over the top of the nut.

"I never got around to making cheese, and I damn sure never heard of goat beer or mead as a jump start for turning goat milk into an alcoholic beverage. Sounds nasty though, like that mare's milk Kickapoo joy juice crap that the Mongolians drink in Tibet, but I give you a try if you're likely." Roland said smiling.

"Likely for what?" GM asked not understanding a southern accent combined with so much worldly wisdom normally regulated to the Discovery Channel.

"Well, I got me this barn that has some living quarters in it. Us folks are not what we appear to be, I am sort of a big dog around here , as John can attest and I got enough meat and potatoes to keep you fit, long enough to try you out" Roland said waiting on John to translate if necessary.

"He means, you get fresh meat occasionally, a bed, a few veggies and a job. I would consider it closely if I were you" John said considering the conversation had gone to all or none state by now.

"You got a formal roster to sign up on, or is my hand good enough?" GM said smiling and proffering his hand to seal a deal for at least as long as his side car treasure took to grow into a worthy animal.

"I am the boss, he is second, no problems, no worry" Roland said offering his hand shake.

"Deal!" Gm said and set about helping to get the pump in place to fuel his and whatever other post apocalyptic vehicles could stomach the gas they were mining at this crucial point in the world.

Swedes Song

"Why in the hell did I ever get talked into going to Florida for a family vacation?" Swede grumbled to himself as he bitched at the traders for the umpteenth time that the size of the steel nuts that they delivered to him were unusable to do his snare creation and manufacturing business.

He should have listened to his buddy Buckshot and had a few spare parts with him to be ready to repair his own commercially made snares, but he had decided the expense was not necessary,

There were only four trappers on the Lake that had a clue of what the difference was of having such an advantage and time and necessity had made them ineffective in producing enough game, because everyone's pre-made air craft steel shit was garbage now from use in feeding others.

He had kicked it with David at one time off a youtube vid about spending 25 bucks on a bunch of snare part repair kits, but never got around to doing it or making a purchase. The things were damn easy to create, but not if you did not have a drill or the materials. What he wouldn't give for a pair of wire strippers now, so he could harvest all those left over power cords going to nothing that would ever work again like toasters or lamps. He remembered his days as a Jet Doctor in the Air Force when lock wiring one nut to another was part of the job and reams of wire were readily available. The purpose behind wiring two nuts together in a special way, was because if one nut loosened the other would tighten.

Just about all the wire that could be had off picture frames had been recycled and it was time to start finding other alternatives.

John and he had tried to make a wire jig and build some conibear traps like David and Boudreaux had, but they hadn't been able to find the right steel to make them.

David had a bunch of different sizes for different animals, but he always said if he could have just one survival trap it would be a conibear 110.

The #110 Conibear Trap is the best survival trap ever made. It can be used for; rabbits, rats, squirrels, muskrats and mink. In An Emergency Survival Situation the #110 Conibear Trap will takes game birds and ducks also. He had even seen Dave fishing with one once also, just to prove how versatile they were.

Asking a trapper what is the one trap he would take into a survival camp is kind of like asking a gun nut what is the only gun to take. The conibear was developed by a Canadian fur trapper Frank Conibear. They are a kill trap that lands on an animal's body, dispatching them quickly and humanely. They are light enough to carry a half dozen in a bugout bag and damn near indestructible. It takes a bit of strength, but they are easy enough to just set by hand.

The conibears are designed to use in trail sets, den entrance sets, and baited sets. The bait all depends on what you are trapping. #110 in a box set baited with garden veggies, will take rabbits. Squirrels really like corn on the cob, or peanut butter.

A properly trained trapper can out do any hunter alive. It is simple math really think about it. A hunter can only be in one spot and not every minute of every day. Now replace the hunter with 12 snares set on 12 different trails 2 miles apart working 24/7 that are always on the job, who do you think is going to be eating good? Common sense when you consider all the possibilities.

If you used them creatively, they could probably be used for wild turkey (this is wildly illegal, but in a survival situation it's no holds barred FYI.) The 110 measures 4.5" by 4.5" and uses a single spring to power the trap closed. This is more than enough to quickly dispatch your prey.

Swede had his own trapping territory that bordered on David's sort of (David dropped him off by sailboat for three day excursions) and Swede had just warned David that a pack of dogs seemed to have moved into the area and were running off the game and robbing his traps.

David had told Swede not to go back to his trap line until he and Boudreaux could go with him to take care of the problem.

David had really reinforced the danger of what a pack of 10 or more starving dogs would do to a lone hunter before he could get more than one or two shots off. These dogs might have already been feral, but they could just be strays with no fear of humans and had possibly developed a taste of human flesh from the dead bodies in the countryside, or worse yet, from some unlucky soul in the wrong place at the wrong time.

David had told Swede that people in Georgia used to practice hunting feral dogs by having someone roll a couple tires down the hill at them, and see how many times they could hit a tire before the tire hit the bottom of the hill. This was supposed to simulate a wild dog attack.

David and Boudreaux were gathering up their big 220 and 330 conibears off their trap lines that they used for beaver and big raccoons. These traps needed a very long pair of tongs to set them, as well as they had him making up as many wolf size snares as he could make up, to help eradicate the problem before the savage dogs threatened the community.

David and Boudreaux were once again having themselves a contest and seeing who could make the best predator bait.

Better them than me, I seen some of that stinking mess they have recipes for, Swede said to himself remembering Boudreaux was trying to find an easy way to grind up some mice and David's jar full of beavertail chunks sitting in the sun.

David had given Swede a couple pairs of military NBC rubber gloves to clean game and such with, but he sure hoped he didn't have to bait any traps and ruin them. He was dang sure not going to be touching that shit with his hands, if they made him help.

Thinking about David reminded him he best locate him another guitar. David had an old Child's practice guitar he had at his place, and when Swede came to visit, David always made him play it and he just felt silly strumming on it. Swede wished for the days of electric amps etc, but those times were long gone now. Maybe he could get Boudreaux to make Dave get a fit house guitar to keep over at his camp, although last time he had brought that up, Boudreaux had snuck a Mickey Mouse guitar into his guitar case at the bar as a joke and wouldn't give his own back to him until he attempted to play a little song on the little thing, to the entire bar's amusement.

5

Plotting and Scheming

David had a moment to himself as Jack, Stewart and Bubba were all in the house looking at the box of trade goods David had left out for discussion as to what to do with them.

David had put up the artificial Christmas tree that Bernie had left behind at his mothers house just after Thanksgiving as his family tradition had warranted, but it seemed a hollow gesture: because only his end of the lake was able to see it and get into the spirit.

The boat landing had a big Xmas tree someone had planted years ago that would be neat to decorate, but it was just too damn cold out to do anything other than decorate it and go home.

The cold was a bigger problem than even food at the moment. It takes a lot of wood to keep a house warm. Many of the families across the inlet had been forced by circumstance to move in with each other to survive the winter and share the labor of gathering firewood. This could cause a lot of friction between the occupants of the houses that was not there this summer, because of the now close living arrangements and petty squabbles it caused.

An idea dawned on David at the moment to solve this and many other problems and he rushed inside to grab him another drink and tell his buddies about it.

"HEY! I got a great idea that's going to set the tone for this season and solve a bunch of worries, too. We are going to have a barn raising!" David exclaimed and grabbed the whiskey bottle to pour himself one.

"Who needs a barn?" Jack asked confused.

"We do of course. Listen up. We are going to build one at the Boat Landing, as a sort of community hall. We can get everybody to tear down one or two houses out on the perimeters of their community and use the wood to build it. The scrap lumber and broken pieces they can use for firewood and a lot of them can move back to their original homes if they got a fireplace, at least for the week of Xmas." David said excitedly.

"Folks been sort of robbing some them buildings anyway for wood, it would make sense for the community to tear down the structures as a concerted effort and share the tasks and the wood." Stewart said brightening to the idea.

"You lend me that tractor of yours Dave and some logging chain and I will show you how quick I can pull one down." Bubba said chuckling at the notion of getting to do a little approved mayhem.

"We could get the kids to beat out and straighten nails. Gather wood for some warm up fires etc for all the workers. That should keep them out of mischief" Jack said contemplating tasks.

David considered that this was a very astute of Jack. The kids seemed to be the biggest bone of contention amongst the community at the moment. This generation of kids that was used to video games and TV to baby sit and entertain them had way too much time on their hands to get up to all sorts of things that set the adults at odds. One of the better things that had been instituted towards the end of summer was a sort of Boy and Girl Scout type organization that all the younger teens and adolescents were required to attend weekly. It taught some traditional moral values they could share and gave them some wood skills they lacked.

"Hell," David said chuckling to himself and the group around him. "Stewart was the one that armed all those little goobers with slingshots, or hand catapults as they say in the UK. It looks like every kid out here emulates Dennis the Menace with one of those wrist rockets in their back pockets." David said pointing towards Stewart.

"It's up to their Mums and Dads to get them to not shoot at one another with them. It did help solve a lot of the food problem." Stewart said defending himself from the looks he was getting from everyone.

"That's true, but that's also why we haven't made them any real bows and arrows either." Jack said sarcastically.

"Melanie had a worse problem, when she taught those kids in her community the story of David and Goliath in her Sunday school class and no one knew how to use a sling. Kids were hurting themselves and not even aiming at each other." Stewart replied.

"Exactly, it was hard enough to keep them from raiding neighbor's gardens or abiding by the scavenging territory laws and not doing the picker thing where they were not supposed to. We started the scouting thing for the mental health of the kids as well as the community. I also did it so I could get some intelligence as to what they were up to once in a while" David said grinning.

Parents not used to sitting down with their kids for dinner or constantly inquiring about their whereabouts were finding they lacked some vital social skills in anticipating what the youngsters were up to or preventing mishaps.

"There is the problem of food, if you got everyone working on your project David" Jack said to bring him back to reality.

"No, I got that covered to some extent, but it's still problematic. Swede said we got a pack of dogs in the area and Me and Boudreaux going to have us a little bounty hunt on them" David said getting him some ice from the fast renewing ice machine.

"You got Ice!?" Bubba said scrambling for the bar.

"Help, yourself, but go light on the cubes." David replied and continued talking about his plan.

'We figure at least 10, maybe more dogs in that pack and if they not sick or poorly, that's a lot of meat" David said looking intently at Jack.

"Well problem solved, they won't know they eating dog, unless you tell them." Jack began

"That's the thing, I could BS them. They wouldn't have a clue if I dressed the meat. But everyone always offers a piece of cooked meat to Boudreaux or Bubba`s dog when we have a feast and they ain't going to eat it" David said before Stewart chimed in.

"What do you mean won't eat it?" Stewart said looking at a slobbering Harley who was looking appealingly at David for another snack.

"Coyotes and wolves eat dogs, but generally speaking, a dog won't eat another dog, cooked or not. These animals are not starved out of their minds so they won't touch it. It is going to freak us out to see them offer it to them, and folks are going to notice something might be wrong." David said finishing his drink.

"So, we tell them then." Jack said guardedly.

"I am not sure that's a good idea. They are going to like the taste of dog after that and might get ideas." Bubba said calling his pooch to his side.

"Not ones they probably not thought about or done. Don't worry about yours, or Boudreaux's, they are pets and respected around here. I will reinforce a few cold realities to the community and kids before we undertake to serve up a dog outside of our community that has not gone back to the wild." David said carefully, not wanting to upset his friend.

"Well be damn sure you get the point across." Bubba said warily.

"I will, you want another drink? I got some Ancient Age whiskey that I have been saving for a special occasion, and I guess planning a barn raising can be the start of one. I know you know construction, but I want you to grab that copy of "Shelters Shacks and Shanties" off my bookshelf and get some ideas to teach the kids about building while we barn raise. That will keep them from wanting to burn up so much good wood as they tend the fires and give them a bit of respect for a 2x4." David said watching Bubbas eyes light up at the thought of some good sour mash whiskey.

"Why does this book say Elemental Historic Collection on it?" Bubba asked eying the book selected, but others were having the same notation.

"Well, awhile back a Prepper had a bunch of old outdated and out of print books in his library that he thought the Prepper Community might like to share. He got the permission rights, did the reformat and edit etc. and brought them back to life as modern printed books that don't fall apart when you try to read them. Other folks did the same with a few of them, but they used blurry scans, these are all printed text, no scans and fully diagramed. I used to put the keyword ELEMENTAL Publishing or Prepper Archaeology in before an old book I wanted to see if I could buy something from the collection or I had not heard about yet and get something for my library. He started something called the Prepper Archeology project to gather up old wisdom, sort of like the Foxfire books, so it wouldn't get lost. There are several titles there on trapping, woodsmen skills etc. that are just great reads or full of preparedness knowledge to acquire before SHTF.

"It always amazes me that you collected so many things in anticipation of events that were unfolding before our eyes, but no one cared more than their afternoon tea about" Stewart said getting in on the review of David's collection of books that he had painstakingly collected over the years and brought all the way to the lake with him.

"You ever going to do a lending library or read in place like a reference room in a library, with these David?" Stewart inquired thinking about business as well as community building.

"It is entirely possible, but let's get back to the barn building plans. The weatherman across the slough said he predicts snow this year." David said letting the fact sink in.

"Hell, they couldn't predict weather on the TV before, what makes him possibly right now?" Bubba said not understanding that it snowed on average every five years in Alabama.

"Lots of things, he does have a barometer and education in that shit. But Jack and I added in the farmer's almanac and my sign reading and I agree with him." David said resolutely.

"I am not meaning to insult you David, but what do you mean by your so called "Sign" reading? Stewart said remembering he had heard the same old superstitious banter among farmers from all over the world in every pub, bar and tavern he had been in.

"Don't, be discounting David. Let me show you something. Look here." Jack said grabbing an old Field and Stream magazine off the table and turning to the pages that showed waxing and waning moons and the best times to hunt or fish.

"People have known that there was something to it for years and game good game guides have proven it"." Jack said in support of David.

"That is like scientific tide maps and times, I want to know what signs David says he sees." Stewart said, taking the initiative of demanding David explain the unpublished weird things that David only explained when he was ready.

"Look Stewart, I forgot about half I used to know about such things but it's like this. I watch nature; have done it all my life. I learned or listened to old country lore and tried it out to see if it made enough sense. For example, the time to plant corn is when the oak tree's leaves are as big as a squirrel's ear, might sound odd to you, but makes perfect sense to me. A big old oak tree is usually the best indicator of climate because it survives. It has survived by whatever Mother Nature instilled in it to know when to put out the first shoots of spring and when to wait a bit for a hundred years or more. If it decides it's safe from frost to put its new leaves out I plant. If I see squirrels gathering more nuts than usual, it's a hard winter coming. If the "mast" (dropping of acorns) is heavier than usual, I got an opinion or a plan. Did you know that you can **tell the temperature by counting the chirps of a cricket**? It's true! Here's the formula:

To convert cricket chirps to degrees Fahrenheit, count number of chirps in 14 seconds then add 40 to get temperature.

Example: 30 chirps + 40 = 70° F

To convert cricket chirps to degrees Celsius, count number of chirps in 25 seconds, divide by 3, and then add 4 to get temperature.

Example: 48 chirps /(divided by) 3 + 4 = 20° C

The idea was first studied by A. E. Dolbear in 1898. He systematically studied various species of crickets to determine their "chirp rate" based on temperatures. Using T for temperature in degrees Fahrenheit and N for number of chirps, Dolbear published his results in the form of an equation -

T=50+[(N-40)/4] This equation for cricket chirping is now known as Dolbear's Law.

"So, do not mess with me, half of what I know has been proved scientifically, or eventually as science progressed thru the ages. Right now I am the closest thing you got to a wizard." David said laughing at Stewart's retort about Granny on the Beverly Hillbillies TV show having a weather cricket and Jack having a match box in his pocket with one inside.

"Look at the ants Stewart; they are more active than usual, gathering in whatever they can get. It will rain tomorrow, mark my words." David said challenging Stewart to a bet he knew he would lose by David's uncanny knack for noticing something about nature and comparing it to his own premonitions proving true.

"You will not get me on one of your sucker bets, David Dupree! The whole lake is still laughing about how you and Boudreaux did your last survival challenge with each other in your underwear in the woods to see who could catch dinner first. I lost money on you saying you could catch a fish on a twig, despite me knowing better to bet a man against his own game. Taking the elastic out of your underwear for a fish line I could anticipate, but tying it to a small stick you sharpened on both ends and stuffing it down a grasshopper and making a fish gorge out of it, surprised even Boudreaux, although I say he still won by stripping buckass naked and shooting the bird out of the tree with his waistband before you even got started.

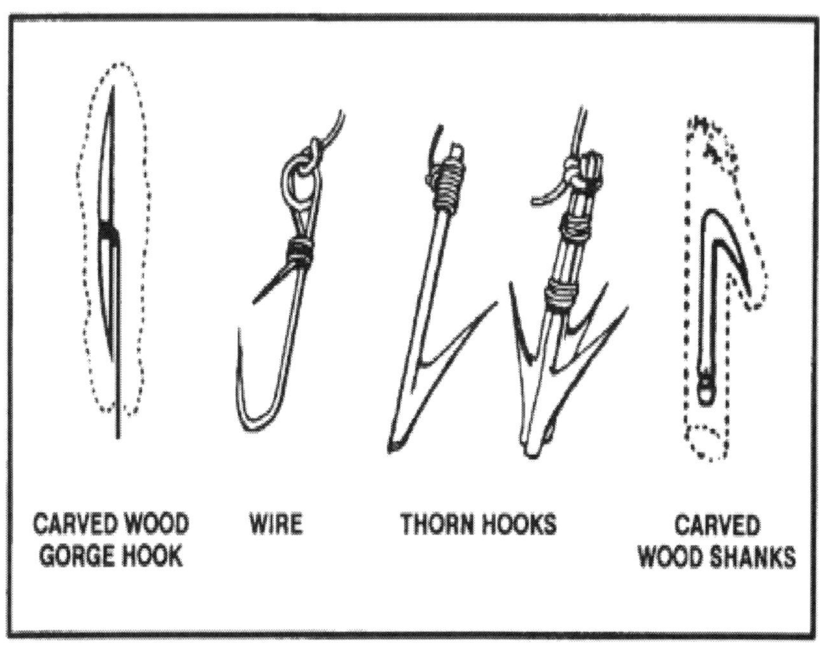

Figure 8-17. Improvised fishhooks.

"O.k. he got me on that one technically, I thought he was going to go get a thorn bush somewhere to make a hook, but I caught a grasshopper first that I could of ate and the judges said I was a winner, because Boudreaux took too long to find a rock for his improvised slingshot. Hell. Man I wasn't comfortable being out in my underwear in front of folks let alone what Boudreaux did." David said resentfully.

I am looking forward to you're bear hunt contest, never realized we had so many black bears in Alabama, until we started to have so many folks spotting them as they increased their numbers this summer´ Jack said offering his bartending services to the three intent revealers to calm them down.

"You remind him, its pocket knife only. No dogs, no boat engines, and uh, no Daniel Boone shit like stabbing one." David said trying to figure out what Boudreaux was capable of.

"That damned Cajun might be able to take a bear with a pocket knife, but I don't think any of the girls is up for sewing him up if he does" David said smiling.

"David, That old Boudreaux has been winning bar tricks off me a while. I want to get even, just a little bit. You mind telling me your strategy, so I can place my bet better with him." Bubba asked looking for an inside track to a possible winning proposition.

"I don't mind at all, if it won't get repeated. You see when I was up in Alaska, I learned me a new trap from an Indian who still uses it.. You split a log in its center and put a stick in the middle to hold the two halves apart after you wire or tie each end of the split to keep it from going further. When an animal steps in the center and knocks out the peg, the two halves come together and catch its leg. I will also probably, do a few spear traps , the falling type, whip type etc. No fancy bow types, though, they take forever to construct and are not very good for this sort of thing anyway.

"Ha. You ought to carve a crossbow before the event with your pocket knife. Technically speaking that's legal. He He." Jack said.

""Good one! But, I would never hear the end of it though." David said grinning.

A Fleet is Formed

David sat and considered how to pull this community through the hard winter and what to do until some crops to come up. There was just no way to crash course a bunch of city dwellers into an effective hunter gather society. Scavenging had been a mainstay to support the community but distance and cold now prevented that as an effective means of supplementing what little game the hunters of the group could provide.

No, something else needed to be done, and done quickly. History had a lesson to teach about the situation they were in. Whole armies had been in the same situation and they had solved it by sending out foraging parties to loot the land. David had always had this solution at the back of his mind, but had avoided it until now.

He did not want to be responsible for creating a warrior nation that got what they needed by force of arms, but options were running out. Of course there were the cities to pillage and scavenge from somewhat. Dump had told him that little fiefdoms had sprung up centered around a food warehouse or a grocery store where groups of people or gangs had taken over a resource as a base of operations and warred on other communities for scant resources, but that was really getting out of hand now that resources had been consumed or stripped so bare that bloody battles were being fought over nothing more than a few cases here and there of food someone managed to still hang on to.

The highways had been the best resource to get food off of. They were safer, had less competition and were not fought over like neighborhoods were. Trucks broke down on the highways had always been a hit or miss proposition though. The just in time delivery of goods for grocery stores often would have one truck carrying nothing but a small variety of items for multiple drops at warehouses. A whole truck of pork and beans had been a godsend that David had found while backtracking his route to Roland's from Montgomery. That seemed like a hell of a lot of food until you saw it distributed out to the trading posts and the needy in the community.

David found it more difficult everyday to share such finds with others as his own clans needs took first precedence and he had made some hard decisions to refuse to distribute more than minimal amounts of surplus to those who produced nothing or lacked ties to the community.

David could train troops though. We had a little 10 man reactionary force that represented the inlet and could come to the aid of the community if threatened by outside groups. They were sort of like the minutemen of old though, scattered about the community and only forming up out of necessity or for the occasional drills David held that everybody hated.

They could not understand why they had to learn to march, do PT (physical training) or learn to stand at attention properly because they were all civilians.

David knew though, it was because they had to get used to taking orders without thinking about it, or deciding if they wanted to do something or not. David didn't want to get in a position where he said charge a group of people shooting at them and he was the only one running towards the danger.

He doubted anyone would have a machine gun nest they had to tackle these days, but that was the way David was taught in the Army, as well as what he tried to instill in his troops as he liked to call them. Blind allegiance to orders is the only thing that saves your but sometimes, and it goes against everyone's commonsense not to run towards someone shooting at you, but somebody has to do it and often times retreat is suicide.

He and Boudreaux had had a blast playing aggressor against his squad of men to teach them the rudiments of responding to an ambush. David had showed Boudreaux how to make flash bang grenades out of MRE heaters and empty plastic pop bottles and when they hadn't charged the attackers and instead tried to retreat, David and he had put a hell of a scare into everyone of the consequences of being driven into a kill zone. He had also lined the ditches on both sides of the road with pinecones to simulate he could of spiked the natural cover offered, he had guessed everyone would take diving off the road and had warned them that it could have been shit dipped pungi stakes in there to greet them.

The order he reminded them was, lay down, take cover in place and return fire, assess situation and get to the edges, or better yet, point men blow off as many rounds of number 1 buck in the direction of attack and everybody just charge to the next place that offers cover or try to overrun the enemy through superior firepower in the ambushers direction. Either damn way, spoil the fool's aim that's shooting at you by making him duck or flinch.

I know what I will do, I will create a marine force. Damn, never thought I would ever choose to call it that branch of service. David mused remembering all the friendly, inter-military rivalries and jokes about Jar Heads he had told about Americas finest.

A foraging group that came in force, was well trained and disciplined was exactly what was needed. Amphibious assault teams could come in at the boat ramps or wherever along the lake and explore the surrounding areas for goods.

"No lose that damn word assault. Mutual protection force, which sounded better would be what David promoted as a term.

A small group or a lone sailor could get into a world of hurt sailing up on another community in exploring or foraging attempts, a show of strength and a parlay would be best if we encountered an organized group we might encounter.

This lake had 750 miles of shoreline and many navigable creeks and rivers flowing into it. I need everyone to lose the Viking attitude though and just explore for empty houses or other communities to trade with.

That is a hard thing to do though, when you have modern scoped rifles that can be pointed at you from either shore and you are getting trigger happy in anticipation of someone taking a pot shot at you to warn you off, or worse.

"I got it! Hell yes! A master plan is taking form here, now how do I do it, in secrecy?" David said to himself as a notion and a light bulb went on in his brain.

David went off to find Jack and Stewart and saw Bubba and his wife Cat sitting on the dock having their morning coffee.

"Good morning!" David called out and Bubba acknowledged him a bit less chipper this morning after a night of carousing with David and way too much liquor for the both of them.

"Your up early" Cat said watching her bobber and surprised David could even stand up this morning after Bubba had bested him in a friendly but drunken wrestling match that no one really remembered how it got started.

"Got some ideas to discuss, glad you feeling worse than me Mr. Bubba." David said still having a twinge in his back from the big heathen laying on him for a count of three that Stewart somehow ended up referring.

"We got to stop that shit Dave, that weird as arm lock you tried on me, got me stove up. You ok?" Bubba said flexing his shoulder to get it better aligned.

"I agree on that, did you body slam me or what

last night." David said doing an odd realignment of his own spine by wiggling about.

"You two are a handful when you get in your cups, hell Jack doesn't even drink and he still was pouring you all drinks the size of what he used to do before he quit and wouldn't listen to us ladies you had enough already. And you instigated that shit David by trying to teach Bubba that arm bar." Cat said to remind David he could be just not right at times if he went on the whiskey trip to far as he and Bubba had both done last night.

"We were not mad, just playing with each other." David said trying to defend himself against the accusation, but wishing he had not indulged so much.

"Two grown men trying to best each other and almost coming to blows over stupidity and alcohol after your long friendship was really stupid." Cat said scolding the both of them.

"I wasn't going to hit him." Bubba started to say protesting before David agreed he had no inclination to do it either.

"You threatened each other when you got hurt, and now look at both of you. Not fit for the work for the day." She reminded the two grinning idiots thinking about a rematch another day.

"Hey, drop the subject for now, it was foolish, but it was all in fun. I got something to discuss here. Hey, where is Harley at?" David said looking around for Bubbas dog that was always around Cat or him.

"Boudreaux arrived an hour ago sleepy head, he had a feral hog he got and is butchering it down at the fish cleaning station and Bear and Harley are waiting on scraps." Cat said still studying her fishing pole bobber and miffed at the boys for playing to hard the night before.

"How big was it? I am soooo ready for some roast pig, he does a cook the hog in the ground you wouldn't believe how succulent it is." David said his mouth watering already for some crispy skin and tasty fat dripping off of it, yummy pork roast.

"Maybe 160 lb, not huge, but he says there are probably 20 or more of the same he wants you to give him a hand with." Bubba said making a drinking motion with his hand when wife Cat, wasn't looking, but David made a hell of a face that said the drinking binge was not starting this early today.

"Look here, we are going to do a regatta for Christmas but not how you think." David said before Bubba asked him what the hell is a regatta anyway?

"Normally it's a sailboat or yacht race, is its meaning. There are also a gathering of boats, such as the blessing of a fleet of fishermen, a gathering of boats for Fourth of July or Christmas gathering etc. The idea is gather up all the boats from the marinas and have an event or celebration. In our case, I am going to get as many sailboats as I can put together, maybe decorate them a bit for Xmas, and we going to sail for Horseshoe bend State Park.

"That was where the Red Stick Indians fought Jackson wasn't it" Stewart said wandering up and over hearing the conversation.

"You know, your history.′ David said surprised

that Stewart had heard of the famous battle.

"Bernie told me about it one day, what's the plan? That area is pretty much all woods and camp sites isn't it? Stewart said helping himself to some coffee from the pot on the nearby fire.

"Not a lot of buildings on it, that is true by a long shot. But look at it this way, if you lived on the lake between here and there, you are going to be watching the waters close. A bunch of sailboats decked out for the holiday, stopping here and there along the way, with as many vehicles as we can move and the trade wagons following on shore is a hello, how do you do, that will be passed on for miles. It is a force to be reckoned with, but also does not seem to be a military invasion to scare who ever lives up that way." David said trying to envision how he would act if he saw such a spectacle coming his way.

"So why Horseshoe Bend?" Bubba asked.

"That has always been sort of our rally point, if we had to bug out of here. I am thinking it might still have game a plenty too if, someone else has not taking the area over as a bug out location. Anyway, I wanted to do a recon of it anyway, its 30 miles or better from here I think, never done it by water. It would be about 50 by land, and we can find out who has made it so far and still living off these shores. That is a lot of foraging territory to open up also, and like I said, I doubt anyone would want to tangle with the little expeditionary force I got planned." David said sitting back and wearing a half smile on his face.

"Let me get this straight, you want to decorate up boats with garlands and such, like those watching a regatta, sail down to the park, and scavenge everything that is not nailed down or occupied between here and there? Well Brilliant I say! Where are you going to get the extra boats?" Stewart said taking a deep interest in the plan like he was the Admiral Lord Nelson or something.

"I have been looking at lake brochures and supposedly there was a sailing school that operated 10 meter and smaller boats about 25 miles from here, about 8 miles from the trading post. I haven't seen any of that sort of craft out on the waters, so I am thinking maybe they are available for acquisition." David said pleased with his plan.

"30 ft sailboats? How many people does it take to crew one?" Bubba asked, getting interested in the plan.

"Just two, actually, one man can do it, but you can carry 8 passengers easy. I don't know how many captains we got around here that can handle one, but we can figure it out and practice without getting anyone drowned. I can operate one somewhat." David said like his little pirate fleet he had proposed was already ship shape.

"Morning Folks!" Jack said wandering up with his wife Lois.

"Jack can you sail?" Stewart asked quickly before he got settled in.

"Yea, David taught me. Sail what?" Jack said interested in any salvage to be had on the lake.

"How about a 30 footer?" Bubba asked, ready to crew one of the boats.

"No he can't, Stewart, you and Bubba are going to take my truck anyway you damn landlubbers. "

David said chuckling.

"What is going on?" Lois asked, thinking correctly David was up to no good as usual and probably going to endanger her beloved hubby.

"You explain it to them Stewart, I am going to see if Boudreaux has ever been to that sailing school or knows where its at and see if Sherry wants to go along on this mission" David responded and rose to leave the little dock party and head towards the back of the neighbors house where Boudreaux had tied his pirogue up.

"Boudreaux! Good Morning! I hear we got pork for supper." David said to the old swamper washing up in the lake.

'"You don't sleep so late, I put you to work helping. She's all cleaned and hanging now. You tell that Bubba that dog of his is a bottomless pit when it comes to eating. He still begs for more after getting a kidney, most of the heart and lungs off that pig. Me dog Bear thinks his Boudreaux don't love him no more, cause I give that big snoot face lion portions to keep him satisfied long enough to finish my butchering.' Boudreaux said finishing washing his hands and arms in the lake and despite his tough constitution, shivering to beat the band.

"Damn, Boudreaux, come on into Sherry's house, you look like you going to turn blue with cold." David told him and picked up his coat and handed it to him.

"No need to tell me twice" He said buttoning himself up.

"You guard" Boudreaux said to his Dog bear, thinking Harley might lose his manners and try for the hog carcass hanging from the rafters of the boat house.

The old Dog lay back down beside the big bulldog and licked him on his head as if to say, he would watch this young pup and then got nudged over by the bowling ball sized head of Harley as he returned the notice.

"Them is a funny pair David. Harley does what Bear say I guess because he is older, but that old Bear save him best scraps as long as Harley polite and let him have his dominance and eat first." He said looking at the two dogs getting ready for a snooze next to the fish cleaning station, probably full enough to bust by now from Boudreaux feeding them various bits after cleaning the hog he had brought.

"Let's let Swede trap those dogs on his own and you and I do the hog hunt , He can set them big boys we got. Although we best teach folks how to rope set one in case someone blunders by one or they lose the tongs." David told Boudreaux, anticipating that sending green horns with Swede around 330 conibears could be hazardous to bones and health.

As elementary as this narrative may be to many who have ever played with one, keep in mind that at some point many of us who had one of these alien looking traps in our hands for the first time wondered: "What is the easiest, safest way to set this thing.

A body grip trap is amazingly strong and dangerous. It must be respected as well as cause no concerns if properly handled.

There are basically three setting options: by hand, with a rope, or with one of several designs of mechanical setters.

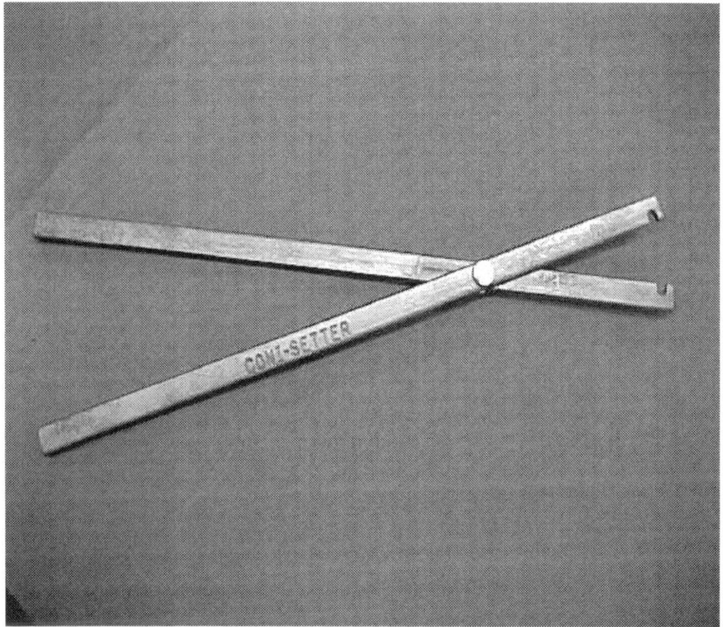

Tongs

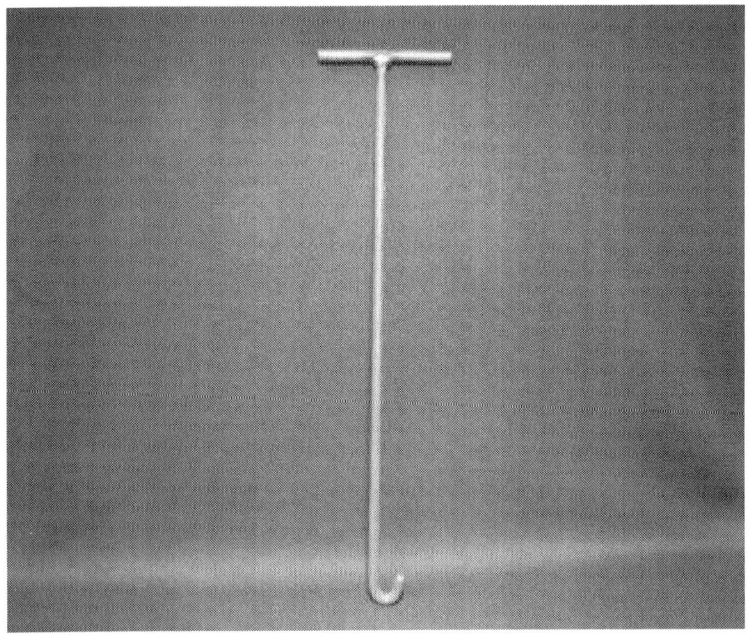

Pull setter (Robbie style)
Stand and pull

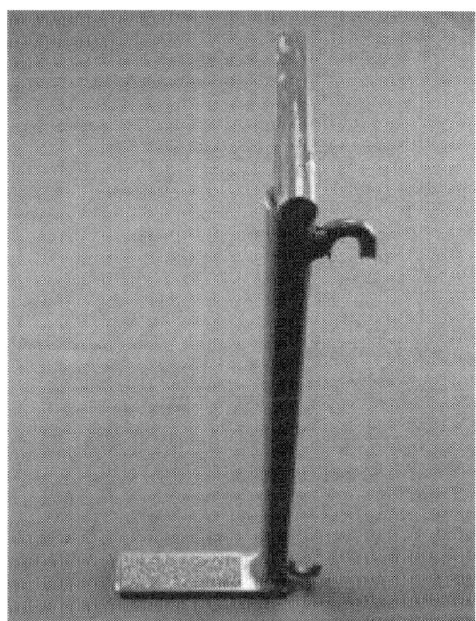
Gemsetter

Stand and pull, safer

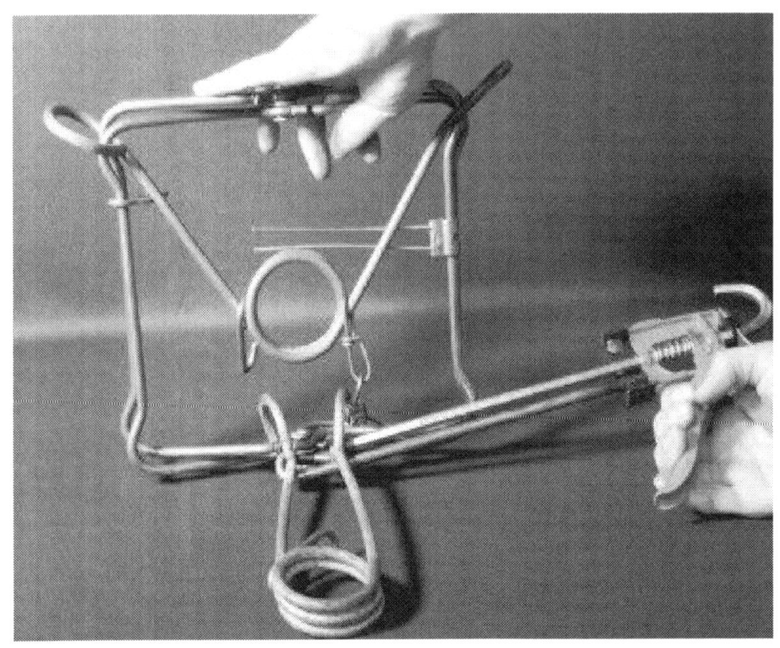

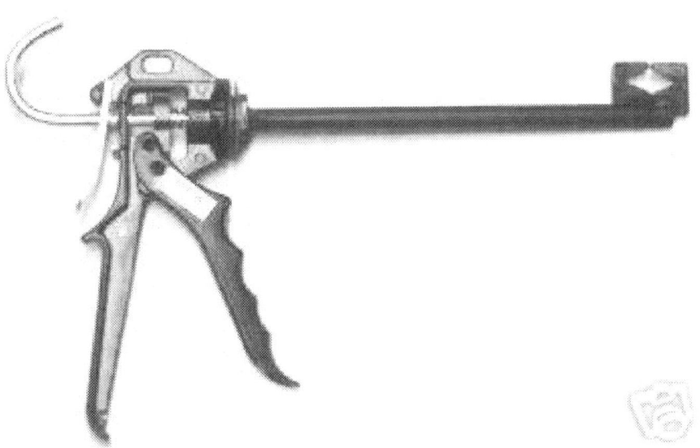

Squeeze setter, or caulk gun type

Setting a conibear trap with rope method is

difficult to imagine sometimes for the uninitiated. You do this by feeding a rope through the inside of both ends of the spring and then crossing the rope back over itself. Then pull the ends of the rope, drawing the spring bars together

#110 & #110-2 Conibear Wildlife Traps

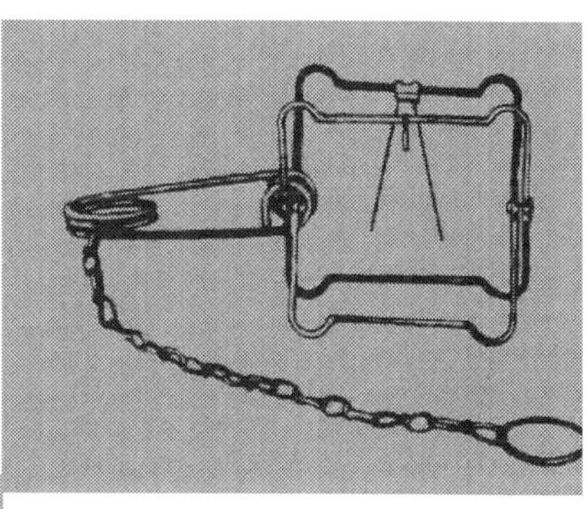

Extend spring so it is pointed directly away from the trap. Then grip and compress the spring.

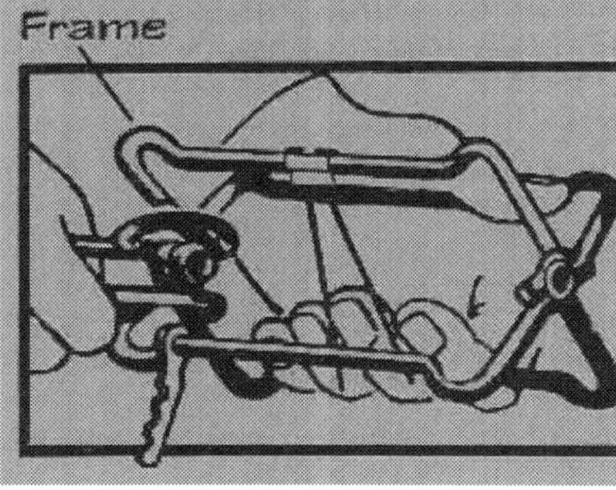

Keeping spring compressed, pull trap frames together with other hand. If a Conibear Safety Gripper is available, set it over the jaws to hold them in place.

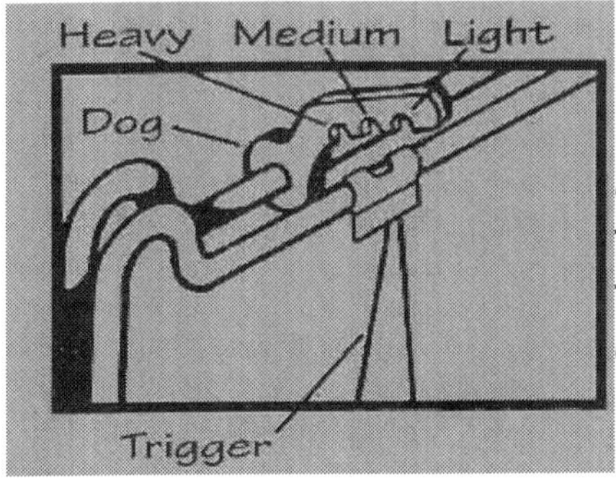

Position trigger and dog at desired location along frame and then set trigger in preferred notch of dog.

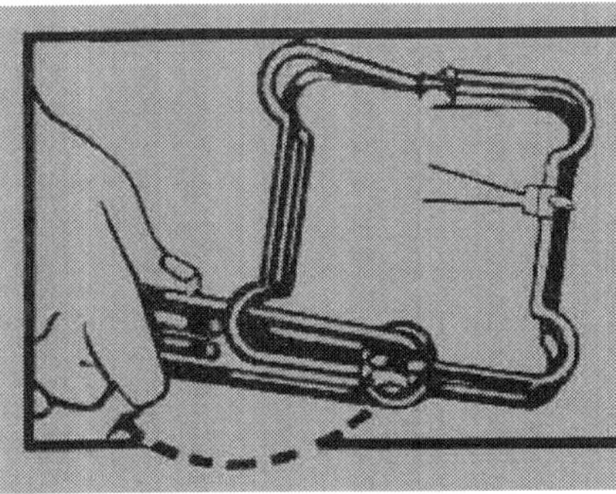

Be sure trigger is secure within notch of dog. Then grip compressed spring and release frames slowly. Release the Conibear Safety Gripper if one is being used. Trap is now ready for use. Spring can be swung to side if necessary for desirable setting position.

#120-2, #126-2 & #160-2 Conibear Wildlife Traps

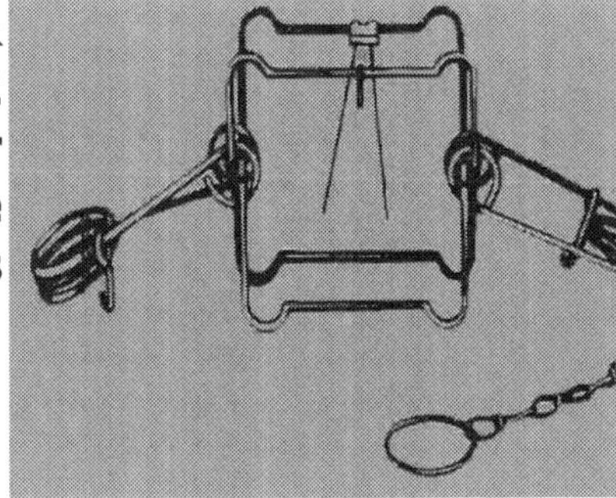

Extend both springs so they point directly away from trap. Grip and compress either spring. Set safety hook to keep spring compressed. Repeat for second spring

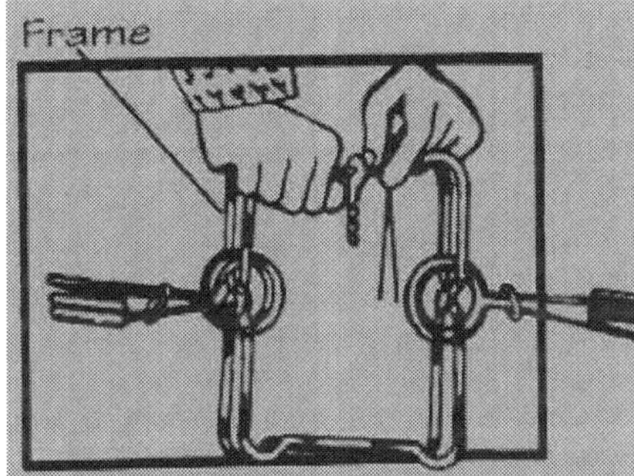

Center springs over hinge and pull frames together with one hand. Keep them together with a Conibear Safety Gripper if one is available.

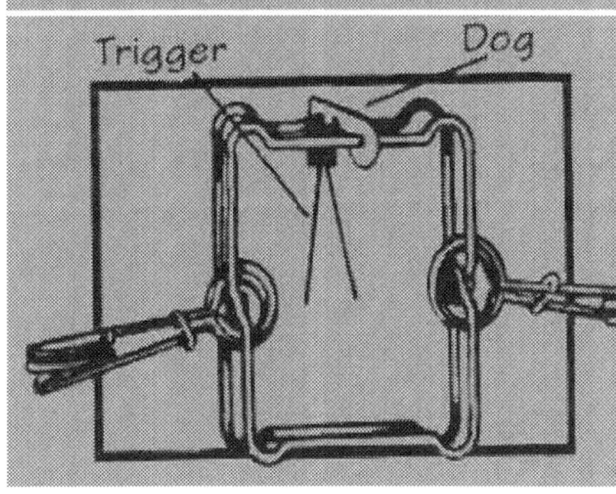

Position trigger and dog at desired location along frame and then set trigger in preferred notch of dog.

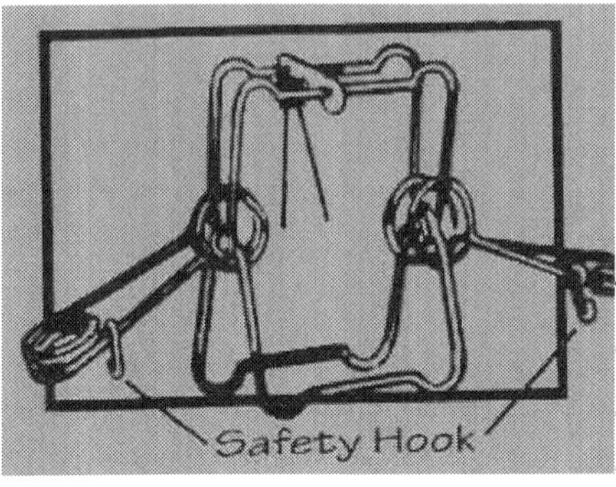

Be sure trigger is secure within notch of dog. Place trap in desired location. Then, keeping hands clear of trap frames, slowly release each safety hook and slide to coiled ends of spring. Release Conibear Safety Gripper if one is being used. Trap is now ready for use.

#220-2, #280-2 & #330-2 Conibear Wildlife Traps

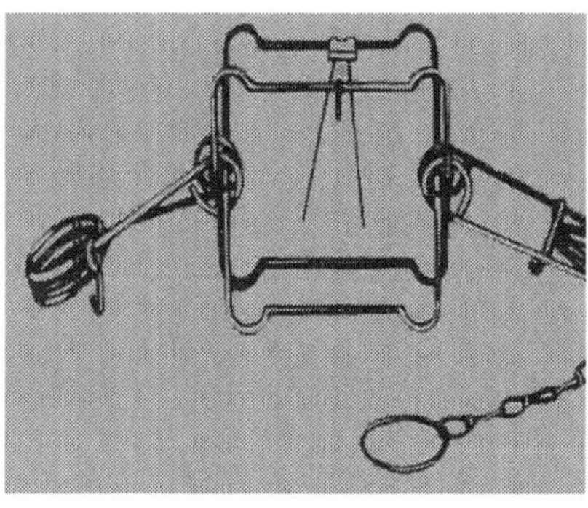

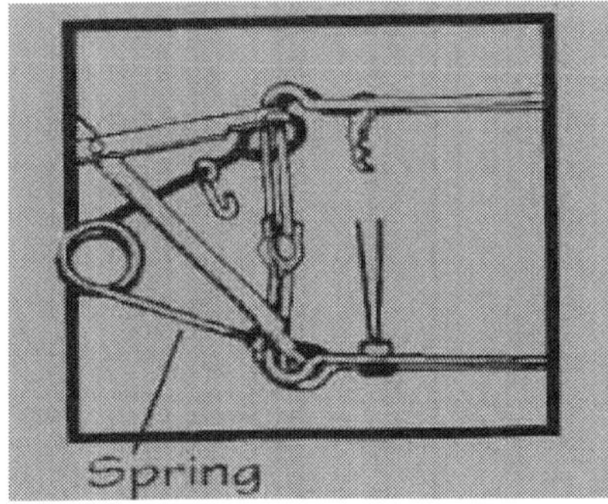

Extend both springs so they point directly away from trap. Hook notched ends of Oneida Victor #0965 trap setting tool over the eyes of either spring and compress. Set safety hook to keep spring compressed. Repeat for second spring. Then proceed as for #120-2 & #160-2 Conibear wildlife traps.

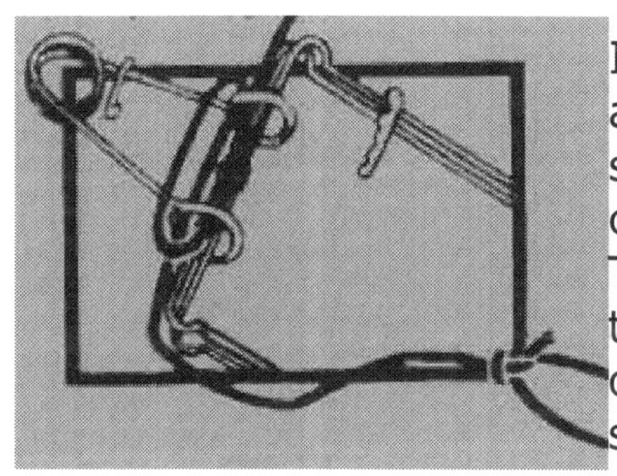

If a trap tool is not available, an 8 foot section of 1/4 inch rope can be used as shown. Tie a loop in one end of the rope and thread the other end through the spring eyes.

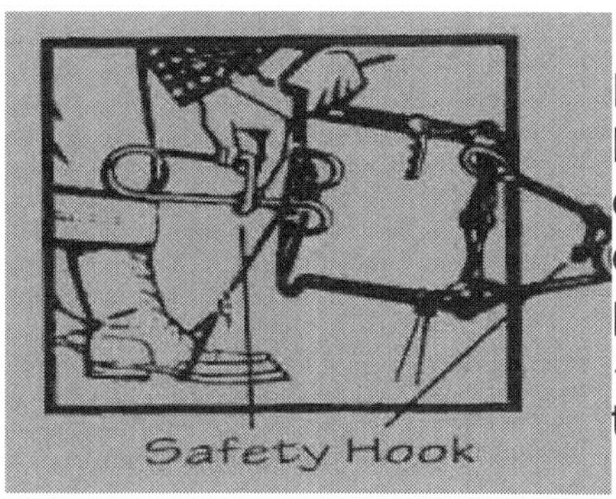

Place foot through the loop and pull the other end of the rope to compress springs. Then proceed as for #120-2 & #160-2 Conibear wildlife traps.

<u>Accessories to Help You Set Conibear Traps</u>

Trap Setting Tool

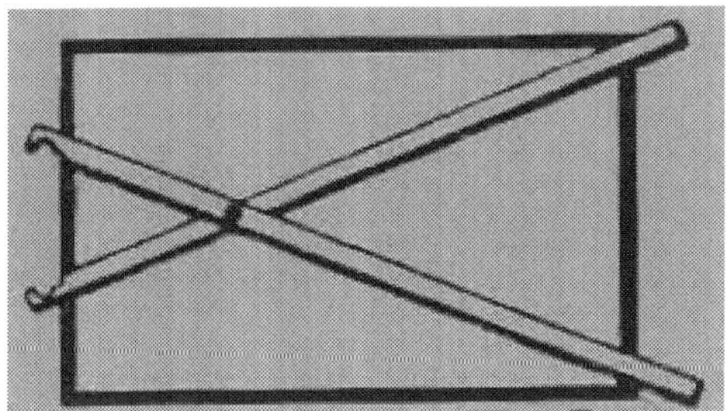

This handy 20" tool lets you apply strong leverage to compress the springs on Conibear and long-spring traps of all sizes. This tool is a good time-saver.

Conibear Safety Gripper

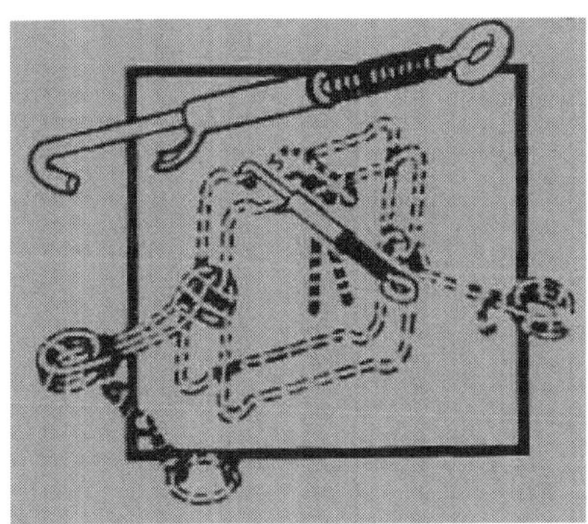

This safety gripper lets you make Conabear sets easily and safely, even difficult underwater sets. If the trap is inadvertently triggered, the Conibear Safety Gripper grabs and holds the jaws

Safety Catches

- An important features of the Conibear trap are the safety catches. The safety catches are s-style hooks that are permanently attached to one side of the spring bar. Once you have the spring loaded (opened), you slip the open end of the s-hook on the opposite bar, holding the bars securely together. I would recommend that once you set the trap that you leave the safety catches in place until you are ready to leave the area.

"We need to demonstrate that rope method to folks that might be hiking in our trap line area if they have a dog with them in case they get caught by accident and they need reminding to carry a piece of rope with them. The small traps won't kill a dog, but they are a bitch to open if you don't know what you're doing. A 220 or 330 if it catches them around the neck is instantaneous death though, so Swede better warn folks if he starts setting close to the community." David said thinking ahead a bit before knocking on Sherrie's door.

"I got a good mind to sky out of here every once in a while David. You and me on our own wouldn't have to work half so hard to feed ourselves if we just had our friends and family to take care of. I know you hate them, but I got my regular leg set traps taken in he can use too.' Boudreaux said of what David considered a cruel device.

"We can't have wild dogs around. You teach him

their use and safety using them and you will hear no complaints from me. We taking a bunch of that snare wire he risked his life for to get them hogs anyway, if he agrees. I ain't squeamish about them traps as much as you think. I just do not use them unless called for. I won't be the one to comfort a mother who had her child attacked in the backyard playing, because I didn't do my duty in eliminating a threat; these are no name dogs and vicious ones. The coyotes are bad enough to contend with, but these beasts have no fear of man, because they were once domesticated. You tell folks to keep the kids close to home until we deal with the problem." David said to visions of snarling teeth in every direction, as he had witnessed before.

"They dang sure ain't muppy puppies and screw anyone that won't eat one, before they eat you." Boudreaux said on the same wavelength David was broadcasting.

"I am thinking we need to fence the community some, but that's another day" David said knocking on the door of the 'girls' house' as he referred to it.

"I got mine barb wired for what its worth" Boudreaux offered.

"Hey Sherry, you all sleeping in today?' David said as she answered the door.

"No, we been up, who can sleep with a Boudreaux in your backyard." She said jokingly.

"Oh, I see no pig cleaning for you? Huh? Well she be done and you ain't out of the woods yet. Get the rest of your brood motivated, because after I have me a warm up and some coffee if you got it, I am going to teach you how to cure bacon and hams." Boudreaux said pushing through the door into the warmth of the house.

"Are you burning pine?" Boudreaux said sniffing the air in the house and drawing David's attention to a smell.

"No. we know better than that. Its pine needle tea you are smelling, good for your gizzard as you say Boudreaux. Its vitamin C rich, want some?" Sherry said as the rest of the house occupants started their way to the house guests' arrival.

"You hard timing Davie? I thought you had plenty of coffee from the trading post?" Boudreaux asked turning his nose up at the proffered steaming cup of turpentine.

"No, Sherry is making sure we don't get scurvy and lose our teeth or get sick this winter, it actually is an acquired taste and not that bad. Lois, get Boudreaux and me some real coffee, if you would please." David said while slumping down in an easy chair and motioning Boudreaux to do the same.

"You want honey in it? Sandra offered while helping Lois get the brew together,

"Where did you find a bee tree at David?" Boudreaux said after telling her that would be nice.

"I ain't that brave yet, I had a 50lb bucket of that I bought as a prep to augment breads and such. It's right handy because it never goes bad, David said declining the addition for himself.

"Sherry, David says you might be able to command a big sailboat and wants to talk about it" Boudreaux said from the kitchen while munching on a left over breakfast biscuit Betsy had passed him.

"How big?" Sherry said hoping David had plans

on building a clipper ship or something with her eyes sparkling at a new challenge and opportunity.

"Calm down, a 30 or 40 footer max, and its formation sailing, not racing" David chided

"Is the boat outside? Sherry said starting towards the door.

"No, its not, might not even be there anymore. I got an idea brewing we going to attempt to try." David said to a somewhat deflated Sherry.

"But f it is there, I can sail it right?" Sherry said gearing up again.

"Hold on a sec, let me explain what's needed here." David said chuckling at her exuberance, but wishing he could stay on subject with her.

"If...and I say IF...the boats I need are still available, we got to go get them and bring them over to the boat landing for mooring and do a few drills with them carrying guards as an amphibious assault force." David said and was amused he got her attention on that last phrase.

"What the hell are you talking about now David? Whose beach you going to storm and why.?" One pissed off Sherry said.

"I told you to chill for a minute so I could explain it all to you. I have no intention of storming anyone's beach, just the capability of doing it, if push gets to shove. Think of this proposal as a Xmas military parade where everyone is cheering for a tank decorated with peaceful seasonal things. We going to sail an "Our end Of the Lake" Navy down the coast and say Merry Christmas along the way." David told her as his weird plan started to get explained by Boudreaux in the kitchen to the rest of the house's occupants.

"So, you going, that is, we are going to decorate those boats; then you put your armed "Marines" on them and sail off to never never land hoping for the best?" Sherry said wondering if David had found some hooch this morning already.

"Don't be so condescending, Sherry. It's a good idea," David objected.

"Mon Cherie, you listen to your David. He has a way bon good idea." Boudreaux interjected while pretending he was Bear begging for another biscuit at Sandra which cracked her and Lois up, and they gave him another from the food reserved for later in the day.

David laughed and tried the same trick towards Sherry, but she was not in the mood for his shenanigans after he just commented on doing an Iwo Jima raid on another boat landing with her as the skipper of the landing party.

"Dang, hard to get a biscuit around here. Sherry, the boats are going to be decorated for Christmas, our intentions are obvious, we ain't flying the Union Jack or Scull and crossbones, peaceful intent, good will towards man etc.. just don't mess with us. Got it?" David said still miffed he couldn't have a biscuit and seeing Boudreaux working on his third and making playful gestures at him in back of Sherry.

"How the hell do you make a boat look like Christmas?" Sherry said not relinquishing her mad quite yet.

"I don't know, that's you alls job. Write Merry Christmas on your damn sail or something with a magic marker. I just need you to sail one to the boat landing, I will get another captain if you don't feel like going." David said resentfully and going to TAKE him a biscuit from Boudreaux, who was having way too much fun waving one in the background at him.

"Sit, David and talk" Sherry said snagging his pants on the way by.

Boudreaux laughed as David dejectedly sat down, but tossed him a biscuit from the kitchen like he was his dog, but David didn't mind he had one now.

"You think it's safe?" Lois chimed in

"Safe as I can make it" David said and reassured her that Jack was staying behind to her great relief to guard the settlement.

"I don't want Sherry exposed like that David, you get someone else to captain that boat" Betsy said and Sandra seconded it.

"I can, but..." David began. Before Sherry made it clear she was the one to make her own decisions whether or not she was going to the group.

"Hey, everybody! At ease for a damn minute! I only need Sherry to move a boat back here and teach others how to sail it, while I am gone hunting with Boudreaux for hogs. You quit your bitching long enough to listen, you will understand the plan and see its merits," David said put out.

"Oh hell, you said the B word, time to go back to checking on the hog." Boudreaux said making a beeline for the door before the fireworks really got started.

Boudreaux was smart, but not that smart; as three irate women immediately blocked his way to escape and wanted to hear this argument to the end and possibly include him in it.

"Look, its safe enough to go get the boats if they are still there, we can decide later if she needs to go with us to Horseshoe bend" David said trying to reason with the group.

"Go help Boudreaux, I will chat with the ladies for a bit" Sherry said letting him escape.

"Ok, I will be back later" David said following Boudreaux out the door.

"Escape at last!" Boudreaux said chuckling as they walked to the boat pier.

"I think it's a good day for a trip, lets get Jack and Bubba to cook that hog and we can go for a sail or something." David offered.

"Sounds good to me, better yet, grab Stewart and let's go to the trading post tavern for a drink. If you take your truck, we can be back by 6 and have us a feast just about ready." Boudreaux said enticing David into just some rest and relaxation time and conversation over a few drinks.

"I haven't snuck off for some R&R for sometime, let's do it!" David said motioning Stewart to come over away from the group to talk to them.

"Stewart, you want to sneak off to the Tavern?" David said whispering at him.

"Sure, I am freezing my ass off trying to just be sociable and talk of trade at the moment. I would much rather sit in a warm pub and talk things over. I think the Weatherman is right, we going to get some snow by Christmas" Stewart replied looking at the gray skies.

"Normally the rarity of a white Christmas in Alabama I would welcome, but not this year. The humidity around here makes for a bone chilling wet cold that's just plain dangerous to be out in. I have lived in Alaska and I swear it feels colder here at times with no snow, than it did up there in that drier climate." David replied turning his back to the wind.

"You ain't taking a boat are you?" Stewart asked.

"Hell no, too hard to stay warm on a boat. I still remember almost setting the boat on fire when one of those emergency heaters I rigged tipped over in rough water. Besides, toilet paper was hard to come by and rubbing alcohol was not all that plentiful." David said advising that they were taking the truck.

Uses:
Heater in Home
Heater in Car during winter months.
Heater for Camping
Heater for your 72 hour kit.

Supplies:
1 empty quart can (you can purchase at any paint store or Wal-Mart)
1 bottle of rubbing alcohol

1 roll of toilet paper (with cardboard removed) paint can opener (you can purchase at any paint store or use a screw driver.)pack of matches or lighter.

Assembly for Use:

1. Remove core of toilet paper
2. Fold the roll of toilet paper in half and stuff into the empty quart can.
3. Slowly pour 1 pint alcohol into can.
4. Light w/ lighter or match.
5. To extinguish, replace the lid.

Instructions for using Emergency Car Heater: Use 70% isopropyl alcohol-any higher percent the flames could be too high. Do not use scented alcohol, it will smell awful in your car. 4 pints of isopropyl will keep a car 60 to 70 degrees for 24 hours. They are extremely safe and don't produce carbon monoxide. The toilet paper acts as a wick and doesn't burn.

Warnings: Be careful the can rim will be hot to touch during and for a while after burning, although the can could be held from the bottom even while the heater is burning. It is suggested that you carry a metal pan or cookie sheet or fold a square of tin foil into fourths to set the heater on. Do not pour more alcohol on the heater while burning. Wait for it to burn out or smother with metal lid. These are very susceptible to wind. Using this outdoors could prove problematic with any decent wind present.

This heater is NOT recommended for cooking! To use as a stove you will need a grate or even a cake cooling rack to place on top of the can This fire will be very hot so all foods will need to be closely watched.

"I will tell everyone we dropping off traps for Swede, go get what you need and I will be back in a minute." Stewart said and headed off to advise everyone we were leaving camp for awhile

Toasting and Roasting

David drove towards the trading post at a leisurely pace. They had stopped and picked up Boudreaux's neighbor and somewhat on again, off again girlfriend Beverly. David was surprised that Boudreaux had suggested it, but he was all for having her accompany them. She could be the one to call 'last call' on them and be sure they got back in time for the "hog in the ground" feast that awaited their return. Derrick Riches, at About.com Guide has some good general instructions on how it's done.

It's one of the oldest methods of cooking. Dig a hole in the ground, fill it with fire, add a large animal, cover, and cook. Most people recognize it as the Hawaiian Luau method. While lots of people do this in many different ways there are a few basic steps you can take to make it turn out right. You can use this cooking method for large hogs, whole lamb, a side of beef, or virtually anything else you have

Digging the Pit: The size of the hole in the ground you need is determined by what you are going to cook. The pit needs to be about one foot larger in every direction. If you have a pig that is four by two feet roughly then you need a hole six by four feet. The hole should be about three feet deep. The size of the hole is going to determine the size of the fire and how much of everything else you are going to need, so you need the hole first.

Lining the Pit: Most pits are lined in stones of bricks. This is done to even out and hold in the heat. Large stones, about the size of your head are perfect. One rule though is to avoid stones that have been in salt water (like the ocean) in geologic time (say the past few million years). These stones have a tendency to crack, break, and sometimes down right explode. If you plan on doing this a lot lining the pit with bricks is a good idea.

Building the Fire: You are going to need a lot of hot coals to do your pit cooking. Traditionally you would fill the pit with logs and burn them down to coals. This process can take the better part of a day. Some people choose charcoal but you are going to need a lot and since the fire isn't going to produce much smoke to flavor the meat you can go with the cheapest solution. What you are going to aim for is about a foot deep of burning hot coals before you start the actual cooking.

Wrapping the Meat: Whatever it is you choose to cook needs to first be flavored and then wrapped. Some people will say that if you are doing a large animal you should place hot rocks in the body cavity. It's up to you, but I haven't found it necessary. What you do need is a secure package to put in the fire. This means tying up the meat firmly. Some people use chicken wire to wrap it together. This makes a good tight package. In the old days an important part of this wrapping was banana leaves (or other large leaves). This provided protection from the fire and moisture to the meat. These days' burlap bags are used to make a damp surface and aluminum foil is used to separate the meat from the coals. You use what you can get.

The basic wrapping instructions are to take the seasoned and prepared meat. Wrap tightly in many layers of foil then wrap that in lots of wet burlap. Finally you want to wrap that in a heavy wire frame. This holds the whole thing together and gives you something to hold on to. Once you have it wrapped tightly you are ready for the fire. One tip, if you are doing a whole hog you need the mouth propped open to let heat through. This is why the apple was put in the pig's mouth.

Loading the Pit: With the help of several strong people and possibly a few 2 x 4's you can now lower the meat into the pit. As soon as the meat is in the pit you need to cover it up. This keeps the burlap from burning by starving the fire of oxygen. The coals will remain hot for days, but you won't have an actual fire anymore. This can be done by covering the pit in dirt, but then you'll have to dig it all out later. You can use a large sheet of metal, but what you need to do is cut off the air from getting into the pit. Otherwise the burlap and then the meat will burn. By covering the pit you maintain a constant temperature that is perfect for cooking.

Cooking Time: This is going to take a while. If you have a very large hog with loads of vegetables (yes you can add these in to the pit too using the same method) you could be looking at the better part of two days. Generally though, the cooking time is going to be around 12 hours. The size of the pit dictated the size of the fire and therefore the amount of heat in the pit. This controls the cooking time. If you built the right size fire you should have about the same amount of time, no matter how much meat you have in the pit. Traditionally the meat goes in the fire at night for eating the next day. Since the meat is tightly wrapped it won't dry out and can tolerate a little overcooking so you have a large window to work with.

"David, is your end of the lake going to do anything special for Christmas this year?" Beverly asked while handing him a beer. *No worries about a DUI or open container these days and David was a careful driver.* She thought to herself

"Wow, where to start on that question. We got plans but they are going in every direction at the moment. That is why we are taking the day off and declaring a bar room discussion over what to do. We were going to do a barn raising, still might, but I don't want folks out in the weather and risking illness or injury. We are talking about sailing up the lake with the boats holiday decorated so nobody takes a pot shot at us. Stewart suggested maybe parading over to the trade post and having some type of festivity Bernie has planned. Jack said we should dress up Boudreaux as the Grinch and do a play.." David said slipping in a jibe that hadn't even been mentioned at the wily old man next to him.

"What is a Grinch? Me no Grinch. how you play a Grinch?" Boudreaux asked suspiciously, thinking it was some type of Scrooge character.

"It's a Christmas cartoon character." Beverly said chuckling and kidding him he would make a very good one, before changing the subject.

"I got some plum preserves that would go right fine with that pig y'all got cooking, or better yet I can make my special dipping sauce if we get back early enough." Beverly said making an offer, but also encouraging them to not stay too long doing the one more, one more time, with their drinks.

"Yum, I love that stuff, I will help you push them out the door." Stewart said ,not to be denied his favorite treat that could make even shoe leather taste good.

"I got some apple sauce and mom said she was making herb bread" David volunteered.

"I got some Goat Cheese that been aging, go nice with that bread." Boudreaux said indicating he wouldn't be too hard to get out of the bar today in anticipation of a fine meal being created.

"I doubt the trade post has any stale bread, but get some Beverly if they do. I will put Betsy on the task of making French Onion soup." David said waiting for Boudreaux to chime in.

"French? She no Frenchman, I see you make a funny at poor old Boudreaux again, but Boudreaux know what that kind of soup you speak of. Beverly, you got any parmesan cheese to make it the magnifique? I now have a craving for it, David you old Devil. I pay for fresh bread too, if we have also to do it." Boudreaux said making his best chefs face of tasting a perfect dish.

"I got some parmesan, David ought to have plenty though, he been buying it up for the spaghetti he loves so much." Beverly said kidding David about preferring just cheese and butter often times on his noodles.

"I will trade you some of that roasted sesame seed confection HopSing made for it." David said knowing he could appeal to Beverly's sweet tooth and save his stash of one of the hardest foodstuffs he had to replace.

"You got some of that? You got to bring that man down to the lake one day David. He can play in my kitchen anytime. Martha is missing out by not learning his tricks. Boudreaux, you find me lots of sesame seeds for my present this year, OK?" Beverly said suddenly being all sweet to him.

"I find you some Mon Cheri; David has honey by the way." Boudreaux said slyly and poked at David's ribs causing him to veer on the road.

"Damn, Boudreaux! Don't be poking at me while I am driving. I will give you some to take with you Bev, but only if I get some flap jacks in the morning and you convince Stewart to donate a jar of that apple butter Martha made up to put on them." David said and Stewart stiffened about being pulled into an unexpected barter.

"You, leave Stewart to me, so we got a deal?" Beverly said not even consulting Stewart.

"Deal!' David said laughing at Stewarts feigned indignation of being usurped by him.

The happy foursome drove along about another 10 minutes, laughing and joking with each other about meaningless things until they had arrived at the tavern. They were getting out of the car still full of merriment when everyone stopped in their tracks to hear the drifting sounds of a song trickling out of the closed doors of the tavern.

"A deep operatic baritone mans voice that sounded a lot like Jim Nabors, was lustily singing in perfect tempo an old Christmas favorite to the accompaniment of a guitar and a trumpet."

God rest ye merry, gentlemen,
Let nothing you dismay,
Remember Christ our Savior
Was born upon this day;
To save us all from Satan's power
When we were gone astray.

[And then a Chorus broke out from the bars occupants]

O tidings of comfort and joy,
Comfort and joy,
O tidings of comfort and joy!

David carefully pulled the door open, and let the beautiful notes of the music flow across the lake. Goat Man was standing by it and motioned them in while hugging his pretty wife Shelly. The late arrivals following David's lead to what must be a Xmas party stood in awe inside the door listening to the finish of one song and start of another song

Do You Hear What I Hear?

Said the night wind to the little lamb
Do you see what I see?
'Way up in the sky, little lamb
Do you see what I see?

A star, a star
Dancing in the night
With a tail as big as a kite
With a tail as big as a kite

Said the little lamb to the shepherd boy

Do you hear what I hear?
Ringing thru the sky, shepherd boy
Do you hear what I hear?

A song, a song
High above the tree
With a voice as big as the sea
With a voice as big as the sea

Said the shepherd boy to the mighty king
Do you know what I know?
In your palace warm, mighty king
Do you know what I know?

A Child, a Child
Shivers in the cold
Let us bring Him silver and gold
Let us bring Him silver and gold

Said the king to the people ev'rywhere
Listen to what I say!
Pray for peace, people ev'rywhere
Listen to what I say!

The Child, the Child
Sleeping in the night
He will bring us goodness and light
He will bring us goodness and light

"Outstanding. really outstanding!" David remarked loudly, still in awe of the scene his people had walked in on. Who is that man singing? He sounds like old Jim Nabors. Irregardless what folks say about his personal life, I liked his voice and songs." David said clapping with everybody else at the wonderful performance.
"It is Chorus night; we are practicing for the pageant" Goat Man said and then added that the clinkers I had heard, were just regulars joining in on the songs.
"Hi, great rendition, you got a good voice; name's David." He said proffering his hand and not waiting on further introduction but Goat Man had disengaged himself from his wife and was following closely.

"David, he brought in a 15 meter sailboat a few days ago full of trade goods," Goat Man said giving David a heads up before the introduction was complete.

"Charlie Flanagan is the name, pleased to meet you." He responded warmly shaking David's hand.

"You didn't happen to get that boat at Lanier sailing school did you?" David asked, thinking some other community had cleaned out all the useful vessels he was about to go after.

"No she is mine. I raced that school before though. Won too, but not because I was fastest. Races are run under the Rules of the U.S. Sailing Association and use the Portsmouth Handicap, so the different boat classes are scored as equals. The best skipper wins, even if he has a slow class boat" Charlie said sipping on his drink and then studying

David for a moment.

"I am sorry to be so blunt, I am losing my manners here, we had thought to salvage a few of those boats from that school, if no one had thought of it yet." David replied looking back at the man equally intently.

"They never had a boat as big as mine there as part of their fleet. I haven't sailed by that marina since the storm hit, or seen one of their boats out on the lake. I did hear tell that Kowaliga, where they are moored has had a lot of problems though, and so I've been staying away from there." Charlie said interested in what David was up to with his line of questioning.

"What kind of problems?" Goat Man asked settling down at the table with them.

"They are at kind of a cross roads for people leaving the cities. They have had some conflicts is all I heard and one little war with some armed group coming through the area. I only heard bits and pieces of rumors coming my way. I heard of this trading post about a month ago and me and my men checked it out first before we sailed our goods in. It seems like you all are the only ones with any pretense of keeping up civilization in these parts.

"It ain't been easy, but we are trying. It seems you arrived at an opportune moment for the choir I didn't know we had until today." David said enjoying the thought of what he called long-laker's (because they came from far down the lake) coming to the post to gather around folks trying to reconstruct a society.

"Oh I sing in the woods to scare the snakes and

bears out of my way, so I figured when we come into port, me and the crew would be singing a little ditty to relax folks as to our intentions. We came in on a Sunday and heard this here chorus from afar and started singing the same song as them like we were sneaking into a church service. That made it easy, sure beats what I had in mind to be bellowing." Charlie said grinning.

"He was going to be singing "What do you do with a drunken sailor" Goat Man said laughing already knowing the punch line.

"That would have been a comedy of errors if you had caught the preacher giving a sermon." Stewart said bring a round of drinks over and introducing himself and Boudreaux.

"Guys, your hospitality knows no bounds, but I got to be sailing before the weather locks me in and the sun goes down" Charlie said motioning to his crew to finish up and get ready to go.

"I look forward to seeing you again, safe sailing." David replied and then asked the old captain what he thought was going on with the weather.

"Well there is an old saw, I tend to follow. In North America:

> *Red sky at night, sailor's delight,*
> *Red sky at morning, sailors take warning.*

In the United Kingdom and the Republic of Ireland:

> *Red sky at night, shepherd's delight,*
> *Red sky in morning, shepherd's warning.*

There is some kind of storm brewing I have no idea about, it's been red morning, noon and night today and its well near nigh that I be getting along. I think we're going to have us a blizzard, as weird as that sounds; but 40yrs of sailing says batten down my hatches and head for home. I would have been gone hours ago, but I think this Christmas celebration is the most important and meaningful thing we can do right now for our fellow man, so I stayed. But now, the singings done and the party's over. I will see you again soon, goodnight." Charlie said and he and his crew left the tavern and made sail.

"I wish he could have hung around longer, I had some trade parlay to discuss." Boudreaux said to David and Stewart staring at the door, the same as he was as the crew departed.

"Me too. Hey Goat Man, we doing the hog in the ground thing this evening; you and your lovely lady want to come to our end of the lake and spend the evening with us?" David asked.

"We'll be having Plum sauce on the pork." Stewart said temptingly and almost drooling.

"What do you think Shelly, sounds like a fine end of the day for me?" Goat man said regarding his wife.

"You going to behave Boudreaux? I ain't forgot about you and David talking my hubby into trying to ride a fire hose, when you got that pump working and you turned it up full steam." Shelly said to the pair who looked chagrined at one of their drunken pranks gone astray.

"We behave. You blame that David though, he told me to crank up the pressure on that hose. We were just playing, we didn't mean for him to look like he was going to outer space riding the thing though. But no one hurt, and it was funny as hell." Boudreaux said with a wink towards David and an obvious wince from Goat Man as he remembered how his butt felt when he landed.

"You can stay at moms and we will be good." David said laying out the groundwork for a peaceful night of just eating well and riding herd on his and Boudreaux's penchant for pranks.

"Ok then, I am in. I got a few jars of watermelon pickles that Sara put up to donate to the cause and there is some hot mustard I made if anyone wants a sandwich later or with their dinner." Shelly said hugging the Goat Man.

"Hey, it's snowing outside!" a customer said wandering in. Several of the Tavern's occupants went to see, but David just grumbled to himself and remembered what the old captain had told him about expecting inclement weather.

It has been a human desire for millennia to make accurate weather predictions. Oral and written history is full of rhymes, anecdotes, and adages meant to guide the uncertain in determining whether the next day will bring fair or foul weather. For the farmer wanting to plant crops, for the merchant about to send ships on trade, foreknowledge of tomorrow's circumstances might mean the difference between success and failure.

"Oh cheer up Dave; you got that nice warm truck to drive home in. At least you ain't riding in the sidecar of a motorcycle like I am about to do." Shelly said starting to bundle up.

"We got room for all, put that old three-wheeler in Bernie's warehouse and ride with us Goat Man. You got to ride in the back with the bug out bags, but that truck has a hell of a heater in it and you won't be getting the sniffles by being silly." David remarked.

"I think I will take you up on that. We can have a couple more drinks and I can talk to the choirmaster before we leave about what song his group is supposed to be singing, when I got to make an entrance wearing that stupid Santa suit and Bernie impersonating an elf in that leprechaun outfit of his." Goat Man said half kidding and half serious.

"Oh, you been dying to play St. Nick for the kiddies; don't be acting like you think its some kind of imposition." Shelly chided him.

"It will be fun, but how the hell did I get stuck with a leprechaun in my sidecar? I thought you playing Missus Claus is a better idea." Goat Man said with a smile that showed he was actually amused at the whole planned event.

"I am going to be Mrs. Claus, just not riding in for the kids to see Santa's arrival. I got to bring him his sled and reindeer in one of those Roland specials dog carts later on. By the way David, you tell Bubba that Harley can be a reindeer, but he ain't pulling my sled and neither is Boudreaux's Bear dog. Those two see something interesting to chase or their masters whistle and I would be on the bob sled ride from hell and I don't trust any of you all not to help make it happen," Shelly said reminding him of his promise that everyone was supposed to behave on that special day.

"I will be the only Santa with a ball bat not meant for a gift if they instigate something." Goat Man said wagging his finger and touching his nose like Santa Claus warning kids to behave, because he knows when you are naughty or nice.

"We agreed we ain't even drinking that day, leastwise until the kids are out of the area. Enough said!" Boudreaux complained and headed towards the door to see what had everyone's attention.

"Aurora Borealis" David overheard someone standing at the door say about the sky being lit up with colored lights.

"Ah hell, not again!" David said jumping up and rushing outside.

It was a seen of wonder that transfixed all of those watching it, as greens and purple hues began to dance across the sky.

Not again! Not again! David muttered to himself while doing a fast paced walk to his car after pulling on Stewart's shirt to follow him. David stuck the key in the ignition and tried it one time. NOTHING! Repeated attempts showed the same results.

"We screwed again Stewart." David said dejectedly and went to the back end to off load his bug out bag that at least this time he had with him.

"CME?" Stewart said looking at the sky and the aftermath of another Coronal Mass Ejection (CME).

"Yup! That's what normally causes the Northern Lights effects we see." David said and feeling like he was going to cry.

All the hard work, all the bright moments in the

recovery process gone in an instant. His solar panels, his portable ice machine, his truck, the radio, gone in an instant.

"Goat Man, try that cycle of yours to start." David yelled to him.

"It's not? Oh hell." he said to his confused wife and David as he tried to use the battery start ignition on his iron horse.

"Got nothing." Goat Man said eying his melted wiring when he had a chance to look for obvious failures in circuitry.

"No Piggy pudding or plum sauce today" Stewart said reminding David that it was a 40 mile walk to home now.

"Oh crap! I am definably in the dark ages now. The bread making machines were probably plugged in. All the houses that he and Jack had run solar lighting to were now dead in the water. Speaking of which, was the "Light In the Lake" connected when this nemeses hit? Time would tell if the light in the lake would ever shine again.

The End

A star, a star
Dancing in the night
With a tail as big as a kite
With a tail as big as a kite

The Season Of The Solar Storm: Christmas Dreams and A Preppers Nightmare

Ron Foster

USA

1

Back out of the saddle

The beauty of the sky's Aurora stood in stark contrast to the fearful moods of the once again stranded survivors of nature's temperament.

"Well buddy, welcome to the world of we ain't got shit again Stewart. No, I take that back, we don't have a working vehicle again at the moment, that's obvious and our most pressing need. However, we also have most likely lost all of our last little bits of technology, that we were reviving from the last go round with mean old Mr. Sun. Looking on the bright side though, at least we are not stuck in the middle of the interstate with no where to go again, so I had better count my blessings and inventory what I got this go round." David said while trying to figure out what the next appropriate move would be. A new solar flare had just whacked his unprotected vehicle's electronics and disabled any electric modern conveniences all over again.

"It would have to start snowing at the same time, wouldn't it?" Stewart said with a bitter tone in his voice that didn't suit his 'oh hell, but what the hell, let's have some tea?' demeanor of accepting the bad, but making light of the situation by taking a thoughtful break and brewing up his favorite beverage.

"I say we that get our prep gear in order and go back in the bar and get drunker than owl shit and decide what to do about this in the morning, you got any better ideas?" David said pulling out his 72 hour kit and also an ALICE backpack with longer term survival items in it.

"If we are talking about me and you possibly walking back to your end of the lake tomorrow, we best reconsider that strongly. You got any way of knowing how much it's going to snow from this freak weather?" Stewart said scavenging around in the back of the 4x4 Jimmy for anything that might be useful and grabbing an old wool army blanket that had seen its better days.

"You got me on that one, I don't have a trick for predicting snowfall, I am a southerner remember" David said eyeing the gray sky and trying to interpret its chances of more snow from the times he had lived in Maine or Alaska, but nothing came to mind to try to guesstimate what the weather might do.

"You got your bug out stuff with you Stewart or did you ass up and leave it back at camp?" David said to Stewart as he checked out the loose bits of gear David was going to leave behind because of weight.

"No I got it, however I never got around to upgrading to a winter version and I find myself lacking a bunch of essentials." Stewart said sheepishly and waited on David to fuss at him how many times he had been told to do it.

"I got extra wool socks and a few other things I can share." David said too tired to even grouse at Stewart's lack of preparedness.

"Let's go see what the Goat Man wants to do, its closer to get to your house than Roland's, but Roland has horses and that engineer John, most likely has several engines in some kind of vehicle that won't be affected by this crap." Stewart contemplated and looked in David's direction for further thoughts or insights on the subject.

"Well, going to Roland's does have some merit; that is, if we were just thinking of borrowing a vehicle possibly or taking a questionable off chance he would be traveling in our direction to help us out. Hopefully he would pick us up before we had to travel too many miles. But no, I think we best just sit tight until the weather breaks and head for home whenever somebody from my compound decides to come get us in a sailboat. Jack and Bubba are more than likely knee deep in comforting the women and making plans for our eventual rescue anyway. Sherry probably needs a restraint jacket put on her to keep her from setting sail already, so like I said, we might as well get cross-eyed and ride the storm out in the tavern." David said looking towards Boudreaux and GM comparing notes on the tavern porch, while their significant others held their own conversation a short distance away.

"That sounds most practical David, the perimeter guards will most likely be coming in soon, or looking for us to send someone with directions. It's hard to tell how devoted to duty those men are times. They being civilians and following their own minds most of the time, tells me they be in soon. Nobody is going to want stay in a tent in a snow camp very long, especially if they have never done it before. I suspect they will be trickling in by ones and twos next day or so, or sooner if we get anything that sticks and makes an inch or two of powder on the ground." Stewart said walking towards the tavern and throwing his hands up in mock dismay to Boudreaux and Goat Man who were looking in their direction as they approached.

"It be a sorry day indeed Davy boy." Boudreaux said petting his old hound that seemed to be enjoying all the excitement about the snow regardless of how it was upsetting the humans.

"Well, the last time this shit happened, I was in a bar and left; this time I get to enjoy being stranded in one!" David said lightening the mood and causing everyone to chuckle.

"Yeah, it sure could have been much worse, it could have whacked us on the way going or coming to the trading post and stranding us on the wood trail." Beverly said giving Boudreaux a hug and evidently being very happy they were together this time to face whatever the cards dealt them for fortune or misery to deal with as a team.

"Don't even talk about it being stranded in the forest, I am not the Daniel Boone or Davy Crockett sort to have been stuck playing lost in the wilderness or going on a cross country hike. I found out what my first fire ant was recently and I don't think I would care to make acquaintances with the other denizens of the woods I hear you all talk about that live out there." Stewart said pulling his coat collar up against the chill wind that had started up even more fiercely.

"Let's go ahead and move inside." GM said as he ushered the group and his wife towards the tavern door and the warmth of a roaring fire." Nothing good will come of us standing out here and wondering about the weather and freezing for no reason, Boudreaux, if my tab is good, I will buy everyone a round ".GM said looking in his direction as the entered the door.

"Today, the drinks be on the house and no stupid needing a ladder jokes, David." Boudreaux said grinning in my direction and creating a cheer from the leftover patrons in the bar that had not left for their homes yet or were stranded there.

"Well brands only!" Boudreaux expressed loudly to keep the revealers from getting into the finer stocks of liquor for free; meaning only standard bar brands would be touched.

"What are you going to do GM?" David asked wondering what he and his wife Shelly had planned.

"I guess we are going to stay for this blizzard party of yours for as long as it lasts. I haven't thought too much further than that. I will monkey with that motorcycle in the next day or two and see if I can get her running. I can't quite wrap my mind around where to start trouble shooting it yet, nor even if there are some kinds of make-do parts around here I can use to get it running again." GM said wistfully, as his concerned wife gave him a pat of assurance that she was confident he would come up with a plan of some kind to set things in a better resemblance of straight for them.

"You could sail with me to our end of the lake when my folks come to get us, or maybe there is someone from the guards that has a go-cart or something to get you back to Roland's instead of hoofing it." David offered, concerned about his friends.

"There is no way in hell I am going to try to hike it back to Roland's. First off, I don't have the field gear with me for that and secondly, why leave here? Someday or another Bernie and Roland will get around to heading this way and give us some transportation back. The guest house at this post I hear is full, so it might not be a bad idea to do our waiting on your end of the lake David. Let's discuss it and create some plans throughout the night." Goat Man said overwhelmed with what had just gone on and the fix he and his wife had just found themselves in.

"We will ride with you David when your people come. The Goat Man and his lady can stay upstairs in my place here as long as they want." Boudreaux said giving GM free rein of his tavern and the tiny apartment on top of it for them to stay in.

"Do me a favor. If this hard winter weather stays with us, we will not be traipsing or sailing over here from the other side of the lake until early spring. When Roland finally gets down this way, I want you to get him to get us one more supply drop from the general store, before we get socked in for the winter." David said to GM and dreading the implications of that statement for all the residents on his end of the lake who were dependant on the trade goods that so far had been managed to be scraped up, and made available to supplement the meager stores and hunting efforts in his community.

"I will look out for you all and advise Roland. Give Shelly a list of what you might think will carry you over for the winter and we Roland and I will do the Valley Forge run to tide you over at least once this winter." Goat Man said not relishing the thought of traveling 40 miles in an open wagon in this bitter cold to ensure that the outward residents had one last roll of the dice, before it became too unhealthy to consider traveling the roads with harsh winds and damp cold all about.

"I would really appreciate that, I am guessing that we are not going to be going out of the houses much further than our trap lines in the days to come and this weird weather is going to have a lot of the animals we depend on for food, staying close to their own lodges." David said wondering about the already depleted game in his area and the ability to depend on them for food close to home.

"This really sucks, we had big plan for a Christmas celebration, now we worry about getting home and having a crust of bread.' Boudreaux said with dismay and looked to Beverly and his hound Bear for comfort.

"Hard decisions and no hopes in sight, that's for sure." David lamented, thinking about possibly having to refuse to share food with the needy residents around the lake, who had become a close knit community that he would normally readily share with. Times being what they were and that were soon going to be worse; austerity, whether he liked it or not, had to be considered. He had been wrestling with himself mentally for days already thinking about the upcoming Christmas celebration. He had been considering if he wanted to share the last two cans of freeze dried turkey he had jealously guarded and saved for the occasion with anyone other than his small group he lived with. A lavish holiday feast was not a smart thing to do anymore, especially if the supply chain was getting cut off. That little bit of turkey was not going to stretch that far anyways amongst the community members, more a symbolic gesture of Dave's goodwill than anything else. David had not seen sign of wild turkey in months and he doubted he would see tracks anytime soon in his area. He had often thought of going to better hunting grounds and leaving the hungry mouths of the community draining the resources and his energy behind him. But these were just the fleeting, momentary, crazy thoughts that pass through anyone's mind when other people become too reliant on the producers in times of adversity to supply them goods or sustenance. There were a lot of different types of folks needing help these days. There were the people that David and the few other hunters and trappers on the lake supplied with game obtained that worked on projects while they were out in the field. Then, there were the lazy worthless souls staying back in the camps that did not contribute anything to the pot or efforts to improve conditions and that had always been a bone of contention and rivalry; but one that made animosity towards them much worse when game was scarce and bellies were empty.

Sharing was always a virtue most folks didn't mind; but now everyone challenged the size of portions and weighed the thought to even do so minimally. The decision to leave someone behind should never have to be considered, but these days it was getting weighed more often than not and was a big cause of concern and dissent. David had hoped the spirit of Christmas coming on would have lessoned the angst amongst the community members, but with this latest threat to challenge everyone's wellbeing, it was clear that was not going to happen.

2

Cold Tavern

"Boudreaux, get some of your help to drag in more wood and find some tarps or something for the woodpiles." David suggested.

"I got a bad feeling about this weather. It could be just a seasonal thing. It snows in Alabama about once every five years and usually doesn't stick but for a day or two. On the other hand, they proved awhile back that solar storms can adversely have an effect on the weather. Europe's 'Little Ice Age' they say was triggered or worsened by a reduction in solar intensity. They attributed this to ultraviolet rays. Now let's look at this with an added twist, solar physicists were surprised by the *lack* of solar activity at the start of this 24th solar cycle, leading to some scientists to speculate we might be on the verge of another Maunder minimum and 'Little Ice Age'. This was in stark contrast to NASA solar physicist's 2006 prediction that this cycle will be a 'doozy' for the 2012-2013 solar maximum.

This leads me to conclude that we still have a long way to go when predicting solar flare events and I started prepping even more towards both events. Loss of technology and a mini ice age occurring closely together." David said probably as confused about all the ins and outs of solar events as the experts and his listeners were. He hoped he didn't have to try to explain about X-ray solar flares versus a CME emissions being only part of the story.

"I have heard of the Little Ice Age from history, is that a similar thing to the mini one you are thinking of?" GM asked.

"Yes somewhat, we will have to get the Weatherman to give us some more science info on that, but basically it just lasts a shorter amount of time.

"How long can it last?" Shelly asked.

"I don't exactly know, maybe up to 5yrs? The coldest period of the Little Ice Age, between 1645 and 1715, has been linked to a deep dip in solar storms known as the Maunder Minimum. We got lots of activity that seems odd to me to compare to." David said contemplating a notion that had just come to mind.

"Hang on a second folks; let me ponder something here for a second." David said signaling the barmaid for another drink.

"Solar Storms don't affect us EMP wise the same as say as the ones generated from a nuclear burst. We get a geomagnetic storm that generates an E3 wave that is the most troublesome with electronics." David said reaching for his new drink and taking a big gulp before continuing.

"Scientifically speaking it shouldn't be shutting cars down without much electronics like it did. I asked John the engineer how he had managed to get a new diesel engine running awhile back and he told me he just used a short length of wire and some alligator clips to bypass the glow plugs that were affected. That got me too thinking, Goat Man you got that CB radio of yours directly hooked to your battery and antennae so most likely that antennae acted like a lighting rod. My truck has the same problem and I bet it just blew out my ignition fuses and maybe my voltage regulator. I say if we can get parts and a new battery, we possibly could be back up in running in an hour or two when we find what we need!" David exclaimed excitedly.

"That makes sense; I didn't have that CB until recently. The last time this crap happened I wasn't affected at all. It sounds like your theory is pretty sound. I see a fix in progress. I still can't figure out what just got us though." Gm said scratching his head on two notions going on at once.

"Scientists didn't realize that a solar flare can get picked up in a solar wind and actually accelerate and change its composition as it can also pick up cosmic magnetic and radioactive dust and plasma on the way. During solar maximum (when the Sun is at its most active), the Earth may be unlucky enough to be staring down the barrel of an explosion with the energy of 100 billion Hiroshima-sized atomic bombs. This explosion is known as a solar flare CMEs are slower than the propagation of X-rays, but their global effects here on Earth can be more problematic. They may not travel at the speed of light, but they still travel fast; they can travel at a rate of 2 million miles per hour (3.2 million km/hr), meaning they may reach us in a matter of hours. We got lots of possibilities going on here that might have never occurred or been considered before. Cripes, the experts have been changing their minds over what is or is not possible for the last 10yrs when they just started really becoming aware of and studying these things." David said waving off further questions on his conjectures because he had no more answers.

"So, you think this cold spell and snow is going to last then?" Gm said speculatively.

"It could, I got no idea how impassable the roads might get with the wind blowing off the lake and all this tree cover. I suggest you be dang careful if we get up and running and watch out for black ice on the roads." David said watching two roving guards coming in the tavern and kicking snow off their shoes.

"Hey, one of you go and get Silas over at the general store for me please." David said referring to the elderly manager of the trading post and the youngest guard went grumbling to do his bidding.

The oldest of the pair came over to the table and shivering in his threadbare layered up clothes announced it was colder than a well digger's ass out there and he doubted we shouldn't have much worry about any raiders tonight.

"For once I agree with you, but you might see a lot of folks trying to make it over here to safety, if they were out on the roads. Warm up a bit and then get ready to go back out, or send some of your younger guards out to pull in the perimeter guards to the bunkhouse. Keep the guard shacks manned though on the two main roads coming in." David said to the crestfallen troopers dreams of hanging out in the bar tonight.

"What the hell you got on anyway bud? I thought as sergeant of the guard you would have some better duds to be wearing out in this weather David said standing to address the man.

"It was summer when this crap hit, I got on multiple shirts and a raincoat, with a towel for a scarf" the man begin before Boudreaux cut him off.

"He had him a good coat we issued him, but he gambled it away. Didn't you, Barger?" Boudreaux said referring to him by his last name, to which the man shamefully hung his head.

"Yea I did. Stupid of me. No excuse." Barger said knowing David would have a lot to say about it, but avoiding or reducing a tongue lashing by giving a proper military response instead of giving whining made up excuses that were meaningless to the problem noted.

"You know when I was in the service you could get an article 15 for getting a sunburn or a tattoo? Your body belonged to the military and if you screwed it up by neglect or stupidity they made you suffer for it. I a going to have some mercy on you today, because you look like you have been suffering enough; but we going to have a talk about this later. I will tell Silas to give you a voucher for another coat and some better winter wear, but I tell you one thing, if you were not Sergeant of The Guard I would stick you wearing that multicolor women's jacket I just got in and make an example out of your dumb ass. As it stands, you can go warm up over at the general store. You got all your issued ammo or did you bet that too?" David said glaring at the shorter man.

"I would never bet my weapon, ammo, or knife." The man said indignantly.

"Don't cop no attitude, any one that would bet their clothes needs asking the question. If you had I would can you on the spot. Now get out of here!" David said pointing at the door.

"Quit smirking Stewart, I know it's not the Army any more, but it might as well be." David said sitting down in his chair but still steaming at the man's incompetence in taking care of himself.

"I just like how you can turn on and off that drill sergeant look you get at times." Stewart said chuckling.

"You are pretty good at." Beverly said and then imitated a stern David pointing at the door and giving him an at ease position military stance, which caused everyone to laugh at the mockery directed at him.

"Ok, I see how you trainees are going to be. Boudreaux don't you need some new KP help for your kitchen?" David said joking.

Just then Silas came bustling in the door and walked over to their table.

"David, why the hell did you have to drag me out in the cold to just tell me to issue a man a jacket?" Silas said looking miffed.

"I didn't, we have other things to discuss. But, while we are on the subject, give him a good one, but charge him double for it. Maybe the hit to his pocket book as well as the cold will make him value it better." David replied and motioned for Silas to have a seat.

"So, what's on your mind?" Silas said after grumbling he had things to tend too back at his store and why couldn't an assistant handle the trader's problems.

"Silas this latest little snafu here has caused us a change in plans." David said motioning at his fellow traders around the table.

"We have had bad weather before, David you know how Alabama weather is. This snow won't be here long. I already sent folks out to pull the guards back, but left a few out to look for your messengers or any travelers that got stuck out in the weather." Silas said complaining still.

"In case you didn't notice, we got no power..." David began before Silas chimed in he had a man working on the diesel generator and battery banks.

"Silas, you danged old office rat! We just had another Solar Storm it appears. Everything is whacked again." David said thumping his glass a bit hard down on the table.

"You got to be kidding?" Silas said peering over his glasses at the front window of the bar that didn't show anything but steady snow to him.

"Mr. Sun threw up again on us." Boudreaux said waving his hand around the room that was just lit up by the various candles and lanterns placed about.

"Well I'll be damned! When? About 2 hours ago the generator quit. Oh, then huh?" Silas said still shaken that he hadn't noticed anything else, but loss of power he had thought was due to snow affecting wiring or the engine.

"We got beaucoup (also boo·coos or boo·koos, meaning abundance, a lot) problems to discuss right here, now sit! Before I stuff you in an onion sack and make you listen." Boudreaux told Silas as he tried to go back to his store to solve problems closer to his hearth.

Silas begrudgingly sat down and listened while David laid out his worries about the weather and told him that this was an unofficial trader's court that could override his authority, if he didn't listen and agree to what the assemblage of traders having goods in his warehouse wanted.

"David, this is not necessary. I tell you the snow won't stick." Silas said looking alarmed.

"You got a barometer at the store? No? Ok let's do an experiment then. I won't know today, but I will start getting me some indications. Anyone got a balloon or a condom?" David said trying to remember his third grade science projects. We got to figure out what this weather is doing." David said while starting to construct a simple contraption.

Aim: To make a Homemade Barometer using simple materials.

Materials Required:

1. A balloon
2. Colored water
3. A straw
4. Tape
5. A piece pf paper
6. Rubber band
7. A jar

Procedure:

1. Cut the balloon in half.
2. Cover the top of the jar with the balloon piece like a lid with the help of a rubber band so that it is completely air tight.
3. Take the straw and attach it horizontally with the rubber lid of the jar in such a way that 1/4th of the straw stays on the lid.
4. Place the jar near the paper and mark the height of the tip of the straw on the paper each day.
5. Compare the markings with the previous days.

Scientific Explanation:

The pressure inside the jar is constant as we sealed it. So when the atmospheric pressure i.e., the pressure outside the jar, increases it pushes the rubber lid into the can. As a result the tip of the straw goes up (Note that the edge of the lid opening acts as a fulcrum). So if the markings are higher than that was in the previous day, the atmospheric pressure is high and vice versa.

Home made barometer

David explained to the group several methods also that did not take an instrument to predict weather, but an observation.

"Long before technology was developed to predict the weather people had to rely on observation, patterns and folk lore to avoid being caught off guard by the elements. If your plans, livelihood or even your survival depend on the weather, it certainly wouldn't hurt to become familiar with some of these methods, especially since you never know when you might be out of touch with the local weather report. These methods aren't foolproof, but they have their usefulness." David said as he tinkered.

Check the grass for dew at sunrise. If the grass is dry, this indicates clouds or strong breezes, which can mean rain. If there's dew, it probably won't rain that day. However, if it rained during the night, this method will not be reliable.

Remember the rhyme: "Red sky at night, sailor's delight; Red sky at morning, sailors take warning." Look for any sign of red in the sky (not a red sun); it will not be a bold orange or red the majority of the time, but that depends a little on where you live.

Sailor's delight

If you see a red sky during sunset, (when you're looking to the west), there is a high pressure system with dry air that is stirring dust particles in the air, causing the sky to look red. Since prevailing front movements and jet streams weather usually move from west to east (see Tips), the dry air is heading towards you.

A red sky in the morning (in the East, where the sun rises) means that the dry air has already moved past you, and what follows behind it (on its way towards you) is a low pressure system that carries moisture.

Look for a rainbow in the west. This is the result of the rising sun's morning rays from the east striking moisture in the west. Most major storm fronts travel west to east, and a rainbow in the west means moisture, which can mean rain is on its way. On the other hand, a rainbow in the east around sunset means that the rain is on its way out and you can look forward to sunny days. Remember: Rainbow in the morning, need for a warning.

Detect which direction the wind is blowing. If unable to immediately detect the wind's direction, throw a small piece of grass in to the air and watch its descent. Easterly winds can indicate an approaching storm front, westerly winds the opposite. Strong winds indicate high pressure differences, which can be a sign of advancing storm fronts. Deciduous trees show the undersides of their leaves during unusual winds, supposedly because they grow in a way that keeps them right-side up during typical prevalent winds.

Take a deep breath. Close your eyes and smell the air.

Plants release their waste in a low pressure atmosphere, generating a smell like compost and indicating an upcoming rain.

Swamps will release gasses just before a storm because of the lower pressure, which leads to unpleasant smells.

A proverb says "Flowers smell best just before a rain." Scents are stronger in moist air, associated with rainy weather.

Check for humidity. Many people can feel humidity, especially in their hair (it curls up and gets frizzy). You can also look at the leaves of oak or maple trees. These leaves tend to curl in high humidity, which tends to precede a heavy rain. Pine cone scales remain closed if the humidity is high, but open in dry air. Under humid conditions, wood swells (look out for those sticky doors) and salt clumps (is that shaker working well?).

Watch the clouds.

Clouds going in different directions (e.g. one layer going west, another layer going north) - bad weather coming, probably hail.

Cumulonimbus clouds early in the day and developing throughout the day - greater chances of severe weather.

Mammatus cloud formations

Mammatus cloud (formed by sinking air) - can form with both severe and nonsevere thunderstorms as well as other cloud types

Cirrus fibratus, aka "mare's tail"

Cirrus clouds high in the sky like long streamers - bad weather within the next 36 hours

Altocumulus mackerel sky

Altocumulus clouds like mackerel scales - bad weather within the next 36 hours. The old sailor's saying for these types of clouds is "Mares tails and mackerel scales, tall ships carry short sails." Another is "Mackerel skies and mare's tails, sailors furl their sails." Mackerel skies and mares tails formations sometimes appear in the same sky. When that happens, rain is sure to follow the next day.

Cloud cover on a winter night - expect warmer weather because clouds prevent heat radiation that would lower the temperature on a clear night.

Cumulus towers (cumulus castellanus) - possibility of showers later in the day.

Observe animals. They are more likely to react to changes in air pressure than we are.

If birds are flying high in the sky, there will probably be fair weather. (Falling air pressure caused by an imminent storm causes discomfort in birds' ears, so they fly low to alleviate it. Large numbers of birds roosting on power lines indicates swiftly falling air pressure.)

Seagulls tend to stop flying and take refuge at the coast if a storm is coming.

Animals, especially birds, get very quiet immediately before it rains.

Cows will typically lie down before a thunderstorm. They also tend to stay close together if bad weather's on the way.

Ants build their hills with very steep sides just before a rain.

Cats tend to clean behind their ears before rain.

Turtles often search for higher ground when a large amount of rain is expected. You will often see them in the road during this period (1 to 2 days before the rain).

A very old wives tale says if birds feed in a storm it will rain for a long time, if they don't it will clear soon.

Make a campfire. The smoke should rise steadily. Smoke that swirls and descends is caused by low pressure (i.e. rain on the way).

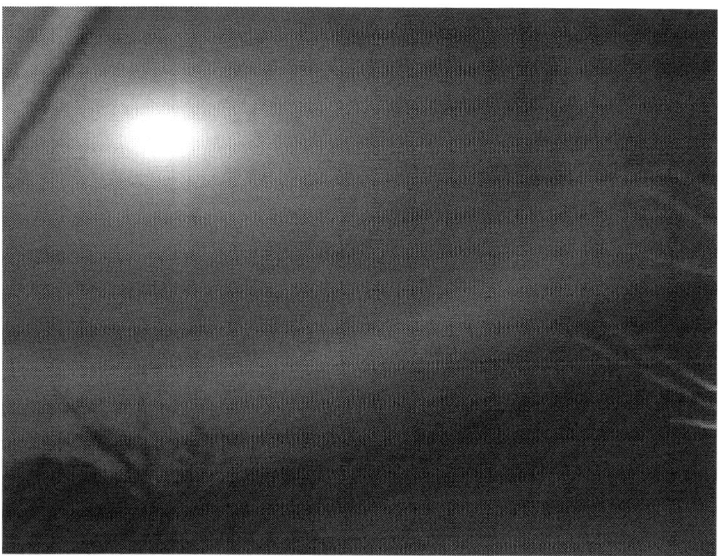

Ring around the moon

Look at the moon during the night. If it is reddish or pale, dust is in the air. But if the moon is bright and sharply focused, it's probably because low pressure has cleared out the dust, and low pressure means rain. Also, a ring around the moon (caused by light shining through cirrostratus clouds associated with warm fronts and moisture) can indicate that rain will probably fall within the next three days. Remember: Circle around the moon, rain or snow soon.

Create your own prediction methods. The methods provided thus far are based around a few key (but very general) principles: Low pressure brings rain, and major weather systems move from west to east. Predicting the weather is all about recognizing the signs of pressure change in your area. While prevailing systems may move from west to east, for example, individual storms in a particular region may not, due to local weather phenomena. Long term residents who spend a great deal of their time outdoors, particularly farmers, commercial fishermen and the like, learn to observe trends that give them clues to long term weather patterns and seasonal changes in their specific geographical location. In the southern United States, for instance, dogwoods are seldom caught off guard by late spring frosts, so when they bloom, you have likely seen the last frost of the season. By being observant, forming hypotheses, and testing your predictions, you can fine-tune your weather predicting abilities beyond what any article could ever instruct

"Now if we had us a real barometer around, we wouldn't be playing about speculating what the weather was going to do next" Stewart said contemplating that David's friend they called the weatherman had exactly what they needed in the form of a real instrument, as well as himself having seen many cheap wall decorations that were still functional in the houses David and he had pillaged on scavenging trips. That was the thing about the lake, folks used them for décor, but he had no idea how they worked or how to read them.

3

Silas Said

"Look Silas, regardless of the weather as it currently stands; we are pulling out our goods for the winter that is if we can figure out transport." David said mindfully and letting the full impact of Stewart, Boudreaux, Dave, their Banker, the community represented moving their trade goods and all the accumulated trade credits they had on the books sink in.

"Why this is worse than a bank run David, I implore you to reconsider." Silas said rubbing his hands together and looking at the agitated stares of those who would be left behind still occupying the bar who had overheard the conversation.

"I didn't say we were going to wipe you out" David said carefully and wishing they had kept their voices lower.

"I am merely saying we are going to make a sizable withdrawal in case this weather remains too obnoxious for travel" David said and did the moving around the room with his eyes thing to indicate this table had too many listeners that didn't need to be included in this discussion.

"Oh now, right then. I know you are reasonable men. We should examine this matter more closely; you had me worried there for a moment. "Silas said, accompanied by much fake response laughter from himself and the table to assuage the fears of the panicky clientele watching their fates being decided.

"We want the wagon I got already packed in my cubicle. I tell Davie, I see blackbirds flying in circles, bad weather coming, and something she is wrong. He no listens, Stewart neither. They send their goods out to other posts with nothing much in stores. Boudreaux smart he kept freight back and now he best trader on lake." The old Cajun said tucking his thumbs into the straps of his overhauls and looking smug.

"You were too hung over to oversee your load going out." Beverly chided before Boudreaux wagged a finger at her.

"No, Mon Cherie hung over...yes. I had a big time night before. Crazy as loon? No, not this old bon gator. Dem birds they got a piece of iron or something in their skulls. It acts like compass and magnet; tells the bird which way to fly, like migration. Them birds were confused, fly in a circle, don't know up from down. I think maybe David tell me geomagnetic storm maybe makes them not see a direction like normal, I did not think of solar storm happening though. Thought maybe thunder storm frazzled their brains. Boudreaux only has 9th grade education, but Boudreaux, he know signs, signs his Pawpaw taught him. Maybe I have iron in my head too, I didn't feel the woods normal this day, no feel for the ways and directions the animals go. I laugh until I got silly at the book David lent me called "Camp Life in the Woods" by Elemental Publishing reprint of that 1800s way of doing the forests business because it remind me of my Pappy's knowledge. It be like you Beverly laughing at the comment some Bjork (stupid person in Cajun) say about your granny cooking book for canning called Every Step in canning, the cold pack method: (Prepper Archeology Collection Edition) printed in the twenties or thirties that he had no value for because not safe for modern folks. Where that ol possum get that from? That book was a bible back then for safe canning and we all still here to prove it! Cold Pack? Folks can't even figure out how to do that no more and it's a fantastic thing to know in a world that lacks ready access to the best modern technology.

'Hell Boudreaux I tried to tell folks about a Zeer pot. Heat rises, and heat will always move toward cooler areas, and if it happens to draw liquid with it, and that liquid evaporates...the inside surface of what just evaporated will be cooler. Solar chimneys, underground cool rooms (the old fashioned cellar), and the zeer pot, are just a few ways that use this to our advantage." David said

The Zeer Pot: $5 Refrigeration Without Electricity

by M.D. Creekmore on Thursday, October 13, 2011

A guest post by Bitsy

Like many preppers, I am always concerned about how to handle refrigeration if the country suddenly goes off grid. Although I don't have any dire needs for cooling—no one in my family needs insulin, we don't have dairy livestock, and ice cream (though necessary in many ways) isn't a survival essential—I do realize that refrigeration could be extremely beneficial in difficult times.

For example, if my family processes a chicken for dinner, refrigeration would allow me to use that chicken for meals on multiple nights (e.g. roast chicken on Monday, chicken casserole on Tuesday, chicken soup on Wednesday) without the worry of spoilage or the need for long-term preservation such as canning or smoking.

In addition, refrigeration also extends the life of fruits and vegetables, which would allow my family to enjoy fresh produce for a longer period of time before long-term preservation became necessary. I feel similarly about dairy. If ever we are able to procure milk and make cottage cheese, I want that cheese to last as long as possible!

In some cases, refrigeration is easy. During the winter months in my mid-Atlantic state, the weather is usually cool enough to preserve food merely by setting it outside in a secure packaging. Anyone who has running water (like a stream or creek) on their property also has easy access to refrigeration. Simply wrap food in a watertight container and sink it in flowing water. But how do you keep your food cool and safe in the middle of a heat wave?

Fortunately, with a few basic and inexpensive supplies, you can construct a pot-in-pot refrigerator that will serve to keep your food at safe temperatures even during the summer months. The pot-in-pot refrigerator—or Zeer Pot—has typically been used in African third world countries in which electricity and other modern conveniences are unavailable.

The creation and subsequent usage of the Zeer Pot has led to a better life for many people in these countries, since reduced food spoilage increases the variety in their diet and helps farmers boost profits. For the prepper, however, the Zeer pot is an inexpensive way to keep food safe when electricity is no longer available to power refrigerators.

Supplies Needed

- Two Clay Pots (one small enough to fit inside the other)
- Clay/Sealer
- Sand
- Towel
- Water

How to make a zeer pot

The inexpensive terra-cotta clay flowerpots sold in nurseries and discount stores are great for use when making a Zeer Pot, although any clay pot will work fine. Make sure the pots you choose are unglazed, since evaporation is essential for the Zeer Pot to properly work.

When choosing your clay pots, the smaller one should fit inside the larger one with some airspace between the walls of the two pots. About an inch of airspace should be enough for most of the typical terra-cotta flower pots, but if you opt for larger pots you may need a little more airspace.

To begin making the zeer pot, plug the holes in the bottom of the pots (if you opted to use flower pots) with clay, silicone sealer, caulk, etc. You can also cover them with tape or anything else that closes the gap.

Place a thin layer of sand—about an inch—in the bottom of the larger clay pot. Then set the smaller pot inside the larger one on top of the sand. Fill the space between the walls of the pots with sand until the sand reaches the top of the smaller pot.

Next, pour water into the sand until the sand is soaked through. A funnel can be useful for this purpose. The sand needs to be completely wet, but it should not be soaked until the water is floating above the sand. It's best to use water that is also pure enough to drink, since the clay walls of the pot are porous. However, if you wish to use water that is not potable for your Zeer Pot, you can glaze the INSIDE of the smaller pot.

Your Zeer Pot is complete! Cover it with a damp towel or an unglazed clay lid. Place the Zeer Pot in a warm spot with plenty of air circulation. Try and avoid any spots that may have high humidity, as this will lessen the pot's effectiveness.

In a few hours, the inside of the ZeerPot should be cool enough for refrigeration. For consistent refrigeration, you'll need to add more water to the sand about twice a day. Depending on outside conditions, the temperature inside a ZeerPot can reach between 15 and 40 degrees.

The Zeer Pot works through evaporation. As the moisture in the sand evaporates, it pulls heat from the innermost and cools the internal temperature of your "refrigerator." This device works best in drier climates. In humid areas, it may be ineffective.

"This is all great info Dave, but you are really putting a hurting on this post. Let's get back to that for a moment. If you and Stewart cash your credits in, what is it that you want in addition to the stock you are making your offers of trade goods rescinded on."? Silas exclaimed looking for his own drink.

"Stewart can fill you in. I will go get you another drink" David said already gathering up glasses on the table.

"Do you have any car and motorcycle batteries?' David heard Stewart say as he ambled up to the bar.

"I want you to free pour a bit for Silas ok?" indicating to Boudreaux's bartender that measured shots were out, and he would appreciate it if the bartender would assist him in pouring more heavily for Silas to make a bad tasting deal go down better for him.

"I got you, happy to help. Silas won't know what hit him." Chuck said grinning and adding an extra measure to all the drinks ordered.

"Hey now, you were supposed to slack off on mine!" David said, while somewhat falsely objecting to an extra strong drink smiling and taking a big swig.

David called Boudreaux to come help him with the drinks after getting his attention and indicating it was an excuse to talk versus a need for actual help.

"Tell Stewart to go to the bathroom or something and we will distract Silas long enough for him to try and get a look at that back storage room he has." David said plotting and scheming.

"Ah! I have been wondering what is in there myself lately." Boudreaux said as he left David to small talk for a minute with the bar patrons.

David returned to the group and handed Silas his drink while noticing his friend Stewart had excused himself and was away from the table on some errand.

David settled in across from Silas to block his view somewhat from the front window and began his banter with the old shopkeeper again.

"You got any grain or flour?" David asked him.

"Well, I am kind of light in that department. Stocks not coming in and the chickens and cattle are getting fed most of the whole or cracked grains. I have maybe about 1100 lbs of flour we can discuss." Silas said stroking his Snidely

Whiplash moustache.

"I thought Roland's railroad kept you a steady supply somewhat?' David said unsure now of how to get the goods he wanted.

"We get very little of that type of item in these days. We mostly are dependant on what the rovers find on trucks on the interstate that broke down. The rail lines might have a 70 car trainload of coal we can't use at the moment blocking access to the rest of the rail line, or a shit load of chemical cars are in the way." Silas said still messing with his moustache and confidant he was going to make some extra dollars off a deal.

"Silas, we have decided to pull most of our goods out of the warehouse and cash in our trade credits for silver so we are well stockpiled to make it through winter and have cash for spring." David said carefully eying the old man.

"What? No need for that." Silas spluttered as a combination of an over strong drink as well as David's unexpected news.

"We think there is a great need for it." Boudreaux said in an even tone.

"If its trade goods you need, then take it in trade, there is little enough hard currency about and I need it for buying from some of the traders." Silas objected and looked very concerned.

"We are traders and we want silver, you can trade us goods for the Bernie bucks we got on the books, but you owe us silver for the balances." David said enjoying making the old skinflint squirm at the thought of having to payout in coin.

"All three of you want cash? Where is Stewart anyway?" Silas said looking around.

"He should be back in a moment. Now then, we know you don't have that much silver on hand so we take gold also. No gems or diamonds etc. though, if all you got is set goods, you can bust the stones out and keep them if you like." Boudreaux said deflecting Silas from inquiring further about Stewart and laying out the terms they wanted.

"Hell, the three of you got over $20,000 on the books in cash, not counting what you have on consignment or notes coming due." Silas said doing a quick mental calculation.

"Its more like $26, 000, you forgot my postal service and my tariff on using my BobCat on Roland's railroad." David said having already done some calculations of the various ventures that the trading post owed him for.

"Dang David, take some more trade stuffs. You are depleting the bank too much. I got to be able to operate." Silas said almost sniveling.

"You said you were low on stock and every time you open that mysterious backroom of yours it costs me double, because you say an item is rare or in short supply. What do you propose to trade? I don't need a bunch of luxury items liked canned blueberries or pickled asparagus, although I will buy some of that off you if you are reasonable." David said knowing he had the upper hand now to negotiate.

"That's right, it's worthless when you buy stuff from us, but gold when you want to sell it" Boudreaux said mockingly and gave Silas an icy stare that caused the poor old shopkeeper to suck down most of his drink in order to not directly look at the agitated Cajun.

"If you're buying in quantity against hard cash, you know you always get a better price." Silas began trying to salvage his profits before David cut him off with a dismissive gesture.

"I told you, we don't need a bunch of gourmet crap. Maybe we get a few little purchases for special Christmas presents, or to change up the diet, but not much more than that. How much real food like Spam or canned ham are you holding out on?" David said lowering his voice so the bar patrons did not overhear.

"Oh I have some to be sure, not much mind you. I got to keep some stock here now to, you can't buy it all." Silas said back to messing about with his mustache as was he won't when he started to price things.

The barmaid came over and replenished everyone's drinks as tensions grew around the table. Stewart came back in announcing that the snow was starting to drift up bad and that one of David's postmen had just come in and handed David two envelopes. The first envelope David dismissed temporarily, it was just his accounting invoice from Philburn's Trading Post, and the second was a personal letter from Dump Truck and Martha. Dump wasn't much of a letter writer and usually got Martha to handle the correspondence for him and tell all the gossip that was happening on the farm after Dump had his say on trade matters. Silas tried to get David to put the letter up for later and continue the negotiations, but David wouldn't here about it and went off to the side to read the note in private first.

Dear David,

I need to request some ammunition from you. The item is in short supply around here now and we are encountering some situations that have required a great deal more of it than we have on hand. Do not worry, everything is under control but you need to send us some common caliber bullets and as much as you can spare.

MeDo had a beautiful baby girl and wants you to thank Sarah for the Motherswort herb and other concoctions Sarah sent. They were most effective but it was a hard birth after all. Mother and Daughter are doing fine now though.

I will be coming to see you in a week and am bringing HeDo with me. We are taking the mule and following the trade wagon, so please think about giving us a ride home later in your truck with the heater lol when its time to come home. You can send the mule back with a trade wagon.

HopSing got grazed on the leg by a bullet that ricocheted off a train that someone else wanted, but it doesn't trouble him much.

Philburn and the Sheriff have given us escorts now to help with bringing back goods and the ammunition I requested is mostly for them.

Martha wants you to come over with Stewart and your group to see the Christmas pageant, if you can. HopSing has managed to trade for two real domestic turkeys he is fatting up and depending on when you come we will butcher one.

Melanie just said she wants to come along and see you and Stewart, so we are discussing transport plans again Lol! HeDo says he can ride his bike and keep up with the mule, but I doubt it, if he gets tired I guess we could throw it up on a trade wagon and he could ride awhile though. Ha! You ready to see that pinkish purple bike again, Dave?

All the best,

Dump, Martha and family.

David was really glad to get the letter, but he thought reading between the lines that things were much worse than Dump had let on. It sounded like they were having more confrontations over disputed goods or the areas they were entering in on scavenging trips had got more dangerous. That was no stretch of the imagination, these were desperate times and more confrontations and necessary caution was inevitable. David just wished Dump had said if it appeared organized or not. Hell, David could bring a small contingent of folks who knew war from their Army experiences if need be to clear out an area to him, but that wasn't the request. *Dump seems to be handling it just fine and he would be happy to see him once again, I still can't help but wonder why they chose dead of winter to make the trip though. Oh shit, it takes at least three days for the mail to run, that means they are likely to be at Roland's or on the road headed here!* David contemplated sipping the dregs of his drink and waving at Stewart to come over and have a word.

"Problems?" Stewart asked and looking at David's countenance that seemed to be only vexed at the moment in not getting the waitress's attention to get him another drink.

"I don't know for sure, but this letter says Dump

and Melanie are on their way." David said handing Stewart the letter and getting up to tell the small talking barmaid to go fetch them a round.

David put Silas off once again as he returned to his table where Stewart sat studying the letter David had given him.

"Are you thinking they are out in this storm?" Stewart asked David whose brow looked quite furrowed to him.

"Might be; the timeline to get here from Roland's covering thirty miles would set them a day out from him or still at his place." David said speculating.

"Wouldn't Roland send a rider out to check on them, knowing they were on the road?" Stewart asked

"If he had one available and if they were willing to brave the storm and freeze instead of waiting it out. Roland has lost three men due to gunshot or sickness lately. I doubt he has anyone readily available at the moment. I would say John would go out on one of those mechanical rigs he has built like the go carts, but he might be in the same position we are at the moment of nothing running. I would send that postman back that way to look for them, but that mans lips looked blue and the horse he was riding was all lathered up from him pushing it to get out of the cold and get here." David remarked and waved Boudreaux over to join the conversation; much to Silas looking extremely put out that trade for the moment was off the tables.

"Why so glum Davie? Stewart tell you what was in that backroom yet?" Boudreaux began.

"No, I think Dump and Melanie might be on the road and they got that Asian boy with them. The way this snow is coming down, I got worries." David said looking out the taverns front window.

"What they using for transport?" Boudreaux asked seeing the concern on everyone's face.

"An old wore out mule and a bike. I guess they didn't expect a snow storm to just come up out of the blue. They came down with the trade wagons convoy from Newnan, but they likely traveling on their own down this way." David said worrying more and more about them.

"Send a rider out." Boudreaux began.

"There is not one until at least tomorrow and I have no idea yet what the conditions will be until I see the roads and check that makeshift barometer we got." David replied.

"They probably stayed over at Roland's and are fine." Stewart said not fully convinced himself of their fate.

"We can do nothing David for now. We tell Silas to offer the big money for a volunteer rescue party to go out tomorrow." Boudreaux said speculating on a possibility.

"That actually makes more sense; that is better than our two old asses to try doing it, we already pulled in the perimeter guards and listening posts. There are a few houses on that road they could seek shelter at, but who knows if they got a woodstove or fireplace. I doubt Dump is packing more than a light weight 3 man tent, if that." David said not trusting Dump's ability to foresee a contingency like this.

"I don't think you're giving him enough credit,

he probably has a bunch of blankets and more." Stewart responded.

"Could be; but he still thinks in that moving light and fast mentality that can get you killed. Not much room for gear on a mule carrying double and a kid on a bike. They should be ok though, barring illness or injury if they press on and find shelter. The ultimate mistake would be to stop and survival camp which I think he might try." David said still staring out the window like he could magically put himself in Dumps position.

'That is a pretty long unsettled road, sometime getting out of the wind is the best idea." Boudreaux offered.

"I can't argue with that, but you can die from exposure when relief is just a few hundred yards away. I don't know if he knows this road or not. How far anyone would keep going is only speculation on my part. I sent him the Elemental guide to shacks and shanties so HeDo could learn to build forts or survival shelters. It's likely that gifted boy already knows the basics of what an immediate shelter and a fire reflector are. You can also use a fire reflector to help cook food or warm yourself, same principle, and it's just not wasting heat by not directing it and letting it escape. I offered this picture from an old Army survival manual to John the engineer one time and asked him if he had comments on modern survival about it. He hemmed and hawed about enclosing the ends of the structure, he said there was no over hang for rain etc. He stated if you had some foil for a reflector on the wood wall it would be better, but he forgot that I made damn sure everyone I knew had one of those cheap emergency blankets I used to buy by the six-pack to improve most anything. The simple answer of putting it on the back end of the shelter escaped him; until I pointed out we would be basting like a turkey if it wasn't cold enough outside to try it out. He wanted to wrap up in it, which under certain conditions you would. Make a cocoon you could freely move about in and insulate it as well with leaves might be much better though, especially if you had one small blanket and a few people.

If you are in a wooded area and have enough natural materials, you can make a field-expedient lean-to (Figure 5-9) without the aid of tools or with only a knife. It takes longer to make this type of shelter than it does to make other types, but it will protect you from the elements.

Figure 5-9. Field-Expedient Lean-to and Fire Reflector

5-32. You will need two trees (or upright poles) about 2 meters (7 feet) apart; one pole about 2 meters (7 feet) long and 2.5 centimeters (1 inch) in diameter; five to eight poles about 3 meters (10 feet) long and 2.5 centimeters (1 inch) in diameter for beams; cord or vines for securing the horizontal support to the trees; and other poles, saplings, or vines to crisscross the beams.

5-33. To make this lean-to, you should—

- Tie the 2-meter (7-foot) pole to the two trees at waist to chest height. This is the horizontal support. If a standing tree is not available, construct a bipod using Y-shaped sticks or two tripods.
- Place one end of the beams (3-meter [10-foot] poles) on one side of the horizontal support. As with all lean-to type shelters, be sure to place the lean-to's backside into the wind.
- Crisscross saplings or vines on the beams.
- Cover the framework with brush, leaves, pine needles, or grass, starting at the bottom and working your way up like shingling.
- Place straw, leaves, pine needles, or grass inside the shelter for bedding.

5-34. In cold weather, add to your lean-to's comfort by building a fire reflector wall (Figure 5-9). Drive four 1.5-meter-long (5-foot-long) stakes into the ground to support the wall. Stack green logs on top of one another between the support stakes. Form two rows of stacked logs to create an inner space within the wall that you can fill with dirt. This action not only strengthens the wall but makes it more heat reflective. Bind the top of the support stakes so that the green logs and dirt will stay in place.

5-35. With just a little more effort you can have a drying rack. Cut a few 2-centimeter-diameter (3/4-inch-diameter) poles long enough to span the distance between the lean-to's horizontal support and the top of the fire reflector wall. Lay one end of the poles on the lean-to support and the other end on top of the reflector wall. Place and tie smaller sticks across these poles. You now have a place to dry clothes, meat, or fish.

"I told Dump a long time ago that survival was based on envisioning and doing, not a book diagram. Why something might work is more important to remember than how to build it exactly. You can forget the means but never a concept as the book Rural Ranger teaches. The grammar Nazis have a field day with that book and that's ok, the old dude talks southern colloquialisms and never learned there were rules to communicate to the brainiacs. He talks to you like you were sitting across the campfire from you, trying to convince that stuffing your shirt, shoes and pants with leaves is not a question of itchy for a moment, but your long term survival to insulate yourself from the cold when you lack proper outdoor gear. In a day or two as your fat reserves are lessened, you will find yourself a connoisseur of which leaves or moss works best and be stuffing more in!" David concluded.

Stewart chimed in with another favorite saying of David's. "Pack light freeze at night" regarding the minimalist value of a poncho and poncho liner was worth as a sleeping bag in cold climates from his army days. David had also told him not to discount it though, especially if you added a space blanket to reflect your body heat back to your body.

"Stewart, I can not carry a full pack, ammo, side arm, rifle, water and food like I could when I was 18. Hell, officers usually only carried a sidearm and no rifle and vise versa. A many an 18 year old I saw in training got wore out on a five mile march and got recycled or thrown out of the Army as not fit to serve. I am well over 50, so are most of us that have very many outdoor skills these days. I carry my brain as my main burden now, I would like to pack extra shit, but I would never get where I am going in time to save my sorry ass; because I would fall out from fatigue. I need speed, demon speed and what bit of reserves I got to get from A to B before age or injury overtakes me. Basics, skills, minimal ammo and small caliber guns. I will be the first man home." David tried to relay as a motto of self preservation.

A brick of 500 hundred rounds of .22 caliber weighs less than and was more useful than any combat load he had ever carried. Sure a blood spattering larger round was more useful in a confrontation with humans or a large animal, but David was not a gun prepper storing up rounds for a war or big game hunt. He avoided those conflicts best he could, or figured most large game was going to be scarce and he most could spoil anyone's aim or throw some well aimed deadly lead out towards a person with a higher caliber rifle. Did anyone not try to duck because a lowly .22 was shooting at them? He thought not.

An old aged prepper was a man of means, both in spirit and in knowledge. One that knew his limitations and one that could rise to the top like butter or cream in a churn.

David always liked the old Kung Fu movies that were done in the 70`s and 80's. They always had some old man hero in them that taught others some needed martial arts or spiritual advisement skills. But, David was not a skilled old master that could outperform a younger generation. He was just a man who was tired, older than he used to be and doing the generational gap method of teaching everyone when they accept that no one truly listens without current need or expectations from those that had already been there, seen it, done it and didn't need any more challenges.

Today was no exception to the age rules, as his former youth conflicted with his practical reasoning? No sense risking his life to prove he wanted to help others, if he might be physically a detriment to the idea. Better to direct and advise others and let the younger folks try their mettle in performing this Samaritan mission.

"We wait, we watch, we talk more." Is all David could offer for the moment? Or was there a solution that had not been considered yet? Perhaps the solution would come in his sleep; right now other matters also pressed his psyche.

4

The Dump Truck Shuffle

The snow flurries were coming faster now as Dump leads the mule and its tired riders. Shelter needed to be found soon, both for man and animal, but he was walking through unfamiliar territory. They had convinced the boy to leave the bicycle behind several miles ago after it got a flat tire, with many assurances they could reinstate it to him later.

"What a Fool I was to take this trip at this time of year" Dump berated himself.

Where were the modern houses on this road? This place was as forlorn in occupancy as he had ever seen. *Just because I look like a whale, don't mean I got enough blubber on me to fight this cold...*

Dump thought about how Alaskan trappers who got caught out doors in a snow storm managed to survive or traveled in sub zero weather. They would dig a shallow pit and make a fire along its length. When the fire burned down to coals they would mound a light layer of dirt over it and line the rest of the pit with pine boughs. Then they would lay their sleeping bag over the whole affair and sleep warm and toasty all night if they managed to get the amount of dirt just right and didn't wake up to a hot seat. He could just make camp in the little tent though and most likely be alright, but that wouldn't help the mule any. Roland had said there was a block building honkey tonk bar on this road he was supposed to use as a landmark that had already been broken into and scavenged a long time ago, but how far it was Dump couldn't be sure.

Dump turned and looked at his traveling companions slumped over on the mule and shivering against the relentless wind. *Got to make a decision soon; Melanie is taking the brunt of the wind head on and HeDo has some protection from it as well as the body heat of the mule and her, but the little boy looked like he was fading fast.* Dump thought to himself as he trudged up a hill.

"There is an intersection it looks like about a mile away." Melanie said pointing from her navigating vantage point on top of the mule as they crested the hill.

"Thank god, there is supposed to be an old bar and a few buildings a quarter mile from there." Dump said putting a renewed effort into his walk to get to shelter.

"I don't see any buildings." Melanie said forlornly.

"We go left at the intersection and around a curve. Then we should see it. I would gallop that mule to it, but we can't fit three of us on it with those supplies. Just hang in there; I will get you warmed up soon. HeDo! How you making out young blood? "He hollered encouragingly.

The boy stirred and replied."Cold Dumpie" in a wistful voice that was full of fatigue.

The Dump Truck Shuffle

"I know, you just hug Melanie tighter and we will get out of this wind soon. You ready for a jiggly ride?" and then Dump started a lumbering jog picking up the pace and Melanie wondered how long the big man could keep it up. Dump surprised the hell out of her by keeping the pace a full mile or more until they got to the intersection.

"Don't get all sweaty Dump, you will get even colder." Melanie said very concerned.

"That actually warmed me up, but you're right." Dump said panting and going to a slow walk.

"I never seen anyone running and putting their arm hanging down to their side for awhile like you were doing, usually people carry them chest height and elbow bent. Are your arms tired from leading the mule?" Melanie asked.

Dump laughed and told her, it was a trick David had taught him called the airborne shuffle. When David went to parachute jump school, everyone had to run at a half step for 5 miles or so. When you start getting tired or cramping, if you drop your arms like that with your fists closed, the motion of your body turns them into a sort of bellows and you get more air in your lungs and feel better to keep driving on during the run.

"Neat trick, I gotta try that sometime. I never liked jogging much, but distance running especially with a pack on is something that might be necessary these days." Melanie said and then pointed.

"There is a white building just around the curve up there Dump." Melanie said relieved.

"I don't smell any wood smoke, but to be on the safe side let me go check it out first. " Dump said looking ahead.

"I say it's safe, no fire equals no people in this weather." Melanie objected, not wanting to stay on the road a minute longer than they had to.

"You can never tell, but I call that a safe bet. Just let me enter first and you keep a tight hold on the reins until I return. Dump said and went jogging towards the decrepit building.

The mule had other intentions though and proceeded to pick up the pace after his master and nothing Melanie did slowed the obstinate beast down.

Dump slowed to a walk and turned back towards them and motioned for them to just come on. The whole world had probably heard that clip clop of steel shod mule hooves already. Dump entered the block building through a broken glass front door and surveyed the inside. Nothing but a bunch of old chairs and tables and one ratty pool table seemed present in the dank interior. Dumps exited and helped Hedo and Melanie off the Mule and lead everyone, including his mule old Saul inside out of the frigid wind.

"I am going to go get some wood, see what's in here to burn or can be broken up and I will be back shortly." Dump said after unsaddling the mule.

"HeDo, get in your sleeping bag up here on this pool table and warm up, while we get a fire going." Melanie said tending to the boy, who was showing definite signs of hypothermia.

Dump was behind the bar looking about, when an idea came to him. He shoved the big icemaker into the middle of the floor and then announced that was what they were going to build their fire in it. He decided they could cover the broken glass door with a poncho and, if he kept a window an inch or two open, they shouldn't get carbon monoxide poisoning and might just be able to warm the place up pretty good with his makeshift furnace.

"I will get some more wood outside in a bit, its time to throw my weight around" Dump said laughing and began stomping the legs off of chairs and breaking shelves as Melanie gathered the wood up and put it in the ice bin of the ice machine.

"Gimme that hand axe, this thing needs a bit of customizing before we light her up." Dump said eyeing the stainless steel contraption and figuring out he needed some vent holes for the smoke and a few for air to keep combustion going.

After the one man wrecking crew got done with his preparations they soon had a good fire going and Hedo had wiggled out of his sleeping bag looking much better and began to help collect wood to keep it going all night.

"This is a cool idea Dump! I can cook on this ledge and if we close the doors on this thing it should burn all night without tending." Melanie said happily looking at an exhausted Dump sitting on a bar stool poking at the fire dreamily.

"I just wish there was still some booze in here." Dump said.

And just then, HeDo popped up from his exploration of the bar and asked, "Beer Dumpie?" and offered two dirty unopened cans he had managed to find.

"I know I brought you along for some reason."

Dump said grabbing a beer and wiping off the top and darn near consuming it all on the spot.

"You can have the other beer Dump, I think you have earned it today." Melanie said giving him a hug, while HeDo beamed a smile at his big friend.

"I won't argue with you about that." Dump said smiling and tousling the boy's hair and taking another big swig from the can he was already holding and reaching for the other.

5

Stews of a different sort.

"We will see what's to be done with the vehicles tomorrow. If we can get something running we will go look for Dump. Where is Swede? At Silas's? He could probably help fix them better than we could." David said speaking to the assembled group.

"Last I heard of him, he was running trap line by your property for those feral dogs that have been drifting this way. He stayed here making snares out of that cable he got on that expedition and he hired two folks to go with him. I suspect he is holed up in some lake cabin around your neck of the woods." Silas said hating to once again get off the subject of barter, as David took stock of his friend's current whereabouts.

"He will most likely make tracks for my compound then, that is if this snow don't let up. Damn, between him and Bubba and three MORE trappers? I ain't going to have nothing in my liquor cabinet time I get home." David lamented.

"Then you need to put that on your list. Boudreaux usually gets first call on stocks coming in. But I got a case of Crown Royal I will sell you for silver." Silas said perking up.

"Why do you think I would even want that over priced shit? I have a connoisseurs taste for cheap whiskey anyway." David began before Silas made everyone laugh by simply stating "Because its alcohol" and grinning at David.

"Alright, that's mine Boudreaux. Hell I will have to share it with you when you visit anyway. What's the price Silas?" David said thinking he was going to see how much of Boudreaux's currently free liquor he could drink up to offset what it was going to cost him.

"Their one ounce silver a bottle and I won't haggle." Silas said back to tweaking on that damnable mustache of his.

"I hate the notion of paying premium for something I don't like as much as cheap but I will take it. I am pretty sure my tractor works so as soon as I figure out how to get home I will be back for it and the rest of our goods. Who has the watch and hunter list so we can see to it we gather everyone in that might have gotten stranded?" David said waving a Chuck the bartender and putting his get even plan in motion.

"Toby does, but I am not so much worried about the woodsman as I am the trade wagons we got out. I am going to have to get me a map and plot the expected arrival times of where they are at momentarily to even figure out if it's possible to send them some help. Your postman are with them most likely David, you should be able to answer that." Silas said putting the ball back in David's court.

"Damn your right, where is Smiley?" David said turning around to look at the taverns patrons and not seeing his Postmaster, he returned his gaze to look at Silas.

"He wasn't around yesterday, he left Roody in charge, said that his wife was sick and he had to look out for her and the kids for a day or two. Anyone has seen Roody about lately?" Silas said towards the Patrons in the Tavern.

"He is most likely at Choctaw ridge; he has been sparking a girl over there and uses every excuse to make his rounds that way." A grizzled old man spoke up.

"David wished he had never hired Roody. He was great in the beginning and then he started slacking off and causing the mail to be late as he traveled the mail drop centers to supposedly bird dog the problems the service had lately. The problem was Roody as near as he could tell. Postman usually got food and booze from the grateful citizens along the way. Roody had made it a lifestyle and being a former sailor seemed to have a girl in every port as it were.

"Great. Just great. No mail, No messengers. No danged horses or wagons onsite when needed. They were still trying to get a telegraph running but the solar storm probably had whacked that to." David said speaking his mind out loud.

"We still got the bonfire and smoke signal system" Boudreaux said scratching his several days' worth of beard.

"That's right, hit I got to do everything around here. Get that idiot of a sergeant of the guard you got over at your store to follow up with the Sergeant Major to light the beacons if they haven't already. Folks will need the guiding lights to get back here, but I doubt we can send smoke up in this weather." David said contemplating a strategy.

Stews of a different sort.

"You got suggestions?" Boudreaux asked

"Well I wish we had some chemicals to change colors of fires but tires burn like crazy and can produce a lot of smoke. Everyone already knows the international Morse code signal for SOS. Three dits form the letter *S*, and three dahs make the letter *O* (· · · — — — · · ·). So I guess those that need help will do it. Rally is just puff, puff, puff, and continuous smoke, one after the other for us. We never spent enough time on that system so I guess we pay for it now.

They will figure it out between long and short signals eventually I guess." David described to get at least some form of communication reestablished.

"I imagine people will be drifting in for days, lets just keep a community pot going at all times and hope for the best." GM said helping with the response efforts that had everyone puzzled as to what to do.

"As long as its hot food, we can just keep adding whatever meat or vegetables we got to it, the heat will keep it from spoiling. It won't be mulligan stew, but it will be hot and nutritious." Stewart said reminding himself of the old stone soup soldier story he had once heard of as a child.

6

A Masterfully Designed Stove

Sherry began lighting the two StoveTec rocket stoves to begin this day's dinner using small twigs. These two sturdy and efficient appliances always amazed her in their practicality and she couldn't imagine life without them. David and her had poured over the manufacturer's website, watched several you tube vids of them in use and had finally decided on a purchase of two top of the line models that burned wood and charcoal. The decision had been carefully weighed against any number of criteria. First off, David was doing the buying with his own funds. True to their own weird little mutual Prepper deal, one was to be his and one was to be hers, as preps were always bought in pairs when they made purchases. David was someday going to live his dreams in Florida and Sherry was staying back in Alabama pursuing her own interests. By purchasing in the way they did, David and Sherry had amassed a sizable amount of preps that could be divided with no remorse should the day for David to leave ever come around. Another advantage to this system was a mutual support and bug out system that many Preppers would be envious of. They shared equally as former boyfriend and girlfriend can only understand. Sherry had purchased two of the water pasteurizer kettles to complement his purchases out of her next paycheck. It was this give and take arrangement that had truly built up their stores and respect for each other.

These stoves were an amazing piece of technology and dedicated craftsmanship. She and David were blessed in that they had the new 2011 models to depend on for the long haul. The old styles were more than sufficient for the tasks they had at hand, but David had gone the extra few dollars to insure that they had the most versatile and long lasting models available because he had predicted the situation they were in now and wanted a lifetime of service.

The 2 door stove, the company had designed by listening to feedback and comments which produced a magnificent prepper cooking resource that resulted in an easier to operate, safer to use, and longer lasting stove. This efficient stove saves lots of fuel.

David had told Sherry that he wanted the charcoal burning feature because they always had a few bags of it around and it suited their hurricane prone gulf coast area the best for short term needs, while the adaptability of being a wood burner made it also the long term survival cooking source they would need. The company said you should always use good quality hardwood charcoal though he had learned and it does burn hotter.

This thing could also actually create its own charcoal! The Ceramic 2 Door Stove efficiently uses wood or charcoal to cook food. Significant amounts of carbon monoxide are burned in the enclosed space above the fire. Frequently, burning wood embers provide enough charcoal fuel for prolonged simmering operations. After creating wood embers, you just close the big door with the fire brick. Then you keep the lower ventilation door slightly cracked open to insure the wood embers or charcoal fuel keeps burning for simmering food.

Hey this was as about as adjustable of a temperature range you can get when trying to cook on wood, unless you were fortunate enough to have grandmas huge wood burning kitchen stove from a bygone era.

David had also figured out how to attach one of those Weber replacement grills to the top and had produced many a fine grilled fish dinner for this compounds residents.

Sherry and the rest of the gang loved the water kettles too. When they finished cooking they always had more than enough heat left to make plenty of hot water for cleanup or the next day's drinking water.

A Masterfully Designed Stove

The pasteurizer container body is made from lightweight stainless steel alloy; the spout above the water line is made of cast aluminum. This product is designed to maximize surface area and optimize heat transferability via its hollow inverted tube design in combination with the rocket stove. Water is poured into the inverted conical walls of the pasteurizer, brought to temperature, and then allowed to quickly cool when removed from the stove. No other product enables you to make 4 liters of safe water as quickly and inexpensively as this pasteurizer with very little fuel.

Sherry went back to the girl's house shuddering at the onset of snow and wind that had somehow came up all of the sudden today. Something was wrong with the bread makers David's mom had said and Jack and Bubba were trying to figure it out. Pretty much everyone had remained inside all day until it was time to get the fires lit and start preparing this evenings meal. It had been a bleak gray sky most of the day and the snow had just started an hour or so ago before she had to take her turn at setting up the cook fires. She glanced at the sky and then stood in awe as a wave of colors started dancing on the horizon. She watched mystified for a moment or two at the spectral lights in the sky until she ran to share it with her friends.

"Come out side and look! The sky is brilliant with colors!" she shouted in to the house through the doorway before turning and becoming transfixed watching the light show.

"Aurora Borealis!" Jack said making it first out the door.

"I thought you only see those in Alaska or something." Lois said watching the swirling kaleidoscope of colors.

"That's not normal, something strange is going on." Sandra said not sure if she wanted out from under the porch for a better look.

"Oh come on, it's just a natural phenomenon." Sherry chided her sister.

"What causes that anyway Jack?" Sherry asked.

"Geomagnetic effects." he began until he and Bubba looked at each other with an "Oh shit look".

"Do you think it's another solar event?" Bubba said reaching for his wife who was now becoming concerned about the look on the two men's faces.

"Gotta be. I just hope that's not why the bread

makers quit. Let me try a radio and I will tell you in a minute." Jack said rushing towards the house.

"Damn it, Damn it! Damn it! Damn it!" Jack said trying to get a signal on the radio and then checking the house light batteries." Jack was looking both pissed off and dismayed at Bubba who had followed his evaluations of the situation carefully.

"We screwed again guy. Would it do any good to disconnect everything else connected, or we electronically cooked already?" Bubba said trying to think of something helpful they could do, but not really having much hope in accomplishing anything useful.

"We need to check everything for possible fires, but I think we screwed, blued and tattooed again." Jack said trying to mentally inventory all the skunk work projects David and he had hooked up amongst the houses.

"I will go and see about David's house, come on Cat, Harley. Jack, you go see to the boat dock and I will meet you down there. Sherry please go unplug everything and somebody needs to see to his Mom's house." Bubba said taking his role as fire manager seriously.

Jack charged off to check the dock and the light system, but couldn't remember if it was hooked to charge or disconnected. Sandra and Lois went to David's mom's house and Sherry and Betsy checked their house and the cook house fixtures.

Bubba searched David's house for any fires and looked out the window at Jack tracing the dock lines and heading towards the Chris Craft to see if the engine would fire.

"The ice machines dead." Cat said.

"The ice isn't though, fix us a drink. We might as well have some use out of the ice before it melts." Bubba said trying to figure out the weird wiring David had on separate systems to light the house or run small appliances.

"I will put what's left of the ice in an ice bucket and we can bring it back to the house to share." Cat said grabbing one off the bar and beginning to fill it.

"Ok, get Jack in here if you would, while I trace back this wire to its origin. David has this drawer locked and I have no idea what he has in it." Bubba said as he was trying to fit his head under the sink with Harley the bulldog trying to see in there at the same time.

"Watch out hound, give me some room." Bubba said nudging the dog out of the way.

"*What the hell is that*?" He mused tracing the wires to a cylindrical metal looking capacitor.

"Ha! I bet this is nothing more than a prank. That's a coil from a car. Let me just connect this up and see if sparks still fly." Bubba said sniggering and waiting on Jack to come be his experimental victim. Bubba remembered how parts store employees used to leave a charged up coil on the counter for unsuspecting customers that couldn't keep their hands to their self and liked to fool with things on the counter. When picked up, it gave them a little shocking surprise.

"What's up Bubba?" Jack said looking down at him laying on the floor and Harley watching him closely.

"What does David have in that locked drawer?

He has wires going to it under here, is it a light or something like a refrigerator?" Bubba said like he was intent on doing his wiring check and turning his face into the cabinet to hide his smile.

"That's David's snack drawer, he locks it to keep me out. I never have seen a light in it. I don't know what he has rigged to it. An alarm maybe?" Jack said reaching over and grabbing the handle to jiggle it before he did the wizard of oz witch thing when she touched Dorothy's shoes and sparks flew off his hand.

"Holy crap! What was that?" Jack said rubbing his hand as Harley and Bubba appeared to be rolling around laughing on the floor together.

"A giant capacitor, an automotive coil that would discharge at a touch. A 'hands off Jack' prank prewired by David, oh that was good!" Bubba said still laughing that he'd managed to scare the hell out of Jack.

"What an ass." Jack grumbled thinking he was going to have the perfect excuse to break into Jacks cracker drawer.

"That was funny as hell! " Bubba said standing up and retrieving his drink.

"Yea and you can't wait until you tell David about it, I know." Jack said watching Bubba and Cat still grinning at him and then noticed Cat holding up a lemon drop she had found next to the ice bucket on the counter to placate him.

"Lemon drop! Yum. Is there more?' Jack said looking like Harley wanting another treat.

"No, that's it. You boys are so mean to each other." Cat said putting the lid on the bucket and handing her hubby his drink.

"Hey that's David's liquor, I know he don't mind sharing it, but I am supposed to keep count." Jack said trying to devise a plan where he could get Bubba to pop the lock on the drawer for him.

"So put me down for one bottle of Ancient Age." Bubba said heading towards the door after grabbing the bottle.

"Hey, we were going to do dinner. I want to see how those stoves do. David said that the company has worked for thirty years to design and build biomass stoves and has completed over 100 projects in 60 countries. That's a substantial amount of know how, that I want to see the results from." Bubba said heading towards the cook house where Sherry was heading towards him with Sandra in tow carrying a bus pan full of spices and sauces.

"What the hell are those giant kettle things?" Bubba said approaching the cooking shelter.

"Water Pasteurizers." Sherry said.

"How is that different from boiling water? I don't understand." Cat asked

"Water pasteurization is a heat process to kill harmful bacteria and make water safe to drink for human consumption. Heating water to 65° C (149° F) will kill all germs, viruses, and parasites. This process is called pasteurization. Pasteurization can be accomplished without having to bring the water to a boil." Sherry responded.

"Ah that is a concept that escapes most. You can use pasteurization from the sun to clean up water by just leaving a sealed bottle in the sun." Jack said wandering up.

"How much wood do those things use?" Bubba

asked studying the operation

"Thanks to a well-designed and precisely manufactured rocket-style combustion chamber, cooks can boil 1 gallon (5 liters) of water in 20 minutes using just three 1.5" by 12" inch long sticks of wood . One additional stick is enough to simmer for another 45 minutes. Designed and built to cook three meals a day, every day," Jack explained.

'I am impressed, it's a lot easier to gather up small wood than get out and chop firewood." Bubba said motioning for Cat to give him a bit more ice before it disappeared as everyone had the last of a luxury not to be seen again.

If you would like to purchase a StoveTec Rocket Stove: I have arranged for my readers and Preppers to use and take advantage of coupon code Prepper1, to get free shipping and $2.50 off a purchase. Go to StoveTec.net and to redeem it and help us both out to get prepared.

A stove like this, fueled by either charcoal or small amounts of wood, is a great back-up to your electric or gas stove and a great Prep.

7

Found By Fortune

Dump woke up and stretched his aching back. A sleeping bag on cold concrete is not the most comfortable thing in the world. He walked over to the ice machine that he had crudely converted into a furnace and pulled back the ice bin door, sure enough it still held a thick hot bed of coals. Melanie and HeDo stirred at the sound of the door being opened and groggily said their good mornings.

Dump threw some scraps of wood on the fire and left the door open so it would throw off some light in the dim interiors of the old block building bar they had spent the night in.

"You have been outside yet?" Melanie asked getting close to the fires warmth.

"Not yet, I am just getting up." Dump responded.

HeDo joined them by the fire and feed it a few more splintered chair legs and then went to the poncho covered door.

"Dumpie!" The boy said excitedly pointing out the door.

"What are you looking at?" Dump said as he and Melanie went to peer out the flap of nylon the boy had raised.

A sea of white snow blanketed everything as far

as you could see. The wind had died down, but they could see many places where it had drifted up during the night.

"That looks like about 4 inches or so on the ground" Melanie said speculatively.

"I imagine so." Dump responded before turning around to the sound of pouring water.

"Oh no you didn't! " Dump said as he observed the mule urinating a flood over in the corner of the bar where Dump had tied him.

"Let's get you outside for a bit before you get a mind to do something else." Dump said slipping on his boots and not bothering to lace them.

"Hold the door Melanie" Dump said as he dragged the mule outside.

HeDo had already donned his hat and gloves and was outside as soon as the mule cleared the door. The boy had never seen snow-covered ground before and stood looking around and alternately kicking and picking up bits of it.

"He doesn't know what to make of it" Dump said laughing and watching the boys wonder.

"We should teach him to build a snowman later." Melanie said sharing a moment of watching the childhood glee the boy was exhibiting...

"I think we are going to wait a day before heading out. Usually this stuff melts in 24 hours or so." Dump said remembering the few times in the past he had experienced snow in the south.

"Of course I have seen it last up to 4 or 5 days though. As long as it don't get any deeper we will be fine." Melanie observed.

"I guess we got time off for a snow day then. I got to find more wood, but we got plenty of supplies. I think I will take Old Saul out later and check out what's ahead, but we got time to do a snowman and make snow angels etc." Dump said enjoying watching the boy frolic around.

Melanie stifled a giggle thinking about what a Dump Truck sized snow angel would look like and went back inside to heat up some water for cocoa.

"Play, Dimpie?" The boy said running up and grabbing Dumps coat tail.

"In a bit. Watch this." Dump said making a snowball and hitting a road sign with it, to which HeDo automatically had to do the same and they had them a little target practice.

"Cocoa is done!" Melanie called out and they went back inside to warm up, hanging their outerwear and gloves on a couple of metal folding chairs she had set up near the fire for the purpose.

"Look what I found" Melanie said grinning holding up a giant waitress serving tray.

"Ha! Ha! That boy is going to have some fun. Think it will work for a sled?" Dump asked.

"I don't see why not, might be a bit hard to hang on to, but I bet he can figure out how to slide down that hill out there once we give him the idea.' Melanie replied.

"Well then, you teach him how it's done and I will watch for awhile and then go to recon ahead a few miles." Dump replied sipping a steaming enamel cup full of cocoa.

"You have to go out so soon? I thought you were going to build a snowman with us." Melanie pouted at him with disappointment in her voice.

"I will later. I will be back in a few hours and we can do it after lunch. I want to see what's up ahead; maybe there is a better place to stay or I can find some drier wood." Dump said assuring her he didn't want to miss out on any fun, but he had responsibilities to tend to.

"Ok, don't stay out long. We worry, you know." Melanie said patting him and then started making whooshing noises holding up the tray and steering it around like she was driving at the baffled boy.

"I don't think they have sleighs in Asia." Dump said grinning watching the confusion of the boy and Melanie's antics.

"Fun is universal and today we are going to have some major fun!" Melanie replied giving Dump a beautiful smile.

"Well let me see to the Mule. This will be one day I bet he don't mind a saddle and blanket. I bet he wouldn't even mind a hat, unless he thinks he will have to work in this stuff." Dump said chuckling and unbuttoning the hood off his Army Fatigue jacket.

"You might need that." Melanie cautioned.

"Naw I got my watch cap and a scarf. I think it will look neat." Dump said and wandered outside to where the mule was tied up.

HeDo poked his head out the door after a few minutes to see what Dump was up to and started laughing and pointing at the mule that Dump had decked out with its ears poking out of the hood and a scarf around its neck.

"I am getting the scarf back, I just tied it on for looks for ya'll to see" Dump said as the mule started braying like it was complaining about the loss of the scarf and causing everyone to chuckle.

Melanie took the serving tray to the edge of the

hill they were on and motioned for HeDo to sit on the big plate and then slid him around a bit. Then she pointed down the hill and back at him and the Boys eyes grew wide with anticipation, as he nodded his head he would give it a go. Melanie gave him a push and he was off. He didn't have the hang of it yet and went wildly spinning into a drift on the side of the road, but came back with the tray and happily gabbling something in his native tongue that ended with a firm "Dumpie Do" indicating he wanted Dump to shove him off this time.

Dump Truck played with them for a while and avoided trying it himself, but watched Melanie go down once or twice having as much fun as her little protégée.

"Well I am off; I will be back in a couple hours. Fire a few shots if you need me." Dump said before setting off to find out what lay ahead on their journey.

The stillness of the white solitude Dump found unnerving. It had been awhile since he had heard the laughs and shouts of HeDo and Melanie playing and now his mind had time to wander back to the here and now. He couldn't believe how stupid he was to set out from Roland's with a bike and a mule. He figured Melanie could ride the bike when HeDo got tired, but the thought of the tire going flat had not even crossed his mind. What was supposed to been a leisurely three day camping trip had turned into hell as the temperature suddenly dropped and the snow had come. He had not originally planned on them being alone either. He thought for sure that Roland or a trade wagon would have accompanied them, but all the stock was out and no messengers or trade wagons had been scheduled to head this way for a week or so. Melanie and he had been impatient to get to David's place and let excitement interfere with common sense, especially with a young one along.

Dump hadn't been too keen on doing a winter trip, but the farmer's almanac had said he was supposed to have warmer weather and besides he had business to tend to with David.

Dump had been entrusted with a man's genuine presidential 18kt gold Rolex watch for trade and David was the only person anyone knew that could value it and get top dollar in trade for it. Being a mechanical movement it still worked and kept precise time. Not that time much mattered anymore. It seemed that everyone had reverted back to keeping odd hours. Stewart had told him that until the modern age, most households had two distinct intervals of slumber, known as "first" and "second" sleep, bridged by an hour or more of quiet wakefulness. Stewart had explained that during the preindustrial era, before the proliferation of modern lighting, people routinely used to wake from their 'first sleep' sometime after midnight to talk with others, smoke a pipe, rob the nearby orchard or bring in the cows etc.. After about an hour or two, he said, people returned to bed for their 'second sleep' until dawn. Having folks moving about at all hours of the night was just a fact of life these days and a sometimes unnerving one at that at times.

Dump halted the mule and sniffed the wind. He had caught a brief whiff of wood smoke and was trying to figure out which direction it was coming from, but couldn't decide. He took the safety off his 30-30 carbine just to be on the safe side and then became more aware of his surroundings as he scanned ahead for a wisp of smoke or any movements. The old mule Saul picked up on his master's agitation and began to periscope his ears around listening for any danger.

Dump reined the mule closer to the edge of the far side of the road and proceeded forward towards the upcoming bend in the road. As he began to clear the bend, he saw a few scattered houses and smoke coming from the chimney from the farthest one. Dump dismounted and began leading the mule towards it, while carefully eyeing what appeared to be empty homes along the way. The house with blue smoke coming from the chimney was just a nondescript brick ranch house, but he studied it in detail before his next move. There wasn't much outside that he could see that gave any clues about the nature of the occupants. No one had been out front or down the driveway, because the snow remained undisturbed.

Dump cradled his gun so as to look non aggressive, but stood next to the bricked in mailbox beside the road to afford him some minimal cover in case the occupants were not happy to see him.

'HELLO THE HOUSE!" Dump shouted towards it. Then he watched the window and door carefully for a response. After a moment or two of nothing, he tried again.

"HEY THERE! COMPANY COMING!" He bellowed.

He saw a corner of a curtain move and waited.

The curtain was pulled back further and he saw an elderly woman's face peering out at him and he waved to her.

The front door opened a crack and then momentarily the barrel of a gun was slowly thrust out and he heard the woman holler to him." What do you want?"

"Nothing at all, just saw the smoke and wanted to talk. I can be going on my way if you don't want to." Dump hollered back.

"Who are you?" The woman called back.

"Just a traveler, I don't need nothing. I got plenty of food and was just passing by." He yelled back.

"Step out so I can see you!" The woman said.

"You lower that gun barrel and I might have a mind too. Look, I am just making my way to the trading post at the lake is all." Dump said still hugging the mail box pillar.

"What trading post? Did things get fixed?" The women said lowering the gun and now poking her head out to get a better look at the stranger.

"No nothing is fixed; it's just a place for folks to do a little business at like a flea market." Dump said getting up his nerve to step away from the brick and mortar edifice.

"You never said your name yet" The woman said now appearing full body in the door.

"Its Bill, friends call me Dump" Truck said stepping out and being sure his rifle didn't look threatening in the least.

"Mr. Dump you come on up the driveway so we can quit yelling back and forth but not too close you hear?" The woman called back.

"Ok!" and Dump lead his mount up the driveway.

"I got to say that's one of the funnier looking beasts I ever seen. Any man who would take off his hood to warm up a jackass on a cold day like today can't be all bad." The woman said laughing at the mules ears poking out of a fur trimmed hood.

"Shush, I told him he looks handsome." Dump said grinning.

"That he does! Well, come on up here. I guess if you were going to shoot an old granny you wouldn't have come bellowing like you were calling the hogs home." She said tucking an old shotgun under her arm and waving him towards the porch.

"Tie that mule up on the far corner of the railing. They ain't got any manners and I don't want a stinking pile of mule mud on my front porch," She said pointing towards the far railing.

"Sounds like you know about mules." Dump said, as he did what he was asked.

"I ought to. Daddy plowed with them a parcel of 50 acres for just about 40 years. My name is Myra Banks. You can call me MeeMaw if you got a hankering to, I haven't had anyone use my first name in a many a year." The woman said extending her hand to the big gorilla in front of her.

"You all alone here?" Dump asked as he lightly grasped the woman's hand.

"You got bad notions boy? Why would that matter?" The feisty old woman said with sparks coming out of her faded blue eyes.

"No, I well, was just curious that's all." Dump mumbled.

"Ha! Got ya! You should have seen the look on your face! Get inside out of the cold. You can stick that mule in the garage later. That is if you stay longer than a cup of coffee." The woman said walking back into the house.

Dump walked into what looked like a well ordered antique store setting of old furniture and smells in the living room. The walls and tables were covered with a variety of photographs and paintings covering several eras.

"Normally I would offer you a seat in here, but I don't need my sofa smelling like mule and you are a pretty big boy so come on into the kitchen." Myra said fearing Dump would probably collapse the springs in her sofa with his bulk.

"I just put water on the wood heater in there, was going to have me a cup of tea. You want coffee though don't ya? Not seen too many men take to tea." She said bustling over to a china cabinet.

"I drink both; I prefer coffee though, if you can spare it." Dump said setting his rifle down in the corner gently so as not to spoil the paint on the wall.

"You do huh? Well, I'd rather give you coffee, tea is just as hard to come by and coffee's what you wish for anyway." She said as she removed a very ornate cup and saucer from the china cabinet and then went to another cupboard to fetch a coffee mug.

"Uh Myra... er MeeMaw? How far is it to the lake from here?" Dump said looking around at the well ordered kitchen.

"What part of the lake would you be wanting? If

you just talking about water its 23 miles, I haven't heard tell of a trading post. I don't get visitors often. Where might that post be located?" MeeMaw said shuffling towards the den where a blue enameled kettle was steaming.

"The post is supposed to be down towards the boat landing on old 97 at the crossroads next to the old Wagon Wheel restaurant." Dump said thanking her as she measured out some instant and poured the water into his mug.

"I know where that's at, you got to go about 36 miles more or less, unless you go the back road and shave off 7 or 8 miles. You say they trading things down there?" She said her eyes brightening with interest.

"They started that... oh I say about 4 or 5 months ago." Dump said sipping his coffee and wondering how the old woman had got by without knowing about it.

"Henry, that was my husband passed away about two months ago, was an odd sort of fellow. He didn't hold with us ever making peace with the Russians and figured we been nuked. We stayed in the storm shelter for about a week when the cars stopped all over the road. He said it was something called EMP and thought a big missile was coming. I eventually talked him out and we moved back in the house. Henry wouldn't let anybody come up to the house and see the food we had stored. He would sit on that front porch with his gun and threaten everyone that said so much as a 'how do you do'. He got a bit whacky towards the end and I hid the bullets from him. He didn't even know his rifle was unloaded. He had diabetes and the medicine run out and he just began dying in body and spirit. Young man, I need you to help me please before you move on. I managed to drag Henry out the door and put him in the garden, but that grave is shallow and the varmints been digging at him. Could you pile some rocks or something over him for me?" She asked tearfully.

"Of course I will! You want me to go do it now?" Dump said starting to rise.

"No. No. sit son. I have made my peace. I just can't stand the thought of a dog digging him up and chewing his bones. They on the prowl out there you know? Don't let your guard down for a minute, they run in packs and chase deer in the woods at night." The old woman said shuddering and looking out her kitchen window.

"You have seen them?" Dump asked incredulously.

"Oh yea, they lead by an old border collie. Used to be, every variety of dogs was in that pack of hell hounds, but now it's thinned out to just the bigger ones. I unloaded on them dogs when they were trying to dig up Pa and killed three of them. They run a buck through my backyard two nights ago and I give them what for again hoping they stay away." The woman told him while offering another cup of coffee.

"You got rocks or bricks handy or do you need me to find some?" Dump asked quietly and somberly.

"There is a low stone wall loosely mortared together around the gazebo in the back. It wouldn't take much for a strong man like you to bust it up with the sledge hammer that's out in the garage and tote them back in the wheelbarrow, so I could do the arranging of them on his grave." She said tearing up once more and looking at him with imploring eyes.

"I will do it, you just tell me how you want them and I will set them in place for you." Dump said extending a bear sized paw to cover the frail woman's hand lovingly.

"That would be such a burden off my mind. I managed to get old Pa Henry wrapped up in a spread and drug him out to the garden where the soil was softer and used a hoe to dig him his resting place, but I just didn't have the strength to do a proper job of it. I was stove up for days afterwards and even thought about crawling on top of his mound and dying myself." MeeMaw said breaking down into a sobbing mass that Dump for the life of him couldn't console or get her to release him.

"Where's your family? I had a MeeMaw myself, usually in the south that means lots of kids or grand kids." Dump said as she settled herself.

"Oh you know how it is, jobs, marriages etc. scattered them all over the country. We had many family reunions, but there is not a living soul left for me ask help from. That's why I asked you. The neighbors have either died off, got foreclosed on, moved away or appear to have been somewhere else when God put his reckoning on us. I think the Hargrove's about 5 miles from here were going to the lake for the summer. Henry walked down there twice to see about them, but no one was at home and he brought their food back for us the second time. I gave him the devil about that. Told him it was stealing and burglary. He said it was necessity and it had been over two months since the Change. What happened? Do you know?" She asked Dump while sitting straighter in her chair.

"It was the Sun; it has happened before in 1856 so get the book of Revelation out of your mind... NASA predicted it and nobody listened, not government, not the people when published in every magazine, not anybody. I got a friend who was an Emergency manager who told me it was even all over Twitter and no one thought it was something to be concerned with.' Dump said trying to allay her fears and explain best he could.

"What's a Twitter? Sounds like a bird or something." Myra said offering Dump a stale cookie from the jar in back of her, which he happily accepted.

"I am not quite sure of what that is myself, I am not technology oriented. It's a thing on the internet that people used to tell others what they were doing on at that moment, best I can reckon." Dump said.

"Why in the world would anybody want to do that? If you got to stop what you're doing to tell others about it how can you get anything done and why would anyone want to follow that?" MeeMaw stated confused.

"I don't know, supposed to have been more popular than a thing called Face book but that's another strange signs of the times I can't comprehend." Dump stated.

"I am all a flutter with you talking technology crap. I didn't understand why I sent money for electronic games to the great grand kids for their birthdays to slay zombies. Henry wanted to send them nice pocket knives, but the parents said no. Those kids used to sit around here at family reunions and complain they had nothing to do! There is 200 acres, a nice creek and a swimming hole in back of this place, what did they mean there was nothing to do?" Myra started before Dump just said it was a different world and kids had a hard time using their own imagination to entertain themselves much these days.

"Bill, you think they have any kind of cab service at that trading post? Lordy, it would be expensive but I am needing some supplies myself. I got a bit of money I could pay." Myra asked carefully.

Dump deliberated with himself for a moment before responding.

"Money isn't what it used to be, values are a bit different now. A green dollar is looked on like trash by some and its how much you got of one thing that someone else might trade for as a value of wealth." He said letting cold facts sink in.

"So a hundred dollar bill is worthless?" said a scared old lady.

"Sometimes...hell to be honest with you most times it is. What would you rather have in time of need, a can of pork and beans or a worthless piece of paper backed by nothing and no store to spend it at? Silver or gold works, if someone has surplus. Ammunition, tools, warm clothes etc. are holding better value at the moment." Dump said not knowing where this conversation was going to lead.

The old woman slowly shook her head knowingly and then stared Dump straight in the eye.

"I can't stay here; I got two weeks at best food

left. No seed to speak of, no youth or energy. I was thinking about playing bait for them wild dogs and being able to get some meat by shooting one, but I am too scared. I got my wedding rings, if you take me to the post and I have some food to give you for your trouble." The old gray haired woman said pretending to adjust her hair bun and not look directly at him.

"Oh shit! How do these things happen?" Dump considered.

"Look, I got a woman and a boy about 6 miles back on this road waiting on me to return. I was checking out what was ahead of us, if, and I mean if, you let us stay the night; we might could work something out. I don't want your gold; I got one mule and a hard row to hoe here. Sorry. Let me go get them and bring them here and we talk about what might work." Dump said overwhelmed at the additional burdens.

"Fine, go get them. Is that your wife and son?" MeeMaw asked.

"No, no one is related, but its family if you can understand that; we are one though. I will get them and hurry back, but to do that I can't take care of Henry today okay? I promise I will do it in the morning or if there is enough light when I get back I will start on it today. Do we have a deal?" Dump said very upset at how to coordinate all the new explanations and burdens he was charged with.

"So you will come back? Guaranteed? Please don't leave Henry unburied. You don't have to take me anywhere; just don't let those dogs chew his bones." Myra implored.

"You got my word. Straight back. Straight to here. You need me to bring in wood before I leave?" Dump said looking at the few split logs by the wood burning heater in the other room.

"That would be a blessing if you would. We had hired someone to cut down two hickory trees that were starting to crowd out the back driveway and split it before the "event" happened and got 7 cords of wood. I can't handle them heavy pieces, but a few at a time. I will make you a great dinner to visit with and this house got four bedrooms that would be warm and cozy, if I open up the damper on a bunch of wood. Please come back, I beseech you. I can make some cathead style biscuits and got some sorghum left to stick to your ribs." She said giving him an unexpected hug and throwing in the bribe at the same time.

" I got a fire to feed then" Dump said scooting his chair back from the table and commencing to carry in arm loads of wood from the stockpile out back.

"Deal then!" MeeMaw said as she started to get out her last stock of flour, soda and salt and was happily humming around the kitchen as the gargantuan man filled up her den with split cord wood.

"Okay, we can survive another blizzard. I am going to go get Melanie and HeDo now." Dump said wiping the sweat off his brow before Myra handed him a clean dish towel.

"You bad about mentioning names; ok so this boy and woman got one now I can identify. He do? Asian you said he was, is that Hay Do? Japanese or something?" MeeMaw said hands on hips.

"Long story, He Do like He does things. Great kid. I think they're probably building a snowman about now. He is not good with English, about 8 or 9, son of a close friend of mine and as helpful as anyone can be. He is a good boy." Dump said eyeing her reception of his little buddy.

"I like good boys, you are one, I already know you like sugar treats so maybe if you hurry back I won't burn your angel cakes, I didn't tell you about." She said giving Dump a welcome to Mama's house hug and a peck on the cheek.

"What is an angel cake?" Dump sad attempting to get a grubby finger on the mixing bowl rim before being rapped with a wooden spoon.

"Its honey, lemon and vanilla with a sprinkling of coconut and you can not have one until you act like the angel I think you are." Myra said defending the treats she was making.

"I am going to be dreaming of angels all the way there and back." Dump said rushing towards the door before pausing.

"If you want to hurry this up, let Saul have some sorghum. He absolutely loves sweet things and will speed up on his own coming back." Dump said before going out the front door.

"Ok, you a tricky one though, is it the mule or you that wants to lick the spoon?" MeeMaw said offering the bowl and spoon to a bug-eyed Dump Truck.

"We share, but that Mule hasn't had any sugar cubes or treats lately. We got to save him something for the return trip." Dump said before getting his paws on a first taste of what he had been denied.

"Hey this has brown sugar in it also" The commissar of Dump Land said studying his finger for anything else to taste." Dump said before the mule stared braying seeing his best friend and encouraging him to share whatever was in that white bowl he was carrying.

"Come on mule we Ride!" Dump said pulling back the reins and turning the animal about while waving at his hostess.

Dump made the six miles back to Melanie and HeDo in record time as he galloped the mule back over its own tracks along the way.

"You're late, we made a snowman already and I finally got him to quit trying to ambush you with snowballs when you got home. Look, I taught him to build a snow fort." Melanie said looking at him mischievously.

"Sorry I been gone so long, but we got us a nicer place to stay tonight." Dump said as he ducked an incoming barrage of snowballs from the fort they had built.

"Ha! Didn't get me you little booger!" Dump said as the child ran to greet him laughing about him falling on his butt avoiding the fusillade he had thrown.

"There is an old woman up the road making us dinner. We got reservations." Dump said making his way indoors to his make shift heater as HeDo babbled to him in broken English and Vietnamese or another language while riding on his shoulders.

"Who are you talking about? You have been off visiting while I worried?" A miffed Melanie complained.

"I arranged for a real bed for you tonight, don't fuss. I got no idea what we can do for her, but she is an old country woman and tonight she opened her heart and doors to us." Dump said pretending he was going to put HeDo in the makeshift furnace to the child's giggles and her admonishments not to be playing like that.

"She is just an old woman, 75 at least, husband died and she wants me to bury him better. We got a nice house to stay in with a wood heater and plenty of fuel I don't have to cut tonight. You will love it, the place looks like an old movie scene." Dump said beaming a smile at everyone and trying to understand HeDo telling him what a wonderful day he had with her teaching him all the fun snow games and tricks.

"What's her name? How many folks live there?" Melanie started asking.

"She is a widower, no one around. She needs us, like we need her right now. "Was all Dump would say as he secured the camp and reloaded the mule.

"Dang it Melanie, we got 6 miles to get back there and this woman is trying to cook for us right now. I got to walk at least 50 percent of the way. Let me get my head together how we are going to make it back in good time. That mule doesn't have enough room on his back for us and all our crap. I am not trying to be hard rushing you, but you got to understand there facts we face. It ain't hard, I am huge, the packs are bulky, child is young and you ain't worth a damn to hump the kind of load I can." Dump said starting to lose it after his initial happiness.

"Damn it, you been gone all day! Then I find out you been sitting around with some old woman while I worried. Now we gotta go on a long trek with out dinner." Melanie started ranting before Dump motioned at the emotional child with them.

Melanie begrudgingly went to comfort the boy before Dump made it clear they were leaving this minute by packing up their belongings and slinging them on the mule.

"I am sorry Dump, your right. We just had so much fun together today I wished you had shared with us. We are ok now" She said brushing his cheek for forgiveness or agreement.

"Fine, let's just try harder, mount up" Dump said gesturing towards the door and rolling the poncho he had put up to block the wind from the outside.

HeDo had already had the best day of his life and not understanding very much English, had no concerns for why adults occasionally fussed as he was blessed in his ignorance of the petty squabbles around him.

"I am glad you had a great day, it will be even a finer day later. I got to lead this mule another six miles by dark and all on foot and it's as the old lady says not my cup of tea to be hiking" Dump said leading out to the road.

Melanie stewed to herself and reflected the first mile or so, and then reflected. Dump had already done at least 10miles today. He had found a better habitat for them and hot food, the only one bitching was her, and that fool had just started that weird airborne shuffle to speed up the progress .That man was a true man in all aspects or theories. However, Dump was going to be obstinate if she didn't say something nice to slow him down, he was going to try to jog along all the way there till he dropped. His heart was made that way, but she had to admit the body was not. He had to take this task at a more leisurely rate, especially dragging a mule along.

"Hey Dump? Could we slow down and talk together. Saul might be tired and I want to apologize for being mean" Melanie said as Dump kept, keeping a steady pace down the road.

"To be honest I am about to fall out, Whoa mule." Dump said slackening up, and panting like a bellows.

"Let's walk slow awhile." Dump said helping her down out of the saddle.

"You really ought to rest a while and have a seat. I am sure that the woman knows it's a long way to her house, especially in this weather." Melanie said concerned he was going to make himself sick.

"I am ok, I need to walk it out and cool off anyway." Dump responded.

"Myra wants to go to the Trading post, but unless a wagon appears out of the blue I think she will just have to wait it out until we send a trader by there. By the way she says there is a wild dog problem in the area so be watchful and don't let HeDo stray.

"I see one more reason you were in a hurry to try to get there by dusk. I am surprised that a woman has not seen a trader yet. Don't they go by her road?" Melanie said slogging along through the several inches of snow on the road.

"No they generally stay on the main road. We

will get to her house in about an hour or so. Hopefully I will have enough light to cover her husband's grave with rocks like she asked me to." Dump responded while scanning the rode ahead.

"Is the house big enough that we all get to sleep in a bed tonight?" Melanie asked hopefully.

"I didn't see the whole house but its pretty good size. We getting closer I can smell wood smoke now." Dump said walking a bit faster and turning to check on HeDo.

8

Tis the Season

David arranged to send a messenger the back way to Roland's and had to pay the man very well to get him out in this weather. David told him to keep a sharp eye out for travelers and in particular Dump and Melanie. Goat Man and David had shoved GM's motorcycle into the warm bar after they had unpinned the side car and GM had been tinkering around with it most of the morning. David's truck had been pushed into the trading posts warehouse and he had a mechanic going over it and working on its electrical system.

Boudreaux and David were over in the corner plotting and scheming something and had already gone through a six pack of beer whilst deliberating what to do next. Beverly had fussed at them for starting to drink so early in the day but her protests fell on deaf ears. She had seen them do this before and wasn't worried too much however. They usually stopped after they had something for lunch and it was just their way of catching a buzz to dream up some off the wall imaginative solutions to whatever it was troubling them.

Most of the bar patrons had gone home or was housed over at the barracks so it remained reasonably quite except for conversations about planning future moves to get home and how to get the supplies there.

"You ready, David? I think I got this thing about as fixed as its going to get. I am going to give her a try." GM said before kicking the motor to life and revving it with a big silly grin on his face.

"Hot Damn! Good going GM." David yelled across the bar after the racket died down and gave the man a thumbs up gesture.

"Well that one worry out of the way and maybe a new something to think on." Boudreaux said smiling.

"I ain't so sure you can drive that thing in snow" David said speculating.

"If he go slow and the snow she don't get too deep that three wheeler make it." Boudreaux said rubbing his whiskers.

"How about it, Goat man? You up for turning that thing into a snow mobile?" David asked smiling.

"Give me one of those beers you all been swilling all morning. I reckon I earned one and this is going to take some thinking." GM said reaching for a beer in the cooler that David had filled with snow this morning.

"Well, my place is closer than Roland's and I'd appreciate it if you will go over there and tell them to bring the tractor and trailer over here; course they probably already thought of that and might be on the way here. You are going to have to decide what's best for you." David said just thinking out loud.

"Well, what's that barometer thing you rigged up say? We got more snow coming?" Gm said drinking the half frozen beer.

"That or rain, I don't trust it much. Either way we got weather coming in tonight or tomorrow." Stewart said from his corner where he had been cat napping.

"Lookee here, the dead have arisen." Boudreaux said looking at a disheveled Stewart.

"If you all had not stayed up all night, or got back started so early again this morning I might have gotten some sleep. I don't know how you do it, I drank half what you all did am hung over as hell." Stewart said going to the water barrel.

"The idea is to not sober up so you don't get the hangovers." Boudreaux said laughing and saying cheers to David as they bumped cans.

"You all are some sick puppies." GM's wife said half jokingly looking up from her conversation with Beverly.

"No, we are booze hounds." David replied smirking mischievously.

"I think it might be best to try to get to Roland's. I will take the bike out for a test run here in a bit and make sure it will handle the trip, but I think I got it fixed pretty well. I can look for Dump on the way and double back quicker than that messenger if I find him." GM said not relishing the notion of watching Boudreaux and David partying all winter if he got stuck at the lake.

"That makes sense, whether its rain or snow you need to be off soon. If it rains, we just are going to get slush and ice for a day or two. We get more snow; I don't know what to tell you. It's never happened that we had such quirky weather this far south." David replied wishing he could gauge accurately what to expect.

"Shelly, I am going to go for a little test drive and then we are going to head to Roland's. You might want to go shopping over at the store and load up on anything special you want to see us through winter, I am not sure when we are coming back this way." GM said heading for the door.

"David! What am I going to do about Christmas? You were supposed to be getting that collapsible fishing rod he wanted and making him a survival snare kit." Shelly said realizing that everyone's plans had gotten altered.

"No worries, I got it out in my truck. I been riding around with your order for a week or so and was going to drop it off at the trading post for you to pick up. The rod and reel look brand new. Its small enough collapsed he can put it in or on his bug out bag and I got you a small pocket size tackle box full of everything he needs." David said smiling.

"Oh that is wonderful, thank you so much. there is no way to carry even a two piece rod on that bike of his with the wind wiping around and he always wanted a telescopic fish pole for his bug out bag, especially with the number of lakes and ponds around here. You're a Sweetie David. Put it in a bag or something so he can't see it, would you?" Shelly said beaming.

"I got Sherry to measure out some Christmas wrapping paper we found and threw in a roll of scotch tape. It's weird what was common now becomes hard to find but I got it all in a brown paper bag. I donated one of my extra ammo pouches for your snare survival kit that Swede made up. By the way, you owe him a cake or pie for that job when you get around to it. I got a few things too I want you to carry back as gifts for the rest of Roland's house guests. You going to be pretty cramped in that old sidecar bucket!" David said laughing and dropping all the worries he had as the spirit of the season made his eyes dance merrily, or was that the alcohol? *She couldn't be sure, but she loved the old prepper immensely at the moment and gave him a hug regardless.*

Boudreaux and I traded for a whole display of fine Schrade and Old timer knives and I finally got John the rarest of the rare he has been wanting and so he won't try to steal mine any more. David said digging in his coat pocket and producing a marvel of ingenuity in an old style woodsmen's knife in a quality leather belt sheath.

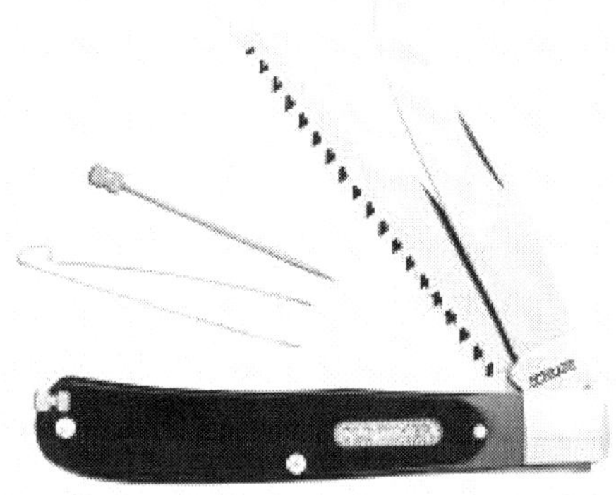

97OT Old Timer Buzzsaw

"Wow! That's handsome. I never seen the actual knife before but I seen you or John wearing it. His wife Sarah has been fussing about him wearing his pockets out carrying a bit of broken hacksaw blade when he hasn't borrowed your knife." She said smiling.

"We community gifting this year, meaning that everyone gives the gift so sign the card. Lol that's another thing hard to find these days. Most all of the Christmas cards we find have already been given and somebody just saved. So, if everybody signs the same card, maybe in the confusion the original sender won't be noticed." David said laughing.

"Most names are common except some of those weird southern or biblical names you have down here so they would be easy to miss. That's a good idea; I made him a card this year." Shelly Responded

"Guess what his starts out with?" David said grinning.

"I have no idea, what?" She asked smiling and getting into the seasonal fun.

"'Love, Boudreaux'" David exclaimed and said it was one of the cards he had given to Beverly a while back that she had donated to the cause. See if the card was just a general Xmas card it didn't matter who signed first. Everyone would just keep adding comas and signing names here or there afterward or scramble them around the page." David said sitting back still chuckling about old Boudreaux getting a nondescript card for the love of his life at the last minute before the stores closed one year and Beverly happily donating it to the cause.

'Boudreaux, go see about GOAT MAN and bring Shelly her present for him out of the truck, if he ain't back." David said giving him a sly wink that

Shelly missed.

"Sure Dave, I am back in a second. Stewart, you got your old mung head back in order yet? You need to go get the rest of our gifts out of storage at the general store while we at it." Boudreaux remarked looking at a sick looking Stewart.

"Yea, I will live now, rather have had me some tea first but I will help.' Stewart said rising and regaining his senses after last night's hullabaloo.

The two wandered out the front door as a cold gush of wind blew snow into the tavern.

"I ain't looking forward to sitting in that sidecar today no matter how slow we go." Shelly said shuddering at the expected bitter cold out in the open mostly.

"Wrap up in a blanket like a sleigh ride." Beverly suggested.

"That powder puff blue down coat David came up with for me is really appreciated, but I think it was made for warmer weather. Its quilted and all, but they were a bit skimpy on the feathers and with that white fake fur trim you can see me a mile away on that OD green colored motorcycle and that's not a good thing these days." Shelly complained.

"I will find you something better when we can, nobody was stocking winter coats when this crap hit." David reminded her.

"Goat Man's heading back." Stewart said poking his head in the door.

"I will go greet him." Shelly said before David countered.

"Hey, look Stewart had your present too stored over at the general store. You are not supposed to know it. Give him a chance to tell GM he has to hide it to." David said with a slight smile.

"OOH! What is it?" she playfully asked.

"I am not telling! You wait till Xmas. Hey GM! How she doing? That old cycle run ok?" David said in a greeting as the Goat Man pulled into the yard.

"Purring like a kitten. No problems. Hey Stewart, put that up! She will see it." Gm objected as Stewart came from the general store with an armload of goods.

"No she won't, I told her to stay inside and Beverly is making sure she doesn't peek." David told him.

"I think its best that you call Christmas early. It is awful cold and it might be the best time to give it to her." David suggested.

"This is magnificent. You made it all by hand?" Gm said fondling the Beaver coat he had requested for his mate.

"Well Boudreaux, John and I caught and tanned the pelts, but the liner was another story. Lois did not have a pattern and that is actually a satin prom dress sewn in there. I think it suits it well looking at the sea green lining on the coat that had a mystifying glimmer.

""I love it, that's almost an emerald green and these pelts I can't see a stitch in. Lois is a fine seamstress, how did she manage sewing leather?" GM said petting the coat.

"We got an old treadle power singer machine for her, but that piecing together of the skins was done on a cobbler's machine. I found an old shoemakers tools that had been stored in a barn for who knows how long and it was the type that did 12 stitches at a pull. Very odd machine, looks like a press and you hand feed through it. I have no idea how it works but Louis loves it. We started saving pelts in September; they ain't prime, but have a nice ruff. Swede tried to donate to the pile but he hasn't learned the art of curing them yet. We going to make a fashion statement I guess this season, amongst me and Boudreaux we got enough to give the girls a coat each after John donated his pelts. We also managed to make Bernie a trench coat length raccoon coat. He! He! I got Lois to make him one of those football pennants of old to wave when he puts it on. That was a style way back in the day to have a floor length raccoon coat. Anyway, when Bernie travels the old man needs to stay warm so we going to deck him out in a fur blanket of sorts." David said proud of the countless man and woman hours put into the special gifts they had prepared.

"Half of me wants to rush in and give it to her now and the other half says wait on Christmas.' Gm said in a quandary as to when to celebrate the day.

"Hey, you can't hide that coat any longer and she has the added advantage of draping Bernie's coat over her legs on the way home. Give it to her now." Stewart remarked.

"Ok you're right. I am going to do it!" GM said proudly starting to head towards the tavern.

"Not so fast, if you declare Christmas today she needs a chance to reciprocate." David said waving a grocery sack in front of him.

"You a sneaky old goomer Dave, did she buy that from you? What is it?" GM said reaching for it before it was snatched away.

"All in good time. Boudreau, if you don't mind go get Silas to give you our end of the lake small presents for our friends." David said smiling.

"One ahead of you Davy Boy already did, but Beverly has to tend to something for us." He said meaningfully.

"We are all going to be in Dutch; unless we let the lady folks organize this." Stewart said straightening his back and getting his diplomat persona ready.

"Go do it Stewart, but no talking it to death. I got to get on the road." Gm stated matter of factly

"You get a Bernie Care kit, 4 cans of blueberries for your pancakes from us, that motorcycle battery and wires you just got on the community tab, and this is from us for your future new year" Boudreaux said holding up a singular seed.

"What type of seed is it?" GM said respectfully knowing Boudreaux was making a point.

"I can't take credit for it, this is one of ten that you get to plant or sell. David brought them with him. Its Seminole squash. Careful where you plant it, I seen vines get 50ft and even climb trees. The squash looks like little pumpkins, but what's neat about them; they keep a long time if the stem doesn't get knocked off. David said he had one on his kitchen counter for a year and a half and it was still good until it got bumped and the stem got knocked off. You can even eat the leaves." Boudreaux said of the longest storing natural prepper food plant he could think of.

"That's really neat. I will fix a place for them along the wood line and let them run wild." GM said

"Shelly didn't like the early Christmas idea too much, but she is going along with it. She said give her a minute to wrap your present." Stewart announced coming back from the tavern.

"I wish I had me a bow or a box or something." GM said trying to think how he wanted to present his gift.

"I don't have any ribbons; Silas will have a box though. Ha! I tell you what, stick it in that Santa sack you were going to use for the pageant and put that Christmas hat on. "David said with a grin.

"She would like that; I will be back in a minute. Keep this thing hid." GM said smiling and heading towards the general store as David put the beaver coat in his side car temporarily.

"Go slip this to Shelly, it's my extra one I had in my tackle box, but I just happened to have stuck in my pocket before we left so I had a can opener with me. She can owe me a cake for it." David said producing an old style fish knife with a scalier and a hook disgorger.

"That's a must around here with all these little bream, fish are always swallowing them small hooks and such." Boudreaux said surprised David was giving up his spare knife.

"I get tired of retrieving his hooks for him when we go fishing, now he is set to do it himself." David replied.

"Ho! Ho! Ho!" GM said walking towards them in his Santa hat and carrying his Santa sack.

"Looking good! Her coat is in your sidecar. Stewart should give us the all clear pretty soon." David said watching the excited man getting ready to present his special present.

"All clear!" Stewart called poking his head out the tavern door.

"MERRY CHRISTMAS!" Goat man hollered as he led the procession into the Tavern.

"Well, Hi Santa!" Shelly said rushing over to kiss him on the cheek.

"Santa has a present in his sack for you" He said hugging her back with the sack slung over one shoulder.

"Oh goody! You got presents to on the table over there." She said gesturing as everyone watched the happy couple sharing their love and special seasonal charm.

"You first!" GM said walking over to the table and seeing the pretty Christmas wrappings.

"Wow! Where did you get Christmas paper?" He said gushing at the special meaning of it.

"Sherry managed to scrounge some up! Really puts you in the spirit of things, Don't it?" Shelly said proud she had managed to source out her special request for real wrapping paper.

"Sure does. Look in Santa's sack and see what he has brought you." GM said setting his bag down on the table.

Shelly opened the bag and looked inside. You could tell she hadn't figured out what it was yet as she begin to pull the fur out of the sack.

"A coat! A beautiful beaver skin coat! OOOOHH! Look at the lining. That is the prettiest green I ever seen." She said admiring it.

A chorus of try-it-on's, forced her to quit hugging her husband and she donned the garment.

"You look lovely" Beverly declared and Shelly blushed with all the compliments everyone gave her.

"Its gorgeous, however did you manage to find it, let alone afford it?" Shelly asked.

"I had it made. That's an "Our End of The Lake" original." GM said beaming.

"Really? Why it looks like it came from a furrier. You didn't really get Lois to sew this up, did you?" She said admiring her sleeves.

"Sure Did! David and I been getting dishpan hands setting so many beaver traps, too! Boudreaux said laughing.

"This is so special. Thank you. Thanks everyone." She said pirouetting around like a little girl showing it off.

"Your turn Baby" She said handing him his first

present.

"I can't imagine what this is." Gm said while unwrapping a box.

"A collapsible fishing rod! I have been wanting one of these for years!' GM said as he telescoped the Rod out and mimicked catching a big fish.

"Thanks Darling!" GM said giving her a kiss.

"I didn't have enough wrapping paper for this, but it goes with it." she said reaching in her purse for a small belt attachable fishing tackle box.

"Cool! This has everything in it!" GM said admiring a variety of hooks, jigs, weights and a couple bobbers.

"Here", she said handing him another small package.

"This is from me, but you best thank David, too." Shelly said as Goat Man unwrapped the fishing knife.

"Ah! This is great! How did you talk him out of this?" GM said admiring his new knife.

"With the promise of a nice nut cake." David said smiling.

"You sure do like her special cakes." GM said pocketing his prize.

"You got one more." She said beaming a broad smile.

"You did far too much already." GM said holding his next package.

"Santa's has been a good boy this year!" She joked at him.

"A survival snare kit! How neat is that? I hope I never have to use it; but we set now baby, if we get broke down again somewhere. Damn! Did I just say that? I best be not thinking about any such thing the way our lucks been running!" GM said hugging his wife and sharing a special moment while his friends laughed and cheered at the impromptu sharing of an early Christmas.

"You best be making tracks now after one more drink. You got to have one with us for the holiday before you leave." Boudreaux said setting down a round for everybody.

"I really hate to leave, especially not knowing when I will see you all again." Shelly said starting to tear up.

"We see you come springtime, now drink up and be merry." David admonished with a smile.

9

The Big Arrival

"Ah Hell! Hold this mule." Dump said handing the reins to Melanie.

"What's the matter?" She said before her blood ran cold at seeing a pack of dogs at the far end of a field up ahead.

Dump took a bead on what he guessed was the Alpha male and emptied his 30-30 in the packs direction.

"I got three of them furry fiends. I don't know if I got their leader or not, but they shouldn't bother us again for awhile." Dump said reloading his rifle from the pocket full of cartridges he had in his coat.

"Its ok, HeDo, Dumpie ran the bad dogs off." Melanie said in a consoling tone to the boy astride the mule.

"Ordinarily I would say we should go cut meat. But I have neither the stomach nor time for it today. Damn I hate shooting at dogs, can't tell if they are former pets, wolves or worse than coyotes. Let's just get on down the road post haste. MeMaw will be worried hearing so many shots." Dump said patting the mule and thinking what a good mule Old Saul was not to be spooked by him shooting at the pack.

They trudged along the road and Dump stopped once to look at the dog tracks that had crossed the road through the snow.

"Hard to tell how many is in that pack, but I am guessing 15 or more. I am sure glad they didn't try to ambush us. I am half tempted to tie HeDo to the saddle. Saul wouldn't have much trouble fighting them off I think, but I doubt the boy could stay on him if started his spinning kicking bit." Dump advised Melanie.

"I doubt I could stay on him if he did that." Melanie said worriedly.

"Well if he ain't too scared, he realizes he has a rider and won't go ballistic. Course on the other hand; he threw me once when he got surprised by a snake." Dump said thinking it was best to not go into detail about that encounter.

"That's her house, the far one on the left with the smoke rising out of the chimney."

"I am so ready to just sit in a normal house and relax. I never realized just how easy we had it when cars were moving. Just turn a key and go, no matter how far and then come back home. Now it takes a day of planning and three days to get where you could in an hour." Melanie said walking into the driveway to Myra's.

"Land sakes! Was that you doing all the shooting" Myra said coming out the front door.

"Yes that was me. I run into that dog pack you warned me about. They weren't attacking, but I wasn't giving them the opportunity to think about it neither." Dump said reaching for HeDo to take him off the mule.

"Hi I am Melanie and that's HeDo." Melanie said

not put off a bit by the old women with the shotgun at the ready still.

"I am Myra, folks call me MeMaw, but I suppose Dump told you that already." the old woman said shaking her hand.

"Pleased to meet you; Dump told us a lot about you." Melanie said as HeDo came up and waved shyly at the woman.

"Well, aren't you the cutest thing." Myra said waving back to him and looking at him appraisingly.

"I am going to put the mule in the garage. You all go inside and get acquainted and I will be in shortly." Dump said leading the animal away.

"Something smells wonderful!" Melanie said as she entered the house.

"I been baking pert near all day it seems like. I have me a big propane tank I ain't used up yet, but that day is not far off. I baked a cake, some bread and some cookies, when I heard a child was coming to visit. Can he have one? Won't spoil his dinner and that tyke looks like he could do with some more weight." Myra said watching the boy politely looking around in amazement at all the antique bric a brac her house contained.

"Sure, he will love it. We been playing in the snow all day and haven't had a chance to eat much today..." Melanie said thinking she wouldn't mind a cookie herself.

"Here you go sonny. You want some to?" Myra said offering a plate of freshly made ginger snaps.

"Yum these are great! " Melanie said.

"Did he just thank me or pray for me?" Myra said as HeDo did a praying hands small head bow in her direction.

"I am not exactly sure what that means; his family uses it as a greeting as well as thanks. Either way, you won a little friend." Melanie said as HeDo carefully approached the woman and took her hand to hold.

"Isn't he just delightful?!" Myra said beaming that the little guy had shown her affection.

"Say MeMaw?" Myra said pointing at herself and looking into his almond eyes.

The boy responded with something that sounded like MamMaw, but Myra couldn't be more pleased.

"He is smart, too! Here have another cookie." She said leading him to the table.

"Where is Dump? He should be back in here by now." Myra said going to the kitchen window and looking out.

Dump had gathered the tools he thought he might need to dress the shallow grave and soon appeared pushing the wheelbarrow towards the site. MeMaw opened the back door and called out to him.

"That can wait, come inside and warm up. I got cookies!" she said trying to get him to relax a bit.

"I will take a cookie, but I need to start taking down that rock wall before it gets any later.

Dump had the wall down in record time and hauled the stones to the grave site before going inside the house.

"I just roughly arranged those rocks; we can put them the way you want later." Dump said entering the house.

"I wish you had taken a rest first, but I am sure happy you got that done though." Myra said showing him a wash basin where he could clean up.

"I was just earning my supper. "I'm so hungry that my stomach is chewing on my backbone!" Dump said grinning.

"I like a man with a good appetite. We got lots veggies, but I didn't have much meat. I put up some hamburger last year and I opened two jars to make a casserole though." MeMaw said puttering around the kitchen.

"I noticed you had two small garden wheelbarrows as well as that big one I was using. You wouldn't happen to want to trade for the big one would you? "Dump said sitting down at the table.

"Well I find it to heavy to use, what do you want it for?" Myra said confused.

"I got me an idea while operating it. I can cut me two poles and lash them to the wheelbarrow handles and make me a travois to haul the kid and our camping equipment in behind the mule." Dump said and then thanked Myra for a cup of coffee.

"Oh? That sounds like a pretty good idea. You can have it then I reckon." Myra said gifting it to him.

"Well I really appreciate that, but I am going to leave you with some supplies anyway. I would love to take you with us, but without a wagon I think its best you just stay here for now" Dump explained.

"You are going to send someone by though to check on me on take me to the trading post in a few weeks though aren't you?" Myra said a bit worried.

"Sure will, or I will come back myself" Dump reassured her.

"That's very kind of you

Pumpkin Pie Spice (1 teaspoon)

Substitute: 1/2 teaspoon ground cinnamon, 1/4 teaspoon ground ginger, 1/8 teaspoon ground allspice, plus 1/8 teaspoon round nutmeg

Allspice, ground (1 teaspoon)

Substitute: 1/2 teaspoon ground cinnamon plus 1/2 teaspoon ground cloves

Apple Pie Spice (1 teaspoon)

Substitute: 1/2 teaspoon ground cinnamon, 1/4 teaspoon ground nutmeg, plus 1/8 teaspoon ground cardamom

- Baking powder...½ tsp. baking soda and 1 ¼ tsp. cream of tartar
- Buttermilk...1 Tbsp. vinegar or lemon juice with enough milk to make one cup

Deodorant2 teaspoons baking soda
2 teaspoons talcum powder
2 teaspoons petroleum jelly

Mix well. Heat in a double boiler over low heat and stir until a smooth cream forms. Pour cream into a small container with a tight-fitting lid, and use as you would a regular cream deodorant

10

Forming the Rescue Party

Bubba and Jack had decided to try to backtrack David's trap line and bring back to camp any steel traps as well as unset some of the deadfalls and snares. No sense leaving an animal to suffer or die unnecessarily if no one was going to be daily running them like David normally did.

"Dang how far does this trap line go anyway? I am freezing out here" Bubba said watching jack damn near get whacked by a spring pole because he got careless unsetting the trigger.

"Damn! That was close! I couldn't quite figure out how that thing worked. I know now." Jack said looking at the vibrating sapling that had just had the tension released from it.

"That was a foot snare. I thought it was a neck snare that the snow knocked down." Jack said dusting some of the snow off the mechanism he had inadvertently set off.

"It liked to have knocked you down. Been funnier than hell if you had of stepped in it." Bubba said laughing.

"I am glad he rarely makes spear traps." Jack said looking around the area to see if he could see any more of David's critter getters before he moved on.

"Shit you didn't mention any of those!" Bubba

said surveying the area more closely.

"He usually only sets them for pigs. Rarely he will do a deer set if the terrain just begs for one. He doesn't make the flying kind of spear traps you're thinking of from Hollywood if that's what you're worried about. He can, but says they are dangerous and inefficient.

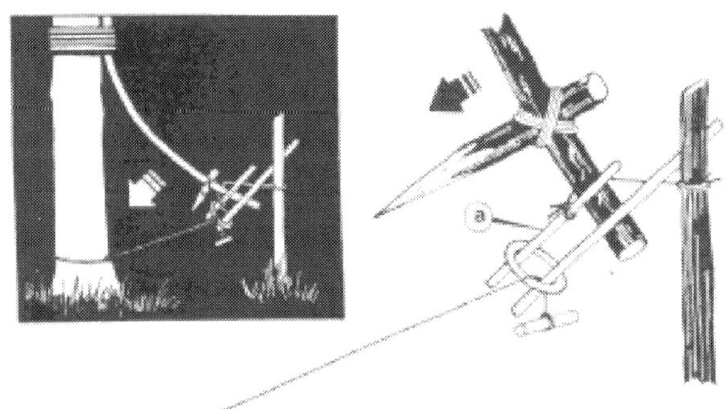

"Getting back to your question though, if he is getting serious about it can swing around in a horseshoe about two and half miles or more. We just follow the blaze marks he cut on trees or be aware of any other trail markers he has out." Jack said proceeding down what he hoped was the right trail.

"HELLO BOYS!" A voice called out from a tree stand David had about 50 yards away and freezing Jack and Bubba midstep.

"Who is that?" Bubba said softly.

"I don't know." Jack replied trying to figure out where the voice was coming from.

"HELLO! Who are you?" Jack yelled

"IT`S SWEDE, I AM UP IN A DEER STAND. HANG ON." He called down to them and began his decent.

"Damn! Scared the hell out of me. I still don't

see him, do you?" Bubba said scanning the woods.

"I can't see him either. David must of just put that stand up I didn't know one was here." Jack said and then started to point towards him.

"There he is, he must have been behind that cedar or up in it." Jack said starting to walk in that direction.

"You two are the nosiest trappers I ever heard." Swede said coming up and shaking the men's hands.

"We aren't out trapping, we are dismantling today." Bubba replied.

"Oh Yea, why? You thinking the snow is going to get worse?" Swede asked looking at the sky.

"The Weatherman living across from David said it might, but that's not the reason. David drove over to the Trading Post and most likely got stuck we think." Jack replied and still wondering where Swede had magically appeared from.

"How long has he been gone?" Swede said concerned.

"Just a couple days, but I bet that solar storm knocked his engine out. Did you see the lights in the sky?" Bubba asked.

"Yea I saw them. I figured that we had another geomagnetic anomaly but I didn't know how bad it might be. I take it you don't have power anymore?" Swede said knowingly.

"Yup! The Sun has just put the proverbial Damn Damn on most of our gear. We back to the darkness once more unless we using batteries or lamp oil." Jack declared and then advised Swede he wanted to see the Deer stand he had just come out of.

"Sure I will show it to you, that things like a mini tree house in that cedar. It ain't been up there long; he has it roofed with cedar branches and their mostly still green. I would of missed it myself if I hadn't seen the steps he has screwed into the trunk to get up there." Swede said leading the way.

"We got one solar battery charging unit that should still work on flashlight batteries but the rest of our stuff is pretty fried." Jack told him.

"Hell man, that's a bummer. I know how hard you guys been working on your setups. Ice Machine didn't get lucky did it?" Swede said as he pointed up to the stand/blind David had set up.

"It's gone." Bubba said forlornly, knowing how bad he was really going to miss visiting David come summer.

"That sucks; well at least we can use some ice trays placed outside the next few days." Swede said telling them to come back down the trail with him a bit too where he had dropped his pack basket and get home bag.

"Where's your crew? I thought you were out fixing the feral dog problem." Bubba asked.

"We were. I sent them back to the trading post when the weather turned bad and started making my way over here to get snowed in at David's bar with you." He said laughing at Bubba taking mental stock on how long David's supplies would last now.

"Well I am glad you didn't bring four more folks with you." Jack said thinking what a disaster that might have been with 5 more mouths to feed and have to bed down somewhere.

"The men I sent back got rations and plenty of

dog meat. They don't mind eating it. I ain't too choosy but if I can avoid it I do." Swede said pulling his gear down from a tree he had it cached in by a hidden piece of Para cord he had looped over a high limb.

"I heard you all making all that racket a mile off. I was bringing David back his conibear traps and removing game from the snares he had set. Which I might add, you all made twice as difficult by scaring game into them. I got 5 rabbits and one deep frozen raccoon that is probably a couple days old by the way. Anyway, I wasn't sure who was up ahead so I cached my stuff and went to have a look see. That's when I saw that stand and climbed up to see if someone had let some elephants out of the zoo." Swede said poking fun at them.

"Come on now we weren't that noisy." Bubba said.

"When someone hollers holy shit a couple times out in the woods next to a lake, you can hear it for miles. What was up with that anyway?" Swede chided.

"Disarming traps that David has set is kind of like mine detecting sometimes. He has some devilishly designed triggers that I either never seen before or the snow disguised them." Jack said sheepishly.

"I could also hear somebody laughing like hell at times." Swede said slapping Bubba on the back playfully.

"Well it was funny as hell mostly." The big man responded, helping Swede gather his things.

"Holy crap, what all you got in that pack basket? That thing weighs a ton." Bubba said hefting it as if he were an Olympic weight lifter with an exaggerated groan.

"David and Boudreaux's conibear 220 and 330 traps as well as some cable snares." Swede replied

"Where did you get the basket to make that thing?" Jack asked.

"It's traditional that trappers carry their stuff in trap baskets. Works better than a regular backpack. I got that old woman who used to re-cane chairs for Bernie's upholstery shop to make it for me. It's split white oak and tough as nails." Swede said proudly of his useful possession.

"I have to see how that's done sometime. I guess they soak those withes to weave them" Bubba said admiring the handy work.

"I didn't get a chance to watch her, but I suppose they do or steam them. It is built tough to last. Great for hunters too. Swede said going over to a brush pile where he pulled out a hobo stick looking affair with all the game he had collected hung off one end.

"That is one frozen raccoon." Jack said looking at the stiff animal dangling next to 5 skinned rabbits.

"I didn't feel like trying to clean him yet. That hide is frozen to the skin most likely. Those rabbits were pretty fresh. Look I will cover the rest of David's trap line for you if you tote most of this stuff back with you." Swede said glad to be rid of the cumbersome load that had wore him down for miles.

"Uh ok. Bubba gets to carry that pack basket thing." Jack said making a grab for the game pole before he could react.

"Hey now! I am already carrying most of those traps and snares we picked up so far." Bubba objected.

"Well I got the survival gear and that damned dog sized possum I swear is probably 20lbs or so." Jack complained back.

"You the one that wanted to bring all that extra survival gear when we were just going on a 5 mile hike." Bubba countered.

"He was right in bringing that extra gear, Bubba. And I am sure you agreed it was smart before you set out. What would you all have done if you had got back and found your camp under attack and been stuck spending the night out in this weather? Tell you what. We divide up the traps I got equally. I doubt David has many more big conibears left out here, and since its cold as hell I will just leave anything he has trapped to come back for later. I should be back in your camp in a few hours. I will fire three rifle shots in quick succession, if I need you. We got most of that pack of dogs but not the smarter ones and I just soon tell you here and now those animals scare the crap out of me. David was right. They have no fear of humans and come on like a Japanese Bonsai attack once they get it in their minds they are going to take something down. They rushed me and Dale checking the trap line and they didn't break off the attack until 5 dogs were down and even then they ghosted the wood line watching us for an opening all the way back to camp." Swede said painting a horrifying picture of the hunter becoming the hunted.

"What did you do with the animal offal when you cleaned that game you got?" Bubba asked as a realization came over him

"I know where you're going Bubba and I am not as stupid as you might think. Yea those dogs are going to get lead straight to your camp following the carcass trail and blood scent. I didn't have any poison or inclination and time to rig any trap sets around the guts and skins. I figured I would have tripped over David out here checking his line and we could have decided what to do. Those dogs are trap wary and gun shy now so it ain't going to be easy to take care of them. I probably did a stupid thing too though and for that it's my price to deal with. Those dogs are lead by a big damned Rottweiler that's smart as hell. He sends his subordinates out first always and watches from afar. When you do get a glimpse of him he is peeking around a tree or something, he seems to understand guns. He also has a nose for steel traps. We have seen where he kicks dirt at them until they spring and takes the bait right out of the area. I been trying to one up that Cujo for several weeks, but he always manages to get away. The dumbest thing I did heading this way was to piss him off so he would follow me and leave my men alone. I peed on everywhere I saw dog sign and my offal piles. Cujo is coming guys and has blood in his eye for me." Swede said finishing his story about a vile beast that had a mutual vendetta with him.

"Sounds like you ought to just say the hell with it and we go back together." Jack said processing the information he had just heard of some killer dog with gang members following his and Bubba's mutual friend.

"That's right; we can go out and finish the line later together. I'd just soon have my 12 gauge, if we got dog trouble headed this way." Bubba said scanning the clearing warily for any movement.

"Nah, that dog I am thinking feels like he is driving me and is waiting until I get tired and let my guard down. What he doesn't know is that my game and his are different. He knows if he can catch up quick, he can get me when I try to turn and fight after he wears me down. I know he has to pick up the pace and he going to get tired also and feels like those dump piles I am leaving are safe, if his friends in the dog pack are not getting hurt maybe. That's hard to say; once a dog goes feral his awareness of anything 'man' increases. He might avoid everything man may try to sort it out about what's safe or not. I know his hunger got to be increasing if he has not hunted, because he is pursuing. The part of the pack that's eating might mess with him for dominance, if they see he gets weaker so now instead of against me, they on my side in a small way." Swede said letting his wood and trapping lore instincts sink into his audience.

"How would it be if I stayed in the stand and shot the old bastard as he came by?" Bubba said hefting his Kel Tec 2000 sub carbine as an exclamation point.

"Might work." Jack offered.

"No, but thanks for volunteering to stay out in this cold. We already stomped the trail down pretty good, so he knows I got friends now that form our own pack against him. I lost my edge of him losing caution and he will be double wary of this spot. I need to separate and go the back trail." Swede said considering his route.

"He can't smell you over that cedar scent, if he gets within 100 yards I will make a point of sending him to doggy heaven." Bubba declared not willing to give up on his theory quite yet. He still thought that he might get at least a pot shot at his friend's nemesis.

"Buddy, that's a good thing you willing to do, but I got something better for ya to give attention to. Go on home with Jack and find a glass bottle and pound it down as fine as flour. Normally I wouldn't do this to my worst enemy but once you got that glass refined lace that coon carcass with that glass powder. If he eats that, it's going to perforate his stomach and Cujo going to die an agonizing death, but that can't be helped and I won't have to be scared to walk in the woods no more." Swede said getting ready to set off.

"Man. That's nasty and dirty too. You don't have any better way to handle this?" Bubba said considering alternatives.

"I don't desire to see any flashing fangs in my sleep. You all got better ideas I am open. Jack set all the traps you got on the perimeter of the compound, because Cujo probably has at least 8 members of his pack still left, and maybe we get lucky to get a few. If we don't, maybe we try the glass thing. You keep Harley inside somewhere and on a leash till this sorts out. That dog can fend for himself, but he might run afoul of our traps or get ganged up on by those dogs. Put his tire that he likes to munch on in one of the houses, he won't be none the worse for wear to stay in out of the cold anyway. Hell, bulldogs are not made for snow anyway." Swede concluded.

"I guess there is no sense in arguing brother, you seem to have the situation thought out some. I will tell the ladies that compound movement should be restricted to pairs also. We doing the outhouse thing again, unless somebody hauls water now, considering those 12v RV pumps you installed to get flow to a toilet from the lake got destroyed this time." Bubba reflected.

"I got an idea; you know how mothballs repel snakes? That Naphtha screws up the pits in pit vipers as David used to tell us they smell with. All these houses around here reek of that stuff like an old lady convention. Could we disguise the traps with that?" Jack said considering the dilemma.

"No thanks when it comes to scenting a trap. A confusion of attraction and diversion to the dogs might work though to channel them in a certain path free from any mothballs." Swede partly thought about before discarding the idea.

"Let's just go with my original plan and I will head out in a few minutes" Swede said dividing up the remaining traps in his basket.

"Ok guys I am off, good luck and stay safe." Swede said.

"I will have a drink waiting on you" Bubba said shouldering his load and following Jack back to camp.

"You think Swede can get that crazy tractor of Dave's started?" Bubba asked

"I done it once or twice and seen him do it a few times. I made him write down how to do it so I didn't hurt myself awhile back if Louise can put her hands on it." Jack said following his foot prints in the snow back to the compound.

"I bet I could do it." Bubba said before Jack reminded him of the cautions David had given him of the tractor sometimes having a tendency to want to bite who ever tried to crank it.

"Well we got to get it started and go retrieve him. I doubt the weather is going to cooperate enough to sail over there. Maybe we can look at the Chris Craft closer and see if we can get it running too. I understand that kind of an engine." Bubba said dodging a branch that Jack had let fly back as he moved it from his path.

"Boy you are dangerous in the woods." Bubba complained.

"Shush or Swede will be telling us we did this or that again by making noise on the trail. I am thinking we try to go retrieve David tomorrow if possible. You staying the winter or heading back to your place?" Jack said letting another branch fly.

"Let me be point man, hell the trail is easy to

follow now." Bubba said getting into the safety zone in front of Jack.

"I want to get back to my place. Cat and I are pretty well set over there and I want a word with Boudreaux about helping to take care of his bar if he is wintering over here." Bubba said seeing a rare opportunity.

"I am letting Swede stay in David's place tonight. You all have mercy on his liquor stock, no telling when he can get a resupply. Maybe Swede wants to go back over to the trading post tomorrow, but I doubt he will want to leave with the dog problem left open. If he does want to go, I am staying to look out for the ladies. You can drive David's tractor over and he can see to getting it back. Tell him to load that trailer up with supplies. I don't relish the thought of having to go back to the trading post until spring." Jack said feeling like his pack straps were trying to amputate his arms already.

"You got enough lamp oil or kerosene to make it this winter for lights?" Bubba asked.

"I don't think so, but we got a bunch of candles we managed to find, and a limited number of rechargeable batteries that should get us through I guess though." Jack responded.

"David said before the crap hit the fan that StoveTec was working on making some kind of lantern attachment for those great stoves you all got. You ever figure out what their lab had come up with?

"No, I know it took a two door stove like we have to work though. He said couple handfuls of fuel and it is bright as a kerosene lantern and burns for almost 2 hours. No fossil fuel required. That would be great for an outside gathering. I have seen an email once when he was chatting with marketing that showed a picture of it in development though." Jack said and then tried to describe it to Bubba.

"I sure would have liked for you all to have gotten one of those. It sounds pretty revolutionary and would have been an exceptional light source for me to have had around camp when I used to do YouTube videos." Bubba said wondering if Swede had snuck some rocks into his pack with those extra traps he was now toting.

"The Preppers on YouTube sure did a great service as well as their subscribers to try to educate the public about a possible event like this." Jack said panting along in back of Bubba.

"Yea but for many it was too little too late. We dang sure gave it a good shot though. I wonder how many people all that work and time saved." Bubba said readjusting the tonnage on his back.

"David said if we reached just one it was all worth it. I think the folks with all those electronic books are singing the blues now though if they never even practiced the bits of knowledge they read." Jack said now dodging a loose branch that Bubba released.

"Sorry about that, either keep up so I can pass the occasional branch to you, or stay far back out of range." He said puffing.

"Hell lets take 10 for a sec." Jack said leaning forward to take the load off his shoulders and rest in place a moment.

"Not a bad Idea." Bubba said doing the same.

"There is a slight hill up ahead. We can sit against it with our feet out and rest with our packs on for a few minutes. I don't want to rest much longer than that or have to sling this pack back on from the ground." Bubba said pointing from the hip as the two crouched over.

"Now you're talking." Jack said straightening and walking up to the spot before settling back to let the hill support his load.

"Older Preppers got pretty good libraries, but lots of folks bought the electronic books thinking they just wanted to learn something new and were going to remember it. I bet you can't tell me off the top of your head like David does how far to set snares off the ground for different animals for example." Jack asked Bubba.

"I can do a few, but I know what you mean. All those tricky snare and deadfall triggers get me. I did print a few of them out for my bug out bag though. I got a nice library at home, but that ain't here." He said wistfully.

"Best survival tool you got is your brain, you can't lose that, and trying out and doing stuff enhances memories so you can call upon it when needed.' Jack said thinking of his own collection of books he couldn't bring with him.

"I always look at the books David managed to bring with him when I visit. He left a bunch behind also he wishes he had, but he has a fair collection of useful info.

"A lot of fiction books got useful things in them. I been reading an old book called A BLOCKADED FAMILY: Life in Southern Alabama during the Civil War (Elemental Historic Preparedness Collection), from the prepper archeology and Elemental collection. It's got interesting info in it like how they used Okra seeds as a coffee substitute and things like that. David borrowed one the Goat Man had called Every Step in canning, the cold pack method: (Prepper Archeology Collection Edition). No one I know of even heard you could cold pack can before he read that. I wish I had their whole collection that they hand picked and reprinted, but that's not to be anymore." Jack said reminiscing.

"David is often heard to say Knowledge is power and power is money. Just think what we could do with all that old time knowledge now. We could barter it, use it, or profit from it." Bubba said shifting up.

"You got that right! Well I guess we burning daylight, let's get back on track." Jack said looking like a turtle trying to right himself as he finally gained his feet.

They heard the crack of a .22 and listened in anticipation for another shot but it did not come.

"He dispatched something. You ever tried to shoot that weird cheap heritage combo 22 he has?" Bubba asked talking about the cowboy looking 22 and 22 mag that Swede used on his trap line.

"Don't knock it until you tried it. I admit is strange to see a safety on that kind of gun, but David gave him that, and it was what he grew up with. They still American made by the way in Miami of all places, or were. They are accurate as hell and get the job done. Kind of pretty too, I like the quality of the wood grips." Jack said.

"What do you think he had to dispatch?" Bubba asked still very aware of his surroundings.

"He didn't have a kill stick with him so could have been anything. I am betting though it was a bobcat that David has been after over that way. Never tried eating one, but I bet if it was a bobcat, Swede will be running a bit late skinning it out for the pelt." Jack said.

"I don't know, if I had that Cujo dog Swede described to us chasing me, I wouldn't be taking the time to." Bubba said getting out onto the paved road and the easy walk home.

"I kind of agree with you, but he been wanting a hat made out of one so we shall see. He sort of gone mountain man if you ain't noticed." Jack said looking at the road in back of him for any sign of tracks or movement while Bubba scanned the road ahead.

"I don't see him as much as I used to, he or I are always making the rounds somewhere. What do you mean Mountain Man? He is getting more frontier like or wild?" Bubba said regarding the expression on Jack's face.

"Bit of Both I guess, He just seems to stay out on the trail longer than most and does more game trading than scavenging the vacated houses. Well at least in my opinion he does, but to each his own. I prefer finding dinner in a can and he rather hunt his down a different way..." Jack said relived he could see the wood smoke from the compound's cabins up ahead.

"Swede been hard at it to provide for his family, he might be just pushing the envelope for Christmas. Hell I thought David and Boudreaux had gone beaver crazy or they tasted like steak or something before I figured out they were collecting pelts for the ladies coats. Then because of the S.O.B.s I had to trade with them to get my old lady one too. Since when did David decide to make a fashion statement and make all the ladies need to start wearing beaver?" Bubba said begrudging David the amount of Bernie Bucks he owed him for Dave's latest marketing ploy.

"I guess because he couldn't catch enough otters. You know him, he enjoys nothing better than to make his own markets and try to control them someway." Jack said laughing, but profiting because his wife was the only seamstress around that could stitch the hides together.

"I guess you are right, he dreamed up that weird fireproofing stuff I do. His latest is he wants me to bend up some sheet metal for reflector ovens.

The reflector oven is a wonderful gizmo to use for camp cookery. It's simple to use, inexpensive and does quite a professional job of baking biscuits, pies, cakes, cookies, pizza, casseroles and other foods.

Reflector ovens were first widely recognized and used in the late 1700s. At that time, they were called "tin kitchens" or "hasteners" by common folk and were used for cooking on the home hearth. Modern reflector ovens closely resemble these early cooking aids

Simply moving the oven can change the temperature.

The principle by which reflector ovens work is actually simple. Heat from the open fire is reflected from the shiny interior of the oven towards the item being cooked. The reflector's slanting top and bottom direct the heat toward the top and bottom of the pan of food being baked, allowing it to brown evenly on upper and lower surfaces. If the cooking temperature seems too hot or too cold, you can move the oven backward or forward to adjust it. If the food cooks unevenly on the sides, rotate the pan.

The best fire to be constructed for the reflector is a teepee fire built to the height of the oven's cooking shelf. If you consider two reflector ovens to be used or are available, place them across the fire from each other so the ovens are facing. This provides maximum reflection of heat.

"Where you going to get tin at to build them? Never mind, we got a bunch of roofs around here." Jack said considering an easy access of materials.

"I am going to go him one better, I know where a bunch of duct work is and already traded me for some sheet metal snips." Bubba explained.

"He has not mentioned that idea to me. I will go on it if you need a partner." Jack said hopefully.

"I might have just messed up; we talked about building a few for Christmas presents." Bubba said catching himself.

"No matter, looks like it be spring until trade starts again. I will spot you some silver if you want to build me some over the winter months though." Jack offered.

"Now I might do that, but its David's idea so you all need to be square on that. Tell you what, you give me those tin bending vice grips I saw in your shop the other day and don't get chincy letting me play with that half gallon of Ancient Age Dave has and I will say we got a previous deal, when it comes to negotiations." Bubba offered.

"I need those tin benders for the skunk works, but if we could maybe job out to you before we make or find another pair that might be ok. I got a bottle of Jim Beam, if you want to trade though. It's not a half gallon, but David's booze is his own and I can't be committing it. How a about a quart of Jim Beam, a liter of RC cola, and use of the pliers?" Jack said doing the stooping and resting thing with his pack.

"You got some coke? Hell, I am sold. You try to get that IOU off him for Bernie bucks though. David might have the ass about us sharing his idea and want it cashed in for cutting wood or digging a ditch or something." Bubba said watching out for a vindictive David.

"He ain't that way, but I will buy your debt out or trade Bernie bucks with him. I want to build some of those steel boxes that look like the Coleman stoves that go on burners, too. You know them, Wal-Mart store type steel boxes with a thermometer on the door." Jack said getting excited.

"No need for those really, you can use an ammo can or a tool box to bake bread if you had to. Where would we get thermometers from anyway?' Bubba asked,

"I have been thinking on that. Grills have got them on them sometimes, but I figure we get some trader who has store raiders, to pick up some oven thermometers. Nobody would have picked them over yet or given them the time of day when the places got cleaned out." Jack said

"Damn! Your right! What else you think might have been overlooked that is useful like that?" Bubba said getting interested even more in a proposed joint venture.

"Oh I got a few ideas, is it a deal then?" Jack said offering his hand.

"As long as David says it's ok or doesn't object much, we got a deal. Hell, even if he does, did he have that oven thermometer idea, too?" Bubba said, deciding it was stupid to stay hunched over talking and he dropped his pack.

"Nope that's entirely mine; your tinworks could also help building pie safes, too." Jack said envisioning sheet metal applications for their venture.

"That's a bit far fetched for demand, but maybe not considering we don't have refrigeration any more." Bubba said stroking his beard.

"Let's finish this trek and talk it over with Swede when he gets in. That boy has a shop, too." Jack said picking up his heavy pack and grunting and protesting like an overloaded camel as he did so...

.

11

The Waiting Game

David scanned the roads leading into and leaving out of the trading post, for signs of activity, but it was all for naught. He had hoped that GM`s motorcycle would overtake the messenger on horseback he had sent out. One of them surely would get word back to him on the status of Dump and Melanie. Little did he know however, that Dump was sitting down to a sumptuous feast and was warm and cozy only 20 miles away from him.

David tried to gauge where Dump was in relation to the time someone could walk several miles, or a horse could gallop the same distance; but the concept was unfamiliar to him at the moment for any kind of math problem. He was a product of modern times and thought of cars and speed limits in regard to distance and time.

He remembered it took his platoon all day to perform a forced march in order to cover 15 miles when he was 18 and in the Army and folks were as fit as they could be then. Add the incentive of being pushed by a drill sergeant to hurry along and taking very limited breaks, he concluded that 10 miles would be about as much as he could imagine Dump doing in a day. No way was he going to make more than 15 miles a day, even if he had to push it in an emergency and that would be if he was traveling light. Traveling with a kid on a bike and a mule packed with camping gear at a leisurely pace. 8 miles was reasonable, maybe a bit short. 12 miles then, he might be anywhere from 25 to 30 miles away then; that is, if they had not had anything catastrophic happening. The messenger wasn't supposed to go above a canter, so he could really look for them; but the cold would push him not to dawdle and he bet he was traveling faster than he should. GM was doing maybe 25 miles per hour on these snow blown roads, so maybe in a couple hours he could possibly find out something about their fate? This is just too much to think about as visions of frostbite or worse crossed his mind.

Nothing to do while waiting, but quit agonizing over it and try to relax he concluded. David decided he could use a drink about then, and went back to the warm tavern.

"I guess we just spend a quiet holiday with the folks on our end of the lake and forget about coming over here for a while. The mechanic said he can get your truck running, he thinks if he can find a voltage regulator. Damn $5 part, but might as well be five million at the moment. No telling when, or if, we are going to find one." Boudreaux advised David.

"Well, look on the bright side; we know it can get fixed. Maybe we can substitute a marine part somehow, seeing that's about the only parts store I know of around here. I will go ask him in a minute to consider it. You and Stewart complete your packing lists?" David said sitting down at the table with them.

"Yes, we going to have to load that trailer to the gills with food stuffs and ourselves, but we will do it somehow." Stewart replied.

"Silas said if we can find some camphor, we can get a better handle on the weather. He wrote out the formulas for us out that old book they use to create different needful things." Boudreaux said handing David a couple sheets of paper.

"I got camphor in my tool boxes so the tools don't rust. It creates a coating from the gases it emits on metal. Mine is in little blocks of what looks like paraffin though and is sold that way specifically for throwing in a tool box. I don't know if I can extract it or not. I can put an order in with the traders; I doubt anyone has looted that item out of a drug store. Never can tell though." David said and started reading the sheets of paper.

Here is a description of a practical storm-glass taken from the book ***Pharmaceutical Formulas*** by Peter MacEwan, published in 1908. The article includes notes to assist in the reading of the instrument.

Chemical Barometer Recipe 1 from *Pharmaceutical Formulas*

Camphor - half ounce
Ammonium chloride - half ounce
Potassium nitrate - half ounce
Rectified spirit - one ounce
Distilled water - two ounces

Weigh the spirit into the bottle and dissolve the camphor, then add the salts and the water (warm). Shake, and when dissolved filter.
Long narrow tubes of glass are filled with this solution and hermetically sealed or corked. The tubes are then affixed to boards by means of wires in the same way as barometers are fixed. The changes of the solution signify the following:
Clear liquid : Bright weather.
Crystals at bottom : Thick air, frost in winter.
Dim liquid with small stars : Thunderstorms.
Large flakes : Heavy air, overcast sky, snow in winter.

Threads in upper portion of liquid : Windy weather.
Small dots : Damp weather, fog.
Rising flakes which remain high : Wind in the upper air regions.
Small stars : In winter on bright, sunny days, snow in one or two days.
The higher the crystals rise in the glass tube in winter the colder it will be.
Interestingly, in a supplementary chapter to this book, another storm-glass recipe was given including a more descriptive set of notes to aid in the prediction of the weather:

Chemical Barometer Recipe 2 from *Pharmaceutical Formulas*
Nearly fill a glass tube 10 in. long and ¾ in. diameter with the following liquid, then hermetically seal:-
Camphor - 2 drachm
Potassium nitrate - ½ drachm
Ammonium chloride - ½ drachm
Absolute alcohol - 2 ounces
Water - 2 ounces

Disolve.

Temperature is the main factor in changing the appearance of the solution. The indications are as follows:-
(a) During cold weather beautiful fernlike or feathery crystallization is developed at the top, and sometimes throughout the liquid. The crystallization increases with cold, and if the structure grows downwards the cold will continue.
(b) During warm and serene weather the crystals dissolve, the upper and greater part of the liquid, becoming perfectly clear. The greater the

proportion of clear liquid, the greater the probability of fine dry weather.
(c) When the upper portion is clear and the flakes of crystals rise to the top and aggregate, it is a sign of increasing wind and stormy weather.
(d) In cold weather if the top of the liquid becomes thick and cloudy, it denotes approaching rain.
(e) In warm weather if small crystals rise in the liquid, which still maintains its clearness, rain may be expected.
(f) Sharpness in the points and features of the fern-like structure of the crystals is a sign of fine weather ; but when they begin to break up and are badly defined, unsettled weather may be expected.
Note: 1 drachm = 3.89 grams.

"Well, that seems simple enough, I guess someday we going in the weather glass business." David said smiling at Stewart and Boudreaux.

"Seem like pretty handy things to have." Boudreaux said while rising to go fix them all another drink.

"We got to figure out this weather or we won't know when to plant or travel, etc. I know how to plant by the signs, but I still been caught by a late frost before. My favorite planting sign is indicated when the oak tree leaves get as big as a squirrel's ear, then its time to plant corn. Oak trees are smart and don't set leaves, until everything is right with the weather." David said sharing a bit of folklore that had proved true for just about every garden David had ever put in.

"I always plant on Good Friday." Boudreaux said sitting back down at the table.

"That's pretty traditional down here, but I been noticing that is getting too late for my tastes as the summers have been getting hotter." David replied.

"Well, you pegged the planting season's right last year, we going to follow your suggestions again this year also I guess." Boudreaux said wondering how late spring would be this year.

"Roland is pretty sharp on when to put his crops in. We got different varieties of vegetable seeds than he is used to though, for a lot of things that we didn't have planted last year. I guess we are just going to poke and hope and stagger out our plantings, until we get the rhythm down right.' David said looking out the window at a light snow still coming down.

"Fishing is going to be horrible. Those fish are going to be in deep water and we are going to have to go out in the boats and freeze, if we want to catch anything." Boudreaux said watching the snow with David.

"I think fishing season is out for me, until spring unless I have to. You and I might have to go stay out in a trapper camp in a more productive game area this winter. We pretty much have been cleaning out the woods close by the cabins." David said wondering which direction he wanted to branch out to.

"Swede said the same thing about his trap line on your boundary. He gets rid of them feral dogs over there and things might get better." Boudreaux replied going to put another log on the fire.

"I wonder how they are making out at the moment. I sort of thought they would have long abandoned the hunt and started back towards here, especially with this frigid weather hanging on and snow covering the trails. He might have headed on over to my place though." David said pondering Swede's whereabouts.

"I f you are going to have him and the hunting party, along with Bubba staying at your compound, you had best go ahead and leave your food here and start restocking your liquor cabinet now instead." Stewart said trying to imagine a week long snow storm party with all those hard drinkers. He couldn't begin to imagine it turning into an extended month long affair with that crew in place.

"I can already imagine the smell of that little get together, too. Those boys been out in the field hunting for two weeks and that bath house rig of yours you built to augment your solar ain't going to be able to be used anytime soon." Beverly said looking up from her knitting and silently commiserating with Sherry and the other womenfolk in attendance at the lake compound.

"Damn. I forgot about that thing running on those 12v RV pumps. Well, the passive solar collector I got up there will still work, but not in this weather. I guess I will rig something up that is gravity fed and wood fired when I get back." David said, wondering if anything was salvageable from his old system.

12

Hitching a ride.

Dump had saddled his mule and decided he would look ahead on the road for a few miles and see what conditions were currently. Snow was lightly falling, but the sky was still gray and hazy.

He continued on down the road and surveyed the forest and fields the road dissected. He spotted a man riding his horse at a fast trot coming down the road in the distance and watched him carefully a moment. Probably a messenger he guessed and urged his mule to pick up the pace and meet the rider.

"Hey, you Dump Truck? I have been looking for you." The rider called out.

"That's me! I take it David sent you?" Dump replied.

"Yeah, he was just worried about you. I am supposed to report back to him or carry on to Roland's depending on what we decide to do." The man responded and looked in back of him as the faint sound of an engine started to grow louder coming down the road.

"Sounds like a motorcycle maybe." Dump said looking off into the distance.

"That's what it is; looks like Goat Man got his bike back up and running." The messenger said shielding his eyes with one hand and looking off in the distance.

"Cool, looks like I got found big time. Nice to have friends looking out for you." Dump said dismounting his mule and the rider joined him to wait on GM to pull up.

"Hidey Ho! Dump, how are you?" GM said in a muffled as he shut his engine off and unwrapped a scarf from his face.

"Doing well. Nice to see you. Hi, Shelly!" Dump said acknowledging GM's wife.

"Hey Dump, where is Melanie?" Shelly asked.

"Oh, she is back up the road a few miles staying with a nice old widow woman. You are heading to Roland's?" Dump asked.

"Yes eventually. David said to look for you on the way and here you are. You say there is somewhere warm a few miles from here where we can talk?" Gm inquired.

"Yeah, house down on the far right. You will see smoke coming from the chimney. Woman's name is Myra. She is a sweet old woman, but she will most likely meet you with a shotgun. Melanie is there though. Just holler up to the house before you open the gate. We will be right behind you." Dump said starting to remount his mule.

"Ok, see you there then." Gm said and started his motorcycle and drove slowly off.

"I didn't catch your name by the way." Dump said to the messenger, as they rode along together back down the Road.

"It's Rob, this is a bit off my route, but I know this road also. Didn't know anyone was living on this section though." He responded.

Dump and Rob chatted back and forth the few miles to Myra's and then turned their mounts into the driveway.

Melanie came out to greet them and said Myra said to stable their mounts in the garage and to come in the backdoor, when they were done.

Dump and Rob unsaddled the animals and Rob shared some grain he had been carrying with Dump's mule before they entered the home.

Myra was distinctly happy to have so much new company and was seeing to it that everyone had some coffee and cookies.

"GM my friend, I want you to do me a big favor, if you would. Could you take Melanie and HeDo to the trading post? Shelly can stay here with Myra and visit until you get back?" Dump asked.

"I have already suggested just that; I will take them after I have had my coffee and warm up for a bit." GM said and began nibbling on a cookie that HeDo was helping Myra had passed him

"That's great. I can head out to the trading post with Rob here and be there sometime around dusk, I am guessing." Dump said sipping on his coffee.

"Well, this day certainly is working out well." Melanie said smiling.

"Yes indeed!" Myra said and then began happily asking a battery of questions of Shelly and getting to know her better.

13

Homeward Bound

HeDo was having the day of his life. Melanie thought looking down at the smiling boy riding in the side car of G'mans motorcycle. He had got him a new adopted grandmother in MeMaw that gave him cookies. He had got to build another snowman with her and Melanie and now he got to ride in a sidecar! Melanie thought about how his parents; HopSing and MeDo were probably beside themselves with worry about the boy and she was sure Martha was having conniptions about them all as well. She was sure Martha's almost supernatural knack of knowing how her loved ones were gave them comfort, but Melanie's heart went out to them just the same.

This had been a magical day she reflected. She was still laughing inside at how Shelly had responded when she asked if the motorcycle could carry all three of them. Shelly had smiled and produced a couple pictures of other sidecar setups that had given everyone a chuckle.

Бременские музыканты. Наши дни.
0:00 / 0:31

Boingky

Don't Ask! ☺

G'man had also told her not to tell David about that first pic of a band, because if she did he would probably have to lend Boudreaux, Swede and Roland his bike for the next party he was planning. He reassured her though that there was more than enough room for everyone and that his side car motorcycle could if need be carry Dump, her and the boy. Myra had provided HeDo with a pair of child's swimming goggles and made sure he was all bundled up before they had set off.

Dump and Rob were a few miles back keeping their own pace after GM gave assurances his wife would be just fine with Myra, until he got back in a couple hours or so.

GM made much better time getting back to the trading post, because he could just follow his old tire tracks and not have to worry about what was hidden under the snow. They waved at the gate guard coming in and proceeded to the tavern door and liked to have got run over by everyone happily pouring out the surrounding buildings to greet them, as they heard the motorcycle's engine coming up the drive.

"GM you are the man!" David called out as he rushed off the porch to hug an exuberant Melanie, as HeDo found the safety of hanging onto Goat Mans leather motorcycle jacket as a sea of well wishers came forward.

"I never thought I would set eyes on you again after you sent me off in Atlanta." Melanie said attempting to fix her wind blown hair.

"Me neither! Hey there is your other friend coming this way!" David said, as he saw Stewart jogging over from the general store.

"Melanie! HeDo!" Stewart cried as he managed to meet both of them running up and embraced them both, as the crowd smiled their approval at such a happy reunion and outcome to the current woes that beset everyone.

"OK! Christmas he comes early this time, Aiee! But, it be my last time for the big Jubilee. You got one hour free drinks on Boudreaux." The old Cajun said to the crowds cheer and he quickly stepped down as they almost overturned the chair he had stepped up on as they made a beeline to the front doors of the bar.

"It sure is great having everyone together like this. I guess Dump will be in a few hours. I haven't heard anything from our end of the lake, but Swede's hunting party made it back here and they said Swede had gone to my compound. They will come get us eventually; meantime, we have some reacquainting to do. "David said smiling at Melanie.

14

Cujo`s Deadfall

Swede reflected that the vicious dog he was waging war with wouldn't be the last of his feral dog problems. There are 100 million dogs in America. He was sure a high percentage of them wouldn't make it, but the ones that returned to the pack instinct, he figured even if is only 10%, that is 10 million dogs to deal with

Dog problems go far beyond attacking and killing wildlife and being a threat to man. "There is what we call in the scientific world direct or indirect effects," Swede considered. "A direct effect is attack and kill, but (dogs) can also spread disease, like rabies. Other indirect effects are harassment, and that can cause stress. So maybe a pregnant deer will abort, or maybe she's so stressed out she can't get pregnant, or maybe she's so stressed out that she moves somewhere else and its poorer quality habitat and she can't eat as much, and so she's in a poor nutritional state. Different things can happen if they start adding humans to their diet, David said always remember shoot the lead dog first! The pack is following him or her and will keep attacking until the Alpha is down or dead.

He had seen that behavior hold true in most encounters with wild dogs, but this pack leader was different. He was tricky like a coyote and used decoy tactics as well as was the one that circled around to attack prey while the pack drove it.

Humm, David must be letting this end of his line be reverting back to nature. He had shot a raccoon

that David had snared with a non-locking snare, but he hadn't seen anything else set. This is a pretty neat setup Swede thought to himself as he saw deadfalls scattered about the trail but they were not set or armed. David could theoretically just come back and arm them when ever he wanted, Swede mused.

David has had a little time on his hands to make all these. Those dogs haven't seen these setups before. Mr. raccoon, you are now bait Swede said to himself as he commenced set and arm a number of different types of deadfalls.

Figure 8-13. Paiute deadfall.

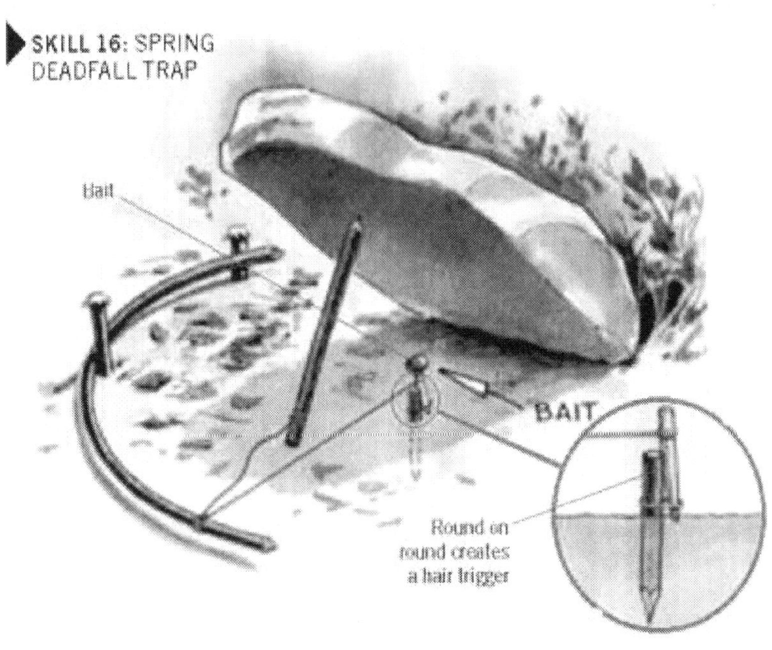

That ought to get at least one of them, Swede said as he crisscrossed the trail setting them and added a few of his snares for good measure.

What's he got over here, oh it's a deer blind, but what the hell does he have rigged to the back of it? Damn it's a bow trap! I thought Jack said he didn't use those he said to himself while inspecting it.

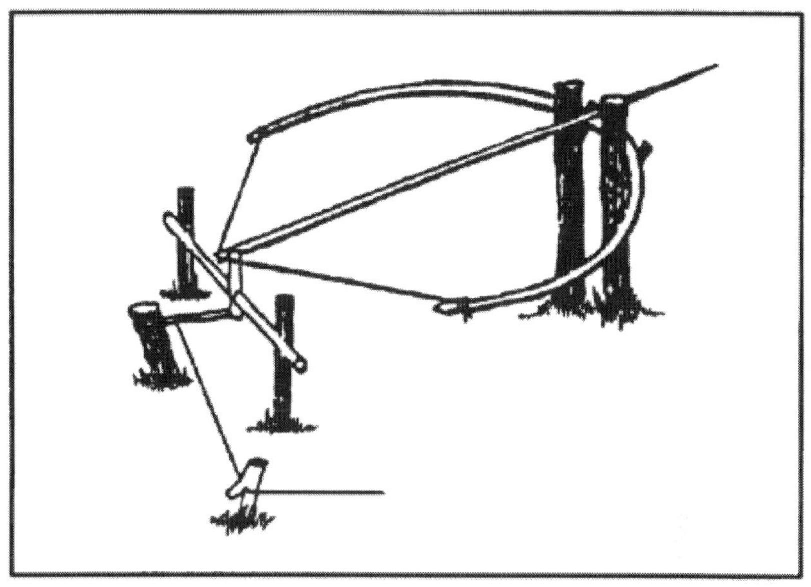

Figure 8-14. Bow trap.

This doesn't appear to be a set for animals; it looks like David had this setup for deterring anyone using his blind and getting the drop on him as he came down his trap line. This thing reminded Swede of a Viet Cong booby trap or something. It wasn't set, but everything was carefully laid out to set at a moments notice. He must have had someone raiding his trap line or was worried about someone in the area. Could be he was just teaching Jack how to build one. No, that trip wire goes to the entrance of the blind. Whatever it was for, Swede now had the perfect use for it and its name was eliminating Cujo. He rigged the bow traps mechanism and was pleased that the sapling for the bow still had plenty of spring to it. A three foot hickory arrow with a fire hardened point was carefully aimed at dog chest level and he looked around the area. Now for the bait. He thought for a moment and then took off his outer layer shirt and threw it towards the back of the blind. There you go Mr. Cujo, that smell will be too enticing and you going to have to go in there to satisfy your curiosity. He decided not to use any of the raccoon carcass on this setup. He didn't want any of their other pack dogs going in here, those dogs would hold back and let the leader investigate that hated smell that symbolized the trapper Swede.

No sense dawdling around here, he decided and picked up his pace to get back to the compound.

Jack and Bubba meantime had finally made it back to the compound after having set snares and Conibear steel traps about a hundred yards back from their perimeter. They explained to the girls the need to be alert and keep their guard up with the feral dogs in the area, but reassured them that the dogs would not be likely to enter the camp; but to be careful about leaving any food scraps around and to burn the garbage pile tonight.

Jack and Bubba were sitting on David's front porch warming themselves by his fire pit, when he came into camp.

"Hey Swede, you must of got you a bobcat, it took you long enough." Jack said thinking he knew why Swede was late getting back.

"No, I was busy leaving a few unfriendly reminders for those dogs. I see you got me a glass ready, Thanks Bubba." Swede said grabbing what appeared to be at first sip, whiskey and instant lemon tea.

"Hey, that ain't too bad." Swede said after taking another sip.

"It beats water and I sort of been acquiring a taste for it ever since David turned me on to it." Bubba remarked.

"Yeah, we have pretty much managed to drink up all the available coke cola around here." Swede responded.

"Hey do you know how to get David's Tractor started?' Bubba asked him.

"No, don't you know how to do it Jack?" Swede said looking over at it.

"I done it once, I made David write down how it was done though for just this sort of emergency though." Jack said handing Swede the directions.

"I am glad you got these, those warnings about serious injuries, if you did it wrong is not something I care to experience." Swede responded handing back the directions.

"I figure you two can drive it to the post, while I stay here and look after the girls." Jack said surveying the wood line for any dangerous dogs or humans about.

"I can stay. I sort of want to see this dog problem to the end, especially considering I might have led that damned Cujo this way." Swede said gulping about half his drink.

"I can handle it until David gets back, unless you just want to hang out. I figured you wanted to get home and get settled in for the winter." Jack said.

"Well, I do need to get back quick; but let's just see what the morning brings. I rigged some special surprises for Cujo and his gang and I want to run the trap line tomorrow morning to see if I did any good." Swede said fixing him and Bubba another drink.

"We set several unique rigs for them ourselves. I didn't know you could set a conibear, but one way until Jack gave me a couple new pointers." Bubba remarked.

"I am going to go try to start that tractor, so we don't have any surprises in the morning. You want to watch?" Jack said standing.

"Yeah, I want to see. I get to drive by the way Swede." Bubba said calling the job before Swede could.

"Have at it. I don't find the idea of starting that thing very appealing, but I want to see it done." Swede said joining them.

After a few false starts and some misunderstood directions Jack managed to have the tractor thumping along nicely.

"That things like a Timex watch, takes a licking and keeps on ticking. Let me drive it around a bit before you shut it down." Bubba said replacing Jack in the driver's seat.

Swede and Jack returned to the porch and watched Bubba playing with the throttle and driving it up the road that lead to the compound.

When he returned Bubba exclaimed that it had more power than he thought and how surprised he was when it whipped his body backwards, when he gunned the throttle too fast.

"I thought you were coming off that seat for a minute." Swede said laughing and nursing his drink.

"What's that you have got there, Jack? Is that a single door version of one of them StoveTec stoves?" Bubba said watching Jack set one down.

"Yeah, David gave me this for my graduation present, when I got my associates degree. I actually prefer it over the two door kinds. You see this has a bigger area to burn odd shape pieces of wood, thorn bushes, pinecones you name it. In an emergency or survival situation you might be burning bits of lumber or furniture etc. so its suits my purposes better." Jack said very pleased with his gift.

"Looks to me like its better for warming your hands in front of" Bubba said watching Jack using a small metal shovel to scoop some coals out of his fire pit and into the stove.

"I am going to make us some rice pudding for desert after dinner. The girls are fixing those rabbits we brought in." Jack said assembling his ingredients.

"David said once that was the way rice was intended to be eaten, but I think he was just sick of beans and rice at that very moment." Swede remarked.

"Wow, you got raisins? You got enough that I can have some? "Bubba asked.

"Yeah, help yourself to a small bit. Raisins are scarce as hen's teeth these days though." Jack replied and started to open some carnation milk.

"We will set out around 10 o'clock tomorrow for the trading post. Depending on how the dog problem appears." Bubba told Swede and Jack.

"It shouldn't take more than an hour and half or so to get there" Jack replied

"That's something I still can't get a handle on. It would take David and Stewart at least three days to walk it this far, but even at a tractors pace it's a pretty quick trip." Swede said calculating how to do what used to be the least bit of traveling, now was thought of as a grueling hike versus a short car trip.

"I am glad that tractor works, I wouldn't care for sailing over there in this weather." Jack responded measuring out some vanilla for his rice pudding he was making.

"That's something you going to have to teach me to do come this summer." Bubba said referring to sailing the 30 ft boat they had.

"Summer can't come soon enough for me" Jack said getting closer to the fire pit.

"You don't think David and Stewart tried to walk back do you?" Swede asked. "It would be seriously dumb on their part, if they did. They would make it just fine; but I think they have sense enough to hole up and watch the weather, while they wait to see if we come to get them." Jack said while adjusting his fire. This wonderful stove was capable of 23,900 BTU of Cooking Power, but he wanted a bit lower cooking temp at the moment.

"You got any tarps around here? I bet David will want to carry back some supplies with him from the trading post." Bubba said planning the trip.

"Good idea. I will get them and some rope here in a minute. You all might want to borrow some blankets too; that is going to be a cold trip riding out in the open." Jack suggested.

'Let's see now, we got Boudreaux, Beverly and David riding back, so that's three blankets. Might want to throw a couple spares in though. No telling who got stuck over there that might need a ride back this way." Bubba remarked and smiled as Jack offered to let him taste test the rice pudding.

"That tastes good, I will be looking forward to it" Bubba said savoring the sweet creamy treat

13

All Are Safely Gathered

Jack, Bubba and Swede set out the next morning in the crisp dawn air. They did a quick circle around the perimeter of the camp checking the traps and looking for any signs that the dogs were in the area.

"I don't see anything but our own tracks going and coming. Let's go check my deadfalls and snares and see if they produced anything. Could be them dogs just moved on to another territory but I doubt it. I saw that pack trailing our trap line or standing off and observing my hunting party from the cover of the woods. That Cujo dog has been quite persistent about tracking my whereabouts up to know. I still think he probably followed me this way." Swede said looking down the trail which had been dusted lightly with newly fallen snow.

"Dusk and Dawn are about the best times to hunt so keep an eye out anyway. If them dogs are in the area they likely will be still moving about even if they been most active nocturnally. "Jack said wishing he was back at home having a good breakfast instead of the dried meat and coffee they wolfed down before setting out today.

"That's a dog track but it ain't that big Cujo hound. Looks like he made himself a big circle away from our camp and proceeded off in that direction most likely. Probably smelled our wood smoke. No signs of a pack though." Swede said studying the tracks in the snow.

"Maybe he is a loner?" Bubba asked eying the suspicious tracks.

"Could be, come on. That Deer blind I told you about is just up ahead. "Swede declared.

Just up ahead they could see the dim outline of it and as they got closer it was plain to see they had got something by the amount of blood in the snow. After they came around to the entrance to it they could see a very large dog transfixed with a yard of hickory sticking out of its chest.

"Is that the one?" Bubba said looking at the huge dog lying on a bloodied shirt.

"That's the one. Looks like he snatched that shirt before the arrow hit him." Swede said examining the ground where the animal had briefly struggled in its death throws.

"That's a relief! If you killed the Alpha male the pack will most likely move on for now." Jack commented.

"I am happy that sucker has gone to meet his maker." Swede said relived that this fight was over.

"I say we just leave him, maybe it will scare off the rest of his pack if they haven't left the area yet. David has enough supplies and I doubt he wants the dog meat." Bubba said not wanting any of it himself.

"Come on, let's go check the deadfalls Bubba, there is one on the far left over there you can check Jack." Swede said as he followed the trail down and examined his sets. One dog had its back broken by a pine log and the rest were still set except for one that had somehow missed its mark.

"Looks like it there were four dogs here. I think that is the Alpha female under that log." Swede said surveying the tracks coming and going into the area. I will disarm the triggers on the rest of these and drag that carcass off in the woods. David can do what he wants when he gets back. Those dogs won't be back in this area for sometime to come I am betting." Swede said and got Bubba to lift the log as he dragged the animal's body out from under it and pulled it a distance away.

Jack had returned from checking his side of the trap line with nothing to report and they headed back to the compound to make ready for the days adventure of going to retrieve David.

While Swede readied his gear, Jack heated water in the big pasteurizer kettle to fill a thermos with hot coffee for them to take on their journey.

"I got a surprise for David when he gets home, the fishing light for the lake wasn't plugged in and we still got a few extra marine batteries that function. I don't know how we are going to recharge them when we put a load on them, but our light in the lake still shines!" Jack said beaming a big smile.

"Man you should just switch that thing on tonight and not say anything about it until you do." Bubba said getting himself some coffee.

"I thought about that, but I ain't plugging it in until we sure this mess is over. It's probably a million to one shot of it zapping us again for a long time to come but I am going to talk it over with him when he gets back." Jack said looking at the sky like he could somehow guess what the sun had in store for them.

"I think that would be best "Swede said agreeing and then went to throw his gear on the trailer in back of the tractor.

"You want me to fire up that tractor or are you going to give it a try Bubba?' Jack said seeing that they had all their preparations done to go on a rescue mission after David.

"You fire it up. I ain't turning it off until we get there." Bubba said

Jack got the tractor started easier this time and gave them the directions if for some weird reason they needed to refer to them.

"Make sure you send those back with David." Jack advised them.

"Will Do, see you in spring." Bubba said and mounted the tractor and had a seat. Harley, Cat and Swede got arranged in the back of the trailer and said their farewells and were off to the trading post to reunite with David and to go to their own respective homes.

A PREPPER MUST HAVE!

StoveTec Rocket Stoves burn cleaner, use less fuel, and are more economical than any other stove of their kind.

Take advantage of a special $2.50 off and free shipping by entering the coupon code Prepper1 at Stovetec.net and support our books and product reviews.

- Bonus biochar generation ability! Burn wood to create charcoal soil amendment
- Optimal for emergency situations: burn nearly any flammable biomass
- 23,900 BTU of Cooking Power
- Rugged Cast Iron Stove Top
- Easy-To-Clean Steel Body
- Sturdy, Heat Resistant Handles
- Steel Stick Support
- Adjustable Pot Skirt

My Readers Might Also Enjoy:

THE RURAL RANGER A SUBURBAN AND URBAN SURVIVAL MANUAL & FIELD GUIDE OF TRAPS AND SNARES FOR FOOD AND SURVIVAL

By Ron Foster

The Modern Day Survival Primer for Solving Modern Day Survival Problems! This book will teach you the techniques to not just survive, but to use ingenuity and household items to solve your problems scientifically with a bit of primitive know how thrown in. A complete and detailed section utilizing explicit drawings and easy to understand photographs covers thoroughly the topic of survival trapping using Modern Snares, Deadfalls, Conibear Traps, and Primitive Snares. This book is dedicated for long term survival in the country or the suburbs to insure you survive and thrive! Build a solar oven or pasteurize water its all in here! Catch your dinner, then cook it or preserve it, too! Food procurement is the name of the game along with purified water in a survival or disaster situation. Are you ready?

Introducing a new series of books for the home library. These books will be consolidated under the **Prepper Archeology Project**. Website will be up soon.

The Prepper Archaeology project is a joint venture between Ron Foster, Cheryl Chamlies, Goat Hollow Press and Elemental publishing to establish a collection of historic preparedness research and information books under the banner of Elemental Publishing. We search the antique book stores and the archives for old tomes of forgotten knowledge contained in out of print or forgotten books and make arrangements to republish them as a resurrection into good quality modern books.

Meticulous care and detail in reproduction is undertaken to preserve and honor the author's original works and preserve the old time secrets and methods used by great pioneers and woodsmen.

The republishing process utilizes good quality low acid crème colored paper and modernized high gloss book covers for durability.

The books included in the collection are hand selected by experts in their field for the Prepper community's enjoyment, so that this historical lore will not be lost and may be reused again to face the disasters of an uneasy world once more.

Every Step in canning, the cold pack method: (Prepper Archeology Collection Edition

The knowledge that our Grandparents, and Great Grandparents knew in their everyday lives, can be a great asset for our use in these ever more difficult economic times. Goat Hollow Press is pleased to make Every step in canning, the cold pack method available to a new generation of home canners!

A BLOCKADED FAMILY: Life in Southern Alabama During the Civil War (Elemental Historic Preparedness Collection)

A Blockaded Family by Parthenia A. Hague is a testament to the ingenuity, adaptability and inventiveness with which a community cut off from outside resources resorts to fending for themselves and utilizing nature's bounty. Less about politics and more about enduring; it contains tips on surviving and making do. From making a coffee substitute from okra seeds, watermelon syrup for sugar substitute, and persimmon seeds for buttons, this book captivates the reader with timeless wisdom.

Deadfalls And Snares (Elemental Historic Preparedness Collection) Annotated (Prepper Archaeology Project)

The old ways of trapping and snaring are forgotten by most today and the times to remember them are once again upon us in these times of economic and disaster uncertainty. This old style survival book of trapping and snaring lore contains one of the greatest descriptive and applicable primitive and modern ways of acquiring game for food and sustenance. The book that was originally published in 1907 has been digitalized painstakingly, not a cheap scan like some offer that is blurry and hard to read. This volume contains information on building deadfalls, snaring with the bits of string you can find or using commercial grade wire snares, portable traps, bear and raccoon deadfalls to name a few. Specific animals are covered and their habits which include, Otter deadfall, Marten Deadfall, Stone Deadfall, The Bear Pen, Portable Traps, various trap and Snare Triggers, Trip Triggers, How to Set, When to Build, Where to Build, The Proper Bait, what to do about traps knocked down, Spring Pole Snare, Trail Set Snare, Bait Set Snares, The Box Trap, The Coop Trap, The Pit Trap, Number of Traps, When to Trap, Season's Catch, General Information, Skinning and Stretching, Handling and Grading, and From Animal to Market.

This is a classic collection from Harding who was one of the first national advocates of scientific wildlife management, conservation and good sportsmanship in the 1900`s. This early work is a fascinating look at a vanished era and skills we can still use today

Camp Life in the Woods and the Tricks of Trapping and Trap Making (Annotated)

This treasure of a historical book, CAMP LIFE IN THE WOODS AND THE TRICKS OF TRAPPING AND TRAP MAKING by W. Hamilton Gibson (1850-1896) was first published in 1881 and is republished here for the education and enjoyment of readers interested in these time tested methods of food procurement using snares, traps, deadfalls and contains many handsomely detailed original illustrations by the author W. Hamilton Gibson of many animals and of the means to procure them for food or for the elimination of vermin and predator. Mr. Gibson describes the characteristics and of the animals, as well as preferred foods, habitat and best trapping method for each.

New up coming titles

Carpentry For Boys: Prepper Archaeology Collection

How to make a shoe: Prepper Archaeology Collection

Check Out The Original Prepper Trilogy

Preppers Road March

A solar storm has just hit the world causing an EMP event. A emergency manager visiting Atlanta

GA must find his way back home after this electromagnetic pulse has stranded him away from his vehicle and his beloved "bug out bag". With 180 miles to go to his destination, David must let his street smarts and survival skills kick in as food and water becomes scarce and societal breakdown proceeds at an unrelenting pace. An interesting and often funny cast of characters from the Deep South helps the displaced Prepper on his way, as he shares his knowledge of how to make do with common items in order to live another day. Ultimately, he acquires an old tractor and heads for home on a car-littered interstate. This is book one of the Prepper Trilogy.

BUG OUT! Preppers on the move!

Book two of the Prepper trilogy finds the disaster planner and emergency manager Dave faced with the choice of bugging out with his cohort of friends and family as he watches the societal collapse and demise of civilization around him after an electromagnetic pulse (EMP) solar storm has taken out the grid. A post apocalyptic fiction series that takes you through the trials and tribulations of survival after the predicted NASA 2012 solar super storm unravels the lives and lifestyles of a group of modern day survivalists. The preppers decide on a lake front bug out with bags in hand as well as a unique group of operating vehicles from a bobcat loader to a lawn tractor. Will they survive? Could you? Let us find out, and join the party down the desolate dystopian landscape of a new beginning in a world without lights or technology.

The Light in The Lake

Book three of the Prepper Trilogy finds our band of refugees from a solar storm safely moved into a several lake cabins and trying to work on their short term and long term survival. The lake is a beautiful place for a survival retreat, but is it safe with roving groups of lake residents all looking for what meager food resources remain after a EMP event has shut down society as we know it. Can society be recreated and restarted here, or will starvation and anarchy take over? Can a simple light in the lake be the solution to survival and the reconstruction of society, or is it merely a symbol of what has been and might be yet again?

Made in the USA
Lexington, KY
08 December 2011